Mary Brendan was born in ~~anag~~ ~~UNTY~~ ~~on~~ but now lives in rural Suffolk. She has always ~~had~~ ~~a~~ ~~fa~~scination with bygone days, and enjoys the research ~~and~~ writing historical fiction. When not at her word proce~~ssor~~ she can be found trying to bring order to a large overgrown garden, or browsing local fairs and junk shops for that elusive bargain.

Don't miss these other Regency delights from Mills & Boon® Historical romance's bestselling authors!

REGENCY
Mistresses

Mary Brendan

MILLS & BOON

All the characters in this book have no existence outside the imagination
of the author, and have no relation whatsoever to anyone bearing the same
name or names. They are not even distantly inspired by any individual
known or unknown to the author, and all the incidents are pure invention.

Mills & Boon, an imprint of Harlequin (UK) Limited,
Eton House, 18-24 Paradise Road, Richmond, Surrey TW9 1SR

REGENCY MISTRESSES © Harlequin Books S.A. 2011

The publisher acknowledges the copyright holder of the individual works
as follows:

A Practical Mistress © Mary Brendan 2006
The Wanton Bride © Mary Brendan 2006

ISBN: 978 0 263 88737 2

052-0811

Harlequin (UK) policy is to use papers that are natural, renewable
and recyclable products and made from wood grown in sustainable
forests. The logging and manufacturing processes conform to the legal
environmental regulations of the country of origin.

Printed in the UK
by CPI Mackays, Chatham, ME5 8TD

A Practical

Mistress

Chapter One

'How dare you even think to treat your sisters so abominably!'

'Now, steady on, Helen, I don't like your tone. You know I am not legally obliged to house you and Charlotte, or give either of you a penny piece.'

'Not legally obliged, perhaps! Morally obliged indeed you are, and not simply to house us, but to keep us in comfort, and you cannot pretend you don't know it.'

George Kingston seemed unaffected by the mixture of disgust and entreaty firing his sister's tawny eyes. In fact, he lounged back in his chair and continued to probe his teeth with a little silver toothpick.

Helen Marlowe, née Kingston, felt her stomach churn with impotent rage as she observed her brother's apathy. Tendrils of raven hair were angrily twitched back from a complexion that, customarily pale as porcelain, was flushed with righteous indignation. 'I know you do not truly want to be mean to us, George, for I am certain you recall as well as I the undertaking you gave Papa. We are not asking for *your* money, all we want is the allowance to which we are entitled. And I need not remind you that Papa stipulated Westlea House was to be a home for Charlotte and me for as long as we needed its shelter.' She paused to drag in breath to deliver a final conscience-pricking truth. 'Our parents would be distraught to know you are planning to sell the roof from over your sisters' heads.'

Helen's small fingers curled into her palms as she realised that her brother was more irritated than swayed by her appealing to his principles. Abruptly she swished about in a rustle of lavender dimity and addressed her sister-in-law. 'Have you nothing to say on the matter, Iris? Are you comfortable, knowing your husband seeks to eject us from our home?'

Iris briskly stepped to a gilt mirror to inspect her reflection. She tipped her hat this way and that on flaxen hair whilst making her snappish response. 'Another house will be found for you both. George has already looked at one. I can't understand why you and Charlotte would want to carry on so. You are comely enough to find a husband to support you,

you know, Helen.' It was said with a slight frown, as though already she doubted the value of her compliment. Dissatisfied with the floral embellishment on her new bonnet she tweaked it some more. 'And Charlotte is quite a beauty. I'll wager the girl could net herself a man with good prospects. Perhaps a banker or the like might take to her.'

'Charlotte has a suitor. She and Philip are in love and want to announce their betrothal, as you well know.'

'How sweet. But he has no money, and no prospects, as you well know,' Iris countered acidly.

George Kingston plunged upright on noticing his sibling's darkening expression. He was well aware that, dainty-built as she was, Helen could act the virago when protecting her own or Charlotte's interests. As his wife and his sister locked combatant stares, he took the precaution of stepping across the rug between the two of them. He stuffed his hands into his pockets and rocked back and forth on his feet. 'It's not as though you and Charlotte will be homeless, Helen,' he coaxed. 'I've found somewhere for you actually. Just this afternoon I arranged a short lease on a property on Rowan Walk. Six months should be time enough for you both to make your own arrangements for the future.'

'Rowan Walk?' The tone of Helen's voice was initially aghast. A moment later she repeated the address in a voice that had lowered threateningly.

'Yes,' George spluttered, conscious of the reason for his sister's simmering fury.

Rowan Walk was not situated in an area where genteel women would choose to reside. In fact, he was aware that it housed a host of females kept in modest style by wealthy gentlemen of the *ton*. Such fellows might like a mistress conveniently close to home, but they baulked at paying exorbitant Mayfair rates. The eastern suburb in which Rowan Walk lay was within easy reach. A lengthy carriage ride would thus not take up time destined to be more pleasurably expended. The neat terraces of townhouses in the vicinity were of adequate size and quality and, because of their association with demimondaines, very good value, too.

'If you think for one moment that Charlotte and I will move into such an area, you must be addled in the wits,' Helen announced. A glance at her sister-in-law revealed her to be maliciously amused. 'But perhaps you have not wasted your money, George. There might be someone you know who would appreciate an available house there.'

George tightened his lips—he understood the allusion to the latest gossip doing the rounds. He stabbed a low-lidded accusatory glance at his wife.

Iris had the grace to flush and flounce about to primp some more at her appearance.

Iris had never used discretion in her quest for powerful and wealthy lovers. Helen often wondered if her sister-in-law relished the attention she got from being the butt of gossip. The fact that George quite obviously resented, yet regularly endured, being made to look a fool by his wife, was also intriguing to those, such as his sisters, who cared enough about him to ponder on it.

'Good grief, Helen, you're a widow, twenty-six years old, and it's high time you found another fellow to look after you and ceased being a burden on me!' George blasted out the reprimand, more in embarrassment than in anger. He had hoped his sisters might still be ignorant of the likelihood of him again being a cuckold.

A sour taste dried his mouth as he dwelled on his wife's current prey. Iris might deny it, but he knew she was infatuated with a man he detested. The same man who had been his enemy for many years.

His sisters rarely socialised; if news of Iris's latest infatuation had reached Helen's ears, then gossip was rife. Abruptly he stalked back to his chair to slouch into it. 'You may live on Rowan Walk or in the poorhouse, it makes no difference to me.' He raised a moody glance to his sister's tense features.

'And it serves you right for choosing to marry a pauper when you might have married well.'

'I thought we might come to that. It was exceedingly bad of me, was it not, to marry a man I loved when I might have married a man old enough to be my grandfather.'

'Scoville was dead within two years of proposing to you. It would scarce have been hardship to be a sick man's wife—a very rich sick man's wife—for such a short time. Had you given the decrepit old fool the heir he wanted, your future at nineteen years old would have been fine indeed.'

'I beg to differ. And I have no regrets that I married Harry. He was a gentleman who did not need money to recommend him. And I am not ashamed to demand again and again that you release to us what our father wanted us to have. If you resent me coming constantly to badger you for money, you have only yourself to blame.' Helen glowered at her brother from beneath eyebrows as lush and black as sable. 'If we are a burden on you, it is you who has made it so by withholding what is rightfully ours.'

George flushed beneath his sulk and snapped his head away from a pair of flaring golden eyes. Imperiously he said, 'If you continue to recommend that our sister encourage Philip Goode, Charlotte will go the same way as did you. Sentiment is all very well, but it doesn't pay the bills. The man has nothing to offer her.'

'He has the most important things to offer her: his love and devotion. Apart from which he is pleasant, polite and totally charming.'

'What a shame such a paragon cannot afford a wife,' Iris murmured with a cattish smile. The bonnet with which she had been fiddling was tossed aside in irritation. Bluntly she informed her husband and sister-in-law that she was going out shopping.

George stared morosely at the closed door before sighing with such unconscious sadness that a little of Helen's anger evaporated. It was ironic that George could, in all seriousness, criticise her for having wed unwisely when his own marriage was a mockery. At least she had been happy for the short time she and Harry had been man and wife.

Helen studied her brother in profile. He was a handsome man, his hair a similar shade of auburn to their sister Charlotte's. Although in his mid-thirties, George's complexion was unlined, yet his youthful demeanour was spoiled by a constant miserable droop to his mouth.

And little wonder he was miserable, for he had married a woman who seemed to relish making him look ridiculous. Yet Helen felt more exasperated than sympathetic. Despite Iris's callous infidelities, George seemed to be in his wife's thrall, for the baggage had no trouble twisting him about her finger.

But her brother was correct in one respect, Helen realised wryly. Sentimental memories were indeed an indulgence when one was struggling to persuade the butcher to extend credit so one might dine on offal. Harry had been kind and charming, but he had died leaving her with little more than her wedding ring and his outstanding army pay.

'Marlowe's been dead for seven years.' George shattered Helen's wistfulness with that harsh truth. 'You've had plentiful time for mourning. Now it is time to be sensible.' The toothpick was again between his teeth. Suddenly he pointed it at her. 'Iris is right: you are passably pretty. Dark looks were the rage last season, you know. I recall when you were eighteen and made your come-out, you received more than one offer that year.'

'My, what a fine memory you have, George!' Helen drily exclaimed. 'That was eight years ago and most of my suitors now have found wives. Besides, if you honour Papa's wishes and the trust he had in you, there will be no need for me to chase a proposal. I am not going to release you from your duty to us. Release our money and have done with it.'

George flushed and flung the silver tool down on

a table. 'I have some unforeseen expenses at present and…and, besides, I am not legally obliged…'

'Ah, we have done that bit, George.' She sighed before saying reasonably, 'I would understand your parsimony if I thought you were honestly in trouble, but I know your wife fritters the money we need for essentials on new Paris fashions.' Helen's eyes slid meaningfully to the abandoned bonnet.

George lurched out of his chair. 'That's enough!' he roared. He strode two paces back and forth. 'You know nothing of my life or my finances and I will not have you speak so of Iris.'

'What would you have me say, then, George?' Helen asked quietly. 'That it is not her new clothes you cannot afford, but her fondness for the gaming tables? Or perhaps her new landau has taken Charlotte's dowry?'

George swung about to stare grimly at his sister. His face now held the expression of a man resentful of unpalatable truths. 'I think you ought go before I say or do something I should not.'

Helen recognised her brother's torment and walked, head high to the door. 'You can dismiss me now if you want. But if our cash is not forthcoming in the next few days, I shall be back. We have no more credit at the merchants and have little stocks left of food or fuel. It is early spring and still quite cold.'

'If you are both determined to be leeches on me, then you and Charlotte can make a few blasted economies!'

Helen managed a smile tinged with bitterness. She glanced down at her waif-like body whilst recalling how plump had looked her sister-in-law's figure. Iris's arms and bosom had fair threatened to burst from the fine silk of her stylish gown. In fact, Helen thought acidly, if the woman did not curb her appetite she would be on the way to becoming fat.

'Charlotte and I have long since cut marchpane from our diets...' Helen noticed George's lips angrily writhe at the reference to his wife's liking for sweetmeats. 'And mutton has become a once-a-week luxury,' she truthfully added. 'What economies would you have us make, George? Already we make do and mend. Shall we boil up potato broth for every meal and live in the cold and dark?'

'A smaller property would cost less to heat and light. If you want to dine well, then it is sensible to move somewhere else.' George's reasoning was accompanied by an impatient whirl of a hand. 'The two of you seem more concerned with pretending you can afford to live in a fine neighbourhood than attending to your comfort.'

'That's not true!' Helen cried, outraged. 'Westlea House is our home. You know it holds dear memories of our parents. How can you be so cruel as to imply we care to keep up appearances?'

George seemed about to speak, but abruptly closed his jaw and showed Helen his back. He was not hiding his face, ashamed of his outburst. Nor was he uncomfortable knowing how frugally they lived, Helen realised. He was simply trying to shield his expression whilst summoning up another excuse for why she and Charlotte ought go without.

Helen felt the fight drain out of her. She felt tired and hungry and keen to go home. George was still musing on a way to withhold their allowance when Helen quietly quit the room.

'Is he to give us our money?'

Helen hesitated in the act of removing her hat and coat as her younger sister came into view. Wearily she shook her head.

Charlotte Kingston bit at her lower lip. 'He won't give us anything?'

It was whispered in a tiny trembling voice that immediately put the bellows to Helen's smouldering anger. Casting her outer garments on to a hall chair, she gave her sister a smile although her teeth were grinding. 'I think…hope he is considering how much he can afford,' she eventually said in a controlled voice. 'I have no doubt that he is embarrassed for funds: Iris was dressed from head to toe in new clothes. They looked French and expensive.'

'But it is *our* money!' Charlotte shrieked, pushing away from her sister's comforting embrace and stamping a small foot down. It made a hollow noise on the bare oak boards in the hallway of Westlea House. 'I cannot have new gloves, yet she has new gowns! How dare she dress in Paris finery at our expense!'

'She dares because our brother lets her,' Helen succinctly answered.

'George would never sell our home so he might settle with her dressmaker. It can't be *our* Westlea House that is advertised for sale in the *Gazette*...can it?'

Charlotte's nervous smile beseeched from Helen a reassurance, but she could not in honesty give it. Her bad news was conveyed in a hopeless shrug as she preceded Charlotte into the sitting room.

A meagre glow in the grate drew her towards the high mantelpiece. Absently she held out her palms to warm them, then looked around. Oh, she could see why her brother wanted to sell Westlea House. It might be spartanly furnished, and in need of some wallpaper and paint, but it was a fine-proportioned property, well situated on the outskirts of Mayfair. Their neighbours included people who could boast an association with influence and aristocracy.

At one time, when their widowed papa had been alive, they had held just such a status, for Colonel Kingston was liked and respected by everyone with whom he came into contact. His friends included gentlemen of all classes: from peers of the realm to low-ranking army officers. It was through her father she had met Harry Marlowe. If Colonel Kingston was disappointed that his eldest daughter had chosen to accept a proposal from an army surgeon, who possessed little money but vast charm and kindness, he gave no indication. The marriage had taken place with his blessing, and a year later, when Harry was killed in action, his distress at losing his son-in-law had been genuine.

But her papa was no longer with them. He had succumbed to influenza within six months of Harry's death. At first their brother had scrupulously adhered to their father's arrangements for her and Charlotte. But then he had married Iris Granville and their lives had changed. Helen sighed and rubbed together her warmed fingers. She stepped to the window and looked out into the cold, bright afternoon. The baker's boy caught her eye as he hurried past, carrying a tempting looking parcel. Her stomach grumbled as she imagined what sort of wonderful aromatic treats might be wrapped within.

She watched the lad cross the road and scamper down to the kitchen door of a house opposite theirs.

It would not have gone unnoticed by the other residents in the Square that tradesmen rarely called at Westlea House. There was no doubt that their straitened circumstances were whispered over, and an embarrassment to some of their neighbours. Helen put up her chin and felt her pride rally. Those people might wish, as George did, that they would remove themselves to a humbler abode, but Charlotte and she were staying put, in the home in which they had grown up.

Charlotte *was* a beauty, Iris was right about that. Given the wherewithal and opportunity to socialise in the proper circles, she would doubtless attract suitors with vastly more to offer than poor Philip Goode could boast.

As though reading her mind, Charlotte whispered, 'If only Philip had some prospects, or an inheritance in the offing. Must I try and find a rich husband to help us?'

'Of course not,' Helen briskly said.

'If we must move out, where shall we go?' Charlotte asked in a quivering tone.

'Our fond brother thinks to move us to Rowan Walk.'

Charlotte's creamy complexion turned pink.

'That's where...where...certain women congregate...is it not?'

'Indeed...' Helen muttered. She chuckled. 'I implied Iris might make better use of it than us.'

Charlotte's eyes grew round. 'You did not dare!'

'Indeed I did!' Helen corrected with some asperity, 'And from the look that passed between them, I'd say that particular bit of gossip is true.'

'She is after Sir Jason Hunter this time?'

'Emily Beaumont said she made something of a fool of herself chasing after him at the Pleasure Gardens.' Helen gave her sister a wry smile. 'Apparently he seemed more interested in bestowing his time on another lady, of rather dubious reputation, too. Mrs Tucker is quite lovely, though. I believe I have seen her once or twice in the shops.'

Charlotte looked scandalized. 'Poor George must feel so humiliated by it all.'

About to snap that their brother was a fool to tolerate his wife's behaviour, Helen simply shrugged. They had their own predicament to worry over. George showed them scant sympathy; let him deal with his own problems. And if, by the end of this week, their allowance had not arrived, she would add to his problems by returning to Salisbury Street to badger him again.

Chapter Two

'Give the lady a smile or she'll never go away.'

Sir Jason Hunter cast a withering look upon the gentleman who had made that ironic plea. He continued absently shuffling the pack of cards in his hands.

'Perhaps I ought invite her to join us. While she's fluttering her eyelashes at you she'll not be concentrating on the game in hand. I might relieve Mrs Kingston of a tidy sum this evening.'

Another quelling scowl met that teasing suggestion. Sir Jason did not appreciate his younger brother's drollery for two reasons: firstly, he didn't find Iris Kingston or her blatant interest in him attractive, and, secondly, his new mistress was becoming tiresome because she imagined she had a rival.

Mark Hunter lounged back in his chair and gave

Iris a glance. 'She's pretty enough, and so desperately eager you'd be a fool not to put yourself at her service….'

Jason dropped the cards onto green baize and shoved himself back in his chair, boredom etched into his features. 'I need a drink,' he bluntly stated on gaining his feet. 'Have you seen Diana arrive?'

Mark retrieved the scattered cards with a swift sweep of a palm. He nodded towards a door that led out of Almack's gaming room and into the corridor. 'She flounced off that way some minutes ago. I'll wager she spotted your admirer before you did yourself.'

Jason jammed his hands in his pockets and blew an irritated sigh through his teeth. Nevertheless, he set off in the direction in which his sulking paramour was said to have disappeared.

As he passed a throng of females, that included Mrs Kingston, he was obliquely aware that fans were being feverishly employed and whispers becoming more urgently sibilant. Despite his reluctance to acknowledge them, his breeding impelled him to nod curtly, to nobody in particular, as he passed by.

About to quit the room, he noticed that George Kingston had propped himself against the wall and was moodily watching him. He and Kingston were known to be openly hostile; nevertheless, Jason diverted to where George was lounging—there was a matter of business that was on his mind. Following a perfunctory greeting, he launched straight away into, 'I understand you are looking for a buyer for Westlea House.'

George found a firmer stance and drew himself up in his shoes to try and equal his rival's height and breadth. Even with his chest fully expanded and his heels out of contact with the floor it was a futile task. 'I'm looking for the *right* buyer for Westlea House.'

'The right buyer or the right price?' Jason enquired, amused.

'What's it to you?' George snarled in response to that.

'I buy freeholds at the right price, as you know.'

Indeed he did know that, George thought sourly. The man he hated, the same man his wife was eager to bed, had a portfolio of the most prestigious addresses in major cities throughout England. Rumour had it he also now owned prime land abroad. 'A price named by you would never be the right price.' It was a poor bluff. If this man offered him what he wanted, he would sell to him, they both knew that.

Jason acknowledged George's petulance with a sardonic smile. It was no secret that the two men had once been friends, but now rarely spoke to one another. A roving glance told him that their conversation was indeed drawing some inquisitive looks.

Most people had assumed that, when Jason gained his title and wealth, George had resented being the underdog. But it was not inequality of status that had stirred such antipathy between them.

Despite their estrangement, Jason was a businessman, not too fastidious to ignore a prime opportunity if it presented itself. Once he had despised George, but the bitter incident that started it all had been mellowed by the passing of a decade. In an odd way, Jason felt pity that the man who once had been a good friend was saddled with a wife who acted like a harlot. It was not past enmity, but Iris Kingston and her pathetic ambition to be his mistress that would jeopardise any reconciliation between them. He returned to the business at hand and something niggling in his mind. 'I recall that your sisters reside at Westlea House…'

'Alternative arrangements for them have already been made,' George said quickly.

Jason nodded and, just for a moment, felt tempted to comfortingly grip his erstwhile friend by the shoulder and tell him that Iris would be wasting her time wanting a simple flirtation with him. But he knew such a sensitive fellow would construe any reassurance on the subject as effrontery. He glanced away to notice a woman he did desire in the doorway of the room. Diana was bobbing her head this way and that as though searching for someone. As her blue eyes alighted on him she instinctively flicked her blonde curls and struck a dignified pose. Jason's mouth tugged into a smile, for she had failed to convince him that she was careless of his presence.

'I expect we might agree on a figure.' He shoved away from the wall against which he had been propped.

George watched Jason saunter away. Inwardly he seethed at the cool confidence of the man, and the knowledge that, of course, he was right. He would sell to him.

'Shall we find some more interesting diversion?'

Diana felt a thrill shiver through her as firm fingers brushed her arm. She swung about in a whisper of pink muslin to glance coyly up into a pair of eyes the colour of gunmetal. She pouted and exaggeratedly glanced about. 'But, Jason, you might disappoint a certain person by leaving here so soon. Of course her husband would be delighted to see you go. He has a face like thunder.' The peevish note to her voice put Jason's teeth on edge. To subdue his sudden inclination to shrug and walk away, he allowed his gaze to linger on what about her was undeniably captivating.

Diana Tucker had a figure of exquisite proportions. She was of above average height for a woman, which suited him for he stood six feet tall. Her body had ample curves, yet retained a gracefulness that was often lacking in full-bodied females. She was blessed with a pretty face, too, and hair the colour of ripe wheat.

The stirring in his loins helped subdue his temper and he soothed her pique with a sensual stroke of a thumb. 'Come, there are better games to be had between us than those on offer here....'

Diana adopted a look of indecision simply to prolong his wooing touch. Alert to his impatience, she soon coyly lowered her lashes and voiced a breathy agreement to leave.

A few moments later, as Mrs Tucker swayed from the room on her lover's elegant arm, she made quite sure that Iris Kingston felt the full force of her bold-eyed triumph.

'Thank you, Betty.' Helen took the proffered letter and gave the serving maid a smile. Once the door had closed, she looked at the black script on the note's address for an indication from whence it came. 'It's from George,' Helen announced, then took another nibble at her breakfast toast before breaking the seal on the parchment. The toast, with so frugal an amount of butter spread on it, felt dry and scratchy in her mouth. Having moistened her throat with a sip of weak tea, she paraphrased, for Charlotte, the note's contents.

'It simply says that George would like me to visit today to discuss financial matters.' Helen sent a smile to Charlotte, who was seated opposite her at their small breakfast table. 'There! I knew he would come to his senses. He is ashamed at having squandered our funds on that selfish harridan he married.'

Charlotte picked up her tea and glumly watched the insipid liquid swirl in her cup. 'I think he has the devil of a cheek making you go there. He has a carriage and ought to come here. Why should you walk a mile or more to see him?'

Helen looked thoughtful at that. It would indeed have been more convenient for her brother to come to Westlea House than for her to be summoned to travel halfway across Mayfair. She shrugged. 'He probably thinks to make us work for our money. It doesn't matter; it is a clement morning and I like a walk....'

Helen handed her umbrella to George's servant, then carefully pushed back the drenched hood of her cloak. As she entered the small study in which her brother was lounging by the mantelpiece, she felt decidedly miffed. 'Really, George! Would it have hurt you to come to Westlea House? I expected you would do so once it came on to rain.' She shook out her damp skirts and heard one of her shoes squelch as she stepped towards the blazing fire to warm herself.'

George frowned at the small puddle forming beneath the hem of his sister's skirt. 'Why in Heaven's name did you not hail a hackney in such weather?'

Helen raked her slender fingers through her sleek black hair whilst glowering at her brother. 'Would you have paid the fare when I arrived?' She gave a grim smile as she saw George's expression.

'Oh, I see, you have no money…I did not think…' George mumbled sheepishly.

'You never do,' his sister returned sourly.

George made a show of gallantly shifting away from the fire to usher Helen towards it.

'You will soon be dry,' he said cheerfully. 'A little bit of rain never hurt a person.'

'It is not a shower, but a downpour. If I catch a chill, I shall blame you,' Helen muttered as she removed her cloak and draped it on a chair-back to dry. Having made herself more comfortable, she turned expectantly towards her brother.

George shuffled uneasily beneath Helen's quiz-zical gaze. Abruptly he strode to the bell pull. 'Let's have some tea. I expect you could do with a nice hot drink.'

'I could rather do with our money. You do have a draft to give me, don't you?'

'Umm…not exactly…' George indicated that Helen should take a chair by the fire. 'But I have some…suggestions to put to you that might ease our problems.'

Helen cast on her brother a deeply sceptical look. 'What sort of suggestions?' she demanded. 'I have already said we have no more economies to make.'

'No…it is not that.' George passed a worrying hand over his jaw. 'In truth, I *would* have come to Westlea House, you know, but I do not want Char-lotte to hear what I have to say.'

'Why ever not? She is nineteen. She is a woman in love…not a child.'

George nodded emphatically. 'It is this *woman in love* that is our problem. It is ridiculous for a girl with her charms to marry a man who can give her nothing when she could have so much.'

'It is as well that Charlotte is *not* in earshot!' De-spite yearning that Charlotte be allowed to follow her heart, as she had, Helen understood the logic in George's words. Nothing was more certain to extinguish romantic love than relentless scrimping and scraping. Helen looked her brother squarely in the eye, hoping he was about to announce that he had managed to reinstate Charlotte's dowry. Briskly she said, 'Charlotte wants to marry Philip.'

'I have been thinking about Philip Goode and how he might perhaps improve his prospects.'

'And?' Helen asked eagerly.

'He is a cousin of Sir Jason Hunter, did you know that?'

Helen frowned her annoyance. 'No, I did not, but what is that to do with anything at all?'

'It is a very tenuous connection. A fourth or fifth cousin on his mother's side, I believe, is his kinship to Hunter.'

'This is ridiculous, George. What of it?'

'Jason Hunter is a rich and powerful man.'

'I hope you are not about to suggest that Philip goes to beg charity from his distant cousin. He is a man with pride and principles. He will refuse to do anything of the sort. But if you were to give Charlotte her dowry…even a lesser sum than the original, it would—'

George interrupted his sister by making an impatient noise. 'Any fund for a dowry will only come from the sale of Westlea House.'

Helen sent her brother a challenging look. 'Will

you have a lawyer put that in writing? If I am to sacrifice my home, I will at the very least want to know that I have done so in order that Charlotte's future is secure.'

'A lawyer?' George exploded. 'Is my word on it not good enough?'

'Indeed it is not,' Helen said equably. 'Were you true to your word, we would not be having this conversation.'

'It is our sister's duty to find a man who can adequately provide for her. If she would socialise properly, she would attract gentlemen like bees to a honey pot.'

'She would also attract many cruel remarks. You know full well that she needs new clothes if she is to socialise in the circles you mean.'

'I'd get her gowns…if I didn't already owe a fortune to every blasted dressmaker in town.' George's features tightened in bitterness. 'None of those damnable things were bought to please *me*. Iris is attempting to impress Hunter with her new finery.'

Helen rose from her chair and approached George to comfortingly take one of his hands. It was the first time he had openly spoken of Iris's infatuation with Sir Jason Hunter. 'You must put a stop to her avarice. We are all suffering because of it.'

George snatched back his fingers. 'I don't need

your pity, or your counsel. We must find a way of clearing my debts or Westlea House is to be sold. I have received some interest in it and cannot prevaricate for long.' George dragged a hand through his hair and snapped, 'For two pins I'd present Hunter with Iris's dressmakers' bills.'

Helen looked shocked, then a hysterical giggle erupted. 'Indeed, so would I if I thought he might pay them. But I've heard that he seems little interested in Iris.'

'Well, you've heard wrong, I tell you! He was flirting with her at Almack's earlier in the week. Anybody can tell that they're lovers.' George's face mottled with mortification for the untruth had easily burst out. He had noticed, as had every other person present that evening, that Jason Hunter barely acknowledged Iris. It had been oddly humiliating for him to witness his wife being shunned in favour of a demi-rep.

'Well, you ought to challenge him over it and take your dressmakers' bills with you!' Helen exclaimed in exasperation.

'I would not give him the satisfaction! I'm sure he flaunts their relationship simply to rile me. Why don't you speak to the arrogant bas—?' George snapped together his teeth before the abuse was fully out.

'Me?' Helen choked a shocked laugh.

George dismissed the subject with a terse flick of a hand and stalked off to glare through the window.

Helen was aware that her brother and Jason Hunter had fallen out many years ago. She had been about fifteen at the time of the estrangement and shielded by her papa from knowing the sordid details. But she had heard whispers that they had fought over a woman. At the time she had felt sad that Jason no longer visited, for she had liked him. More honestly she had harboured a juvenile *tendresse* for him. But now all that was inconsequential. Over a decade had passed and there were far more vital matters at stake than two grown men sulking over past slights.

'This is quite ridiculous.' Helen sighed. 'It is reprehensible of you not to have done your duty by us.'

'And it is reprehensible of you not to have done your duty by me!' George thundered. 'Do you think that I would have promised our father to support you had I known that seven years later you would still be a burden on me? Father was under the impression that, after a decent mourning for Marlowe, you would remarry, and so was I.'

Helen's face grew pallid. 'Papa didn't say that…'

'Indeed he did.' This time not a hint of shame betrayed the untruth that flew from George's mouth. 'He thought that by the time Charlotte had left the schoolroom, and was ready to make her début, you would have done the decent thing and removed yourself elsewhere. You accuse me of selfishness! You ought to look to your own behaviour.'

Helen stared, stricken, at her brother. 'Papa never mentioned anything of the sort to me,' she cried. 'I was always welcome in his house…'

'He probably thought he did not need to be blunt. He probably thought your conscience would guide you on it.'

George eyed his sister with calculation. 'Hunter wants Westlea House, he told me so at Almack's. I detest the man, but I shall sell it to him. I need cash quickly and he has a plentiful supply of the stuff.'

'You can't!' Helen emphatically shook her brother's arm.

'Indeed I can! Philip Goode ought to swallow his damnable pride and beg his cousin for assistance. Hunter has connections in the city. There are lucrative positions to be had in banking and so on.'

Helen stared at her brother, silently entreating him to reconsider.

'I can tell you think Goode too spineless a fellow to act. Believe me when I say Hunter is a different kettle of fish. He is a ruthless man and, once the deal is done, he would not hesitate in sending the bailiffs to evict you.'

Chapter Three

'What?'

Jason Hunter turned his grey eyes on his aged servant. He wasn't certain that he had correctly heard the message, for his visitors were creating a din that had smothered Cedric's croak.

The old fellow whispered again, 'A lady is here to see you, sir.'

'Yes, that much I gathered. What name did you say?'

Mark Hunter's second ribald anecdote caused the gentlemen congregating in Jason's library to resume guffawing.

'Mrs Kingston.'

Jason heard the husky sibilance through the noise and his mouth thinned before a low oath exploded through touching teeth. Enraged by the damnable audacity of the Kingston woman to bother him at home, he gave Cedric a curt nod and snapped, 'Put her in a side room and tell her to wait.'

Cedric dipped his wispy head, understanding exactly why his master was so put out. His weary bones might not allow him to venture far from the house these days, and his deaf ear might prevent him getting all the gossip, but he knew that a woman named Kingston was making a fool of herself over Sir Jason. Brazen hussy she was, too, with her haughty look. All airs and graces! He'd known her station straight away. Ask her to wait, indeed! It wouldn't have happened in the old master's days. Cedric wagged his head to himself. Oh, he'd find the baggage a place to wait!

'What was that all about?' Mark demanded as he watched Cedric slowly amble from the room.

'None of your business,' his brother rebuffed bluntly. He refilled his glass from the decanter and asked Peter Wenham what price he wanted for his hunting lodge. The Wenham estate edged his own land at Thorne Park and the lodge and surrounding fields would be a fine addition to his Surrey acreage. A quizzical smile met the ambitious price his friend cited, but Jason gave that more charitable consideration than the accursed female waiting for him below.

He would see Iris…eventually. But he'd let her kick her heels. Perhaps a little blatant incivility would finally penetrate her vanity; she might come to understand that, far from finding her attractive, her behaviour disgusted him. If she could not take the hint, he would have to clearly tell her some truths. He was sick of being stalked and spied on when out; he certainly did not intend having her hound him at home. If she repeated to George what must, of necessity, be an unpleasant incident between them this afternoon, so be it.

One hour and five minutes later, when his brother and their friends had noisily departed, Jason descended the stairs of his opulent mansion in Grosvenor Square. He quite hoped his unwelcome visitor had tired of waiting for him and had removed herself. However, that would leave matters unresolved. He swore beneath his breath in exasperation. It would be as well if Mrs Kingston were still loitering about the place somewhere. Not by nature inhospitable, he nevertheless hoped that Cedric hadn't been plying her with refreshment to wile away the time. Within one step of the marble-flagged hallway he halted, and watched curiously as Cedric emerged, shaking his head, from a cloakroom.

Cedric glanced up and, seeing his master's bemused expression, hobbled across to glumly impart, 'I am afraid she has gone, sir. Mrs Kingston can't be found.'

'Did you think she might be lurking in there?'

The mildly amused comment caused Cedric's loose jowls to take on an unusual sanguinity.

Jason had hoped that Iris hadn't been mollycoddled; from his butler's guilty look it seemed he had little to fear on that score! 'Where exactly did you show her to wait?' he demanded to know.

Cedric's withered lips puckered mutinously on understanding the reprimand in Sir Jason's tone. He had been working for Hunters before this fellow was a twinkle in his sire's eye. He was the old master's servant, not this young pup's. Sir Gordon Hunter had been happy to leave the welcome…or otherwise…of uninvited callers to his discretion. Had Sir Gordon been alive, the Kingston woman wouldn't have put one foot over the threshold, let alone been given the courtesy of a seat. 'Bold as brass and looking at me with those cat's eyes…' he mumbled out defensively. A watchful, watery eye slanted at his employer. He had been subjected to that scowl before, and caught the sharp side of the fellow's tongue. Cedric now knew to quickly curb his insubordination, for he was aware the boy kept him on simply because his father had said he must.

'Cat's eyes?' Jason echoed exceedingly quietly.

'Eh?' Cedric cocked his good ear towards his master.

'You said she had cat's eyes.' Jason's tone held much volume and scant patience.

'Yellow…like a cat.' It was a statement accompanied by a wag of Cedric's head. He continued to mutter to himself. In his opinion he'd put the baggage where she belonged.

Jason frowned. He took little notice of Iris Kingston, avoided her when possible; nevertheless, he had been close enough at times to know her eyes were blue.

'What else can you recall of her appearance?'

'Thin…black hair…prim.' Cedric listed out each trait as though it was a sin.

Jason's eyes narrowed as he pondered on whom it could be the old fool had insulted. 'And she gave her name as Mrs Kingston?'

'Gave her name in full, she did. Mrs Margo May Kingston, she told me.'

The furrow in Jason's brow deepened. He knew no other Mrs Kingston. If for some bizarre reason an impostor were masquerading as the Mrs Kingston he did know, she surely would introduce herself correctly. Noticing that Cedric was sliding wary glances at him, he dismissed him with a flick of a hand and a caution. 'We'll speak further about this.'

As Cedric trudged away Jason took out his watch. Diana was expecting him to traipse around the warehouses with her this afternoon and he was already late. If his tardiness provoked a fit of the sulks he might be sorely tempted to go instead to White's and find some uncomplicated male company. He strode to the door, the question of his visitor's identity now submerged beneath thoughts of another exasperating female. At times he doubted Diana's delightful attributes were compensation enough for her juvenile nature.

'Please accompany me inside, Jason. How am I to know if you would rather see me in blue satin or lemon silk…?'

Jason felt tempted to honestly say that he couldn't care less in what Diana chose to garb herself. The only reason he paid for any woman's finery was to see it in a crumpled heap on the floor. 'If you can't decide between them, buy both.'

Diana showed her pleasure at his generosity by sliding along the phaeton's seat to rub her hip on his thigh.

Jason acknowledged the artful caress with a cynical twitch of the lips. He then tilted his head to watch a man beckoning him from across the street. 'I'll join you inside in a short while. Peter Wenham's over there and I want to speak to him on a matter of business.'

Diana limited her pique to a pretty pout. A most pleasing aspect of having hooked such a distinguished and wealthy protector was being able to show him off to envious females. There was no better place to parade her triumph than in Baldwin's Emporium, for women of every class were to be found browsing the sumptuous array of wares.

Diana's sulky expression brightened when she spied an acquaintance of her own. Mrs Bertram was approaching with a servant trotting behind. Obviously the woman had started shopping early, for the poor maid was bearing evidence of numerous purchases.

Georgina Bertram was the mistress of Lord Frobisher and an erstwhile playmate of Diana's. The two young women were of similar age and had been reared in rags in the shadow of the east London docks. Both had been blessed with abundant female charms and a most canny instinct on how to exploit such assets to escape the drudgery their mothers endured. They engaged in quite a good-natured rivalry when it came to finding rich gentlemen to keep them. With an affectionate squeeze for Jason's arm, Diana nimbly alighted, with a groom's help, from the smart phaeton. 'Don't be too long,' she breathily nagged over a coquettish shoulder. Soon she was entering the shop arm in arm with Mrs Bertram.

Jason sprang down from his high-flyer and, with an instruction for his groom to handle the horses, made to cross the road. He'd barely taken two paces when a rickety vehicle pelted past, far too close. He fell back against his phaeton, aiming a voluble string of oaths at the cab driver's head.

The jarvey seemed unaffected by being so eloquently damned and, with barely a look at his victim, continued blithely on his way. Obliquely it registered in Jason's mind that a female passenger was within the contraption and that she seemed vaguely familiar. Suddenly she shifted closer to the window and from beneath a wide bonnet brim glared at him with large topaz eyes.

Helen sank back into the battered upholstery of the cab with her heart drumming wildly and a startled look on her face. She had not set eyes on Sir Jason Hunter for years, yet had recognised him instantly. Less than an hour ago the odious brute had snubbed her in an outrageous manner. He had allowed her into his house, then made her tarry in a cloakroom for an audience she was certain he had never intended bestowing. Hah! He'd been destined to see her after all! And be punished for treating her so abominably!

Now that the shock of the close shave had passed,

she allowed a throaty chuckle. *The Lord pays debts without money,* her papa used to quote when some misfortune was visited on a deserving recipient. Sir Jason Hunter might have escaped being flattened by her conveyance, but he certainly looked as though his dignity had taken a knock.

On rare sightings in the past she had exchanged a nod with Jason Hunter. A feud might exist between him and her brother, he might now be rich and important, but he was gentleman enough to be polite. Or so she had previously thought when appreciating his good manners. Now she knew differently. He had become an arrogant boor since last they had acknowledged one another. It was a pity his uncouth character didn't show in his appearance. She might have only had a brief look at him just now, but he was undeniably still a fine figure of a man. Suddenly a thought entered her head that made her squirm: she could understand why her sister-in-law was so smitten by him.

She quelled that thought by dwelling on the appalling incivility dealt to her less than an hour ago. When she had been shown to a seat in a cupboard filled with packing cases she had imagined that the butler had simply been confused, for he seemed a doddery old cove. When forty minutes later he put his head about the door and told her, with a crafty squint, that Sir Jason still wasn't ready to receive her, Helen came to the wounding conclusion that she was being intentionally insulted. She had quickly deduced that Sir Jason was spiting her because he hated her brother. With her head held high, she had swiftly exited the house without leaving a message of any sort with the footman who showed her out.

She had dredged up every ounce of courage she possessed to go and visit the swine. She had set out without a cogent plan, only hoping he would listen sympathetically to her family's predicament. She had considered requesting he delay buying their home, at least until her sister's marriage to Philip Goode could be arranged. To persuade him at that point she might have made much of the fact that the prospective bridegroom was one of his own kin. Such a squandered effort that would have been! She doubted such a man would care a fig for the nuptials of an impoverished distant cousin. It would have been better to set out this morning to again do battle with George, for this ridiculous situation could no longer continue.

Her brother might plead poverty and pretend to be an injured party but he lived well, far better than did Charlotte and she. He might not have ready cash, but he had assets to sell. The new landau in which his wife sashayed around town was just one such valuable item.

The cab drew up outside Westlea House and Helen handed over some coins to the jarvey. She gave his impassive wrinkled countenance a sharp look, wondering whether she ought to bring to his attention the fact that he had almost knocked down one of the *ton*'s most notable personages. She decided against it and, unusually, added a small tip to the fare.

Helen removed her grey velvet gown and carefully hung it on a hook. She had dressed with such care that morning in the few garments she possessed that were elegant, if dated in style. She had not wanted Sir Jason to see her looking like a waif and stray come abegging. A small smile twisted her lips; she might just as well have called on him dressed in her washed-out twill; all her painstaking *toilette* had been in vain.

Feeling chilled, she quickly donned her old day dress, then knotted a woollen shawl over it for warmth. She studied her reflection, lips tilting wryly at the incongruous sight of her faded blue gown hanging loosely from her slender hips whilst her hair was still primped to perfection. Briskly she removed the pins from her sleek coiffure and brushed through the silky coils. As she was about to loop it into a neat chignon, a loud noise startled her. She heard the doorknocker again being forcefully employed.

There was only one person she knew of who felt entitled to so imperiously announce himself: Mr Drover, of Drover's Wares and Provisions in Monmouth Street. Helen had been expecting him to call for a week or more. She felt sure she knew what the grocer wanted, and was tempted to pretend nobody was home. But that would simply delay the inevitable and deny them further supplies. With a sigh she quickly went below, her mind foraging for plausible excuses for delaying payment of what they owed whilst inveigling for another delivery soon.

'May I come in?'

Helen sensed her heart stop beating, then start to hammer in a rapid irregular rhythm. Obliquely she realised she had been terribly rude in instinctively pushing the door almost shut. She strove for self-control as she made wider the aperture by a few inches to blurt, 'What do you want, sir?'

Jason tilted his head to try and see more of the petite woman stationed behind peeling green paint. Merely a tantalising sliver of her figure was now visible and her features were concealed behind a curtain of loose dark hair. 'What do I want? I want to know what you want, Mrs Marlowe…apart from trying to assassinate me with a hackney cab….'

Helen jerked the door towards her and gazed at him with large astonished eyes. 'I did not intend you harm! It was an accident! And had you been civil when I called on you earlier, you would by now know what I want.'

Jason found himself confronted by a fragile woman garbed in a dress that looked as though it had seen far better days…probably when it had fitted her. Now it was too large and as shabby as the shawl she was gripping tightly about her slender arms. His gaze returned to her face and lingered. She'd been bonny as a child. Now a hungry look had pared flesh from a heart-shaped face framed by hair as lustrous as black silk. But it was her eyes that mesmerised him and he realised that old Cedric's sight must be failing too if he thought them yellow. They were the colour of fine cognac.

Helen felt herself flush beneath his silent, searing appraisal, certain that she knew what prompted it. *He's wondering whether I had the cheek to arrive at his grand house dressed like this.* The thought brought slashes of colour to highlight her sharp cheekbones and for a long moment she simply met his slate-eyed gaze with haughty belligerence. Had he taken the trouble to see her, he would not need to speculate on how she'd been attired.

'May I come in?' Jason repeated. 'It might be as well to have this conversation out of sight of prying eyes.'

Immediately Helen's gaze darted past him; it certainly would give the neighbours something to gossip over should she be seen trading accusations on her doorstep with a distinguished gentleman of the *ton*. For barely a moment longer she dithered, undecided whether to send him away. But in truth she knew she ought make some sort of explanation for her unsolicited call on him. She also had been presented with a prime opportunity to do what she had really set out to do: to tell him that she and Charlotte were not willingly quitting their home, no matter what business he had hatched with her brother. Besides, now he was here, she had no intention of letting him go without taking a flea in his ear for treating her so vilely!

Helen crisply stepped back allowing him to enter the cold and gloomy interior of Westlea House.

In the parlour Helen indicated a chair by the unlit fire and then took the seat that faced it. She watched as Sir Jason Hunter perched his large frame, with effortless elegance, on the edge of the cracked hide.

After a tense moment in which Helen could think of nothing sensible to say because his eyes were so unnervingly fixed on her, she announced, 'I would offer you some refreshment, sir, but my serving maid is out at present.' It was true Betty was out; it was also true that only limp grouts, twice used already, were what she had to offer any visitor.

Jason moved a hand, dismissing the apology as unnecessary, then leaned back in his chair. From beneath subtle lids he considered Helen Marlowe and her intriguingly fragile beauty.

He had not spoken to her for ten years or so when he and her brother were still on good terms. He had heard she had married, and been widowed, but they no longer had any mutual friends who might bring them into proper contact. He racked his brain to try and recall the last occasion he had seen her at a distance and where that had been. He thought it had probably been in Hyde Park over two years ago. He wondered if she had then been as waif-like as she looked now.

Helen clasped her quivering fingers in her lap. She was sure she knew what he was thinking, for she was acutely aware of it, too: their status and social circles were now vastly different. Once he had been welcomed in to their home and she had been invited to Thorne Park to play with his sister, Beatrice.

Those past halcyon days were a world away from how she lived now. Now Charlotte and she socialised with people of their own station: people whose financial status limited their entertainment to simple at-homes. Outings to the theatre or exhibitions were treats that came rarely, for even the cost of travelling to such venues was beyond their means.

From the top of his glossy dark head to the toe of the gleaming leather boot in her line of vision, Sir Jason Hunter exuded an air of affluence and power that was stifling in its intensity. She had dared to go and see him, uninvited, to tell him he could not have this house. With wounding clarity she understood that, if he wanted it, he would take it. She raised her head and a flitting glance about her beloved, faded room encouraged her that he might decide Westlea House an unattractive investment after all. Her musings were brought abruptly to a close by a cultured baritone voice.

'I must apologise for the poor welcome you received when you called on me. My butler was confused as to your identity.'

'I'm not sure why,' Helen returned coolly. 'I gave my name.'

'What name did you give?' Jason asked. He leaned forward, linking his fingers and resting his forearms on his knees. He felt tempted to rub together his palms. The room was stone cold and a pale spring afternoon let little light into it. Nevertheless he could see her exquisite eyes watching him.

'I said I was Mrs Marlowe, née Kingston,' Helen answered him. 'I fail to see what is confusing in that.'

Jason's mouth took on a wry slant, for suddenly

he understood how the sorry episode had come about. Helen Marlowe had a softly spoken, melodic quality to her voice. *Marlowe, née* had sounded to his deaf butler like Margo May. 'Cedric announced you as Mrs Kingston.'

'Why? Can he not hear?'

'Not very well,' Jason admitted with a ghost of a smile. 'Nevertheless, that is no excuse for his bizarre interpretation of my instruction to show my visitor to a side room. The incident won't go unpunished. I have long tolerated his eccentric ways. It is time, I think, to let him go.'

'I would not have you do that on my account,' Helen immediately objected. 'He looks to be an aged gentleman. I doubt he would get another position, especially if afflicted with poor hearing.' Helen knew too well the rigours of possessing little money; she didn't want it on her conscience that she had robbed an old man of his wages in his twilight years. She gave Jason a trenchant look. 'Besides, even if the draughty cloakroom was not your idea, I imagine the lengthy wait I endured was.'

Jason looked at the proud tilt to her sculpted little chin and felt utterly despicable to have subjected her to such discomfort and humiliation. 'I'm afraid it was,' he honestly said. 'And I am hoping that in some way I can make amends. I won't have you think I indulge in petty spitefulness because your brother and I don't see eye to eye.'

Helen met his gaze challengingly.

'That is what you think, isn't it?'

'It was,' Helen replied, 'until you clarified matters a moment ago.'

Jason's grey eyes narrowed on her. 'And what do you think now?'

'I think you believed my sister-in-law had paid you a visit. I think you decided to punish her by keeping her waiting for you. Why? Had you had a lovers' tiff?'

Chapter Four

'Lovers' tiff?'

The query was mildly quizzical, yet Jason's eyes resembled flint.

Helen felt her mouth become dry and her tongue trembled moisture to her lips. Moments ago he had said he would like to make amends for showing her such poor hospitality earlier that day. It was unexpected, but most welcome news. A favour from this man was *exactly* what she wanted, but ladies…even those of shabby gentility…did not speak of a gentleman's *amours*. Such impertinence was hardly likely to cultivate his goodwill.

Since Helen learned she had been mistaken for Iris Kingston a single thought had dominated her mind and she fervently wished she had curbed her inclination to voice it. Sir Jason had believed

George's wife to be his visitor and his intention had been to eventually oblige her with his presence. Was Iris so besotted with the arrogant man that she would have allowed him to humble her in such a way?

Helen had good reason to dislike her sister-in-law, yet felt oddly piqued on her behalf. She was also a little indignant on her own account. How was she to know if, as Mrs Marlowe, she might have been turned away from his door?

The room was dim, his face in shadow; nevertheless, Helen winced on noticing a definite mocking slant to his lips. She feared he knew of her regret at having acted with such spontaneous vulgarity.

Iris had succeeded in her ambition to become his mistress. George had said they had been openly flirting earlier in the week…blatantly flaunting their affair. Such behaviour was sure to invite comment, thus Helen's face was beautifully prim as she announced, 'I am afraid I cannot pretend ignorance of your liaison with my sister-in-law. I have heard the rumours…' A hideous idea made her falter and demand, 'I hope you do not imagine I intentionally set out to impersonate Iris in the hope such a ruse would get me over your threshold.'

'Had you announced yourself simply as Mrs Marlowe, it would have guaranteed that you not only got over my threshold, but got my immediate attention.'

A cluck of disbelief dismissed that. 'You would not have known who on earth Mrs Marlowe was. When last we conversed, I was Miss Kingston.'

'Be assured, I would have known who you were.'

Helen's eyes darted to his at that husky affirmation. But still he made no remark about her impropriety. No doubt he considered it beneath his dignity to do so. But she could tell the matter had affected him. His composure could not completely camouflage that he was annoyed.

A tense silence ensued and Helen was conscious that he might now take himself off without questioning her further. Perhaps he had deduced from her attitude that she had gone to his house with the intention of interfering in his affairs. Sibling loyalty—however inappropriate—could conceivably propel her to confront the man who was making a cuckold of her brother. He had apologised and soothed his conscience, something she had yet to achieve for her own.

She was alert to a slight movement he made, sure it meant he was making ready to leave. 'I must say sorry, too,' Helen blurted. 'I was rude. I should not have been quite so explicit…that is…I accept that your association with George's wife is none of my concern. My brother is able to fight his own battles.'

'Is he? It occurs to me that perhaps he sent you to see me.'

Helen tensed at that observation and a surge of guilt stained her cheeks. It had indeed been her brother's angry challenge—whether uttered in jest or not—that had prompted her visit.

'Why would he do such a thing?' Helen flicked a nervous gesture. 'You would be hardly likely to pay attention to my opinion.'

'I'm doing so now….'

Tawny eyes sought to read his expression in the half-light. He had not sounded sarcastic, but it was hard to tell. 'If you are being sincere, sir, I must take advantage of the opportunity to…to…' She faltered, frowned at her fingers with the strain of being diplomatic. Her opinion, should she honestly give it, was hardly likely to be well received. How much attention would he want to pay to the fact that Charlotte and she endured hardship because his mistress was avaricious and selfish?

The loss of their allowance, and Charlotte's dowry, the imminent sale of Westlea House—all had come about since George took a gold-digger to wife. The thought that now she must petition the gold-digger's lover in order that she and her sister could have some basic necessities made ire burn in her blood. But she would not again make mention of the dratted woman. Rather she would concentrate on keeping her home.

'My brother is being dunned by his creditors and that is why he wants to sell this house. It is home to me and my sister Charlotte.'

Jason gained his feet in a lithe movement. 'And you have heard that I want to buy it.' It was a neutral statement.

'Yes,' Helen said, very conscious of the height and breadth of him as he passed her chair.

'You don't want me to have it?'

'It is rather that I do not want to lose it,' Helen said carefully.

Jason turned his back to the empty grate and cast up a glance at a ceiling meshed with cracks. 'I expect you will prefer living elsewhere. The upkeep of a property such as this is high.'

'It suits us to stay,' Helen interrupted firmly.

'George has arranged other accommodation for you and your sister, yet you'd rather stay here?'

'Indeed I would.' Helen breathed fiercely. So he knew that George wanted to locate them in a seedy neighbourhood. 'Our home might be rather shabby, but I am afraid even a flash house on Rowan Walk would be unacceptable. In fact, I have no intention of being dispatched there.'

Jason moved closer to the petite figure that had jumped to its feet. He could tell from her raised chin and tight fists that she was furiously embarrassed.

And he understood why. 'Rowan Walk?' he echoed in disbelief. 'What the devil is he thinking of housing his sisters in such an area?'

'He is thinking of what he can afford,' Helen retorted immediately. 'I am sure he would have chosen somewhere more salubrious had his wife not squandered so much on gowns and hats and other selfish whims in order to hook you—' She abruptly bit at her lower lip to stem further angry complaints.

'Go on…' Jason quietly invited.

'Very well, I shall.' The declaration was child-like in its defiance. 'My brother is being dunned and I am to lose my home because your mistress is a selfish spendthrift. Whether you know it or not, sir, indirectly you are a reason we suffer.'

It was too late to perhaps phrase things more tactfully, but there was less volume to Helen's voice when she continued, 'George has dressmakers' accounts and so on that he simply cannot pay…'

'And I am to blame?'

'I have just said so.'

The impenitent statement elicited a mirthless laugh. 'You are a very loyal sister, if blinkered to your brother's faults.'

'On the contrary, I have no illusions as to George's character. He is weak and foolish to allow his wife to constantly manipulate and humiliate him. It is to my sister, Charlotte, that I owe my loyalty.' Helen moved closer to him, hoping the blaze in her eyes and the tenor of her voice would impress on him the strength of her outrage.

She looked into a face of raw-boned masculinity. Even as she glared at him, prepared to continue her tirade, she could not block the thought that he was breathtakingly handsome. 'You are aware that Westlea House has been owned by Kingstons for generations. It was Papa's intention that it should be home to Charlotte and me for years to come. Even had we both settled elsewhere with husbands, my father would have expected George to keep it in the family. He would be distraught to know his son married a shameless adulteress and, as a consequence, the house his wife loved must be sold for a paltry sum.'

'You think I intend to cheat you of its true worth?'

Helen was very aware of his grey gaze lowering to her face with that remark. 'You are a businessman, and very successful I have heard. I can't pretend to know much of commerce, but I'm sure you will want to negotiate terms favourable to you.'

'I'll pay a fair price for the property and George cannot withhold what is due to you and your sister from the proceeds.'

'We have no pecuniary claim on this house.' Tears of frustration sprung to Helen's eyes at that awful truth and she swiftly swung her face away. The movement caused black tresses to fly out and momentarily skim silkily on his dark hand. 'This property belongs in its entirety to George. We have nothing other than the memory of our father's wishes with which to bargain. Already George has broken his undertaking to dispense our allowance.' Helen turned to him, then held her breath as his eyes settled on her mouth. Abruptly she became aware of how close they now were. Barely a few inches separated her faded cambric bodice from the splendid wool of his jacket. She distanced herself with a small backwards step. And then took another.

In a moment of unguarded bitterness she had disclosed far too much that was private to a man she barely knew and certainly could not trust. He was her brother's enemy…hers, too, perhaps. It niggled at the back of her mind that he might use the intelligence she had just provided to his advantage. She might lack business acumen, but she understood the rudiments. It was extremely foolish to disclose one's desperation when negotiating a deal. Far from paying George what was fair for their property, perhaps she had just provided Jason Hunter with the ammunition he needed to haggle.

Helen sensed her spirit sapping. She felt like slumping into a chair to weep. She would not do that, of course, for Charlotte would fret to see her upset. Charlotte! She had forgotten about her sister's imminent return.

Should her sister come in and find her in the company of an imposing stranger, it would be certain to provoke a host of questions, the answers to which could only be depressing. 'I must ask you to leave, sir. My sister will soon be back from visiting her friends and…it is best no explanations are needed for your presence here.' Without awaiting a response to that, Helen walked, with confident step, to the parlour door and opened it.

Jason dipped his head slightly, ruefully accepting his dismissal. In the hallway he turned and stared significantly at wallpaper drooping loose close to the coving. 'You intend to stay here?'

'Indeed, I do.' Helen had bridled at his tacit disparagement. 'This property holds very happy memories of my parents and my childhood.'

Jason nodded absently, glancing about. 'I remember those days…I remember you…' Abruptly his eyes swerved back to her.

The look he gave her was lingering and penetrative and caused her again to blush. He remembered her… A decade ago her face and figure would have been attractively rounded by sufficient food. Her clothes would have been new and stylish. At fifteen she had been beautiful.

His quiet acceptance of her wretched appearance now was hard to bear. Had he displayed surprise or distaste at her deterioration she might have preferred it.

Having been in his company for some while without worrying unduly that she looked a fright, she was suddenly acutely self-conscious. She was ashamed of her worn dress and her locks wild about her shoulders. Belatedly she inwardly railed at fate. Why had he not arrived on her doorstep just five minutes sooner, when her hair was in its pins and she had been still garbed in her good clothes?

She jolted her mind from pointless wishes to say, 'I bid you good day, sir, and please take with you my apologies for the mishap on the road. The cab driver could not have seen you, I fear. Thankfully it seems no harm was done to you.'

A corner of his finely moulded mouth tilted, causing heat to return to her cheeks.

'I appreciate your concern, Mrs Marlowe.'

For some minutes after the front door had closed Helen remained staring at its paint-peeling panels with the sound of his softly mocking voice echoing in her ears.

* * *

'Mr and Mrs Kingston are about to dine, sir.' The manservant whispered that with a concerned frown. One didn't expect a caller at this hour, especially when it was a gentleman of such eminence. Robbins quickly deduced it must be a matter of some moment to bring Sir Jason Hunter here with an angry glitter in his eyes and his mouth clamped to a thin line.

Robbins had been in the Kingstons' employ long enough to know of the hostility that existed between this man and his master. He also knew that, whereas Mr Kingston didn't like Jason Hunter, Mrs Kingston did…rather too much, if gossip was to be believed. The idea that a pillar of polite society would flout etiquette and visit his mistress at her husband's house caused Robbins to almost snort his disbelief. He transformed the noise into a cough. 'Are you expected by Mr or Mrs Kingston, Sir Jason?'

'No, but I will not keep Mr Kingston long from his dinner. Please tell him that I should like to see him on a pressing matter of business.'

Robbins still seemed thoughtful and immovable.

'Tell him…' Jason urged gently, but a terse flick of his head betrayed his impatience.

The manservant needed no further prompting; quickly he hurried away.

* * *

'Have a care! Why are you haring about like that?' Iris snapped tetchily as she stepped from her bedroom to almost collide with Robbins.

Breathlessly the servant gabbled, 'There is a gentleman to see Mr Hunter…umm…I mean there is a gentleman to see Mr Kingston. Sir Jason Hunter is below.'

A wondrous look immediately lifted Iris's sulky countenance. So explicit was her excitement that it caused a sardonic twitch to her servant's lips. When the lady of the house inelegantly pushed past him to fly towards the top of the stairs, Robbins shook his head in disgust.

'Sir Jason…such an agreeable surprise…I hope…no, I must insist…you stay and dine with us.' It was coyly said and Iris posed with a white hand fondling the banister before swaying towards him in a whisper of sky blue silk. She kept her eyes lowered until close enough to coyly peep up at his face. What she read in his expression made a hand flutter to her pearly throat and a budding smile wither on her ruby lips.

'Thank you for your hospitality, but I am not here on a social call, madam. Where is your husband?'

Iris flinched from the ice in his voice, but was reluctant to relinquish the fantasy that he was really here to see her. His brusqueness she explained away: he was uncomfortable with her knowing he longed for her company. And Heaven only knew it was folly to visit her at home when gossip about them was already going around. When they were in public together he could appear aloof but that, too, was a simple ruse to camouflage his tumultuous feelings…a tumult she provoked! She was sure he would soon succumb to those secret yearnings and discreetly proposition her. After all, he could not possibly prefer that common baggage. *Mrs Tucker!* The harlot had never been wed! Diana simply sought to protect her worthless reputation by claiming the status of a widow and everybody knew it.

Iris smoothed her jewelled fingers over the shimmering silk of her skirt, pleased that she had chosen to wear it. She knew the colour matched her eyes and the snug fit to the bodice enhanced her bosom.

'What do you want, Hunter?'

George had been in his study and had just received his servant's breathless message that Sir Jason Hunter requested an audience. George's eyes narrowed suspiciously as he noticed how close together were his entranced wife and his unwanted caller.

'I want to speak to you,' Jason returned in a voice that was low and clipped. He stepped past Iris without giving her another glance.

'Can it not wait till tomorrow? We are about to dine.'

'Your wife has invited me to stay and join you. Shall I do that, or shall we attend to business so I might leave you in peace?'

Iris's lips tightened in annoyance for she knew full well George would rid them of Jason's company as soon as he could.

'Would you mind terribly leaving us, my dear?' George drawled the request, but a significant stare had Iris blushing. 'Ask Mrs Jones to delay dinner for a little while. This will not take long.'

After a twitched smile and a tiny bob Iris flounced away. Before disappearing below, she watched George show Jason to his study.

'What the devil is this about, Hunter? We were just about to sit down. Have you no notion of proper behaviour?'

'I was just about to ask you the same thing.'

'Me?' George choked an astonished laugh as he went to his desk and used the decanter. 'Well, just to impress on you that *I* am a gentleman with certain standards…would you care for a drink?' Without awaiting a reply he thrust a glass of brandy at Jason.

'*A gentleman with certain standards,*' Jason mimicked sarcastically. 'Why is it, then, you allow your sisters to exist in conditions more often found in Whitechapel than Mayfair?'

George gulped too quickly at his brandy and wheezed a cough. 'Explain how you know… What do you mean?' he hoarsely corrected himself.

'This afternoon I went to Westlea House.'

George looked warily at him. 'You ought to have made an appointment for that. You had no right to go there uninvited.'

'You have sent me a contract to sign. I have every right to survey what I am buying.'

'Perhaps; but you have no right to study my family. How my sisters live is my business and none of your concern.' George sipped more sedately at his drink.

'Is that right?' Jason drawled. 'I've recently been told that not only is their plight my concern, but my fault. What is it you really want to sell me, George? Your house or your sister?'

Chapter Five

'That is an exceedingly strange thing to say. Am I to take it as a joke?' George frowned in studied thoughtfulness.

'If it were a joke, it would be in poor taste.'

'I'll take it as a joke, then,' George drawled with heavy irony. 'If I were to take it seriously, I should act as a good brother and defend Helen's honour.'

'How did you know to which sister I was referring?' Jason's teeth flashed in a silent laugh as George's complexion became ruddy. 'You've no need to answer.' His tone was husky with mock sympathy. 'Obviously I realise how you know, you sent Mrs Marlowe to see me.'

George snatched up his drink and took a swig before delivering a curt response. 'That is another exceedingly strange thing to say, Hunter, and not at all funny. It appears you have no notion of what is good taste.'

'It appears you have no notion of how to act as a good brother.'

George's mouth thinned. 'So you have this afternoon been talking to my sister Helen,' he snapped. 'What of it?'

'You sent her to see me. Why?'

'I did no such thing,' George angrily refuted. 'If you knew Helen better, you'd realise that she does as she pleases. A fine day it would be, and no mistake, if she followed my dictates.' He barked a laugh. 'If she did what *I* told her, she would by now be remarried.'

'And thus no financial burden on you.'

'Indeed,' George retorted without shame or remorse.

'I gather you were entrusted with the care of your sisters after Colonel Kingston died. Yet they seem to be fending, not very successfully, for themselves.'

'I'll not discuss any of my family's private business with you!' George thundered and slammed down his glass on a table that became beaded with brandy. 'How my sisters go on is none of your concern.'

'But you'd like to make it so. You're wasting your

time, Kingston. If you have a clear conscience over it, I don't see why I should give a damn.' Even as the callous words were uttered Jason flexed the hand that remembered her touch. A phantom caress from ebony hair was again on his skin and a faint redolence of lavender water teased his senses. He cursed beneath his breath as fingers curled about the brandy George had given him. The amber spirit reminded him of the same soulful-eyed woman. Abruptly he put down the drink and walked to the door, aiming a contemptuous stare at George as he passed him. He halted with a hand gripping the handle.

'I've offered you a generous price for a property in need of extensive repair, and with tenants who are unwilling to leave.'

'There is no need for you to fret over my sisters' accommodation. I have already explained that I have made other arrangements for them.'

'And the dilapidations? The house has obviously been neglected for many years.'

George's mouth disappeared into a thin line. So that was what it was really all about! Money! Hunter had come to haggle over the price now he knew the condition of the property. George had expected to expediently conclude the sale confident that Jason would rely on a memory of Westlea House in its elegant heyday. 'Are you about to renege on the deal?

If you have named a price beyond your means, please say so....'

'I think you know I have not,' Jason enunciated very quietly.

George fiddled nervously with the lawn knot at his throat, for Jason's icy grey gaze was unrelenting. He already regretted having resorted to using scorn. George knew, as did most people, that little was beyond this man's means. The knowledge was galling, yet he was wily enough to know when to retreat. 'Westlea House might now appear a little drab, but it is basically sound and will be grand again. When I have payment you will have vacant possession.'

'You think that your sisters will accept being moved to Rowan Walk?'

George made an exasperated gesture. 'I've had enough of this! You are being damned inquisitive and impertinent over matters that are not for discussion. You are not the only party interested in such a prime piece of property.' Smugly he crossed his arms over his chest. 'Bridgeman has made an offer on it.'

'But not at the figure I gave you. Nobody will match the sum, and you know it.'

George's smirk collapsed—his bluff had been immediately trumped. Colin Bridgeman's offer was far lower and George had been hoping nobody but he was aware of it.

George glowered at his adversary from beneath heavy lids. Hunter hadn't come here simply to complain that Westlea House was rundown. What was bothering him, George was sure, was his meeting with Helen. A crafty smile was imminent, but it withered as Jason stepped purposefully back into the room.

'Before I leave, it is timely to comment on some gossip whilst we are discussing family affairs. It seems your sister is under the impression that I am conducting an illicit relationship with your wife. She has heard a rumour, she said.'

George turned pale, but made no other indication that the subject affected him.

'I'm sorry to have to speak so bluntly, but this matter needs to be addressed,' Jason continued levelly. 'Let me make absolutely clear that I have no romantic interest in your wife. You and Mrs Kingston must deplore the nonsense that is being bandied about to the contrary.' Jason waited, but a rapid tic at the corner of George's compressed lips was all the response he received.

'There has been enough bad blood between us, George. I will not be falsely accused of a dalliance with your wife.'

George turned his back on his visitor. So! Helen had not minced her words with him. He now sensed that sly smile tug at his lips as he wondered whether she had gone so far as to demand he settle with Iris's confounded *modistes*. 'I'm surprised you think a mention needs to be made of it,' he slung over a disdainfully elevated shoulder. '*I* never comment on pathetic concoctions doing the rounds. What I will say is that my eldest sister at times forgets her breeding. She can be far too outspoken and act outside her role. I shall not apologise for her impertinence, if that is what you hoped.'

'You have no need to do so, Mrs Marlowe apologised on her own account.'

'When was that? When she called on you or when you paid a visit to her?'

George's tone held an insinuation that made Jason's eyes narrow to stony slits.

'I was otherwise engaged when your sister paid me a call. I was thus not able to speak to her until I surveyed the house.'

'I'm sure you took a thorough look at it all.'

'I always do when someone is too keen to sell me something.'

The threat George saw in Jason's countenance made him reconsider riling him further. He simply asked innocently, 'Are we to renegotiate the price because of the dilapidations you saw or the insults you heard?'

'I'll honour the sum first agreed on one condition: you find decent accommodation for your sisters.'

George examined his fingernails. 'What's it to you where they live?'

Indeed, Jason wryly thought, what was it to him? But the memory of Helen Marlowe's fragility cocooned by a threadbare dress was again in his mind. Despite her ugly clothing and unbound hair, despite her furious embarrassment when telling him she was to be sent to live on Rowan Walk, she had exuded a quiet pride…a stubborn grace. He recalled the feverish flush he had more than once brought to liven her marble-white complexion. There was meagre satisfaction in knowing that by discomfiting her he had momentarily kept her warm.

Helen Marlowe was neglected because her brother was weak and selfish and unable to control the grasping harlot he had married.

Jason wondered how Iris Kingston would like living in a freezing house, clothed in faded cotton. He wondered how she would withstand feeling hungry, for Helen had looked as though little nourishment passed her lips. He felt tempted to sneeringly voice his thoughts to her inept guardian. Instead he bit out glacially, 'I'll not have people think I'm in any way involved in putting two gentlewomen on Rowan Walk.'

'In case it's imagined you have a…shall we say, special interest in one of them? Both of them?'

Jason allowed that sneer to curl his lip. 'I've never yet housed a paramour so poorly. The fact that you would consider settling your sisters in such surroundings disgusts me.'

'I'm sure you know that your opinion of me counts for nought.'

Jason smiled his contempt on turning away. 'I'll let you get to your dinner…and your lady wife.' In the corridor he halted to say, 'Mrs Marlowe was alone when I visited. I didn't see your younger sister Charlotte. How old is she now?'

George looked startled at that question. 'Charlotte's nineteen. She's quite a beauty…'

'I'm sure,' Jason said drily. He enjoyed a leisurely moment before allaying George's anxiety. 'No need to fret, George, you chose the right one to send to me.'

George stared at the door for some moments after it had closed. He did not immediately go to the dining room to partake of his dinner. He returned to the decanter and poured another brandy. With a frowning countenance and a hand plunged deep into a pocket, he ambled to the fireplace to contemplate the smouldering embers. He tipped up his head to stare into a mirror soaring above the mantelpiece. A corner of his mouth lifted before a huge grin displayed his triumph. He raised his glass, saluted his reflection then downed the cognac in one swallow.

'He won't go, Mrs Marlowe,' Betty announced, with an air of resignation, from the parlour threshold.

Helen looked up from Mr Drover's account, hand delivered that very morning and accompanied by a terse, if ill-spelled, demand for payment for provisions delivered to date. Her eyes were fleetingly drawn back to the postscript in bold print: he would be back for payment before close of business today. Helen doubted it was an empty threat.

'Oh, for pity's sake!' Helen exclaimed in irritation. Pushing the papers away across the table, she jumped to her feet. She glanced over at Charlotte, who had raised her head from her embroidery on hearing her sister's vexed imprecation.

Bored with her stitching, Charlotte tossed the sampler aside and followed her sister into the hallway. Diversion, even of the variety that might conclude in unpleasantness, was a relief from monotony and hunger pangs.

Helen marched towards a grimy face cocked about her front door—it was the sum of the fellow she could see on her step. With a yank the door was fully opened and she looked fully at the mucky, pungent person. 'Look, my good man, my maid has already told you that we have not ordered a delivery. I'm afraid you are at the wrong house.'

'No, I ain't.'

'You are, I tell you!' Helen contested with strengthening volume and impatience. 'I do not even hold an account with your company.

'Bin paid for.'

'Well, in that case those...' a wagging finger indicated the coal sacks '...are most certainly not mine. Go to your depot and check your records.'

A blackened hand dived into a pocket and the coalman thrust a paper at Helen. A tantalising redolence of dusty warmth wafted to Helen's nostrils from his coarse fingers.

'Wot's that say?' he demanded.

Helen tilted back her head to focus on a scrawled address. 'There must be another Westlea House...'

'Not in this square, there ain't.' He tapped black dust on to the scrap of paper. 'That's what it says... see.'

A glimmer of an idea...extraordinary as it was... entered Helen's mind. She took the note and scanned it for clues. 'Did Mr Kingston arrange for this delivery and pay for it through his account?'

'Might 'ave bin 'im, but not on account. The yard

clerk took cash.' A white slash appeared in his dusky complexion as he grinned. 'That's more'n good enough. No questions needed to be arst. Where d'ya want this put? I got other places to go, y'know.'

'Here is George now,' Charlotte whispered. 'He must have been feeling most generous. I expect he's come to make sure the coal has arrived.'

Helen looked from the merchant's surly countenance to the smart rig that had stopped behind a cart laden with oily-looking bags. 'So it is,' Helen muttered with an amazed little huff of a laugh. Never before had their brother taken it upon himself to order a stick of wood or a quarter of tea for them. Prising the money from him in order that she might do so was the routine they had invariably followed till now.

'I suppose there is a first time for everything. Heavens! I hope he has not come to ask for his money back,' Helen muttered, not wholly joking. 'He might have been in his cups when the guilty feelings took hold of him.' Stepping back from the door Helen instructed Betty to deal with the delivery while she and Charlotte went to the parlour to receive their brother.

George had barely stepped into the room, his hand hovering at his coat buttons, when Helen burst out, 'Why have you done such a stupid thing, George? You have paid cash? *Cash?*' she stressed angrily. 'Did it not occur to you that half of what you have spent on fuel might have been used for food? Do you think we might eat coal? And I am quite capable...as ever I have been...of ordering in my own supplies. I know what we need better than do you. Had you given the money to me, I would have used it far more wisely and—'

'What in God's name are you going on about?' George demanded. 'If you think that coalman is my doing, you are very much mistaken.'

Helen looked amazed, then distraught. As the consequences of what she had heard penetrated her mind, she dashed to the door. 'I knew it! It *is* the wrong house,' she muttered, appalled at the knowledge that the merchant would be in no mood to want to remove his wares from her bunker.

George caught at her arm as she made to fly past him. 'I doubt it is the wrong house and, if it is, it is that fellow's error, not yours.'

Helen saw in her brother's eyes a gleam of something akin to amused satisfaction. She was further convinced he was pleased with himself when he gave her a bright smile. Helen chewed at her lip. Past experience had taught her that it boded ill when George looked smug.

'Do you know more of this than you are letting on, George?'

George recommenced unbuttoning his coat and

seemed about to shrug it off. As though suddenly conscious of the chill in the room, he pulled the woollen lapels together to cover his chest. Dropping his hat and gloves on to the table, he informed her with a slanting glance, 'Sir Jason Hunter came to see me earlier in the week.'

Helen felt her complexion heating beneath her brother's significant stare. Helen was aware of Charlotte's mystified frown at their brother's odd declaration. She had not mentioned to her sister anything about her meeting with Sir Jason. The opportunity to improve Philip's prospects had been forgotten and she felt rather guilty about that.

'Mr Goode and Miss Goode are arrived, ma'am.' Betty had again appeared in the doorway.

Charlotte immediately smiled shy pleasure at that news, unaware that her brother had muttered disparagingly beneath his breath on learning who were the visitors.

Helen was well aware that George had little time for Philip. On the few occasions they had come together at Westlea House in the past, George had made little effort to be friendly.

Once ushered into the room, Philip bowed courteously to the ladies, then immediately strode towards George and extended a hand. 'We have not met in some while, sir. It is good to see you.'

With scant enthusiasm in his greeting, George briefly shook hands before withdrawing and striding to take up position by the empty grate.

Undisturbed, Philip drew forward his sister, Anne, and introduced her to George. George managed an approximation of a bow to the plain young woman before drumming his fingers on the mantelshelf.

Anne Goode blinked rapidly, sensitive to the snub. Philip took his younger sister's arm and patted it into place on his sleeve, his smile still present.

Helen felt her temper rising at her brother's churlishness. Quickly she said, 'How nice to see you both. I had no idea you were to call by.' Helen slid a look at Charlotte to see her sister blush.

Philip might manage to appear impervious to George's moods, but he was unable to ignore his beloved's consternation. Quickly he said, 'Oh it was not arranged. Anne and I just thought to call and ask if you would like to take a ride. It is a sunny day and quite warm too.' He looked expectantly at Charlotte, who immediately gave a little nod. Gallantly Philip turned his attention to Helen. 'And you, Mrs Marlowe?

'I thank you, no,' Helen said. 'I have a few matters to attend to.' She gave her boorish brother a sharp glance. 'By all means get your coat and so on,' she told Charlotte. 'There is nothing much to keep you here this afternoon.'

Without further prompting, Charlotte quit the room.

Having watched her go, Philip cast a nervous glance at George. He suddenly took a deep, inspiriting breath and stepped away from his sister.

Helen drew Anne into a little chat, but was nevertheless more interested in hearing the intense speech to one side of her.

'I wonder if I might beg leave to visit, sir,' Philip began in a voice that shook slightly with emotion. 'For some time I have been meaning to come and see you on a matter that is very dear to my heart…'

George shoved away from the mantel against which he had been lounging and interrupted Philip in a voice that was cold and clipped. 'You can find me at my club, sir, most afternoons.'

This time Philip blushed to the roots of his fair hair at such an obvious rebuff. He managed a stiff bow before removing himself to hover close to the door. Within a moment Charlotte appeared. 'I am ready… shall we go?' she said quietly, having noticed from Philip's bright complexion that all was not well.

Once the trio had departed, leaving Helen and George alone, Helen rounded on her brother. 'I cannot believe that you acted so rudely.'

'And I cannot believe that the man has the effrontery to want to bother me at home to ask for my sister's hand in marriage. He has nothing. You only have to look at him to see that!' He barked a laugh. 'His shirt cuff! Did you see it? Frayed!'

'Like this, you mean?' Helen snapped and yanked down one of her own cotton sleeves for his inspection. 'Philip's sister cannot have offended you, yet you treated her with the same lack of manners.'

George tersely flicked away Helen's furious accusations and turned his back on her.

'I am ashamed of you, George. It is getting to the stage when I am loath to admit, even to myself, that we are related, for I am not sure that I like you.'

George pivoted back to glare at her. 'I do not want Charlotte seeing him any more. Make that clear to her or I will make it clear to him. And, as you have just noticed, I shall not stand on ceremony when I do so.' His face was livid when he added, 'I am sick of the burden of two ungrateful sisters to support. I will never countenance being saddled with a good-for-nothing brother-in-law, too.'

'I wish Charlotte had gained her majority and you no longer had power over her life.'

'She is nineteen and I am her guardian. She can do far better than marry him. In fact, perhaps she has already done so.'

'What do you mean by that?'

'I mean that I would hazard a guess that she has caught the eye of an extremely eligible gentleman. I would go so far as to say that it is to that particular wealthy gentleman you are obliged for that delivery of coal.'

Chapter Six

'You are talking in riddles, George. Charlotte knows no extremely eligible gentleman. We do not frequent places where she might meet such a person.'

'She has not needed to go anywhere. Recently a man came here, did he not?' On observing Helen's startled look, he added, 'There's no use in denying it, I've had the news firsthand.'

'Has Sir Jason Hunter asked you if he may propose to Charlotte?' Anticipating a dilatory response Helen came to her own scornful conclusion. 'I know he has not; but you'd like to make me think differently, wouldn't you? You might not like Philip, but this is truly absurd, George!' Helen's large golden eyes demanded a retraction from him, but a smug look was all she received. Helen sighed disappointedly. 'Apart from the fact that a delivery of coal would be an extremely odd courtship gesture, Jason Hunter did not even see Charlotte earlier in the week. She was not at home when he called.'

'I know she was not here. He mentioned that he missed seeing her…amongst other things.'

Helen stared at her brother, perplexity arching her dark brows. 'What exactly did he say?'

'That you were rude to him.'

'I was not!' she spluttered, but with guilty spots of colour seeping into her cheeks. 'I simply told him some truths, and you cannot deny you didn't want me to!' She felt depressed from knowing Jason Hunter had immediately tittle-tattled about her to George. She had not believed him to be that sort of mean character. 'In any case, it ill behoves a libertine to preach about good manners.'

'Never mind about that now,' George airily dismissed. 'Whatever you said, I think it might have had a most beneficial result. Hunter came to see me within a short while of leaving here. He spoke of Charlotte in a way that makes me certain he finds our little sister…interesting.'

'What did he say?' Helen demanded.

'I recall a mention was made of her beauty…' It was a statement calculated by George to imply that the compliment had not been his. Briskly he continued, 'Hunter made a point of asking her age. It is as well Charlotte has gone out for I wanted to speak to you in private. Do you think that he has recently spied her out walking with friends and taken a liking to her?' George subdued a smile on noticing his sister's deep concentration. 'It might end in a family feud if Hunter takes her on. But at least Goode would be saved the indignity of going cap in hand to his cousin.'

'Oh, be quiet, George!' Helen exploded, unimpressed by her brother's drollery. 'Now I think sensibly on it, I see it is just another deluded fancy of yours, concocted in the hope of securing someone rich to clear your debts. None of it alters the fact that Charlotte loves Philip.'

'And Hunter won't give a damn either way.' George bestowed on his sister an extremely patronising smile. 'I realise you were not married long, Helen; perhaps that explains why you often seem too naïve.'

A suspicion of to what her brother was alluding made Helen's soft lips slacken in disbelief.

'Jason won't countenance getting leg-shackled to a woman with nothing to offer but her looks.' George snorted a coarse laugh. 'I know of several ambitious chits with good dowries who would forgo being a duke's wife to marry that particular baronet. He's planning to use his cash to lure a high-born filly and found a dynasty.'

Alarm and anger vied for precedence in Helen's mind now she clearly understood what her brother meant. If Jason Hunter wanted to buy his heirs a nobler lineage, so be it. She was not interested in his aspirations. But the prospect of her sister's ruination was very much a concern close to her heart.

For a few fraught moments Helen played over in her mind all that had passed between Jason Hunter and her when he had come to Westlea House. Had she been so obsessed with lambasting him over his relationship with Iris that she had missed vital clues that he was preying on someone far dearer to her? Her conclusion was that there had been no word or deed of his to make her suspect him a callous seducer of innocents. When she had asked him to leave because Charlotte would soon be home he had not attempted to find an excuse to loiter, and surely he would have done so if he were attracted to their young sister.

With shocking and depressing insight she realised it was not Jason Hunter she mistrusted, but her own brother. 'I cannot believe you would accuse a gentleman of being capable of anything so despicable!' She glared at George, but he simply returned her an impenitent smile. 'Sir Jason might have a reputation as a rake, but I'm certain he leaves maids alone.'

Helen's mounting outrage had made her slender body tense as a spring and her censure increasingly vociferous. In fact, so absorbed had she been in railing at George that for a moment she was unaware that his attention was riveted elsewhere.

What wounded Helen most was the knowledge that their brother—the person their father had trusted would protect and care for his sisters—considered Charlotte's degradation would be a *surprisingly beneficial result* to recent dealings with Jason Hunter.

Helen whipped about to face her brother and was momentarily struck dumb. Betty was, once more, hovering awkwardly on the parlour's threshold, her red countenance bearing testament to her having overheard rather too much of the contretemps between sister and brother.

'There is a gentleman caller, Mrs Marlowe,' Betty announced in a croak, her eyes gliding to the side to indicate the hallway.

Obviously the visitor had also heard Mrs Marlowe shouting like a fishwife. Helen took a steadying breath and submerged her regrets at having been caught out in such unladylike passion, beneath a soaring optimism. She offered up a silent prayer that Samuel Drover had returned to collect his payment and was in no mood to be fobbed off. Fervently she wished the grocer might today succeed in cornering George into settling his account.

But Betty's next whispered words withered any such hope and sent icy fingers to momentarily squeeze still Helen's racing heart.

'The visitor…umm…he…it's…Sir Jason Hunter, ma'am,' Betty concluded.

Helen felt a strange mix of dread and defensiveness coiling cramps in her stomach. It was possible Sir Jason had not heard his name mentioned, or discerned the nature of their heated exchange. But certainly he had heard her sounding like a raucous harpy. She darted a glance at George; his expression betrayed a peculiar ruefulness. Jerking her faculties into action, Helen tilted up her chin and instructed clearly, 'Please show him in, Betty.'

'So, you think my theory absurd, do you? I wonder what brings him here?' George peered closely at Helen. 'Try and make yourself presentable, for Heaven's sake. You have dirt on your cheek. Hunter will think you a slattern.'

Helen's fingers spontaneously jumped towards her face. She gave a tut of dismay as she noticed that the very digits she had been about to employ to remove the spot bore evidence that they had caused it. It was likely the dust had come from the scrap of paper the coalman had given her.

Quickly she wiped her stained fingers on her skirt just as she heard George announce, 'Hunter, fancy seeing you here....'

'A pleasant surprise, I'm sure....'

It was a wry retaliation to her brother's sarcasm and made Helen wince. She raised watchful eyes to Jason's face and again marvelled at features that were both ruggedly masculine yet finely proportioned.

Perhaps aware of her regard, he turned to look at her. Helen proudly tilted her chin and quickly clasped her mucky hands behind her back.

If he was aware that he'd figured in the argument he'd overheard he gave no outward indication. He looked no less cool and composed than he had when last she had seen his sartorially splendid physique stationed in her shabby parlour. And she looked… only slightly better than she had on that occasion, she realised. The bulk of her thick hair was still in a chignon, and her serviceable brown skirt and crisp cotton bodice were an improvement on her faded blue cambric. But on that previous occasion at least her face had been clean. Whilst the two men exchanged a few words Helen casually brought the cuff of a sleeve to her cheek and scrubbed. Her hand dropped back to her side as she heard her name spoken in a husky male voice.

'I trust I've not called at an inconvenient time, Mrs Marlowe.'

It sounded innocent enough, but there was a gleam of amusement in his grey eyes letting Helen know the nicety was ironic. Blood fizzed beneath her skin, but instinctively she sketched a bob in response to his greeting. 'Unfortunately you have, sir,' she boldly told him. 'My brother and I were in the middle of discussing some important domestic issues. I'm sorry to seem inhospitable, but—'

'Helen! Where are your manners?' George interrupted with a reproachful tone and an easy smile. 'There is nothing we were talking about that can't wait for another time.' Pulling out a heavy gold watch, he consulted it with a regretful sigh. 'Look at the time! Much as I would like to tarry and be sociable, I must be on my way. My attorney is expecting me to call on him in Cheapside and after that I have to attend to pressing business in Holborn. Why do you not get Betty to fetch some tea, Helen? I expect Charlotte might soon be back and join you.' He sauntered to collect his hat and gloves from the table before carrying on towards the door.

'Perhaps Sir Jason might think *you* rather impolite,' Helen sharply addressed her brother's back. 'Will you not stay just a short while, George, and keep us company?'

'Of course I should like to, but I'm late already. Besides, I doubt Jason is come to see me. Anything in particular you must say to me, old chap?' he asked with affable charm.

'Not a thing.'

There was again an inflection to her visitor's tone that made Helen sure the two men were tilting at one another. But her overriding desire was to get her brother to tarry long enough to give her an opportunity to slip away and tidy her appearance.

Having come and violently upset her, George was going to insouciantly depart and leave her to deal with the awkwardness of Jason Hunter's untimely arrival. The slippery devil was also going to avoid a confrontation with Mr Drover this afternoon. George was once more about to wriggle free of providing the wherewithal for some provisions.

For some moments after George's slick departure from Westlea House, the only sound in the cool parlour was the rhythmic tick of the mantel clock. Helen managed to subdue her anger at her sly brother for long enough to remember to offer what meagre hospitality was available. 'Please do sit down if you wish, sir.'

Whilst her visitor was seating himself on the ancient leather chair he had used once before, Helen was finding another reason to despise George. His blithe assumption that she had refreshment to give a guest was a typical example of his careless ignorance over how his sisters existed at Westlea House.

Suddenly she pounced on a useful memory. In the dining room was a decanter half-full of Madeira. George kept it replenished in case he fancied a tipple when dropping in on them. Conscious of grey eyes steadily observing her profile, Helen announced with the aplomb of a competent hostess, 'If you would like a drink, sir, my maid will be pleased to fetch you a glass of wine…'

'I thank you, no,' Jason said with a crooked smile. 'I shall endeavour not to outstay my welcome.'

Helen again felt blood tingle beneath her cheeks. Perhaps his voice held no humour and she was simply too sensitive to being mocked.

She resisted the urge to press her fingertips to her face where skin felt singed by eyes like charcoal embers. She knew he had noticed the smudges on her face and the knowledge irked enough to make her prickly. 'Is there a reason for your visit, sir?'

'Indeed there is. I have come to advise you that I have arranged for a load of fuel to be delivered. Has the coalman already been? You look a little sooty…'

Helen inwardly winced, but nevertheless brought her mucky fingers into view and wiped them, very deliberately, with a handkerchief whipped from a pocket. 'As you can see, sir, the delivery has indeed just arrived and, being unexpected, was inconvenient.' She rolled the stained cloth into a ball and hid it in a fist. 'Whilst not wanting to look a gift horse in the mouth, perhaps you would care to explain why you thought to interfere in something that is not your concern.'

'But it is my concern, Mrs Marlowe,' he softly corrected. He leaned back in his chair, lifting a boot to settle at an angle on the other leg. His long lashes screened the expression in his eyes as he said, 'Maintaining this house is now my responsibility. The structure is damp and I have decided it would benefit from some warmth in the rooms.'

Slowly Helen absorbed the awful significance of what she had heard. 'Westlea House is now your property?'

'Yes.'

'The deal is all done? It is finalised so soon?' Her voice was little more than a horrified whisper. As though the full force of the news had finally penetrated, Helen allowed a startled glance to flit about the parlour, as if trying to imprint every faded feature on her mind.

'The sale was finalised a few days ago. I'm surprised that your brother has not already found an opportunity to tell you of it.' Jason paused, looking thoughtful. 'Has George said anything at all to you about the terms and conditions we agreed?'

Helen absently shook her head. She cared little for knowing the details of the deal. Besides, she could guess that the terms and conditions to which he referred centred on the speedy ejection from the premises of George's sisters.

Suddenly she perceived exactly why her brother had been so eager to immediately leave when this man arrived. George had cravenly scampered away lest the news slip out and cause a bad atmosphere. He would not like his sister to harangue him, in front of such an influential acquaintance, over the indecently hasty sale of their childhood home. Helen grimly realised that, had her brother been still within range, she might have forgone a verbal assault in favour of a physical one. Her fingers unconsciously wrung the handkerchief until it loudly yielded. She looked down at the shredded linen, then carefully put it out of sight in a pocket.

It was useless blaming Jason Hunter for depriving her of her beloved Westlea House. It was all George's fault. She walked in a daze to the window and gazed out sightlessly at a smart phaeton. Her trancelike state prevented her from noticing that a neighbour out walking had hesitated to peer inquisitively between the expensive equipage and her front door. Suddenly Helen whirled about to launch some breathless questions. 'Must we leave here immediately? Is that the real reason you have come today? To give us notice to quit?'

Having accepted the comfort of a chair for barely a few minutes, Jason was again on his feet. He shoved his hands in his pockets and, tipping up his head, frowned at the ceiling. 'No, that is not the reason I came here, Mrs Marlowe. I was actually speaking the truth when I said I wanted to tell you a merchant would be calling.'

Helen flushed beneath the tacit warning that he resented the implication he was a liar. But she was to anguished by the loss of Westlea House to offer an apology. All she would now deal in were hard facts. 'When must we leave?' she demanded to know, struggling to sound coolly polite.

'You may stay here until your brother finds you suitable accommodation.'

Helen smothered a laugh with the back of a quivering hand. 'You must be a patient man then, Sir Jason, for I will never find Rowan Walk suitable.'

'Then George must rent another property. If he fails to do so, he will forfeit a sum of money. It is a condition of the sale, signed and witnessed, that you and your sister are housed somewhere that is acceptable to you.'

Helen's fists tightened at her sides. 'And that condition was your idea?'

Jason signalled a brief affirmative with a lazy hand and an expressive lift of his dark brows.

'If you are expecting me to thank you, sir, I am afraid I cannot. If you withhold George's money, he will use that as an excuse to continue to keep us short. Besides, *this* house is the one acceptable to us.'

'If it is really what you want, you may stay here.'

Helen's topaz eyes flew wide in astonishment. A moment later they had narrowed suspiciously. George's theory on this man's interest in Charlotte niggled mercilessly at her mind. Gentlemen did not offer shelter to young ladies unless they were relations…or the target of lustful intentions. 'What do you mean…we may stay here?' she enquired in a glacial tone.

'I mean that your brother must rent you somewhere to live. This house is now mine and I would consider granting a tenancy on it.'

'You would not when you discover how little my brother would be prepared to pay you,' Helen said with a brittle laugh. 'The property on Rowan Walk is taken for six months and he will not squander the expense of that. I told you he had committed to it when last we met. Perhaps you had forgotten what I said.'

'I haven't forgotten one thing you said to me, Mrs Marlowe. And, I repeat, if you want to remain here, I'm sure something can be arranged.'

Helen again felt an alarming *frisson* race through her. Had she misjudged and berated George unfairly? Her brother might think her too naïve, but unbeknown to him she had personal experience of the negotiations between rich men and poor women.

Two years ago she had received, and rebuffed, a proposition from a gentleman wanting to offer her his protection. Colin Bridgeman had written to her of his respectful admiration and of how he was confident that *something could be arranged* between them. Helen had felt at the time quite angry when Mr Bridgeman had ignored her curt note of refusal and written again, coaxingly, of the benefits she would receive. She had been on the point of telling George to speak to the insufferable lecher. Now, of course, she was glad she had kept the matter private—doubtless George would have insisted that she take up Mr Bridgeman's kind offer.

Helen shot a wary glance at Jason's face. He returned her regard with quite pleasant directness.

She had spoken to him once before in a blunt way that would guarantee her ostracism by polite society should they ever know of it. Taking a deep, inspiriting breath Helen blurted out, 'I must beg your pardon, sir, and your forbearance, but I find I must again speak to you in a way that will be considered shockingly improper.'

'Please say what you must. I'd rather there was no misunderstanding between us.'

But having boldly got that far, even his gentle prompting could not bolster her courage. Looking up at his worryingly handsome face, she decided first to try and prise some clues from him. 'When you arrived here today...I expect you overheard...that is...I'm sure you know George and I were arguing.' Large amber eyes peeked up through a web of inky lashes to discern his reaction.

'I admit I was aware of a heated exchange.' Jason's mouth tilted, but he seemed unwilling to elaborate.

'I'm not sure how much you overheard...' Helen probed.

Jason felt tempted to smooth back the lustrous strand of hair that clung stubbornly to her soot-smudged cheek. Instead he murmured, 'Please don't embarrass yourself by mentioning it further, Mrs Marlowe. Suffice to say that I was not disappointed on hearing your opinion of me.'

Helen felt fiery blood rush beneath her complexion.

Seeing he had heightened her confusion, Jason

soothed softly, 'My intention was *not* to embarrass you, Mrs Marlowe. Let's say no more of it.'

Helen cleared her throat. 'I find I cannot just dismiss it, sir, for I'm not now sure that George deserved the ticking off I gave him.'

'And what has changed your mind?'

'Something you have said…'

Jason twisted a slight smile. 'Ah, I see. You no longer think me a principled rake…just a rake. Will you enlighten me as to how I have disgraced myself in such a short while?'

Helen nodded, but his mild mockery had made words again awkwardly clutter her throat.

Jason walked to the cold marble mantel and braced a lean hand against it. 'Let me hazard a guess and save you the ordeal of telling me. You think that any benefits I have offered will be subject to unpleasant conditions. Let me reassure you. I do not need to coerce widows in straitened circumstances into sleeping with me.'

Helen's beautiful eyes shot to his face as the awful truth registered. He thought she was hinting he found *her* attractive.

'*Me?*' Helen gasped in a voice that hovered between ridicule and outrage. 'Oh, no! I don't think you want me at all. I think it is Charlotte you're after.'

Chapter Seven

'Charlotte? Your younger sister?'

Helen had to admit that his astonishment seemed genuine. His brow, visible beneath a fall of dark hair, had furrowed, and he looked ready to laugh. Feeling unaccountably nettled by his reaction, she gave a curt nod.

'You think that I have designs on your sister's virtue.' It was a toneless statement and he now looked far from amused.

Helen felt her pique wilt beneath his latent anger. She chewed nervously at her lower lip and tried to avoid the ominous glitter in his eyes. But still she wanted to hear his denial. 'Are you saying you didn't intend to attach strings to your generosity?'

'Is there any point in saying anything at all? It seems I've already been found guilty as charged.'

'No! That's not true. I told George I did not think you capable of callously seducing a chaste young woman.' She had come closer to him in her agitation and a small hand raised as though she would clasp his forearm in emphasis.

Just for an instant their eyes coupled, travelled together to her outstretched fingers. Helen quickly curled the slender digits into her palm and the fist dropped to her side.

'But you think my leniency extends only to untried maids,' he stated quietly.

'I do not think you a callous man at all,' Helen briskly said with a crisp back-step. 'I'm sorry if I have offended you, but I did warn you I had nothing pleasant to say. Charlotte is just nineteen and hoping soon to get engaged. A hint of scandal would ruin her reputation and her future.' She hoped that her apologetic explanation had sweetened his temper, but received no such sign.

A finger fiddled a bothersome curl behind a small ear. 'I'm sorry I mentioned any of it. It is just that…someone said you were showing an unusual interest in Charlotte.'

'I wonder who it was?'

The question was soft, sardonic, and Helen knew that trying to shield George was pointless. Jason was perfectly aware who had sown that particular poisonous seed in her mind.

The best form of defence is attack, her papa would have counselled had he known her predicament. And she did have a grievance of her own to air! 'I know you went to see my brother after you left here last week. He told me so this afternoon.' She gave him a reproachful look. 'I had already apologised to you for being impertinent that day. Perhaps if you had not gone off telling tales to him my sister's name would not have arisen and thus no misunderstandings either.'

'So I'm not only suspected of being a brute, but a tattler, too.'

Jason shoved his hands deep into his pockets and slanted a searing look at her from beneath curved black lashes. 'Do you seriously think I would waste an hour of my time bleating to your brother about how horrid you had been to me?'

Helen winced at the dark irony in his voice. 'I realise you had other matters to discuss with George, too,' she tartly allowed.

'Indeed, I did,' Jason drawled. 'Actually, I must thank you, Mrs Marlowe, for bringing something to my attention. It seems that a comment from me was long overdue on a slanderous rumour going around.

I have not cuckolded your brother and have no intention of doing so.'

Helen's heart jumped a beat, then started an erratic tattoo beneath her ribs. She had certainly not expected *that* to be one of the topics he had discussed with George. 'Be that as it may, sir,' she breathed, 'you have only yourself to blame that people have assumed differently. If you flirt outrageously with my sister-in-law, you ought know gossip will ensue.'

'I abandoned flirting a decade or more ago, Mrs Marlowe. And you ought know that, where I am concerned, your brother is a regular mischief-maker. I suspect his wife is, too.'

He was correct, of course, in his assessment of her kin. Moreover, she believed he had been wrongly maligned, and thus could have made much more of a complaint than a taciturn observation on the devious natures of her brother and sister-in-law. Nevertheless, Helen instinctively bristled at receiving even a mild rebuke from him. She blinked and moistened her dry mouth by delicately tracing her lower lip with her tongue tip.

His steady, penetrating appraisal flustered Helen and she fought to equal his calm demeanour. She wished he would go, yet, confusingly, was reluctant to lose his company. There was something about him that was daunting, yet very appealing. He seemed in no rush to leave despite having done his duty and advised her of the coal delivery. Perhaps he was allowing her an opportunity to raise objections to his criticism of George and Iris from consanguinity. But her selfish sister-in-law deserved no such championship, and she baulked at the level of hypocrisy required to defend her brother.

Unspoken words seemed to whisper between them in the tense silence. She sensed he was daring her to voice the thoughts haunting her mind. Persistent phrases crept again to teeter on her tongue-tip. *Why do you stare? Is it me you want?*

Helen compressed her shapely lips into a tight line as though forcibly preventing any such shameful utterances from escaping. Jason Hunter had told her earlier, with faint scorn, that he had no need to coerce widows in straitened circumstances into sleeping with him. But what if they needed no such persuasion?

Helen averted her face, hoping to conceal the blush she again felt staining her complexion. It was not his potent presence that caused her embarrassment, but her own unquiet mind. She had never before considered herself conceited, yet a silly fantasy that this gentleman might desire her would not quit her thoughts.

Helen knew, as did the rest of polite society, that Jason Hunter had selected Mrs Tucker to fill the role her sister-in-law coveted.

Some months ago, when she had been out walking with Charlotte and a friend of theirs, Emily Beaumont, she had observed a beautiful young woman alight gracefully from a shiny carriage drawn by a pair of splendid greys. Servants in smart black livery had been in attendance and the ensemble had drawn admiring glances, not only from Helen's party, but from other people promenading, too. Emily had whispered that Sir Jason Hunter had provided the lady's transport. It was at that point that Helen learned from Emily the identity of the favoured lady and why Sir Jason would be so generous.

Diana Tucker had soon made her way, with confident step, into a shop. Helen had pensively studied her stylish outfit, thinking that, with her superior air and elegant bearing, she might have been a nobleman's daughter rather than a notorious courtesan.

In her mind's eye Helen could again see blonde curls dancing over blue velvet shoulders and a pretty face shadowed by a plumed hat cocked to a jaunty angle. In her nostrils was a faint redolence of an exotic perfume that had wafted in Mrs Tucker's wake on that particular afternoon.

An involuntary glance down at her appearance took in her drab skirt and frayed cuffs. Her critical eyes spotted the soot smudges on her hands and she absently rubbed her fingertips together. She recalled that her face was similarly grubby and her hair dishevelled. At that moment she was conscious of how very risible was her idea that she might attract a disturbingly rich and handsome baronet. It prompted her to stutter into the silence, 'For…forgive me, sir, but it seems we have said all we must. My sister will soon be home, and…'

'And you would like me to leave,' he finished for her in a wry tone.

Helen nodded and managed a grateful smile. She was on the point of summoning Betty to show him out when the maid poked her head about the door. The housemaid was holding the handle close to her body with just her face and mobcap visible at an angle.

'What is it, Betty?' Helen asked quickly, alarmed by her servant's odd appearance.

Betty took a nimble sideways step over the threshold and tried to immediately shut the door behind her. It was to no avail. She was suddenly sent flying as the door was shoved fully open and a stout gentleman barged in to the parlour. He was garbed in a brown wool coat and beneath a burly arm was squashed his hat.

'Is this him?' Samuel Drover loudly demanded, forgoing introduction or explanation for his outrageous intrusion. His balding pate was snapped down in the direction of Jason. 'Is it him?' he again insisted on knowing. His scalp remained low and pointing straight ahead, although his eyes had swivelled to bulge at Helen.

Helen blinked rapidly, momentarily shocked to speechlessness.

'I told him you was prior engaged with company, ma'am,' Betty mumbled, miserably aware of her mistress's petrified consternation. 'He don't never listen. He just pushed past…uncouth he is…'

Samuel Drover was unaffected by that slur on his character. 'Is this the poor fellow?' he purred sarcastically. He eyed the imposing gentleman stationed by the mantelpiece, a dark hand braced on pale marble and a faintly bemused expression shaping his beautifully stern features. 'I must say he don't look to be on his uppers.' Mr. Drover subjected Jason to a calculating inspection. 'I reckon this person could find fifty-three pounds two shillings and five halfpenny in his pocket right now.' With that he whipped a bill from somewhere inside his coat and begun to stride purposefully forward.

Having finally shaken herself from her daze, Helen said in a quaver, 'Mr Drover, please wait in the hallway and I will—' She broke off to skip over the oak boards as Samuel Drover continued his menacing advance towards Jason.

Helen deftly interposed her petite figure between the belligerent grocer and the muscular physique of her new landlord. She stood with her chin elevated and her back to Jason as though she would protect him from assault...or having his pockets picked. With her countenance alternating between shocked pallor and pink mortification, she announced, 'Mr Drover! Listen to me! This gentleman is most definitely *not* my brother, I cannot impress on you strongly enough that I resent...' Helen's impassioned plea was curtailed as firm hands, gentle as a caress, enclosed her upper arms. Suddenly she was lifted a little way off the ground and then deposited carefully at Jason's side.

Mr Drover tottered back a step as a broad hand suddenly shot towards him.

'I don't think we have been properly introduced. I am Sir Jason Hunter.'

Samuel Drover glared suspiciously at the five elegant digits extended towards him.

Having clapped his eyes on a gentleman with dark hair and a handsome visage, at his ease inside Westlea House, Samuel was impressed enough by the likeness between the couple to have decided this must be the tight-fist to whom Mrs Marlowe was related. 'How can I be sure you're not this lady's brother?' he queried whilst giving a single pump to Jason's hand.

'Should you demand proof, my mother, I think, would attest to my legitimacy, having first planted you a facer.' It was no empty jest. The Dowager Lady Hunter was renowned for a fiery temperament that remained unabated despite her having recently reached the stately decade of a sexagenarian.

Samuel Drover's eyes squinted upwards in consideration. Defeated, he muttered, 'Well, whoever you say you are, I want my cash. And don't try to pull a fast one and take your custom elsewhere. I'll tell every other merchant hereabouts to avoid your business. Don't think I won't.'

Numb with humiliation Helen could only watch glassily as Jason suddenly took Mr Drover's shoulder in what looked to be an exceedingly firm grip. Five fingers bit further into brown wool as the man tried to shrug him off.

'I think you have made your point,' Jason said.

'If you're not Kingston, where is he? Do you know?' The grocer gave Helen a hard stare. 'Mrs Marlowe thinks to keep that information from me. I'll find out his direction and set the duns on him.'

'I understand your predicament, sir,' Jason said equably, steering Samuel about with one hand in quite a facile fashion. 'However, as you can see, Mrs Marlowe's brother is not here, so you appear to be wasting your time and your threats.'

'I'll take back the sack of potatoes, or what's left of it, that my boy brought here last week.' Mr Drover aimed that over his shoulder at Helen as Jason propelled him towards the door.

'I'll bid you good afternoon, Mrs Marlowe,' Jason said as he paused for a moment on the threshold. His easy stance seemed in no way affected by the restriction he was imposing on the fidgeting merchant.

Helen fleetingly met his gaze and a flicker of gentleness in his eyes put a peculiar sensation in the pit of her stomach. *Don't pity me!* It was a silent, heartfelt demand that threatened to burst the sob swelling in her chest. Quickly she lowered her prickling eyes to her tightly laced fingers. Unaware that Jason had nudged the florid-faced grocer forward into the hallway, she managed an imperceptible nod at an empty doorway. 'Yes…good day to you, sir….'

'You look as though you've lost a sovereign and found a shilling.'

Jason scowled at his brother as he passed him. By the time Mark Hunter had turned on the sweeping staircase, peered at his brother's flying heels, then hared after him, Jason had strode the length of a thickly carpeted corridor. He slammed into his study, downed two shots of whisky one after the other and was refilling his glass when Mark appeared.

'Bad time at the tables?' Mark's tone was sympathetic as he speculated on a possible, if unlikely, cause of his brother's dark disposition. He helped himself to Jason's decanter and, after a couple of gulps from his glass, realised his commiserations remained unappreciated. He tried a blunter approach. 'Devil take it, Jay, if you've not lost at cards, what's up with you now? It's too much, I tell you, having to continually look at your long face. You've been odd for weeks.'

Jason let his lean frame drop into the chair positioned behind a grand oak desk. Having settled himself with his boots resting on the table edge, he slanted his brother a stare over the rim of his glass. 'When did my moods become your damned business? And why is it every time I come home, you're here? I don't remember inviting you to move in.' His brother's pained expression caused him to blow out his cheeks and gesture apology with a flick of a hand.

'I know the old goat wants shooting for acting so blasted idiotic,' Mark intoned with some indignation. 'But, even if the two women are good friends, it don't just affect *your* mistress, y'know. Every bachelor in town is cursing over it, so no need to take it out on me if Diana is being tricky.'

Jason grunted a laugh at his brother's oblique and garbled reference to a rumour that he'd personally found amusing rather than irritating.

He had heard the talk that his paramour was jealous of her friend Mrs Bertram. That woman had, if gossip was to be believed, secured a promise from Lord Frobisher that he would make an honest woman of her before the year was out, thus making her a lady in name, if not in nature.

Jason carefully placed down his empty glass, feeling a little the worse for alcohol. On the way home he had called in at White's and loitered, drinking, for an hour or more, hoping that George Kingston might turn up, simply so he could knock down the mean bastard.

'It's nothing to do with Diana or any foolish aspirations she might have,' he told his brother.

'Relieved to hear it,' Mark replied with a grin. 'So what has upset—?'

'Mark…go away,' Jason advised with guttural gentility.

Mark noticed a flare of threat in his brother's eyes and shrugged. He knew from past experience when it was wise to retreat and leave Jason alone to brood. He strolled to the door, whistling.

Jason rested his dark head against the hide chair-back and stared sightlessly at the ceiling. His features were tensely set, but a muscle moving close to his mouth animated his mask-like visage.

His brother's instinct that a woman was stoking his frustration was quite correct, even if he was ignorant of her identity.

Helen Marlow had unexpectedly come back into his life and he couldn't chase from his mind the exquisite woman who had emerged from the bonny child he'd known. He wished now that he'd sought to renew their acquaintance sooner. He could have done so, for he'd spied her at a distance on odd occasions. It would have been simple enough to approach her and ask how she fared. But the feud with George had driven a wedge between them years ago when she was still a schoolgirl. Later, when she returned to town as a young widow to live with her father, it seemed too much time had passed and they had slipped back to being virtual strangers.

It had been more than ten years since he had come within touching distance of her. From the moment she had opened the door of Westlea House to him and tried to hide her dishevelled appearance behind the wood panels, he had been robbed of his peace of mind. In truth, he resented the loss.

Yet his thoughts continually revolved around

finding excuses to go back and see her again. The urge to do so was not primarily altruistic and therein lay the root of his torment. He wanted to improve her lot in life, but he desired her, too, and she knew it.

He gave a lopsided smile at the ceiling as he recalled the way she had instinctively leaped to defend him when the grocer got belligerent. Feelings of tenderness had engulfed Jason as she'd stood before him like an intrepid waif prepared to do battle. He'd also felt a sense of relief, for she had proven—unintentionally, he imagined—that she was not completely set against him. She was indebted to him through no fault of her own and she sensed that made her vulnerable to his lust. In just a short while she had displayed wit and courage and dignity. She had also showed her selfish brother more loyalty than George would merit in his lifetime. But acknowledging Helen had fine qualities had not subdued the throb in his loins.

He had a perfectly adequate mistress. Why would he want the trouble of wooing into bed a well-bred woman who thought him a rake and seemed unwilling to trust him to act ethically? Something else was nettling him. Jason knew he was playing too easily into George Kingston's hands. He was allowing George to manipulate him, yet seemed unable to put a stop to it. George wanted him to take over the financial burden of his sisters' keep and he was achieving his aim with such ease that he had begun to dispense with the need to be subtle. Filling the empty grates and larders at Westlea House was not his responsibility. But he had taken on the task, just as George intended he should. George had gambled on a meeting between Helen and him paying spectacular dividends, and he had won. George was now basking in his victory. He was goading him, blatantly challenging him to choose between pride and lust.

Jason knew that soon he would have to make a decision before gossip started. Evicting Helen and her sister from Westlea House was out of the question, but it would not be long before it was common knowledge he owned the property. Risking a stain on Charlotte's reputation was also out of the question. The obvious solution would be to establish a position in his life for Helen.

Wife or mistress? George Kingston would not care either way. If Mrs Marlowe became a kept woman, polite society would be provided with a tasty morsel of gossip for a week or two, but they would not ostracise her. Helen's reputation was protected by the status conferred by her late husband.

Thus, it was his choice which role he offered to her after such a limited renewal of their acquaintance. Certainly she fascinated him and he was sure he liked her, but he had felt that way before about young women who now he could barely recall to mind.

Jason got to his feet, only half-aware that he had come to a decision as he stretched out his stiff muscles. A rueful smile tugged at a corner of his mouth as he realised that the only objections he was likely to receive to an offer of *carte blanche* was from the lady herself.

Chapter Eight

'What on earth is the matter?'

Helen had been attempting to compose a letter of apology to Jason Hunter while Charlotte was out. The scuffed leather surface on the bureau was littered with crumpled scraps of paper, testament to the difficulty of the task she'd set herself.

But now Charlotte was back and looking very dejected. Pushing away pen and paper, Helen swivelled on her seat. Charlotte was plucking at her hat strings with vibrating fingers. Once free of her thick tresses, the bonnet was forcefully discarded on to the sofa. Charlotte sank down beside it, her red-rimmed eyes concealed by her palms.

'What is it, dear?' Helen immediately went to her. She crouched by the side of the chair with an anxious frown crinkling her ivory brow. Charlotte's hands were gently eased from her face and Helen comforted them with her own. 'What has happened? Is Philip not with you?' Helen glanced at the door. Philip invariably came in for a short while when he brought Charlotte home from an outing. 'Have you argued?' It was a doubtfully tendered possibility. Charlotte and Philip usually seemed a very harmonious couple.

Charlotte raised her watery brown eyes to Helen's face. 'Philip won't ever come here again. He won't marry me now. Why would he when I have such a hateful brother?' she gritted out through small pearly teeth. Charlotte again hid her freshly streaming eyes with her fingers.

Helen sank forward on to her knees as an inkling of what might be ailing her sister put a guilty sigh in her throat. So obsessed had she been with dwelling on her fraught encounter with Jason Hunter and Mr Drover that she had neglected to give any more thought to a worrying incident that had occurred before either of those gentleman had arrived.

Helen cast back her mind a few hours. Charlotte had been from the room, collecting her coat, when George had cruelly curtailed Philip's attempt to make formal his suit. No doubt Philip had felt injured enough by George's churlish rejection to tell Charlotte of it.

Helen remembered, too, with heavy heart, that George had not been content to leave it at that. Once their sister had quit the house with the Goodes, George had more doom to deliver on the subject of the courting couple. Or rather, he had anticipated that she would do his dirty work for him. His curt dictate echoed in her mind: *I do not want Charlotte seeing him any more. Make that clear to her or I will make it clear to him. And, as you have just noticed, I shall not stand on ceremony when I do so.*

'Was Philip annoyed that George was short with him? He had every right to be…'

'What did he say to Philip?' Charlotte interrupted, scrubbing the heel of a hand across her eyes. 'Tell me, please! I sensed something unpleasant had occurred while I was getting ready to go out. Philip is too agreeable to make a fuss, but I guessed something was wrong, even before George came over and was horrible to us in the park.'

'You saw George whilst you were out?'

Charlotte nodded. 'I'm sure George only turned up in Hyde Park because he guessed we had gone there. Why does he hate Philip? He has never taken the trouble to get to know him.'

Helen tightened her grip on Charlotte's shivery hands. 'I'm sure he does not hate him,' she soothed. 'It is just that our brother is…' She struggled to find words that might mitigate George's boorishness. 'I know our brother has an unfortunate manner at times,' she lamely concluded.

'*Unfortunate manner?*' Charlotte shrieked and stamped a foot to emphasise her outrage. 'He is a swine! He deliberately humiliated Philip in front of his sister and me! The park was quite crowded too and a lot of people witnessed what went on. A horrible fellow started laughing at us.' Charlotte's voice wobbled as she recounted, 'Poor Anne was so upset she started to cry, although she pretended she just had a speck in her eye.'

Helen's wide eyes revealed her astonishment at what she'd heard. Usually George sought to keep his shameful behaviour out of public display. 'What exactly did he do?' she demanded to know.

'We had stopped by the lake to watch the swans and George just appeared with one of his cronies. George got out of his carriage and stormed over to us. With no more ado he ordered me home. Philip was startled by his rudeness, but took it in good part, I thought. I'm sure he knew George was slighting him because he doesn't deem him good enough for me.' She paused to wipe a hand across her feverishly flushed cheeks. 'Philip offered to immediately bring me back, but George stared at him as though he was dirt beneath his shoe. He snapped out that he would directly take me *safely* home himself.' Charlotte pulled a scrap of linen from a pocket. She furiously applied it to her glistening dark eyes. 'Philip was…he looked so mortified when George made me get out of the gig. That's when I heard his friend laughing.' She gurgled a sob, then wiped her dewy nose. 'I tried to reassure Philip that I was disgusted too by George's behaviour. I said I would be pleased to see him again later in the week. But he avoided my eye and said, in a strange voice, that he didn't think that would be possible.' Charlotte blinked away fresh tears. 'He doesn't want to see me again. It is finished between us, I know it is.'

Helen shot to her feet. 'George brought you home? Where is he?' she demanded and flew to the window to peer out into the street.

'He is gone. The whole way home he wouldn't speak to me, even when I shouted at him that he was overbearing. When we turned into the Square he cast on me one of his black looks.' Charlotte pursed her lips mutinously. 'He said he would never give his consent to a man of Goode's standing and I might as well get used to it. That's when I told him he was the vilest man alive and I would marry whomever I chose and *he* might as well get used to it. After that it was as much as he could do to help me down from the carriage. He was so rough with me I feared he might pull my arm from its socket. Before Betty had let me in he'd set off up the street.'

Helen observed Charlotte's distress and her heart went out to her. It was difficult to comprehend why any decent person would deliberately make a spectacle of a gentleman as inoffensive as Philip Goode. But then George, she reluctantly admitted to herself, had not acted very decently in a long while. Despite knowing it, she still felt lurking within her a sibling's sadness. A corrosive resentment of the contented, and a grasping wife, were destroying the personable brother who once had taught her how to ride her first pony and fish the streams in the Surrey countryside.

Helen retraced her steps to the sofa and sat down close to Charlotte. 'From what you have said it seems George has made himself, rather than Philip, appear ridiculous. It is George who needs our pity,' she added gravely. 'Perhaps if he had made a successful marriage he might not be so sour at life.' She enclosed her sister in a hug and planted a kiss on her luxuriant, auburn tangles. 'We are the lucky ones, Charlotte. You and I both have known what bliss there is in being cherished by someone we love. Poor George! I think at times he knows what he misses and is bitterly jealous.'

Charlotte rested her head on Helen's slender shoulder. 'I wish Papa was here. He would have liked Philip. He would have given us his bless-ing…just as he did to you and Harry.'

'Yes, he would. Philip is very like Harry. I ex-pect that is why I took to him from the start.' With a wistful smile she looked down at her young sister. 'But our papa is not here. Neither is dearest Harry.' She put Charlotte from her and said briskly, 'So we must look after ourselves and not let our brother scare the fight out of us.'

'I do love Philip, you know.'

'Yes, I do know. And that is why, somehow or other, you must marry him,' Helen answered softly. She looked off into the distance with a slight frown drawing close her ebony brows. 'I expect Philip wants very much to see you again, but fears spark-ing another ugly scene with George. And who could blame him for that?' She gave Charlotte an encouraging smile. 'The best thing will be for me to go alone and pay the Goodes a visit. I shall let them know that they are most welcome to call on us at any time. If George gets temperamental over it…well, he shall have me to contend with.'

'Beg pardon, Mrs Marlowe, but he is back again.'

Helen peered over her sister's tousled head at Betty. Her maidservant was, once more that day, sta-tioned in the doorway with an apologetic look on her face. Helen sensed her heart falter and then a burst of terrified exhilaration made her feel quite light-headed. In a breathy rush she demanded, 'Who is it, Betty?'

'Oh, not the gentleman, ma'am,' Betty said with distinct disappointment. 'It's Mr Drover. He won't say what he wants, so I've left him on the step this time.'

Within a moment Helen was briskly walking to the front door. 'My brother is still not here, Mr Drover,' she announced without preamble. 'And I am not expecting him to arrive any time soon. I'm very sorry, but I cannot help you.'

'I've not come about him.' The grocer shifted on the stone step, fingering the brim of the hat that he was banging in rhythm against his knees. 'I'm sorry for acting hot-headed earlier…end of tether, you understand.' He cleared his throat. 'The other gentleman settled my account.' His tone was level, but a sly glance slanted up at her before he again meekly studied his shoes. 'I've fetched over that order you sent with my boy earlier in the week.'

'Sir Jason Hunter has settled the bill…' Helen whispered. It was not really a question at all. Since Jason had been rudely petitioned to pay for her groceries, she had wondered if he might indeed do so.

Helen suddenly became conscious that Betty was hovering behind her. The young woman's gaping mouth and bulging eyes indicated her great interest in the proceedings. Before Helen could dismiss her entranced maid, Samuel Drover supplied both women with another piece of riveting information.

'The gentleman left cash on your account, too, so you're not to fret on this load.' He gave a sideways nod at his cart. After a silent few seconds he politely queried, 'Shall I start to bring it in?'

'Please do.' It was a firm instruction from Helen, issued after only a tiny hesitation.

Mr Drover lowered his head and humbly backed away a step or two before setting about his task.

Helen proudly elevated her chin. 'Please set fires in the parlour and the bedchambers. Then when the provisions are checked we will plan what to prepare for dinner.'

'Yes, ma'am,' Betty agreed in a buoyant tone.

Charlotte's bright words, issued from the parlour's doorway, reassured Helen that her sister had observed, if not heard, what went on. 'Heavens! Do you think that George is feeling so guilty over his foul behaviour this afternoon that he has paid the bill at last and sent us some food?'

Helen subdued the sour laugh that scratched at her throat and limited her response to a wry smile. She did not intend to lie to her sister over the source of their improved fortune. But omitting to mention who was their benefactor might be wise until she had a notion of how to present it all to Charlotte.

Besides, Charlotte now seemed too embroiled in her own tribulations to bother with mundane domesticity even if a tasty meal and a warm bedchamber were finally in the offing. Helen could tell that her sister was again lost in her own thoughts as she fiddled with her hat ribbons and sighed loudly. 'Why do you not go and freshen yourself, Charlotte? Put a brush through your hair and wash your teary cheeks before we dine.'

Charlotte sucked in a rejuvenating breath. With a little nod she turned towards the stairs. Halfway up the flight she pivoted towards Helen with a plea that proved her thoughts were indeed fixed on her beloved. 'Will you promise me that very soon you will go and see Philip? Please tell him that I am so sorry and that—'

'Hush!' Helen interrupted Charlotte, but she gave her an indulgent smile. 'I have said I will go there and so I shall.'

In a moment Charlotte had skipped out of sight and Betty had bustled into view with the coal scuttle.

Helen quite expected to hear the sounds of Mr Drover whistling and Betty humming a tune. She felt heat flood her complexion as she imagined what occupied their minds as they happily went about their business. The grocer and her servant had come to the same conclusion about what prompted *the gentleman's* intervention in her domestic affairs. It had improved their attitudes enormously to think that she was paying in kind for her keep. Helen didn't for one moment blame either of them for suspecting such an arrangement existed. Had she not already challenged Jason Hunter to clarify what motivated his benevolence? She had received no proper answer from him and was still unsure what prompted him to be generous. But the thought of accepting his charity or his pity was anathema to her.

She could, of course, leave the food on the cart and the coal in the bunker. Charlotte and she could swallow their pride and scrape an existence on Rowan Walk instead of in Westlea House.

Helen felt tranquillity trickle through her as an inner battle ebbed. In her mind it was settled, and there was nothing new or daring about her plan. A host of women before her had resorted to a discreet liaison to keep themselves and their families clothed and fed. He seemed honest and generous and there was nothing about his person that revolted her... quite the reverse... As to her part, she was sure that she could adopt a brazen attitude and willingness. She glanced at her dowdy appearance and gave a wry smile. Perhaps a little artifice with a needle and a rouge pot might not go amiss either.

A little breath caught in her throat as she contemplated the decision she'd made. She might try to be rational and practical, but there was no denying Sir Jason was a powerful and exciting man. What if her proposition was rebuffed, or worse, mocked? Helen felt a fluttering in her abdomen as she imagined dealing with the humiliation of his rejection. The feeling strengthened as she imagined dealing with his agreement to her suggestion! She felt heat seep into her complexion at the haunting memory of making love with Harry. Would she want to again have the sensation of a man's hot skin welded to hers when, perhaps, he might not even like her very much? She quickly concentrated on Jason's kindness to her, the intensity of his grey gaze when he looked at her. He liked her at the very least, she was sure of it!

'It looks as though Bridgeman has forgiven George for not selling him Westlea House.'

Mark Hunter's cynical observation drew his brother's interest. Jason dropped the opera glasses from his eyes and turned to look to his left.

Colin Bridgeman and George Kingston were indeed looking very cosy together in one of the boxes.

Bridgeman had his head tipped back and was guffawing. Of Iris Kingston there was no sign, although Jason had seen George and his wife arrive together. Jason's coach had drawn up outside the opera house at the same time as had George's. The gentlemen had coolly acknowledged one another with a nod. The ladies had exchanged disdainful summarising stares. Diana's audible aside that a far superior harlot would be needed to put *her* in her place had made Jason inwardly smile as they proceeded to the stairs in the King's Theatre.

The house had been scintillating with light and laughter as Jason and Diana took their seats in one of the green boxes just before the performance started.

Now the curtain had fallen on the first act and a buzz of conversation was again growing louder in the auditorium. The performance had been pleasing, but now the main entertainment had begun as people flitted from place to place to pose with friends and gossip over the latest *on dits*. Mark Hunter had moments ago ambled in to speak to his brother, leaving behind in his own box his current amour. The abandoned actress was with her gallants, yet her soulful eyes were constantly straying to Mark despite the fact that he appeared oblivious to her attention.

Soon after Mark had arrived in Jason's box, Diana had left it. Jason had made no objection when one of his mistress's young admirers had entered his domain. The fresh-faced boy had politely asked if he might escort Mrs Tucker to Lord Frobisher's box where her friend Mrs Bertram was holding court.

The appearance of the eager young buck hovering behind him had started Jason reminiscing on his own youth. For the past few minutes he had been idly training his glasses on the pit to watch the boisterous gentlemen congregating there. Fifteen or more years ago it would have been he and his friends—George Kingston included—laughing and joking whilst fixing a lascivious eye on the elegant females up in the boxes. It had been a game amongst young bloods then, as he imagined it was now, to compete for a lady's signal. Wagers had regularly been laid on who would be first to be beckoned by a society beauty to indulge in a little flirtation…perhaps more than that before the night was out.

Jason had been following, with some lazy interest, the interaction between Michael Langham and Lady Corbin. The ageing countess had finally given up on subtlety. Her bosom was spilling from her gown as she hung over the edge of her box, frantically jiggling her fan at the object of her desire.

But now Jason lounged back in his chair, bored with the mating rituals of the beau monde. His eyes narrowed on the two gentlemen to one side of him, still deep in conversation.

'I'd not be surprised if George were negotiating some sort of deal with Bridgeman,' Mark suggested with a quirk of a dark eyebrow. 'Can't be selling him his wife, though.' He gave a coarse chuckle. 'I hear Bridgeman's had Iris for free.'

'As have above half the gentlemen here tonight,' Jason murmured on extending his muscular legs comfortably in front of him.

'I saw those two together in Hyde Park yesterday. Kingston made quite a spectacle of his youngest sister, and the people she was with, much to Bridgeman's amusement.'

Jason slowly drew himself up in his chair again and rested his elbows on his knees. He turned his face to Mark and gave him his full attention. 'What happened?' he asked.

Mark shrugged. 'At a guess I'd say George was casting aspersions on the worth of the young gentleman taking his sister for a drive. I don't know why, he seemed mannerly, and there was another lady present so the niceties seemed to be in order.' He frowned thoughtfully. 'I was ready to intervene when I eventually recognised the poor fellow's identity, but it would have simply prolonged the hubbub. We may not be close, but there is a family connection. Goode looked ready to explode with embarrassment and his sister, Anne seemed to be crying. Kingston can be damned insensitive.'

Jason stared at his linked fingers, then slanted a steady gaze at his brother. 'Philip Goode was taking Charlotte Kingston for a drive?'

Mark gave a nod. 'For the last time, I'd say, judging by Kingston's reaction. If the lad had ideas above his station where George's sister was concerned, I'd say he's been knocked severely back into place.'

'Which means that Kingston must have another candidate in mind or he wouldn't stir himself to bother,' Jason muttered. He took a thoughtful look at George Kingston's box.

Mark read his brother's mind. 'I've heard that Bridgeman is in the market for a wife.'

At that point Diana swept into Jason's box in a haze of cream muslin and gardenias. She pouted her thanks at her ardent gallant for safely returning her whilst keeping an eye on Jason to detect a reaction. The fact that there was none, and Jason continued conversing in a low voice with his brother, made spots of colour burn in her cheeks. She settled herself in her chair with much rustling and sighing.

The curtain began to open on the second act and Mark took his leave to return to his own seat.

Jason looked at Diana; she rewarded his indolent attention with an extremely seductive smile.

'Mrs Bertram and I were just saying that the soprano sounds shrill tonight.'

'Do you want to go?' Jason suggested bluntly.

Diana's lashes lowered to screen a sudden brightness in her blue eyes. 'I'm not bothered if we do leave. I know you'll always find us something pleasing to do. Are you bored? Have you something nice in mind?' She whispered huskily.

Jason straightened his spine against the chairback, then lithely gained his feet. Courteously he extended a hand to Diana. 'Nothing in particular,' he said lazily, his eyes on the dim outline of George Kingston's box. 'But I've seen enough....'

Chapter Nine

It had been some months since Helen had set foot in this house, but she saw straight away that the broken hallway chair was still propped against the wall. An air of faded elegance imbued the vestibule of the Goodes' residence much as it did the interior of Westlea House. Walters, the family's old retainer, closed the front door behind Helen before turning to give her a stump-toothed smile.

'Miss Anne will be pleased to see you, Mrs Marlowe.'

'I…actually, is Mr Philip Goode at home?' Helen asked. 'It would be nice to see him too whilst I am here.'

'He is at home, Mrs Marlowe but he has an important gentleman with him at present.' The information was imparted with a hint of confidentiality and a twinkle in the eye. Walters was plainly impressed by the fellow's identity if not about to reveal it.

'Helen! It is good to see you. Is Charlotte not with you?'

Helen twisted about to see Anne Goode flitting down the stairs. 'Charlotte is indisposed…a slight headache, but nothing to worry about,' Helen quickly added as Anne showed concern. 'Perhaps I ought come back another time as you have company.'

'No, please stay!' Anne urged. 'Come to the drawing room. Philip will like to see you.' She linked arms with Helen. 'I had just slipped away from there for a second to change into my best shawl when I thought I recognised your voice.' Anne gave an absent stroke to the lustrous silk swathing arms that were lightly freckled. 'I think our distinguished visitor is only planning to stay a short time. Do come and say hello for it might delay him. I'll wager he is too mannerly to take his leave soon after someone new is introduced.' Anne gave a little giggle. 'It is hard to credit that we are related to such a grand family. In fact, it is so long since Goodes socialised with Hunters that I had quite forgot our connection.'

'Hunters?' Helen's tone held sharp enquiry.

Helen abruptly halted and Anne was jerked about to face her, for their arms were still entwined as they took a promenade along the hallway. Being so close Anne spontaneously hugged Helen in excitement.

'Sir Jason Hunter is visiting us. We are distant cousins, you know,' she proudly informed her.

A startled tenseness shaped Helen's features on discovering the identity of the eminent guest.

'Do you know the Hunters?' Anne asked on a frown.

Helen managed to execute a jerky nod. 'Sir Jason and my brother, George, were friends when younger. When we lived in Surrey our house was quite close to Thorne Park.' The explanation was brief and abstracted—already Helen's mind was attending to the consequences of what she'd heard.

She had promised Charlotte that she would relay a message to Philip today, but she needed an opportunity to be alone with him. With Jason Hunter present there would be even less chance to engineer a private conversation and discover if her sister was to have her heart broken.

But there were other issues besides Charlotte's happiness rotating dizzily in her mind. When she had left Westlea House this afternoon her first task had been to take to the post a letter for Jason Hunter. In it she conveyed her regrets at Mr Drover's conduct, but its proper purpose was to ask him to again visit her. She was reasonably confident that her phrasing and his sophistication would ensure he understood her objective.

Infuriatingly, the two gentlemen with whom she had pressing business were in the immediate vicinity, yet nothing would be gained by seeing either of them now.

It seemed an odd coincidence that Jason Hunter should have recently renewed his acquaintance with her and also with distant cousins he had not seen in an age. Helen felt inclined to ponder if it was connected to the association between Charlotte and Philip.

Charlotte had defiantly told their brother that she would marry Philip despite his objections. George did not like to be thwarted and could bear ferocious grudges. The roses, put in Helen's cheeks by her brisk walk, faded away. Her reasoning veered between possibility and probability. Had George stooped to enrol Jason's help in ensuring Philip stayed away? There was no love lost between her brother and Jason Hunter, but she had bitter proof that they could successfully deal together in business.

'Are you well, Helen? You look very pale,' Anne said anxiously.

Helen reassured her friend with a smile.

'Will you come to the drawing room and join us?

You need not feel overawed by Sir Jason,' Anne advised helpfully. 'Indeed, he is terrifyingly distinguished and handsome.' A little shiver of delight accompanied that observation. 'But he is not at all uppity.' Anne inclined her head to whisper, 'I think I have a crush on him already and he has not been here above half an hour. I know his brother Mark is handsome, too. I've heard that Emily Beaumont has quite a hankering for him.' She sighed. 'It is a shame that Mama is gone out. She will be distraught to have missed him.'

Gently Helen disengaged her arm from her friend's. 'I shall not stay, Anne.' The idea that she might manage to politely converse with Jason in company, knowing that her explicit summons was even now on its way to his door, was enough to make her complexion flood with blood.

Anne skimmed the back of her hand over Helen's cheek. 'Heavens! First you seemed too pale now you look very flushed. I hope that you and Charlotte have not taken a chill.'

'I shall be on my way, Anne. I only called in as I was passing this way to go to the library.' It was a little fib that she could make truth by entering that establishment on her way home. 'Charlotte is on her own, so it would perhaps be best that I do not tarry.'

Once back in mellow sunshine Helen descended

the stone steps and turned in the direction of home. As she passed the phaeton at the kerb she hesitated. Belatedly she recognised it and chided herself for having overlooked it when she arrived. Twice recently this very vehicle had been idle outside Westlea House. She glanced at the young groom holding the reins of the fine chestnut horses as she walked swiftly on.

Jason accepted more tea from Walters and wandered to the window with it. He glanced down at the street scene, half-aware that Anne had returned and was bestowing on him another coquettish smile. His mouth tilted in response as his cup travelled upwards. Short of its target the vessel hovered, then was replaced softly on its saucer. He turned fully to gaze through the glass at the girlish figure skipping quickly down the stone steps. The young woman lingered by his phaeton, long enough for him to clearly identify her, before hurrying away.

In Anne's absence he'd had an enlightening conversation with her brother. By calling on them today he'd finally broken the ice that had been set half a century ago by their warring kin. He'd remained an acceptable amount of time. Now he was ready to take his leave.

* * *

Helen had been walking quickly, her face lowered against gusts that whipped her hair into her eyes. She had slowed her pace to pick away the irritating tendrils and clear her vision. Now, as she raised her head, she glimpsed him just in time to compose herself.

The phaeton had drawn to the kerb a little way in front of her and Jason was leaning against the shiny coachwork, watching her approach.

Helen felt her stomach somersault at the sight of him. There was no doubt that Anne was correct: Jason Hunter, despite his casual stance and his dark fringe blown awry by the breeze, was terrifyingly attractive.

She remembered that she had planned on looking sophisticatedly groomed the next time they met. She knew the rudiments of applying cosmetics and could make an adequate job of tinting her lips and complexion. She had also been rather pleased with the way her thick tresses had been teased into a stylish coiffure when she had practised with the tongs earlier in the week.

With a wry inner smile Helen acknowledged that today she looked simply bedraggled, whereas he looked ruggedly windswept. But her steps didn't falter as she brushed the black tangles from her white skin and neared him.

He was watching her, a slant to his mouth, and she knew he was amused to see how she would react to this unexpected meeting; whether she would stop and talk or simply nod and walk on by. But then he had not yet received her schematic note and had no idea that, in fact, a meeting between them was exactly what she wanted. It was merely the time and place that were wrong.

Her chin tilted and she boldly traversed the pavement to stand before him. 'Good day to you, Sir Jason. How are you?'

Jason inclined his head. 'I'm very well, thank you. And how are you, Mrs Marlowe?'

'I'm well, too, sir, thank you.'

'And the weather seems quite fine for this time of the year,' he added smoothly. Slate-grey eyes skimmed the perfect oval of her face as she attempted to gather the loose strands clinging to her complexion. 'Though it is perhaps a little too windy.' It was a murmured observation.

Helen felt her face burn where his darkly humorous gaze lingered.

'Why did you not stay longer at the Goodes?'

'Anne mentioned to you that I had called?'

'No. I saw you leaving from the drawing-room window.'

'Oh…'Helen caught her lower lip in small perfect teeth. She settled on being honest. 'I…I wanted to speak privately to Philip about something, but it didn't seem that I had chosen an appropriate time.'

'I thought perhaps Anne mentioned my name and you sped away to avoid seeing me.'

'Yes, she did. But, no, I didn't…run away, that is. Actually, I have wanted to see you and have today sent you a letter.' Helen abruptly pressed her lips together. She had not meant to so boldly disclose that fact. But he had guessed correctly her evasive action, and it had nettled her into rashness. She strove to limit the damage. 'I…I wrote to you because there is something on my mind…but please don't ask me to explain now,' she quickly besought as his eyes became narrow with interest.

'Perhaps I can guess what it is,' he softly said. 'You want to know what ulterior motive prompted me to settle your grocery bill. Is that it?'

He was not quite correct, but his thoughts were certainly travelling in the right direction. She backed away a step, said in a strangled tone, 'It is not a good time or place to talk, sir.' She glanced about, noticing that people passing by were sliding inquisitive looks at them. No doubt they were wondering why an elegant gentleman, in possession of an expensive equipage, would be in tense conversation at the side of the road with an unstylish young woman. As

Helen noticed two plump matrons give her a scan-
dalised stare, then put their heads together, a shocked
breath filled her lungs. Surely nobody thought her
to be soliciting! The thought that next jolted into her
mind crushed her indignation and her pride. Procur-
ing this man's protection was exactly her intention;
she had simply hoped to proposition him out of sight
of prying eyes.

Jason's head tilted so he might study her lowered
face. 'If you have taken the trouble to write to me
about your concerns, they are obviously important.'
He held out an arm to her. 'Come, if you will allow
me take you home, we can talk there—'

'No…' Helen swiftly interrupted, her eyes glancing on his. 'Charlotte is at home today and I would
rather not…'

'I understand. I'm sure I can find a place en route
to Westlea House that is neither too secluded nor too
public. A drive through the park is sure to turn up a
quiet spot. We can stop there and look at the view
without attracting attention.'

Helen needed little persuasion to agree. As soon
as he returned home he would have her note…and
her measure. It would be best to surge ahead with
what she'd started. If she had misjudged his interest
in her, and her forwardness irritated rather than
pleased him, she might never see him again. She

knew that he found Diana Tucker desirable and, Heaven only knew, she was as far removed in face and figure from her as a woman could be. As Helen took his arm to be courteously assisted aboard his phaeton, she drove down any regrets at having despatched the letter at all. The deed was done, and done after much inner debate that had kept her restless throughout last night.

She had been expecting that, once on the move, he would immediately try to prise some snippet from her. But she was wrong. It was several minutes later that Helen abruptly broke the silence. She had become far too conscious of a muscular thigh encased in fawn fabric close to her hip. Feeling flustered by his proximity, she slid a few inches away on the seat before angling to face him. Briskly she marshalled her courage and her thoughts. She might just as well open proceedings and contrive to lead their conversation towards revealing herself…as a brazen hussy. Quickly she blurted, 'I know that you are related to the Goodes, sir; forgive me for asking, but what prompted you to visit them after so long an estrangement?'

Without losing speed, Jason skilfully manoeuvred a path between two weighty coaches. Once the road was clear he reined back the plunging horses and gave her a glance. 'Are you asking whether the friendship between your sister and Philip Goode might have spurred me to go there?'

There was very little hesitation from Helen before she owned up to that. 'Yes, sir, I suppose I am.'

Jason smiled his appreciation that she'd not prevaricated. 'I suppose I could say I simply thought a family feud of some decades' duration had run its course, and it was time to extend an olive branch.'

'But?'

'But it wouldn't be the whole truth.'

Emboldened by his honesty, Helen continued to probe. 'Did you know that Philip has been quietly courting my sister, Charlotte?'

'I had heard something of the sort.'

'From George, I take it.' Her spontaneous response was curt enough to make Jason frown.

They had passed through the gates of Hyde Park. The earliness of the hour and the buffeting wind ensured that few other people were about to enjoy the spring sunshine. Jason drew the phaeton to a smooth halt in a quiet avenue. Soft afternoon sun filtered through swaying branches to lightly gild them.

'I first learned of it from my brother, Mark,' he eventually answered her.

'Your brother?' Helen echoed in surprise.

Jason turned on the seat to face her. He leaned back against the side of the vehicle. 'Mark witnessed a rather unpleasant scene in this park. It involved your brother and sister and our cousins. Mark interpreted what he saw as George displaying disapproval of Philip Goode squiring your sister.'

Helen looked at her gloved fingers, regretting having spoken snappishly before. 'That is exactly what did occur and Charlotte was mortified by the incident. She told me that George made a spectacle of them all in front of passers-by. You have confirmed our fears that gossip might ensue.'

'And are you about to confirm my fears? I get the impression you think I might have today gone, at George's behest, to tell my cousin to stay away from your sister.'

'George is determined to kill their love and find Charlotte a wealthy man. He will do whatever it takes to achieve that.'

'And you think I might help him in his ambition?'

'You do business together,' Helen said crisply, unwilling to appease the anger she sensed in him. They were being truthful with each other and she had no wish to deviate from that.

'I don't consider my cousin's courtship to be my business. But Philip and Anne Goode are kin and I take against their being made to look ridiculous. Mark was annoyed at what he saw and was tempted to intervene.'

Helen winced at the grit in his voice. 'I'm sorry if I have jumped to a wrong conclusion, sir,' she said. 'But I'm glad that your brother did not become involved. It would undoubtedly have resulted in more of a rumpus.'

'Indeed,' Jason agreed drily. 'Mark felt exactly that way.' He gazed upon her sculpted profile for a moment, fighting down an urge to reach out and feel beneath his fingertips skin that looked pale and pure as alabaster. Abruptly his gaze sought the horizon. 'Today I let Philip know I'd heard about the incident and that I deplored Kingston's conduct.'

Helen immediately swerved her golden eyes to him. She might not have had an opportunity to speak to Philip, but perhaps she could discover what Charlotte wanted to know from another source. 'Is Philip still feeling humiliated? He has every right to be angry.'

'He seemed philosophical. If you went there today to discover if he still carries a torch for your sister, the answer is that he certainly does,' Jason told her softly.

A small sweet smile from Helen displayed her gratitude at knowing it. 'Charlotte will be very happy. She was sure George had succeeded in destroying Philip's devotion.'

'If he had, perhaps it was infatuation and not worth having.'

'Oh, it's true love, I'm sure,' Helen said earnestly. 'But even so, I wouldn't blame Philip for giving it up as a lost cause. He needs George's consent to a betrothal and you've no idea how abominably rude our brother can be to him.' Helen smiled ruefully. 'A stoic temperament and an unflinching love are minimum requirements for a gentleman of limited means wishing to wed a sister of George's.'

'Was Harry Marlowe just such a man?'

'Indeed, he was, sir.' Helen felt a surge of shame that her beloved Harry be mentioned at such a time. What would Harry think of her wanton plan? A moment later she said briskly, 'Of course, my brother was then much younger and much different.' She suddenly realised that they had not yet touched on the subject of the note she had sent him.

'Are you going to tell me what is in your letter or would you rather I read it?' Jason asked as though his thoughts were in tune with hers.

Despite willing herself not to, Helen sensed a blush stain her cheeks. 'I can tell you the gist of it.' She drew in an inspiriting breath. 'First I must apologise for Mr Drover's behaviour. It was unforgivable of him—'

'But understandable. If he spoke honestly, he has been a patient man.'

Helen nodded her acceptance of that truth.

'Have you eaten well since?'

He was awaiting her reply as though her nourishment was of serious concern. 'Yes...thank you, sir, we have eaten very well. The house is warm, too.'

Jason nodded and was absently looking over parkland when he murmured, 'Good.'

'The comfort you have provided is what prompted me to write to you.' Her opening gambit was out, if uttered in an unsteady voice.

Jason picked up the leather reins from where they had rested on the seat and idly transferred them from hand to hand. 'I've explained, Mrs Marlowe, that George is due a payment from me following our recent business. Any sums I settle on your behalf will be deducted from his account. That is all there is to it. You don't owe me a damned thing.'

He was obviously irritated by this conversation to have used strong language in front of a lady. Or...perhaps he had guessed she was about to disclose she wasn't a lady. Helen drew in a breath and blurted, 'I don't think that is absolutely true, sir.'

'What is true, then?' It was a terse demand that terminated on a laugh that sounded hollow and humourless.

Helen knew it was time to choose between acting the jade or the coquette, but unplanned words just tumbled out. 'I...I think that you have been generous to us because you have a liking for me. My reason for writing to you is…I want you to know that I have no objection to your interest. In fact, I should like to encourage it.' Her proposition ended on a soundless sob of relief that it was done.

She felt her heart thundering and inwardly she blenched—she knew her solitary attempt to win a protector had been extremely amateurish. He seemed unimpressed, too, for he remained silent, studying the leather reins crossing his palms for some while before replying.

'Perhaps if I tell you something else, Mrs Marlowe, you might reconsider some of what you've said. During our talk today I learned from Philip that he is seeking a position. I know of an opportunity in the city that might suit him. In short, if he takes up the offer, his prospects ought to improve enough for him to take a wife.'

'I am very pleased about that,' Helen said huskily, with some understatement, for her heart was soaring. 'But still I am prepared to—'

'Put yourself at my disposal?' His tone veered more to anger than irony.

'No…' Helen finally turned to look directly into his eyes. In their profound blackness she discovered a glow that calmed her. She managed a shy smile. 'No…' she repeated softly. 'I am prepared to shun modesty and propriety. Virtue has its merits, but not for someone like me; I shall not regret its loss.'

She prayed that enough was now established between them for him to take over and allow her some pride and gentility. But her hopes were dashed.

'I'm not about to make this easy for you, Helen. If it's what you want, ask me....'

Chapter Ten

'**W**ould you make me your mistress?'

'Yes.'

'Do you not want to think about it for a moment?' Helen offered quietly.

'No. Do you?'

'No,' Helen murmured, barely faltering.

'Are you sure about that, Helen?'

'Yes…'

She had been a schoolgirl when last he had used her given name. She had always liked the way it sounded spoken in his gruff, cultured voice. Far back in her mind stirred a memory of how he would smile at her and make her feel at the same time awkward and elated and intuitive of a promise of excitement hovering between them.

But he was no longer her brother's friend, welcome in their home, and she was no longer a fanciful maid of fifteen.

She might be unpractised in such negotiations, but she knew that a gentleman was encumbered financially when he took a woman under his protection. She had anticipated that such an arrangement would necessitate a conversation between them lasting longer than a few minutes. But he seemed to have settled into staring moodily into space.

Helen was obliquely aware of his detachment whilst reasoning on what must come next flitted through her mind. Unless he intended keeping her in the background, a mistress was usually a social companion, too. Once it became common knowledge that they were lovers she would be barred from some areas of his life, but accompanying him to the theatre or a shopping trip and so on would be in her scope. Her clothes were dated and shabby. She would need an allowance for new garments in order to look acceptably stylish when partnering him. And, of course, they would need a discreet place to meet. Although he now owned the property, visiting her at Westlea House would be out of the question. Her teeth settled painfully into her lower lip as she came to shameful awareness of how naturally mercenary thoughts had occupied her. But, of course, such practicalities kept at bay the apprehensiveness that was making moist her palms and parching her mouth.

Sir Jason Hunter was to be her lover, to know her body as intimately as would a husband. Goose bumps rippled fierily over her limbs in response to the wild images that ran amok in her mind. Although they were not touching she felt intensely conscious of his muscular physique and the clean fresh scent that emanated from him.

She took a glimpse at his profile, acutely conscious of his silence. Perhaps his odd humour sprung from the fact that he had been the quarry. He had a reputation as a womaniser. Was he a Hunter by name and by nature—a man who liked being a predator? She might have pricked his male pride by audaciously approaching him. That train of thought lead to something else. Perhaps a woman brazen enough to start the chase was expected to bestow an appropriate token of gratitude for her victory. She glanced swiftly about; there was certainly nobody in the vicinity to witness a little wanton behaviour. 'Would you like me to kiss you?' she softly volunteered.

Jason tipped up his head and barked a hoarse laugh at a canopy of dancing branches. 'Of course…though perhaps not here…'

But Helen had already slid dutifully towards him to comply.

She had pressed her body close to his, so close that his thigh felt like immovable rock against her soft yielding flesh. She heard a muttered oath and was lifting her face to investigate what now had vexed him when her jaw was cradled between his palms. That first softly sensual caress caught her breath in her throat. For a lengthy moment their eyes met, then Helen's lashes dropped and she felt his mouth cover hers.

It was so long since a man had touched her in passion that his virility overwhelmed her. His kiss was confident and clever; her mouth was parted and his tongue stroking its silky warmth before she had fully accepted their intimacy. But she participated when he led her to do so. A hand deftly infiltrated her cloak, caressing her midriff through her dress and she curved closer. She felt his thumb sweep the underside of her breast, then extend upwards until it brushed against her nipple. A surge of warmth enveloped her as his hands and mouth worked their devious magic. She felt her head eased back against his arm by the increasing pressure of his kiss. Her lips clung, widened when he urged them to do so and a throb low in her pelvis instinctively made tight her abdomen whilst relaxing her thighs. The core of her femininity felt hot and dewy and a rasping breath was welling in her throat. But within a moment the exquisite tension was ebbing. He had taken up the reins and set the vehicle in motion.

Inwardly Jason cursed Peter Wenham to damnation even as he wryly acknowledged that his friend's inopportune arrival was probably a godsend. He had been on the point of losing control and Hyde Park was certainly not the best place for an al fresco romp with a respectable woman. Helen wasn't a seasoned harlot, she wasn't even right as a mistress, but her sweet seduction had swept from his mind any noble thoughts he'd had of saving her from herself. He wanted her. His loins were afire and, no matter how he strived to be rational, what dominated his mind was finding another quiet place to take her…so he could finish what she'd started….

When Helen observed the smart curricle approaching she was still dazed with heady languor. Slowly she came to vague awareness of the occupants who looked to be a modish young couple. She blinked as Jason and the gentleman acknowledged each other with a word and a nod as the vehicles passed. Then they were out of the park and Jason calmly tooled the horses to a trot on a busy street.

Helen touched two vibrating fingers to her pulsing lips. For her, their first kiss had been unexpectedly shattering, the memory of it consumed her mind. Jason seemed undisturbed by their intimacy and that stirred a peculiar feeling in the pit of her stomach.

The phaeton soon got up quite a speed and Helen pulled her cloak closer about her to ward off the chill of fast-flowing air. Her gloved fingers tweaked her small hat forward to shield her face.

'Are you cold?'

'A little.'

'Grosvenor Square is not far.' A ghost of a smile touched Jason's mouth as he realised that lust had, after all, surrendered to decency. He'd settle for conversation this afternoon. 'We can go there and resume—'

'No.' Her sharp interruption made him arrow a look at her. Her apology was limited to a wavering smile. 'I fear I might be colder still if your butler again shuts me in that cupboard,' she weakly joked.

'That was very bad of Cedric,' Jason said, matching her levity, but his eyes were delving deeper into her brusque refusal.

Helen quelled her misgivings. In fact, she inwardly mocked herself. Had she expected a notorious rake to go into raptures over a quick kiss in the park? Suddenly she felt rather silly to have instigated it at all. He had told her he had done with flirting years ago; clandestine embraces in public places probably provoked in him similar ennui. Inwardly she squirmed for she was never more aware of her lack of womanly sophistication. 'I ought return home immediately. I expect Charlotte will wonder where I am.' Her defensiveness made her sound rather haughty.

'I shan't keep you long at my house.' His tone was adamant and her tawny eyes widened in alarm.

Abruptly he reined back the horses to a slower pace. 'I make it a rule never to ask a mistress to entertain me in my own home, especially not when my sister is in residence. Yesterday she came up from Surrey with her husband.'

'I didn't mean…that is, I know you would not expect…' Helen frowned as she vainly scrabbled to find words to smooth the situation.

'You don't know what I expect, Helen,' Jason softly emphasised. 'And that is one reason why we need to resume our conversation. Had you not distracted me…' he shot her a lightly amused look '…we might have concluded our talk in the park. Another thing we need to speak about is your ulterior motive in all this.'

Helen blushed to the roots of her silky black hair. He sounded as though he was about to accuse her of being a crafty harlot. 'I know you must think me shockingly brazen to proposition you…but I have my reasons.'

'I'm not that easily shocked, sweetheart,' he said on a dry laugh. 'Nevertheless, I'd like to hear your reasons.'

Her wind-parched lips were moistened with a flick of her small tongue. She had not been expecting an inquisition. He knew her husband was dead and that she lived frugally. Surely he could use his imagination as to her motives? She had assumed that, if he desired her, little else about her circumstances would bother him. Perhaps he was used to women hinting at having an uncontrollable *tendresse* for him or flattering him over his handsome looks and social position.

'I have no objection to explaining myself, but I would rather not go home with you and meet your sister. It would be unseemly, when soon we will...' Her explanation faded away.

'Beatrice would remember you as an old friend she has not seen in a long while. As of yet there is nothing unseemly to fret over.'

Helen sank back against the seat. Humiliation stung colour again into her cheeks—suddenly it occurred to her that he might have changed his mind. Perhaps he had been little impressed by her seduction and was trying to wriggle free of his agreement to care for her. A penetrative glance at his profile was not enlightening, but she felt her pride rally. 'If you think you made too hasty a decision and want to reconsider, I would understand and never again mention the matter.'

His muttered oath was inaudible to Helen for her gasp of alarm had filled her ears. Without warning, but with expert skill, Jason had turned the phaeton in the road. Helen found herself clinging to the side of the spinning vehicle that was soon hurtling back towards Hyde Park.

A few minutes later Helen was glancing about to see that the phaeton was stationed in the same quiet spot as previously. The avenue was once more deserted.

He turned to look at her with stormy eyes. 'If we can't go to your house or to mine, we shall need to stop here a while longer. What have I said to make you think I no longer want to sleep with you?'

Helen blanched and slid him a glance that appealed for a little more delicacy.

'Don't be coy about it, Helen,' he said quietly. 'We both know what this entails. I shall provide you with *carte blanche* in return for the privilege of sharing a bed with you whenever I so desire. Or is it that you are only now giving serious thought to the consequences of being my paramour?'

'Of course I have given it serious thought!' Helen cried with stifled indignation. 'If you think I would have lightly humbled myself to proposition you, sir, then you are wrong!'

'Jason.'

Helen glanced at him in confusion.

'My name is Jason. We're now on familiar terms, aren't we?'

'Yes,' Helen breathed. 'Jason.'

He grunted a laugh at her mutinous expression. 'Far from not wanting you, my dear, you've made me an offer I can't refuse. But I need to be sure you understand the ramifications of becoming my mistress.'

'I do understand,' Helen readily affirmed. That brave statement was not entirely true and her mind pondered on latent messages. The more she pondered, the more she was sure their brief kiss had disappointed him and he was implying she might prove an inadequate lover. 'I expect you know I was not married for long. But I am not too unpractised in the passion and pleasure to be had between a man and a woman. I recall enough to—'

'It's not that,' Jason brusquely interrupted. Then added in a soft drawl, 'But thank you for such delightful news.'

'Don't mock me!' Helen's voice held both a plea and a command.

Jason simply smiled and lazily shifted position on the seat. 'I was referring to the impact this will have on your present way of life. When it becomes obvious that you're my mistress, gossip will ensue, although it should not last long. Some of your present neighbours and acquaintances might shun you if feeling fastidious. There will be social events to which it would not be appropriate to take you.'

'I have thought of all of that.' Helen said. She squarely met his grey eyes. 'And in case you are too gallant to mention it so early on in our dealings, I shall say it for you. I know you will tire of me eventually. And even before then I expect you will be reluctant to remain faithful. You need not fear that I will nag or become fretful if you do not devote yourself exclusively to me.'

Jason threaded the reins through his fingers. 'I'm not sure you are suited to be my mistress, Helen. You sound to me like the perfect wife, my dear.'

'I would rather you did not make of it a joke, sir. I am simply trying to be fair and practical.' She had thoughtlessly reverted to using a formal address and it made him quirk an eyebrow at her. 'If I seem calculating, Jason,' she deliberately, stiltedly, used his name, 'I do not mean to appear so. But neither do I want to be accused of being a hypocrite.'

'And what about love and marriage?'

Startled, Helen glanced at him. She had certainly not expected him to bring up any such emotive subject. Briskly she put his mind at ease. 'I promise not to embarrass you with any such declarations or demands.' A private little smile sweetened her solemn demeanour. 'I feel fortunate to have known the love of a fine gentleman. I was a wife just a short time, but I was very happy and have no wish for another husband. I am content with my memories.'

Jason's expression remained unreadable a moment longer, then he gave her a slow smile. 'And what about me? Or perhaps you think love and marriage pass rakes by.'

Helen blushed at that mild sarcasm. 'Not at all, sir…Jason,' she glibly corrected herself. 'I know you have a…lady friend…and I assumed that, if you had a deep affection for her, you would decline to take me in her place.'

'In her place?' Jason echoed so quizzically that further words were unnecessary.

Helen twisted together her fingers. He was starting to needle her, quite deliberately, she imagined. On a deep breath she said, 'I imagined that if you loved Mrs Tucker you would not want to hurt her by giving her a rival.' She was unsure why his response was so important, but found herself awaiting it with bated breath. But he remained uncommunicative and his ruthless gaze made her seek something else to say to shatter the silence.

'I also realise you will one day marry a nobleman's daughter and wish to start your family. I have promised already not to make a fuss when it is finished between us.'

'You have given it a lot of thought,' Jason murmured. 'What makes you think I'll marry a nobleman's daughter?'

Helen did not want to reveal that George had told her of Jason's ambition to marry for pedigree. It might stir more enmity between the two men. She gave a vague shrug. 'It seems sensible to me to conclude that a rich gentleman would choose to do so.'

'It seems sensible to me to conclude that a rich gentleman would not need to do so…unless he was in love with the lady.'

'Are you in love with someone?' Helen blurted.

'I'm not sure,' he answered, seemingly unaffected by her impertinence in asking.

Helen swallowed a lump that had suddenly formed in her throat. She was not so naïve as to suppose that a wealthy bachelor would not keep a mistress simply because he was in love with a débutante. But she felt a fool for not having anticipated that might indeed be the case. He obviously socialised with the best families. 'I'm sorry to pry, but if your affections are engaged and you soon will take a wife, I'm not sure that I—' Helen clamped together her lips for she had been about to blurt that she might not be able to bear it.

'You're not sure how philosophical you would still be about it all?' Jason suggested mildly.

Helen nodded and found she could not look at him.

'If I decide I am in love, Helen, I promise you'll be the first to know. Likewise if I decide to marry.'

'Thank you,' Helen murmured.

'As you have concluded I will tire of you, I take it you have a plan for what to do next?'

Inwardly Helen winced at his ironic tone. Outwardly she gave a single nod. When she could no long avoid looking at him she turned, chin up, to face him.

'And?'

'I will ask you for a settlement. I believe that is not unusual or avaricious in these cases,' she said levelly.

'As we are being very honest and practical, shall we discuss it now?'

The question was equable, almost gentle, but far back in his eyes was laughter and Helen felt her fingernails score her palms. He had the benefit of wealth and security and found her lack of those things amusing. She snapped her head up and gazed into the budding trees. 'I should like the deeds to Westlea House and a sum that I might invest for income…say, one hundred pounds per annum for three years.' She slid him a glance. 'Is that fair?'

'If you're satisfied with that, I'm concerned that I've been vastly too generous in the past.'

'It's enough…all I need,' Helen said quickly.

She suddenly felt anxious to be home—she craved respite from his latent mockery. 'I really ought go now. Charlotte has been alone for some time and she is poorly.'

'You were going to tell me your reasons for instigating all this,' Jason reminded her. 'But I dare say it will wait for another day. I'll start to make the necessary arrangements, shall I?'

Helen vigorously nodded whilst frowning into the distance.

He took up the reins, but hesitated in sending leather undulating over the backs of the beautiful chestnut horses. He addressed her without turning his head. 'Just tell me this…did you decide to offer yourself to protect your sister from me?'

Helen swiftly looked at his unflinching profile.

'Tell me the truth. Do you still believe I have nefarious intentions towards Charlotte?'

He was still staring straight ahead and Helen put a light hand on his arm to make him turn to her. 'I'm very sorry I ever was taken in by such a ridiculous tale. Certainly it has no bearing on my proposition.' She glanced down at her lap, for his steely gaze was now upon her. 'You know, of course, that George sowed that seed in my mind. I want to believe his motive was not all bad. I expect he hoped I would persuade Charlotte to quickly marry someone of influence and forget Philip.' She tipped up her head and an involuntary little sigh escaped her. 'George is right in one respect: until she is married Charlotte is vulnerable. She does need a husband to provide for her and protect her reputation. George might be her guardian, but he has no shame in letting it be known she cannot rely on his care.'

'And neither can you.'

'And neither can I…' Helen echoed and turned to look over the lake as the phaeton left the park.

Jason watched Helen slide a swift peek over a shoulder at him before disappearing into the sanctuary of Westlea House. A rueful smile touched his mouth as he regarded the front door being rapidly closed. Then he set the phaeton in motion, but instead of heading towards Grosvenor Square he turned again towards Hyde Park. For the third time that afternoon he brought the vehicle to a stop in the same spot. It was fast approaching the fashionable hour for the beau monde to parade within the environs of the park. Although strollers and vehicles were more in evidence, Jason sat gazing out over the greensward oblivious to the company.

His brow furrowed with the intensity of his thoughts. Having decided just a short time ago that he would approach Helen Marlowe and offer her his protection, he was not sure why her timely proposition had unsettled him. Certainly he wanted her. Just a ghost of her scent and warmth remained on his clothes from when they had kissed, yet the pulse in his groin was unabated. The torment was keen and, with a frustrated mutter, he bowed his head towards hands that were clasped close to his knees.

He could have approached her some time ago, but had hesitated without giving proper thought to why he was delaying. Now he understood that he had never fully accepted the decision he had made regarding Helen's role in his life. At the back of his mind had always been an idea he might ask her to marry him. Now he didn't know whether he was regretful or thankful that he had kept those thoughts to himself.

Barely an hour ago she had made it perfectly clear that being his mistress was preferable to being his wife. Helen had no wish to remarry, for she was still in love with her dead husband. But she would sleep with him. Not only that, she would not interfere in his life. Nor would she make any demands on him other than he keep her until she had earned the deeds to her home and a sum to scrape by on. And just in case he wasn't convinced that she was seriously prepared to humble herself in such a way, she had attempted to act the wanton.

And it had worked; despite her nervousness, despite him knowing she was simply behaving in a way she thought was expected, he had been enchanted by her artless seduction.

Jason sighed and abruptly tipped up his head to watch clouds travel over cerulean sky. He imagined his conscience was bothering him...or perhaps it was his pride. He didn't believe himself egotistical, but he knew there were several young women of good family and fortune who would be elated to have him propose marriage. Yet an impecunious widow would rather have him as her lover than her husband. If he thought she desired him, it would be easier to bear; but he feared she would tolerate making love with him as she would any other duty to be discharged.

To retain pride and dignity and some control over her life, she had come to him rather than await his approach. Yet despite knowing it all he still wanted her, and inner demons taunted him with the knowledge that, in any case, he could seduce her into lust and after that...why care?

Chapter Eleven

'It is quite beautiful, Charlotte.' Helen swept a thumb across a cluster of rubies adorning her sister's finger.

'Philip just took me to the terrace where we could be private and presented it to me.' Charlotte's eyes glistened with happiness. 'It was enough for me that we were today officially betrothed. I did not expect such a wonderful surprise as this splendid ring.' She wiggled her finger to admire the gem. 'He bought it without any idea what I would like. Yet it is perfect! I could not have chosen better myself.'

'Philip has excellent taste, my love.' Helen gave her emotional sister a soothing little hug. 'One can tell that from his choice of wife.'

Iris Kingston was with her husband, a little way distant from her sisters-in-law, and making scant attempt to mask her boredom. But George had insisted they both attend Charlotte's modest engagement party, held in the prospective bridegroom's drawing room.

Now Iris's expression livened, for she had noticed Charlotte proudly displaying her hand. She sidled closer, manoeuvring into position for a better view of what glittered on Charlotte's finger. A buxom hip was interposed between the slender figures of her sisters-in-law. Snatching hold of Charlotte's wrist, she elevated it to inspect her ring. A disdainful grimace took her plucked eyebrows beneath a fringe of blonde curls. 'It is sweet. But personally I would have expected a love token to be a trifle larger.' Charlotte's arm was released as though it had become hot. Iris flexed her fingers so her jewellery caught candlelight. It was an ostentatious display that shaped her lips into a moue of satisfaction.

Helen fixed feral eyes on her vicious sister-in-law. 'Of course, your build is not so delicate as Charlotte's. Something of less elegance and more substance is needed for a big hand, else there is too much flesh on show.' Helen ignored the glaring blue eyes boring into her; her attention was devoted to admiring her sister's rubies.

Charlotte was too blissfully ebullient to have taken much notice of Iris's cattish remark. Her creamy cheeks were rimmed with excited colour. 'I'm so happy, Helen, I feel fit to burst.'

'Well, I beg you will not!' Helen said with mock alarm. 'Your guests are still arriving. Emily Beaumont is here…and Heavens! It looks to be her brother, Tarquin, accompanying her. I'm sure Emily will be dying to see your wonderful betrothal ring.'

Charlotte pivoted about, her auburn curls jaunty about her shoulders. With a parting smile for her sister, she was soon gliding serenely towards the newcomers, stationed just inside the doors of the drawing room, chatting to Philip and Anne Goode.

Iris peered that way too and a look of distaste puckered her face as she stared at Tarquin, a tall gentleman of about Helen's age with a distinctive shock of flaxen hair. 'I'm sure I have heard about that wastrel,' Iris announced waspishly. 'Is he not the fellow who was lately residing in the Fleet for unpaid debts?'

'Yes,' Helen succinctly confirmed. 'But I do not consider him a wastrel. It is an affliction he has, for he desperately wants to curb his tendency to gamble.'

'What very odd company you sisters do keep.'

'Do you think so?' Helen said. 'Our relatives, then, are probably equally strange. I recall George fretting the duns would have him thrown in debtors' prison. Perhaps he might have shared a cell with Tarquin. But I expect you would have pawned a bauble or two to keep your husband from such ignominy, Iris. Wouldn't you?'

Iris's lips formed a carmine bud. She flicked an encompassing glance about the faded appointments of the Goodes's drawing room. 'It is a nice house Philip has here. Such a pity the interior does not quite match the fine address. One can rarely estimate a person's standards.'

'Philip has done an admirable job in retaining the property and caring for his mother and sister since his father died.' Iris seemed unwilling to let her escape and kept step with Helen as she tried to distance herself.

'A betrothal ball would have been more befitting to people of our standing. This is rather a shabby little affair. But then nothing about this entire episode is *comme il faut.*'

'I agree,' Helen said coolly. 'Were things *comme il faut,* George would have shared the cost of this celebration and not left the entire burden of it to Philip.'

Friends who had come to congratulate the newly betrothed couple were laughing and chatting, creating a buzz of good humour throughout the drawing room. Helen revelled in the atmosphere for a moment, then turned to her sour-faced sister-in-law. 'In this instance, I think I'm grateful for George's parsimony. I'm thoroughly enjoying this shabby little affair…'

Helen's lavender skirts were given an ungentle twitch. 'Ungrateful! George paid for *this* and for Charlotte's new gown.'

'He has certainly taken the credit for doing so, yet I think the sum involved is less than what we are owed in unpaid allowance.'

Iris's complexion glowed beneath her powder. 'And George has been unwisely generous in allowing Charlotte to marry beneath her,' she snapped.

'He has not, for Charlotte is not marrying beneath her,' Helen returned icily. 'Philip is of excellent family. He has had hard times, but his fortunes are now improving. Were they not, I doubt George would even have consented to listen to Philip's suit.' Helen turned to move swiftly on, but bumped straight into George. He immediately held aloft two glasses to prevent the drinks spilling. One was given to his wife and he sipped from the other. 'I ought have fetched you a drink, Helen. Sorry…' he absently remarked.

'You are wasting any such consideration.' Iris gave Helen a significant stare. 'She was just complaining how meanly you treat her and Charlotte.' Iris turned an elevated shoulder on Helen. 'Surely we have done our duty and can now go,' she muttered peevishly to her husband. 'We have been here above an hour already. Sonia Lancaster is having a card party in Hertford Street. It starts late…'

'I'll fetch your cloak.' George watched golden wine swirl in his glass, then speared a look at the doorway. 'That is, if you're sure you don't want to stay and greet our future brother-in-law's patron. It seems he has after all graced us with his presence.' He gave a theatrical sigh. 'I suppose I should make a point of thanking him for easing my burden.' He deliberately slid a look at Helen. 'Perhaps I might yet lose it entirely,' he added slyly. His next comment carried more volume. 'I just hope Goode hasn't frittered the whole of the salary Hunter advanced to him on those rubies.'

Iris immediately swivelled towards the doorway. Her blue eyes took on an excited gleam and she nipped her lower lip between her teeth.

'You don't seem quite so bored…or so keen to leave, my dear,' her husband remarked cynically before strolling away.

Helen deserted Iris too, but walked swiftly in the opposite direction to her brother. Once by the wide doors that opened on to a small terrace she hesitated and let the cool evening air soothe her feverish skin.

Philip had mentioned that he had issued an invitation to his benefactor. Helen had imagined Jason would decline it due to the delicacy of the situation between them. He had made a point of telling her that there would be occasions when it would not be appropriate for them to socialise together. She knew he had been referring to times when their families would be present. Although news of their relationship was not yet out, she imagined he would start as he meant to go on. But not only had he come this evening, he had brought his brother with him, too.

It had been a few weeks since she had propositioned him in Hyde Park and, although they had communicated by letter, she had not again seen him. They had parted, she thought, in an atmosphere of subdued harmony that sunny afternoon. After a few days she had received a letter from him enquiring whether she would like an advance on her allowance. Helen had considered that carefully before putting pen to paper to decline his premature generosity. The following week another missive arrived, asking if she desired choosing her own residence and staff or whether she would want him to deal with it. His mode of writing echoed his wry speech and she had managed a little chuckle on reading his assurance that she could trust him to spare her Rowan Walk. She had dashed off a note to him instructing him to please go ahead.

Certainly they had not exchanged *billets-doux,* but Helen had sensed a fragile amity burgeoning between them. She also had realised the clandestine nature of the prologue to their affair was piquantly thrilling. But, of course, it would not always be just a game, or a secret. At some time they would be lovers, sharing bed and board on occasion, and everybody would know it.

But when? As the weeks had passed, it had occurred to Helen that Jason might be purposely postponing because he was satisfied with things the way they were. He had made it woundingly apparent that Mrs Tucker's services were not to be dispensed with. Had his current mistress got wind of developments and coaxed him to keep the status quo? Once or twice Helen had considered again writing him a note to probe for clues as to the delay, but her pride would not let her. She had humbled herself to proposition him—she certainly would not chivvy him to make a date to sleep with her.

'Charlotte's rubies are beautiful.'

Helen started from her introspection to swirl about in a rustle of lavender satin. Emily Beaumont's eyes were on a level with her own for they were of similar height. She gave the pretty young woman a smile. 'Indeed, it is a magnificent betrothal gift.'

'I'm glad it came right for them both,' Emily said.

'And so expeditiously! Anne told me weeks ago that she feared your brother had taken against Philip and would never give his consent to the match.'

'In truth, I did, too,' Helen wryly admitted. 'But as soon as George learned of Philip's improved situation…well, suffice it to say he has undergone quite a wondrous change of heart. He is keen for them to set an early wedding date.'

Emily cocked her head in the direction of the two distinguished dark-haired gentlemen who stood beneath the room's central chandelier, encircled by a group of people. 'Tarquin tells me Sir Jason Hunter has taken his cousin under his wing and made all this possible. I had no idea that the Goodes were related to the Hunters.'

Helen glanced that way too and immediately noticed that her sister-in-law had lost no time in pressing close to their honoured guest who, she had to admit, exuded magnetism. His dark jacket was excellently tailored in fine raven cloth that enhanced his impressively broad shoulders. The tailcoat was significantly narrower where it skimmed over his lean waist and hips and complemented his grey trousers. He looked, Helen mused, as though his muscular physique owed a lot to strenuous masculine pursuits. An irrepressible image of certain nocturnal exercise had stolen into her mind, making her cheeks warm. She forced her thoughts to fencing and sparring whilst recalling how well toned George had once been when keen to participate in sporting bouts.

'Did you know of the connection?'

Emily's sweet voice infiltrated her mind. She was looking curiously at her…probably to divine the reason for her blushing cheeks, Helen guessed.

'Ah…indeed…I was aware of it,' Helen quickly confirmed. 'It is a distant kinship and one, I believe, that is not widely known, for it has been rather strained in the past.' Her eyes darted again to Jason to see that he was now watching her.

An astute look from Emily veered between Sir Jason and Helen's quickly averted face. 'Sir Jason seems interested in you. Are you acquainted with the family?'

'Our family lived by the Hunters's estate of Thorne Park…many years ago now,' Helen quickly answered, then neatly evaded answering any more of Emily's questions by asking one of her own. 'I think *I* ought ask whether you are acquainted with the Hunters.' She gave Emily a teasing smile. Helen liked Miss Beaumont. Charlotte socialised more than Helen and so was more of a friend to Emily. But Emily was, at twenty-four, nearer Helen's age. Helen had always thought her a personable and attractive young woman and had wondered why Emily was still single. 'Philip's sister told me that you hanker after Mark Hunter.'

'Cheek! I do no such thing.' Emily's eyes had darkened in annoyance. 'Well, perhaps that's not entirely true. I do hanker after wringing his neck!' Her fair head dipped towards Helen's ebony tresses. 'He is the *gentleman* who set the duns on Tarquin and landed him in the Fleet.'

Helen's amber gaze flicked anxiously towards Tarquin. She certainly did not want her sister's betrothal party ruined by any hostilities. 'I expect Tarquin must feel quite bitter about that,' Helen whispered back.

'But he does not,' Emily spluttered with a perplexed frown. 'Tarquin said a gentleman is entitled to call in his vowels. I think he quite likes him. Heaven knows why! Last time I spoke to Mark Hunter I found him vastly arrogant and—'

'Did I hear my name mentioned?'

That softly ironic query put space between blonde and black locks. Both young women had snapped their heads up to see a gentlemen smiling at them.

'Mr Hunter…I…it is a very long time since last we met,' Helen said quickly. She politely met his extended fingers. 'And I believe you are acquainted with Miss Beaumont?' Helen exchanged a subtle smile with Emily.

'Of course…Tarquin's sister. I'm pleased to see you again, Miss Beaumont,' Mark said mildly.

Emily refused to touch his hand and slipped into a bob. 'I'm afraid I cannot echo that sentiment, sir. It seems the pleasure is all yours.' Her blonde ringlets rippled as she swung her head to the side. 'Ah, I see Tarquin is beckoning me. I hope he does not already want to go. But his health was not improved by his odious incarceration in the Fleet. He probably feels unwell.' With a smile for Helen and glaring insolence for Mark, Emily was soon on her way.

'Tell me, Mrs Marlowe, am I being overly sensitive or did you also find Miss Beaumont's attitude towards me a tad frosty?'

Helen bit her lip to quell her smile. He shared his brother's sense of irony as well as his striking good looks. 'I believe there is an icicle thawing above your head even as we speak, sir.' More soberly Helen added, 'Emily is very loyal to Tarquin and rightly or wrongly will defend him.'

'I recall you and I dealt together quite well on those occasions you came over to Thorne Park to play with Beatrice. I expect you think I must now be a cruel miser to have had Tarquin imprisoned.'

'I expect Mrs Marlowe is too polite to comment, but Miss Beaumont might have no qualms over giving you your answer.'

Helen turned to see Jason slightly to one side of her. Their eyes coupled for a long moment before he gave her a polite nod. 'It's nice to see you again, Mrs Marlowe, and at such a happy celebration.'

'Indeed, it is a fine occasion, sir,' Helen said rather breathlessly, for her heart had begun erratically pumping. Obliquely she wished she had noticed him approach—she felt silly and girlish to be so discomposed by his sudden closeness. As his eyes lingered momentarily on her mouth it began pulsing beneath phantom pressure. Simply for something to say she blurted on a bright smile, 'But it will be finer still to see them married.'

'Indeed it will,' Jason said softly before his grey eyes were levelled at his observant brother. 'Why do you not go and try to revise Miss Beaumont's opinion of you?'

Mark flicked a glance between Jason and Helen. Suddenly a look of enlightenment flickered over his features. 'Could you not have set me a feasible task, Jay? Reforming Tarquin might be simpler.'

As Mark Hunter moved away Jason strolled closer to Helen, so close that she could sense his heat through the delicate fabric of her new gown.

He leaned back against the wall next to her and she saw him make a sweeping perusal of the company. She had, seconds ago, made a similar swift check to see if they were being observed so understood his scouting look. Only Iris seemed to be darting intermittent glances their way.

'I…it is a long time since I have seen your brother.' Helen made a little light conversation to attempt to curb the fluttering in her stomach. 'I don't think he has changed one bit in looks.'

'Not in looks, perhaps.'

'I remember Mark used to be quite a carefree character,' Helen warmed to her theme and felt relaxed enough to broach the subject of Emily's antagonism towards Mark. 'He has apparently treated Tarquin quite harshly. Does he not like him?'

'Actually, he is fond of him.' Jason slanted Helen a rueful smile before explaining. 'Gambling is like an opiate to Tarquin. Only a true friend would bother to have him forcibly removed from Almack's before he brought himself to complete ruin.' Jason stared off in the direction of where were Tarquin and his sister. 'Mark took away his liberty, it's true, but he also freed him from the tables for a while. Mark has brought a lot of opprobrium down on his head…not least from the Beaumonts. Perhaps they would prefer to watch Tarquin lose his dignity along with the shirt from his back.'

'I hope, then, that it has not all been in vain. I did know of Tarquin's problems, and that he tries to resist temptation.'

'As do we all…' Jason sighed out in a tone replete with irony.

Helen stole a glance at him. His eyes were kindling, making the butterflies in her stomach again take flight. She found another topic of conversation. 'I…it would have been nice to have seen Beatrice this evening. I'm sure Philip intended the invitation be extended to your sister, and her husband, too.'

'I believe they declined due to a prior engagement.'

Helen sensed that was an invalid excuse and suddenly her agile mind pounced on a reason for Beatrice's absence. Immediately she knew she would voice her suspicions whilst they were alone, for there was an opportunity to discover what steps had been taken to make formal her role in his life.

'Has Beatrice chosen to stay away because of…what we discussed in Hyde Park?' It was a leading question she hoped might yield other answers, too.

'As far as I am aware, nobody but us knows about it, unless you have mentioned—'

'I would not!' Helen interrupted in a fierce whisper. 'It is hardly something that I am proud to boast of—' She abruptly bit her lip and her lashes screened her eyes in regret. It was a very unguarded comment to have made.

'Indeed…it's something you're ashamed of, isn't it, Helen?' Jason said softly. 'Which reminds me that I'm still waiting to hear what has driven you to choose such a course of action.'

'And I have said that I will tell you,' Helen returned in an undertone. 'But my sister's betrothal party is perhaps not an appropriate place.' Gathering her skirts in quivering fists, she tilted her head to squarely meet his eyes. 'I think I ought to now circulate amongst the other guests.' Helen managed one step towards the company before Jason moved, blocking from view her fragile form with his powerful height and breadth. He inclined a little towards her and held out his arm. 'I think this guest deserves just a little more of your time, Mrs Marlowe. Come…accompany me to the terrace. I think we need a little fresh air.'

Chapter Twelve

'I hope you have not simply brought me out here so we might bicker.'

'You may rest assured that arguing with you was the last thing on my mind.'

'Well, that is good news, at least,' Helen said with constrained levity as they proceeded towards the railing enclosing a moon-dappled terrace. Her demeanour became again quite serious. 'I beg you will let me first thank you for helping Philip. Had you not done so…well, I am aware that Charlotte's marriage to him would still be a distant dream.' She gazed up at Jason; although his expression was veiled by shadow, she was conscious of his potent allure. 'Whatever happens between us,' she said huskily, 'I would just like you to know that I will always be grateful to you for that.'

A mere dip of his dark head acknowledged her thanks.

Helen turned to look out over the darkling gardens, her small hands gripping the iron balustrade. 'Did you put in a good word for Philip with George, too? Our brother seems very different towards him.'

Jason leaned on the railing close to her and stared up at the sparkling stars. 'What help I've given is Philip's due: a favour to right a wrong done to his family by mine. My great-grandfather caused the rift between the Hunters and the Goodes when he stole the wife of one of Philip's kin some sixty years ago.'

'But…'

'Hush, Helen,' Jason said softly. 'Your sister is happy; my cousin is happy. There's no reason to analyse how it all came about.'

Helen again started to speak, but he interrupted her with, 'You look very stylish this evening.'

Helen brushed a gloved hand over the sleek lavender satin of her skirt. It was the first time he had seen her well groomed since she was a child. Oddly she felt piqued rather than pleased by his compliment. She rested her slender hips against iron, boldly facing him. 'Why, thank you, sir,' she said with acid sweetness and arranged her gossamer shawl about her shoulders. 'I suppose I ought to have warned you that I do brush up quite well.'

A grunt of laughter preceded, 'Indeed you do. I never doubted it for a moment.' He watched her from beneath lazy lids. 'You always look delectable. But it is the first time in a long while I've seen you in a pretty dress.' He raised a hand to gently cup her sharp little chin. 'I have just one small criticism to make…' A pin was eased from her glossy coiffure and an ebony curl spiralled slowly on to a milky shoulder. 'I like your hair loose…'

Helen gasped and attempted to snatch back the pin to anchor the ringlet again into place. But Jason was not done ruining her careful *toilette*. A thumb leisurely traced over her soft lips. 'And you don't need artifice,' he murmured. 'Besides, it's likely to arouse suspicion if I go back inside sporting rouge.'

'Jason, you mustn't…someone might come…'

An imprisoning arm settled either side of her and Jason brought his head inexorably closer. His mouth tracked hers until, done with half-hearted evasion, Helen turned to him of her own volition. Her lips parted and her eyelids drooped in languid anticipation. After a moment, when all she could sense was his body warming hers and a lemon scent enveloping her, she flicked a glance up at him. She understood the demand in his searing look and immediately complied by going up on tiptoe. About to press her soft lips against the hard contours of his mouth, a bark of laughter made her jump. Immediately one of his hands moved to rest, cool and confident against the silk of her jaw, encouraging her to stay still.

But the moment was lost. Helen jerked back against the balcony whilst peering anxiously in the direction of the doors that opened into the drawing room. Laughter erupted again, sounding disturbingly close. Jason's splendid waistcoat received a little thump as Helen attempted escaping to a respectable distance.

Having first cursed beneath his breath, Jason murmured, 'I've missed seeing you.' He pushed himself back from the railing, allowing her liberty.

'Indeed? You know where I live,' Helen tartly rejoined whilst keeping a vigilant eye on the moving figures she could glimpse between the stirring edges of the curtains.

A smile tugged at one side of his thin mouth. 'That encourages me to think that you've missed seeing me, too.' It was stated with an amount of throaty satisfaction.

Helen bit back the spontaneous denial that had sprung to her tongue. There was no point in acting the coquette. He didn't bother with flirting; she imagined he might also be out of patience with women who feigned indifference to him. With that thought in mind she blurted, 'I was expecting to hear a while ago that you had made certain arrangements. Have you been too busy to give much thought to it?'

'I've thought of little else.'

Helen's eyes soared swiftly to his face. 'Is it all finalised?'

'Why do you want to continue with something that you fear will damage your self-respect?'

Helen was momentarily stunned into silence by his acuity. Then briskly she said, 'I think you presume to know too much about me. If you think I will cry wolf once you have gone to the trouble and expense, I can assure you I will not. I promise you I am at ease with our...new relationship.'

'Are you?' Jason said drily. 'Well, I am not sure that I am.'

'You don't really want me at all, do you?'

He gave a grunt of harsh laughter. 'If that were true it would solve a lot of problems.'

'Then why are you delaying...?'

'I'm flattered by your impatience, my dear. But you did promise not to nag me, Helen,' he drawled in mild rebuke.

Regret and humiliation swept over Helen. She had obviously made herself sound like a shrew as well as a desperate wanton. A cool hand flew to a flaming cheek to gauge how obvious was her mortification.

Jason understood the gesture and with a low imprecation enclosed a fragile wrist with long fingers to draw her comfortingly close.

Helen immediately flung him off. 'If this is a game to you, sir, it is not to me,' she hissed in a low breath. 'If you are content with just Mrs Tucker as your mistress, you only have to say…'

'I want you, dammit, and you know it,' he gritted out in immediate response.

Helen sent a startled look at him, then at the French doors, but it seemed that the people who had stationed themselves just inside had moved away.

'So again I have answered all your questions,' he said with harsh self-mockery. 'I certainly think it's time you answered mine.'

Helen nervously laced her fingers, then just as quickly jerked them apart. 'Very well,' she burst out. 'I shall start by saying that I suspect you find awkward this unforeseen aspect to my character. I am no longer the innocent child you once knew. I suspect also that you would rather I had not propositioned you at all. But I have, and I do not regret it.' Helen gazed boldly at him before her tawny eyes swept away to the velvety blue horizon. A scudding cloud made hazy the moon, deepening the dusk. 'I know our families once were close. My father liked you and was upset when you and George were no longer friends. Perhaps you think that because I am of gentle birth I ought to find a genteel solution to being poor. I expect your conscience would be easier if I were to support myself by finding respectable employment, and apply to be a governess or a companion to a lonely lady. Perhaps I might find a position in a shop.'

Having listed out her prospects, she swallowed and turned to him. 'The truth is, I do not want to do those things. I have had a husband who cherished me and, although we had little money, I had my own household. Even before then I kept house for my papa from when I turned seventeen. In short, I have long been my own mistress, and now I would rather be yours than be despised as inferior by employers who are no better than me.' She clutched again at the railing and watched the silver disc shed its fleecy coat. Her wistful face became bathed in milky light. 'So, you see, my self-respect is more under threat from being good than being bad.'

'I'm the lesser of two evils.'

Helen frowned her regret at the horizon. She had not at all intended that it would sound that way, but, in essence, it was true.

Having read her answer from her expression, Jason swung away. He threw back his head to contemplate the stars, and whether to make light of the blow to his ego. But the poignancy in her quiet re- flection had subdued him, made him feel churlish for even considering using flippancy to disguise his wounded pride. How much greater would have been the damage to Helen's self-worth had those fears she'd confided been realised. She had not lied or ex- aggerated in what she'd described might be her fu- ture. Many young women who were poor relations endured just such a miserable existence, sometimes at the hands of their own kin. A sudden surge of ha- tred for George swayed Jason on his feet.

He thrust his hands into his pockets and looked at her for a long moment. 'You need not resort to being bad, or to being employed, Helen.' With just a hint that she would welcome his proposal he would ask her now to be his wife.

Helen swirled about to face him. 'What would you have me do then, sir?' she snapped with subdued volume. 'You know very well that George has squan- dered our allowance and is heavily in debt. Would you have me transfer the burden of my keep to my new brother-in-law? He already has his mother and sister depending on him. I need not beg for a home, I know the offer will be freely given. But Philip and Charlotte deserve their privacy and their honeymoon years. I will not live with them.' It was a vehement statement that brought a sheen of tears to her eyes.

Helen swallowed the ache in her throat. 'And before you offer it, I do not want your charity. But again I must thank you for your concern. You have recently provided more for Charlotte and me than has our own brother.'

'You ought to marry,' Jason stated more roughly than he intended. 'Harry Marlowe would want what is best for you.'

Helen nodded, a faraway look in her topaz eyes. 'Yes, he would,' she dulcetly agreed. 'And Harry would know that a loveless marriage is not right for me. I would far sooner have my independence and my widow status than a roof over my head and a life-time of disappointment with a husband who remains a stranger.' She gave him a wry smile. 'Do not fret for my virtue and try to find someone to make an honest woman of me.' A little chuckle escaped her. 'Harry used to say I was too romantic and not nearly practical enough. And so I was.' She glanced at Jason. 'He would be quite amazed at how reversed are now those traits.'

'And what became of your romantic nature?' Jason asked quietly.

Helen cocked her head to one side and held out her hands before her, slowly intertwining her slen-der fingers. 'Oh, I am still a romantic on occa-sions…' A sweetly shy smile flitted to him. 'Have you not noticed how enchanted I am by Charlotte's betrothal? She has the most wonderful engagement ring…rubies and diamonds, and soon we will shop for her trousseau and discuss a wedding breakfast and flowers and so on…' She absently rotated her plain gold wedding band. 'Oh, there is still a lot to enjoy that is wonderfully romantic.' Aware suddenly of a quiet protracting between them, Helen neared him and looked calmly into his eyes. 'I have told the truth. Has it put you off having me as your mistress?'

'No.'

She smiled up at him, marvelling again at how extraordinarily handsome he was. 'We have been honest in the past. I like being able to speak plainly to you. I was not nagging you earlier, it is just…'

'You don't want me to ruin your plan.'

'And will you?'

'Of course not.' He smiled at her before dipping his head and taking her mouth in a swift, hard kiss.

Helen was still reeling from that bruising assault when he said, 'At least you consider me the devil it's better to know. I'm not sure everyone would agree with you.'

Helen looked earnestly up into his dark, long-lashed eyes. 'I do not think you a devil at all,' she said with husky sincerity. 'You have been considerate and kind and it will certainly be no hardship to—' She broke off, aware of being a word away from reassuring him with indelicate candour.

'Go on…' He turned her face up to his with relentlessly firm fingers. 'We speak plainly…don't we?'

'It will be no hardship to be intimate with you…to sleep with you.' It was uttered almost defiantly and she boldly held his gaze. 'You are not a repugnant character or physically ugly. In fact, you are quite handsome, as I'm sure you know.' She felt her cheeks warming beneath the sudden glint of humour in his eyes and whipped about her head to frown at the moon.

'Thank you, Helen, for that compliment. And you are quite beautiful, as I'm sure you know. There…in one respect we make the perfect couple,' he remarked drily. 'I think that the theatre or Vauxhall Gardens is probably the best place for our first outing together. Have you a preference?'

Helen swiftly shook her head and murmured, 'No.'

'I'll send you a note detailing what I've arranged,' Jason said. 'I've taken a house on the outskirts of Chelsea that I think you will like. We will finish the evening there, if you're agreeable. I imagine you would want to return to Westlea House and not leave your sister alone at night?'

Helen nodded and chewed her lower lip before sending him a wavering smile. 'It would be best if we are very discreet about our times there, at least until after Charlotte is married and moves in with Philip. I would not want her to be shunned should it all leak out.'

'Of course.'

'Thank you.'

'I think it's time we went inside.' Jason extended a hand to her; their progress towards the French doors was timely, for a couple strolled out. Mr and Mrs Bond were neighbours of the Goodes and they exchanged a few words about the happy occasion before Helen and Jason continued into the drawing room. Without another word passing between them, Jason led Helen towards her sister and ten minutes later politely took his leave.

'What in damnation is *he* doing here?'

Iris swung her blonde head towards her husband, then followed the direction of his astonished glower. 'I invited him.' It was a brisk response, for her china blue eyes had returned to a more fascinating sight than Colin Bridgeman's late arrival at Charlotte's engagement party.

Some fifteen minutes ago Iris had noticed Jason and Helen go to the terrace. She had imagined he was simply being courteous, for Helen had the appearance of being flushed and in need of a little air. But now they were back inside and Helen seemed the opposite of refreshed. Slashes of pink were more vividly highlighting her cheekbones and her eyes were extraordinarily bright. Not only that, her new hairstyle looked in disarray, with tendrils draping about her face. Iris was an expert in the art of covert dalliance in company and could easily spot the signs that betrayed when others had indulged.

Iris narrowed her eyes on Helen's distinguished escort. Of course, Jason seemed unruffled…as ever he did. Iris pursed her lips—insufferable thoughts were pricking at her mind. Had the skinny little drab managed something she so far had failed to achieve and hooked the *ton*'s most charismatic rake? It seemed too incredible to contemplate one moment longer and yet… Helen was a needy widow. Iris looked back to her sister-in-law to make a thorough female assessment. A fierce glint fired in her eyes: the conclusion to which she came was that Helen had the radiant aplomb of a woman who had just secured a wealthy protector.

'You invited Bridgeman to Charlotte's betrothal party? Why, in God's name?'

George's angry demand interrupted Iris's agitated thoughts. 'I deemed it the least I could do,' she exploded in exasperation. 'You virtually implied Colin could have Charlotte as his wife. It is best we smooth things over with him. We do not want to lose his friendship.'

'*I* do,' George said with sour significance. 'You have so many friends, my dear…all gentlemen. Surely you could lose just the one?' George looked past his wife's shoulder to see that the unwanted guest appeared to be making his way relentlessly towards them.

Colin Bridgeman was about George's age, but there ended all similarity. Bridgeman was of average height, fair of complexion with sandy hair. George was tall and swarthy. Colin was thin and favoured peacock colours whereas George was beginning to spread about the middle and dressed quite conservatively.

George had never really liked Colin, but they were old acquaintances and, with few friends between them, he was a ready companion when no better was to be had. Before George married they had gone roistering about town. Now more sedate pastimes of dice and cards, or taking a tipple, drew them together at the clubs.

When he turned thirty, Colin had taken a sizeable inheritance from his grandfather's trust. But years of having little in his pockets had left him close-fisted. Then, recently, George had unexpect-edly found a way to prise apart Bridgeman's fingers, and in doing so he had opened a can of worms.

When Colin offered to forward him a loan to keep the duns at bay…and a little in reserve…in return for permission to pay court to Charlotte, George had thought it perfectly acceptable. He was even pleased to think that Colin's approach meant he had not taken offence at having had rejected his quite reason-able offer for Westlea House. Had Jason Hunter not offered handsomely for the property, Colin would be the new owner.

Now George wished he had not taken a penny piece of the man's cash. He would not have done so, he commiserated with himself, had it not seemed that Charlotte's swain was destined to remain a pau-per. George had no real wish to see his young sister unhappy, but neither had he any intention of contin-uing to support her financially. He therefore had de-cided to be practical. It had occurred to George, and had been an added incentive, that were Bridgeman to marry a woman younger and prettier, his wife might be abandoned by her latest conquest.

In that affair, George exonerated Colin. He had come to accept that it was his wife who instigated her liaisons. Once he would have denied such knowl-edge, finding it humiliating and distressing. George watched his wife simpering as her paramour came closer and suddenly realised he no longer cared very much what she did.

On the strength of the two men soon becoming brothers-in-law George had thus accepted substantial financial assistance. Rushing to lay hands on the cash, he had heedlessly signed the contract before properly checking the clauses. Now he knew that the rate of interest charged to him was extortionate; not only that, but the loan was also repayable on demand. And he had just that morning received such a demand: Bridgeman wanted his money immediately returned with interest.

Had he realised the precarious position he would land himself in, he would not have given Philip Goode his permission to marry Charlotte. But Jason had made it clear that Philip had his patronage and was destined for success. George might not like Jason, but he was one of the *ton*'s most influential and affluent gentlemen. He had happily pondered on being showered with plaudits for being canny enough to welcome a wolf in sheep's clothing into the family.

George scowled to himself as he saw his young sister laughing with her future husband. Goode might be destined for success, but he seemed destined for disaster! If he could not pacify Bridgeman and wheedle a little time to pay, he might yet find himself languishing in gaol....

'The blushing bride-to-be looks exceptionally charming this evening.'

George gave a well-feigned start as he turned to Bridgeman. 'Colin...there you are...'

'Of course, here I am. I'm sure any betrothal party is not complete without the jilted fiancé putting in an appearance.'

George noted his wife wince at that sarcasm and swiftly steered Colin away a few paces. 'Now steady on, Bridgeman,' he hissed. 'No such arrangements were ever properly made. God's teeth! You didn't even call on Charlotte once.'

'Not for want of trying. Whenever I said I was ready to pay a visit, you told me to wait for your instruction on it. Then you instructed me she was to marry this whippersnapper.' He cast a derisive look in the direction of Philip Goode.

'Her choice, Colin; her choice,' George sighed out. 'A brother can't interfere with the workings of a sister's tender heart.'

'That's not what you said in Hyde Park when you dragged her home and sent the boy off with a flea in his ear,' Colin reminded him acidly. He gave George an estimating look. 'I would say it has more to do with his cousin's money than anything else. You prefer Hunter's coin to mine, just as you did with West-lea House. So be it,' he snapped. 'Give me back mine, together with the interest you owe, and we'll say no more about it.'

George blanched. 'I will repay it as soon as I can, you know that.'

'That might not be soon enough,' Colin said with a gleam of malice darkening his eyes. 'I want it by noon tomorrow or I'll have you dunned.' He cast a look towards where Helen and Charlotte stood centrally within a group of friends. 'Of course, you have more than one sister…perhaps we may yet find a solution…'

George gulped and Colin's profile received a drop-jawed look. '*Helen?* You want to marry *Helen* instead?' As he digested that thought, his features relaxed into a wondrous smile.

'Marry her? I don't think so. She's past her prime and a might too spirited for what's nice in a wife. But I'll be happy to take her to bed and pay for the privilege.'

Chapter Thirteen

'You want to proposition Helen?'

'Yes.' Another brooding stare sloped from under Bridgeman's sandy lashes at the group of young women chatting together.

George's eyes swivelled nervously as he realised someone might have overheard their shocking exchange. He quickly manoeuvred Colin by the elbow to a safe distance. 'We are men of the world so I am not about to take offence even though the lady in question is my sister,' he rattled off in an undertone. 'In fact, *I* know it for a sensible solution. If she won't find a husband, what's to be done?' His shoulders elevated as far as his ears. 'An informal arrangement with a gentleman is all that's left unless she's content to grow old pinching pennies.' George's brow corrugated in vexation. 'Trouble is,

Helen can be damnably headstrong and uncoopera-
tive at times.'

'I know,' Bridgeman sourly agreed. He recalled
the terse notes he'd received years ago when she'd
rebuffed him. He had not thereafter pursued her; his
pride would not let him. But he had not forgotten her
either, and the lust to possess her was as strong. It was
a while since he'd seen her and he could detect some
physical changes. Her face was more sharply honed,
and her body less curvaceous, yet for him she still
held an irresistible allure. Her full rosy lips were
presently parted in an appealing smile and hands that
seemed pale as porcelain, and equally fragile, were
expressively gesturing whilst she talked. As though
sensing she was under observation, she turned her
glossy dark head and her joyful smile withered.

Bridgeman's fleshy mouth twisted sardonically.
She hadn't warmed towards him. She certainly
would not have liked the idea of him as a brother-
in-law, of that he was sure. But the piquancy of wedding one sister whilst brooding on bedding the other
had certainly given him a reason to consider marrying a chit with no dowry.

Colin came to awareness of George curiously
eyeing him, no doubt wondering what kept him so
moodily quiet. 'I take it she has never told you that
I offered her my protection a few years ago.'

George's jaw lengthened almost to his chest.

'She turned me down. It's up to you to make sure she doesn't again do so. There's only so much injury a fellow can take before being inclined to retaliate.'

George looked startled by the unsubtle threat. 'If she won't have you, she won't—there's nothing I can do about it!'

'But you are her brother,' Colin stressed silkily. 'And I have every faith in your powers of persuasion.' He gripped George's shoulder. 'I'll give you a little time to work your magic. In case you need an incentive to be diligent...' he gave a terse nod at a group of young gentlemen '...why do you not go and ask Tarquin Beaumont how he liked the Fleet?'

Helen settled into comfortable squabs and, stripping off her gloves, her warm fingertips pressed dents into the supple hide either side of her. Her eyes darted about the interior of the coach. Before this evening such a luxurious conveyance had been unknown to her. Realising that her hands were lightly quivering, she clasped them together in her lap.

Many hours ago, when Jason had arrived to collect her in this plush carriage, she had noticed curtains twitching in the houses opposite, yet she had continued to feel quite calm.

But now the evening was drawing to a close and she felt less serenely confident. She swayed on the seat as the coach smoothly negotiated a rut whilst conveying her to Chelsea and a new life as a gentleman's mistress.

They were just a short time from being lovers, but he had not rushed her to leave the theatre and embark on the journey. In fact, she had been the one to suggest they left a few minutes before the final curtain to beat the crush of carriage drivers racing to get the Drury Lane crowds back to the suburbs. She had made the remark like a veteran theatregoer, yet something else had been her prime motivation. She had run the gauntlet of speculative stares when entering the theatre; she had no wish to do so again on leaving it.

But the sly glances and whispers were to be expected, and, in a way, perhaps it was best to encounter them early on. The sooner the gossip started, the sooner it would be finished. In a few weeks another scandalous *on dit* would be doing the rounds and talk of whether or not Sir Jason Hunter had brought Mrs Marlowe under his protection would be less diverting.

Helen guessed that polite society had not made up its mind if Jason was squiring her because his cousin was marrying her sister or whether his interest in her was more personal. During the intervals those with uncontrollable inquisitiveness had invited themselves in to Jason's box with the sole intention, it seemed, of finding out. Amongst others, whose names she had forgot, Helen had been introduced to Lord and Lady Silverston and Viscountess Montague. Then Lady Mornington and her spinster sister had swept in and begun a bold interrogation. Helen had marvelled at Jason's skill in answering a question without revealing a thing. The twins had thus surged out as the curtain rose on the next act, no wiser about Mrs Marlowe's claim on the eligible baronet's affections than when they had arrived. On the surface everybody *seemed* charming; but Helen had long been adept at spotting insincerity.

Yet, on the whole, she had enjoyed her first outing with Jason. She slipped a glance from under her lashes at the lounging figure opposite. Why was she suddenly feeling awkward and anxious? He had acted no differently towards her this evening than at any other time since they had renewed their acquaintance. Whether shielding her from malicious eyes and tongues or fetching her refreshment, he had been unfailingly courteous and attentive. She had no reason not to trust him to treat her kindly in bed, too. It would be different, of course, to the intimacy she had shared with Harry. They had been lovers in the truest sense of the word. Jason desired her, treated her with respect, but she wanted a little affection, too.

'Is it far?' Helen glanced through the shadows at the gentleman opposite looking to be perfectly at his ease.

'We are nearly there,' he answered and she heard the gentle humour in his tone.

Helen felt warmth flood her cheeks. 'I… It is just I am quite hungry, that's all. Are we dining first?'

'Of course,' he said softly. 'Do you think me an uncouth barbarian?'

Helen smiled at his self-mockery and relaxed a little. 'Not at all. In fact, I was just appreciating how gallant you are. I never doubted that you would do every thing quite properly, sir,' she lightly teased him.

'Well, to prove you wrong, I am about to do something quite irregular.' Slowly he unfolded his crossed arms and held them out. 'Come and sit with me,' he huskily invited.

After a fleeting hesitation Helen relinquished her seat and settled close to him. Immediately a muscular arm came about her and she nestled her head quite naturally against his chest. She could sense the hard masculine lines of his body beneath his fine clothes and the verbena cologne he used was pleasantly soothing. Within a few moments her heartbeat had steadied to a more regular rhythm and, feeling cosy and content, she slipped a hand on to the large fingers resting on his knee. He turned his hand, welcoming her tender touch with a brush of a thumb before his lips also saluted her fingers. Slowly he returned their clasped hands to rest on his thigh.

'People will be whispering about us now, won't they?'

'Yes…'

Helen gave a little sigh and nodded in resignation.

'Have you been worrying about it?'

After a moment Helen said, 'Not really for I can imagine what they might be saying. But nobody knows for sure how it is between us…only us.'

'Has your sister quizzed you over it?'

Helen nodded again and choked a little apologetic laugh. 'As we are speaking plainly, I know you will not mind if I tell you something quite shocking. I am afraid Charlotte is wholly under the impression that your interest in me must be honourable.' She knuckled a laugh into submission. 'I have not had the heart to tell her that her hints about double weddings and so on are wildly far of the mark.'

When Jason remained quiet, she twisted her face up to look at him, fearing he might not, after all, have found it an amusing anecdote. His eyes were blocked from view by an angular jaw that looked dusky enough to need a razor. Helen subdued the temptation to sense his skin graze her palm. Instead she angled her head to see his expression and interpret his mood. 'Are you angry? I would not have mentioned it to you, only I thought…I thought it might make you laugh,' she weakly explained. She swallowed, feeling rather foolish. 'I hope you do not think I have said something to make Charlotte think that…'

'Why would I suspect any such thing? After all, you have made it clear to me that you have no wish to remarry. Have you changed your mind?'

Helen's gaze was locked to darkly gleaming eyes that seemed able to probe her soul. She had loved and married Harry Marlowe; she would never want anyone else as her husband…would she? 'No…of course I have not changed my mind,' she whispered. The denial was out, but with devastating insight she abruptly knew it to be false. There *was* a man she would marry, if only he would ask her…

Obliterating years fell away and she recalled being in her teens and daydreaming of Jason Hunter. Those girlish fantasies had faded when they no longer saw one another and then had extinguished beneath her love for Harry Marlowe. Now she could quite painfully recall sitting on the grass in Surrey pulling petals whilst chanting…he loves me, he loves me not…

'No harm is done. And I don't think it will hurt to postpone dashing Charlotte's hopes, do you?' Jason's voice splintered her poignant reminiscence. 'Once she is a married woman, she might be inclined to see things differently.'

Helen managed a single nod, but her alarming self-knowledge had left her mind reeling and her body weak. She made to slump into the seat by his side to ponder on the discovery that Harry didn't, after all, have sole claim on her heart. But he again drew her against him. He tilted up her face and just before their lips touched she sensed she was submerging in eyes like glittering pools of desire.

Helen felt an exquisite ache low in her abdomen start sapping strength from her limbs, for his mouth was moving on hers with wonderfully erotic expertise. Her cloak was loosened and his fingers skimmed her midriff, trailing fire in their wake. Helen felt her anxieties drift away and abandoned herself to the sensual delight he was bestowing. Slowly a small hand crept up to curl about his nape and when next his tongue slid seductively on her lower lip, she flicked hers to it in welcome.

Jason sensed Helen melting beneath his caresses. She was moulding her body against him and igniting in him profound passion. His kiss became slow and deep, his hands swift and confident. Her bodice and chemise were deftly opened and tantalising fingers stroked over silky warm flesh that instantly rose to fill his palms. Jason's slick lips slid to her throat, to the tender nook at her shoulder, before finally claiming the aching little nub her bowed back begged him to soothe.

His tongue moved with skilful slowness, flicking, touching, circling until Helen felt maddened, delirious with delight, and her little guttural cries seemed to well from deep in her throat.

Jason felt a burst of tenderness moderate his urgent need to immediately possess her, for five small fingers had again intertwined with his to clasp together their hands. Besides which, he had no real wish for their first loving to be quickly consummated on the seat of his coach when they were barely fifteen minutes away from a feather bed and many hours of sensual pleasure. He raised his dark head and eyes like smouldering coals roved over a beautiful face set in rigid lines of desire.

Jason continued to kiss her as he brought together the edges of lace to cover her breasts and marvelled that she could be such an intriguing mix of innocent and wanton.

And that conundrum started unwanted thoughts rotating in his mind. Helen Marlow was a woman who didn't want a husband, but who needed a lover.

A perfect paramour…under normal circumstances. But this wasn't normal for him. He was different. He was falling hopelessly in love and he didn't want Helen to be his mistress—he wanted her for his wife.

Her brother's thievery might have precipitated her into finding a protector, but he sensed she would, in any event, have been ripe for seduction. He was reasonably sure he was to be her first lover since her husband, and Harry Marlowe had been dead more than half a decade. There was a raw hunger in Helen that made her pliant and responsive to his touch. He kissed her again with sweetness and felt her immediate thrill of anticipation as to what he might do next.

But perhaps it was not just *his* touch she wanted or needed. He was prepared to marry her, but she might have allowed the first philanderer to call by to share her bed so long as he had a few pretty compliments and enough cash to keep Westlea House for her. Even as the disturbing thoughts tormented Jason he knew them absurd. Helen Marlowe was the antithesis of a vain courtesan susceptible to flattery.

And he would have sworn *he* was not a jealous man. But a savage new emotion was poisoning his mind and defeating his restraint. Deft fingers swept up her skirt to expose lissom milky legs before spreading to explore the sensitive darker skin on the inside of her thigh. His kisses coarsened and deepened, widening her mouth.

Helen's hands instinctively drove between them and she jerked back her head. A reproachful look held his defiant gaze and then, with a sigh, she wound her arms about his neck and lay her dusky head against his shoulder.

With a low oath Jason sank against the seat, a powerful arm anchoring her to his side. His head fell back and his lids drooped low as he realised he had after all proved himself an uncouth barbarian. He'd startled her, yet the residue of sensual languor in her stayed. Glancing down at her, he could see dark lashes fanned on pale cheeks and a mouth that looked slick and swollen and achingly inviting. He forked a tender hand over her chin, a thumb brushing soothingly against her turgid lips. For some reason it was the closest he could come to apology.

He had wanted to savour their first loving in every respect. He had wanted them to share conversation and dinner, and leisurely mutual pleasure. Instead he had acted like a callow youth with a hair trigger. The guilt in him made him feel unworthy to again touch her. He smiled ruefully at shadows moving on the roof of the coach; but he knew he would, for, guilt or no, wanting her was ungovernable.

Helen slowly relaxed beneath the thumb sweeping an arc softly over her cheek. She knew he regretted losing control, but she was not disgusted to know he could be less perfect and more human at times. Once or twice Harry had loved her swiftly and selfishly, then had sheepishly told her that carnality could tempt a man to savagery.

'It is as well it is too dark for me to see the sight you look with rouge smeared on you,' Helen lightly teased. As she sensed rather than saw him lift a testing hand to his face, she giggled, shattering the tension between them.

Jason dropped a kiss on her sleek crown of hair before chuckling, for he had just recalled that earlier that evening he had complimented her on refraining from using it. In a voice of velvety roughness he said, 'I'm sorry….'

'I…I am sorry….'

'It is forgotten,' Jason glibly lied and eased her head down against his shoulder.

Helen immediately sprang up again and a cascade of ebony hair caped her nude white shoulders. She looked down at the handsome dark face starkly outlined by a pristine pillow. She had ruined everything. And it had been so perfect between them up till a few moments ago…

The townhouse to which he had brought her was

cosy and elegant. They had enjoyed a delicious meal
served up by footmen who flitted discreetly to and
from a candle-lit dining room. The grand table had
been decked with the finest crystal and china and
gleaming silverware. A warm atmosphere that owed
little to the blazing logs in the grate had blossomed
between them. Helen had felt her inhibitions and
her nervousness melt beneath the pleasure of just
being with him. When eventually they had eaten
their fill and talked into amicable quiet, Jason had
asked if she would like yet to go upstairs. It had
seemed the most natural thing in the world to agree,
and a young maid had shown her to a magnificent
bedchamber in which reposed a vast four-poster.

Helen had gently declined the young woman's of-
fers of assistance in preparing for bed. She had
wanted time alone; not only to make herself ready
but, like a child on a fascinating excursion, to explore
her surroundings.

She had brushed velvet bed-hangings with rever-
ent fingers, taken puffy pillows from the bed to peer
beneath at the silky white sheets. And then she had
found the gossamer negligee draped on a chair beside a dressing chest that held a selection of oils and
perfumes and silver-backed brushes.

Helen had tested a scent in a pot on a wrist, wondering if it was the perfume that had wafted in Mrs

Tucker's wake on the day she had seen her alight from her stylish carriage. She had accepted, with a twinge of melancholy, that Jason was probably as generous to all his mistresses, but nevertheless she had appreciated being treated well. And now she had ruined everything…

She touched a finger to his face, feeling the stubble on his jaw. She wanted him to open his eyes. 'Please look at me. I…it is not nothing. I would not have liked it at all if you had…I mean, if you had called me Diana at such a time I would have been insulted.'

Jason gazed up at her. 'I'm not likely to do that, *Helen.*' Her name carried a certain stress that told her his nonchalance was poorly feigned.

As though he read her knowledge and it irked that he had betrayed himself, he swiftly turned, drawing her down and beneath him. Slowly he linked brown fingers with white then carried their clasped hands to where the black silk of her hair tumbled over snowy pillows.

'I said it doesn't matter, Helen… Shall I prove it to you?'

Helen felt an odd surge of tears clog her throat, for indeed she wanted him to.

Earlier Jason had made love to her with a skill that had transported her to a level of sensation unknown to her. With a poignant ache she understood how he had acquired such expertise. Diana Tucker, and numerous other women who had come before her, had also gasped and cried out beneath such lavish sensuality. But, when teetering on the brink of explosive tension, had they all remembered to rightfully name the man who had so inflamed them?

Her late husband might not have loved her as slickly as Jason, but such tenderness had existed between her and Harry that they had communicated softly even at the height of passion. And this evening she had called his name again....

Chapter Fourteen

'How much longer are we to endure this?'

The petulant demand snatched Helen's interest from the pearly silk slipping beneath a sensitive palm. 'What is the matter, dear?' she asked Charlotte.

Charlotte shot a fierce look to the other side of the shop's counter. 'They are talking about us, I'm certain of it.' Charlotte gave Helen a glimmering look. 'Or rather, they are gossiping about *you,* I suspect.'

Helen glanced at two fashionable young women who were peeking in their direction. Curious eyes were intermittently visible between the filigree edges of Brussel's lace suspended from rolls shelved on high. Linking arms with her sister, Helen urged her to move on towards the selection of velvets at the other end of Baldwin's Emporium. 'They will soon grow bored and find somebody more worthy of their snooping.'

'I doubt it!' Charlotte announced pithily. 'Sir Jason is very eligible and handsome and the débutantes will naturally want to know whether or not he is taken.' She gave her sister an arch glance. 'I have to say, Helen, I think it is time your beau gazetted a notice.'

Helen felt her cheeks prickle with warmth, but said levelly, 'Sir Jason is not my beau; he is simply a good friend of mine. I have said that you must not hope—you certainly should not say to anyone—that there is more to it than that.'

'Sir Jason intends there be more to it than that, I'm sure,' Charlotte flatly opined. 'He has been calling on you and escorting you around town for two weeks. Everyone has noticed how taken he is with you. Emily and Anne are so excited! Anne has already hinted at how nice it will be to welcome you as a new cousin. She quite thinks of the Hunters as family now, you know.' Charlotte slid a significant look back at the gossiping ladies. 'Not everyone will be so thrilled, of course. But I shall be most surprised—and disappointed—if soon you are not sporting a huge betrothal ring.'

'Charlotte!'

Charlotte was unperturbed. 'I'm not so innocent and naïve that I'm ignorant of what people imagine is going on between a rakish gentlemen and a young

widow…who happens to be my sister,' she added
primly. She gave a cautioning nod and set her auburn
curls to bouncing. 'Especially when it gets out how
very generous your admirer has been in providing
comforts for us at Westlea House.' Under the pre-
tence of examining a bolt of blue velvet, Charlotte
stole a peek to see if others found them noteworthy.
'I've no doubt Sir Jason has his pride. He is probably waiting for a little sign from you before he pro-
poses. You must encourage him, or you only have
yourself to blame if people start making up lies about
the two of you!' Charlotte gave her elder sister an extremely old-fashioned look before taking a more
genuine interest in selecting fabric for her trousseau.

'That colour would suit you,' Helen said, desperately bright, as she attempted changing the subject.

'I know you're in love with him,' Charlotte
breathed insouciantly whilst trailing her fingers over
plush gentian pile.

Helen dropped her eyes to the cloths and in agitation yanked a length of apricot velvet off the roll.
But in her mind rotated thoughts far removed from
a new gown.

Charlotte was correct in one respect: Jason's generosity had altered her routine and her spending. Obviously it had been noticed that she shopped more and
that clue, coupled with her outings with Jason, had

naturally aroused speculation that they were more than friends. She was not extravagant, but neither could she mix in polite society dressed in her old clothes. New stockings and gloves had just a short time ago been unaffordable luxuries. She could now purchase a dozen bonnets at a time should she so wish.

George, of course, knew that her upturn in fortune was not the result of his conscience finally troubling him. In fact, she was most surprised that her brother had not been by to express his gratitude that she had found a man to support her.

And, indeed, she was being lavishly supported. She had received a note from her bank of the astonishing sum that had been credited to her account. Her monthly allowance from her lover was more than her sweet papa had estimated his daughters could comfortably live on for a year.

So her plan for her future security was a success: she had acquired a gentleman to keep her, and a promise that in the future Westlea House would be hers. Charlotte was shortly to be married to Philip, who now had excellent prospects. Jason Hunter had within a short time bestowed so much. She had got what she wanted, she again impressed on herself as she absently wandered between rolls of jewel-coloured cloth. For the first time in many years she felt pampered and attractive. Jason treated her with respect and, if not prone to display overt affection, she was sure he was fond of her. He invariably complimented her on her new gowns when he came to collect her from Westlea House. But his patient, polite socialising for a few hours could not mask the fact that he'd sooner go to Chelsea and see her naked. His desire for her was as yet undiminished and sharing a bed and mutual pleasure was her bittersweet role... But he had promised to tell her if he fell in love, or was ready to wed, Helen poignantly reminded herself.

She glanced up and saw the débutantes had not yet conquered their inquisitiveness. At first she ignored them, but then could not help but wonder if either of those pretty young women might capture Jason's heart. He was now thirty-five and, although no further mention had been made between them of his marriage, she knew he must want eventually to settle down with a wife and raise his family.

'Let us go, Charlotte.' Helen abruptly turned to her sister, making Charlotte frown enquiringly at her. 'It is quite warm in here,' Helen excused her need to avoid the nubile young ladies. 'Let's go to the tearoom. We can return here later for another browse.'

Charlotte smiled agreement and linked arms with Helen.

They had barely put a step on to the pavement when Charlotte let out a groan. 'Oh, no! Iris is coming this way with that Bridgeman fellow. We will never manage to dodge her.'

Helen squinted into the glaring sunlight and a sigh of disappointment escaped her, too. Iris had seen them and obviously had no intention of walking on by. Her buxom silhouette was looming at them through the incandescence. Helen blinked and saw that her sister-in-law was dragging her escort along by the arm.

'We're doomed to speak to her, I'm afraid,' Helen muttered to Charlotte just before Iris and Colin Bridgeman came to a halt in front of them.

Iris's blue gaze ranged quickly over Charlotte before sharpening on Helen. 'Have you not bought anything?' she demanded, looking significantly at the sisters' empty hands.

'No…we have not…' Helen began.

Iris let out a shrill giggle. 'Heavens! You have much to learn!' she amiably sneered. 'With such a *friend* as you have acquired, surely you must be able to find something in Baldwin's on which to spend his money?'

Helen felt her cheeks sting and noticed that Charlotte had blushed bright red.

'I expect Mrs Marlowe is a lady of certain taste

who likes to take her time before making her decision,' Colin purred into the tense quiet. 'Sometimes waiting makes possession the sweeter…do you not think, Mrs Marlowe?'

Helen gave him an icy glare, uneasily aware of the insinuation in his tone. 'We were just going to Millie's Tearoom,' she clipped out. 'Good day to you,' and, with a curt nod, she made to propel Charlotte along by the arm.

Iris was not about to lose her quarry so easily. 'I should like some refreshment.' She began to determinedly trail in their wake.

'There's George.' With a relieved sigh Charlotte waved urgently at their brother. He was making slow progress in his carriage for there was a press of vehicles in the street.

George saw them and steered the rig to the kerb then nimbly alighted. If he resented seeing his wife arm in arm with her lover, he gave no sign. In fact, he tried to avoid meeting Bridgeman's eyes at all. When eventually their glances collided, an unspoken message passed between them. George was first to look away and he immediately turned his attention to his sisters.

'Where are you two bound?'

'We were going to take tea in Millie's Rooms, but I think we shall instead go straight home,' Helen said.

Charlotte nodded her agreement to aborting their shopping trip.

'Well, I was just on my way to Westlea House,' George said. 'I'll take you home and save you the hackney fare.'

'I don't think Helen is now short of such a paltry amount, do you?' his wife sourly muttered. Iris was annoyed at George's interference, for she saw the chance slipping away to interrogate Helen.

George barely looked at Iris. He proceeded to help his sisters alight.

When they had been journeying west for a few minutes, Charlotte asked idly, 'Was there a special reason for your visit to see us, George?'

'Yes,' he succinctly replied after a momentary silence. 'And I won't say more on it till we are indoors,' he finished ominously.

Once back home and in Westlea House's parlour, Charlotte stripped off her bonnet and gloves and lobbed them on to the table. She sank wearily into the sofa. 'A wasted afternoon!' she peevishly complained. 'I feel too cross about it to go to Vauxhall this evening,' she dramatically threatened. 'Why did we not stay in the shop? I could have bought the blue velvet for my honeymoon outfit.'

'If things don't come right for me, you won't need a trousseau; leastways, not for a marriage to Philip.'

For the duration of the journey home Helen had sensed that George was in a fit of the sulks brought on by self-pity. From that she had deduced that he probably had got himself into more financial troubles. But she had not expected him to sink low enough to use Charlotte's happiness as a bargaining tool. And she was sure he was about to reveal a plan.

'You have no right to say such a thing!' Helen sharply rebuked him, for Charlotte's face had turned chalky on hearing his muttering. 'You have given your consent to Philip and cannot now retract even if you have got yourself into another muddle.'

'I would not get into muddles at all if it were not for you two leeches!' George snapped defensively. He paced back and forth, ignoring the withering look Helen shot his way.

'Well, you might as well say what you must,' Helen urged in exasperation. 'You obviously have something unpleasant on your mind. What is it?'

'*Who* is it is what you ought to have asked me.' George brought a fist down on the mantelpiece. 'Damnation! If I had known that Goode would eventually cosy up to Hunter, none of this would have come about.'

'You're talking in riddles, George. What have you done?' Helen insisted on knowing whilst keeping an eye on her sister's fearful expression. Charlotte was batting glances between her and George as though trying to estimate the course of an, as yet, unspoken debate.

'I borrowed money from a fellow to pay off the worst of my debts on the understanding that I'd permit him to marry Charlotte.'

Helen snorted in outrage. Quickly she put a comforting arm about her sister's shoulders. 'Well, that was an astonishingly stupid thing to do—you must have known that Charlotte would refuse him.' She suddenly turned a disgusted look on George. 'It was Bridgeman, wasn't it?'

Charlotte burst from her sister's embrace and, fists clenched, confronted her brother. 'I would rather run away than have that weasel for my husband.'

'Fortunately he will consider another solution…' George said so hoarsely the words were almost inaudible.

Helen frowned until George's uneasiness and downcast eyes gave her a blinding insight as to what the *solution* was. Her eyes grew round with horrified disbelief. Turning swiftly, she instructed Charlotte, 'Ask Betty to make some tea, please.' She gave her sister a reassuring smile. 'This foolishness will not affect your wedding plans. George must sort it all out.'

Charlotte backed towards the door. 'I swear I will run away if you even say that scrawny coxcomb can call on me!' she shouted at George before rushing from the room.

Once sure that Charlotte was out of earshot, Helen announced tightly, 'If you think I will in any shape or form contemplate a relationship with Colin Bridgeman, you are addled in the wits.'

George gripped the mantel with both hands till the knuckles showed bone. 'I am in serious trouble this time,' he obliquely wheedled for her to reconsider. 'Bridgeman isn't a piddling merchant, waving his invoices. Contracts were signed and he immediately wants back his money.' George looked forlornly at Helen. 'He'll set the duns on me. I might be in the Fleet as soon as next week.'

'How dare you try and prick my conscience. All of this is your own fault!'

George hung his head between arms braced on the mantel. A sudden sound stopped Helen from quitting the room. She spun about, but did not retrace one pace. She addressed her snivelling brother from the threshold. 'How much do you owe him? I have some cash in the bank…'

'Four thousand pounds,' George immediately supplied the figure in a gurgle. 'Plus some interest, too…'

A Practical Mistress

Helen repeated the amount in disgust.

George made an instant recovery. He pushed away from his support and swiped a hand over his eyes. 'Don't lecture me!' he spat irritably. 'You're hardly Madam Virtue, are you?'

Helen's complexion became grey with rage—she knew to what her brother referred, just as he intended she would. 'No, I'm not,' she whispered. 'I'm what you made me. You forced me to support myself and I am doing so. Your schemes worked. You have Father's money all to yourself, just as you intended, and now you have the outrageous cheek to moralise.'

'How much might you be able to loan me?' George plaintively asked.

'I have at the moment just over one thousand pounds…'

'It is not enough!' George despairingly shook balled fists at the parlour's cracked ceiling. 'Besides, I suspect Bridgeman wants you more than his cash.' He speared a glance at Helen. 'Why did you not tell me that he had approached you before?'

'Because I knew you would try to bully me to accept him, just as you are doing now.'

George looked affronted. 'I've only ever wanted you to be practical. You're not a blushing virgin, after all. And Colin is not such a bad chap. Would you not…once or twice…?'

Helen said icily, 'No, I would not.'

George resumed his pacing about the room, frowning at ceiling, door and wall. Suddenly he halted and spun to face Helen, a grin splitting his face. 'Of course! Hunter would advance you more if you ask him. He is renowned for being generous to his women. You could find a romantic little spot in the Pleasure Gardens this evening and ask him nicely for me.'

'I shall do no such thing, for he has been more than generous thus far,' Helen said in a cold, quiet voice.

'So you will not help me? You refuse to do a thing,' George whined.

'What I *will* do, when next I see Bridgeman, is tell him exactly what I think of him. I'll see if Betty has made the tea.' With that Helen quit the room without a backward glance.

'You're quiet this evening.'

Helen slanted Jason a faltering smile as they promenaded the Long Walk in Vauxhall Gardens. 'I have been engrossed in Charlotte's wedding plans, that is all.' She pressed a little closer to him to indicate she was content. 'Shall we go back and find Philip and Charlotte? The music must soon be due to start.'

As they turned on the path to retrace their steps, Helen's thoughts were once more occupied with her family's troubles.

Before they left the house earlier that evening, Helen had tried to pacify her sister. Persuading Charlotte that no good would come of relating George's sorry tale to Philip had not been an easy task. But Helen was sure it would be best to keep the matter private. Although he was a placid gentleman, Philip might take it into his head to act manfully to protect his fiancée. Gossips were already having a fine time at Helen's expense. It would not be prudent to give them something new to crow over and risk a stain on Charlotte's reputation.

Helen glanced at the tall gentleman at her side. An aura of power seemed to emanate from Jason and she was tempted to confide her worries. If she asked for money, he would give it to her. But such a sum would beg a question and she had no wish to lie. Neither did she intend disclosing that her brother was venal enough to sell one or other of his sisters to Bridgeman to keep his liberty. Her continuing loyalty to George seemed wasted, as did attempting to shield him from Jason's disgust. But a stubborn scrap of caring seemed entrenched in her soul.

The peacefulness of the Long Walk receded as they neared a more populated area of the Pleasure

Gardens. Helen glanced up and sensed her blood freeze. Not more than twenty yards away she spied Bridgeman's thin profile, his mouth agape in a grin. He was with George and some other fellows. A little further on was a party of young people grouped about Charlotte and Philip. Should Charlotte panic at the sight of him she might yet cause Philip to confront Bridgeman.

'I didn't know George was coming here this evening,' Helen breathlessly said, urging the muscular figure at her side to accelerate his step.

'Are you so keen to see him?' Jason drily asked and took a look down at Helen's countenance, now puckered in anxiety.

'No,' Helen muttered. 'In fact, I wish he and his friends had taken themselves off elsewhere this evening.'

Jason caught Helen to him and gently turned her about. Although her body faced his, her amber eyes were immediately looking over her shoulder. She anxiously eyed the group of gentlemen lounging against a supper box in which were several attractive ladies. 'What's the matter?' Jason asked. 'You have been preoccupied since we arrived.'

Helen sensed Jason's strengthening concern and gave him a wobbly smile. 'It is nothing, really... George upset Charlotte this afternoon,' she blurted in explanation. 'It might be as well to keep them apart. I shall just go and warn her he is here.' Helen looked into a darkly handsome face. A slight lift at a corner of Jason's mouth did little to convince her that he was satisfied with her answer.

'Your brother is heading this way.' Helen's dusky head briefly nodded to the left as she noticed Mark Hunter's distinguished figure weaving towards them through the crowd. 'I shan't be more than a moment,' she said, slipping her hand from Jason's elbow and darting towards Charlotte.

'I don't see anything of you in an age then, delightfully, we meet by chance twice in one day.'

Helen gasped and twisted about to see Colin Bridgeman's pale blue eyes on her. About to nod and immediately hurry on she hesitated and haughtily faced him. She had told George earlier that she would tell this man what she thought of him. Perhaps now was the perfect opportunity to do so.

Chapter Fifteen

'*I*s it a chance meeting?' Helen bluntly demanded to know.

Colin Bridgeman's bulbous lower lip protruded in amusement. 'I see you're a lady who knows when not to act coy. I like that.' He eyed her appreciatively from beneath stubby lashes. 'I take it from your attitude that George has revealed he is heavily in debt to me. Do you understand how perilous is his predicament?'

'Indeed I do, sir,' Helen breathed in a voice made virtually inaudible by wrath.

'He is a hair's breadth from a stay in gaol. But I can be persuaded to be lenient…did he tell you that?' Bridgeman asked whilst his eyes lowered to Helen's pert bosom, and his wet tongue crawled on his lips.

'He did tell me that. And I will relate to you my

response. I have no intention of saving him by becoming your harlot.'

'You'd rather remain Hunter's whore, would you?' Bridgeman's top lip lifted in a sneer. 'That's what people are calling you…did you not know?' he enquired with mock surprise.

Helen swallowed and glanced about, her face white and strained. 'Other than to let you know I despise you, I have nothing more to say to you,' she whispered hoarsely and took a step away from him.

'And *I* have nothing more to say to you,' Bridgeman echoed carelessly. 'Now I think on it, I'd sooner speak to your sister. Charlotte is younger and has the full figure I like. I'll warrant the sweet maid is more tenderhearted where her brother is concerned, and anxious to keep him from the Fleet.' His pale eyes swerved to slyly study Charlotte. 'A virgin, too…' he reminded himself, but with sufficient volume for Helen to hear.

'You will leave my sister alone!' Helen fiercely gritted out. Bridgeman simply winged a ginger eyebrow at her, and made to strut in Charlotte's direction. Helen blocked his path. 'You will not bother Charlotte! She is betrothed and is soon to be married.'

'Betrothals have been broken before when a family crisis demands it.'

Helen darted a furtive look about to see if they were drawing attention. Her golden eyes pulled to the spot where Jason and his brother had been standing, but they had gone. Next she glanced in Charlotte's direction and was relieved that her sister still seemed happily oblivious to Bridgeman's presence. George appeared to be flirting with a young lady in the pavilion upon which he was still supported, negligently, by an elbow.

Helen's attention moved to the odious man close to her and for a moment she simply glared at him. She didn't want to spend another minute in his company, but she feared he was not bluffing. Should Bridgeman carry out his threat to approach Charlotte so soon after her hysterical outburst this afternoon, chaos was likely to ensue.

Sensing her imminent capitulation, Colin purred, 'Come, my dear, we ought not be bad friends. Let us take a little walk along the paths and be free from prying eyes. It will only take a few minutes more to establish if we might arrive at a mutually acceptable arrangement.'

About to reject his suggestion out of hand, Helen hesitated. There was scant chance of them finding common ground. Nevertheless, going with him would prevent him bothering her sister and might even, if she was astutely eloquent, gain George some time to pay up. She allowed her hand to hover above his sleeve—the idea of touching him was repugnant. A moment later a graceful raven-haired woman and her dandified escort could have been mistaken for a couple out for a romantic stroll as they merged into the shadows on the pathway.

Helen's hope that they had departed unseen was far from realised. In fact, several people had noticed her slip away with Colin Bridgeman, and reactions to their disappearance were varied.

Charlotte had been sharing a joke with Emily Beaumont when Emily suddenly began frowning over her shoulder. Charlotte had turned to see what interested her friend and had been agitated to see her sister with the horrible man who wanted to usurp Philip as her husband.

George had also been keeping a sly eye on the proceedings between his sister and his main creditor. His heart had soared as he saw Helen take Bridgeman's arm. But it was short-lived euphoria; his conscience began to worry him at about the same time he noticed the disquietingly saturnine demeanour of the imposing fellow a few yards away.

Jason had moved towards the orchestra podium to greet Peter Wenham and some other friends, but had nevertheless kept an eye on Helen's progress towards her sister. From the moment Bridgeman had intercepted her, Jason had been ready to intervene if necessary.

Helen was an independent woman and Jason was not a character to stalk a mistress and be thought overly possessive. Nevertheless, at one point, when Helen seemed flustered, he had started towards her. A moment later he retraced that step, for Helen had moved very close to Colin before glancing about as though to check they were unobserved. She had obviously felt reassured by her furtive survey—he'd watched relief smooth her brow as she took Bridgeman's arm. There was no doubt in his mind that she'd gone willingly with him into the dark.

Jason had never liked Colin Bridgeman. Since Mark had told him of the incident when Kingston had humiliated Philip in Hyde Park, and Bridgeman had found it amusing, he liked him even less. The man was renowned to be callous and lecherous.

Jason accepted he was hardly fit to judge, for he had long been ruthless in business and predatory with women. But if recent events were anything to go by, he was in danger of becoming not only a reformed character but content with his mellow persona.

Thus he stood for several minutes more, surrounded by his jovial friends, attempting to control the gnawing jealousy he felt. Helen had every right to promenade with her admirers and flirt with whomsoever she pleased. She had promised him nothing more than her body in his bed and that she would not interfere in his life. And she had been true to her word. If she cared what he did, or whom he saw, those evenings they were apart, she gave no sign. It had never occurred to him that perhaps he ought ask what *she* did whilst he sat quietly at home, thinking of her.

Abruptly he excused himself from his brother and his friends and strode towards the walkway. As he passed George Kingston, their eyes briefly met before George shifted his gaze. The wine within George's fist was so abruptly upended into his throat that, some distance on from him, Jason could still hear him choking. A humourless smile tugged at Jason's tight lips. George had looked guilty and if there was any skulduggery afoot, George was certain to be embroiled in it.

Thus, some minutes after Helen and Colin Bridgeman disappeared, Jason did, too.

'I think we have come far enough, Mr Bridgeman.' Helen's fingers recoiled from proximity with his hairy knuckles and swiftly she removed herself to a spot some distance away. The pretty globe lamps swayed high up in the hedge, illuminating the rustic bench framed by an arbour. 'I have but a few minutes to spare, then must return or I will be missed.'

'Come…let us be seated,' Bridgeman coaxed whilst sidling close.

Helen immediately evaded him and moved the other side of the seat. 'I must first ask you to please show my brother a little tolerance. George told me that he was negligent in checking the terms you offered when you made him the loan. Had he wholly understood the document—'

Colin interrupted her with a theatrical sigh. 'You do George no kindness in making him sound such a fool, my dear.' He took a surreptitious step, then another, craftily penning Helen into a corner of yew. 'Do *me* a little kindness, however, and I promise it will pay dividends for that doltish brother of yours.'

'I have made myself clear over that,' Helen reminded icily. She attempted to dodge behind the bench, but it was set too far back into greenery to permit her to escape both him and injury. 'I will never sleep with you.' She put up her chin, intrepidly confronting her persecutor. 'So, if you have no sensible arrangement to offer, you are wasting my time.'

'But *I* think my arrangement is sensible,' Bridgeman cooed. 'And perhaps when Hunter is finished with you, you might not be so precious over it all.' He grinned as he saw her reaction to that. 'I know your rent at Westlea House is waived courtesy of your trips to Chelsea.'

Helen nipped her soft lower lip between her teeth.

'Ah...I see you thought nobody wise to your little love-nest.' Colin's eyes glowed with satisfaction, for he understood what provoked her stricken expression. 'I made it my business to find out,' he admitted with a flick of a limp wrist. 'I followed you there when you and Hunter left the Beaumonts' *musicale*. Extreme tactics I'll own, but that's how you affect me, Mrs Marlowe. I want you and, now I know you're not too prudish to be bought, I will have you.' He eyed her, his head cocked in consideration. 'I could soon ensure the drawing rooms are abuzz with details of how you earn your keep.' He chuckled lewdly. 'I know you don't stare at ceilings in Chelsea every night. On those occasions Hunter prefers the company of a blonde, *I* could take his place.' He hooted in derision. 'Don't look so melancholy, my dear. Did you not know that Diana Tucker is still firmly ensconced in one of his houses?'

Helen felt her throat throb in anguish, but nevertheless whispered, 'My brother is less of a fool than are you if you expect me to stay longer and listen to your—'

Her scorn was not fully expounded, for, with surprising strength and agility, Bridgeman suddenly leaped the space between them, forcing Helen back against the hedge. His moist mouth pounced on to hers and a few fingers delved forcefully into her bodice.

'Am I intruding on a tender moment?'

Colin pivoted about on hearing that glacial sarcasm. His chest was heaving with exertion and thwarted lust. A foul curse scratched his throat; next came a gasp of triumph as he identified the silhouette in the gloom. 'I think you ought ask the lady that…or judge from what you saw with your own eyes, Hunter.' He leered at Helen's shocked countenance. 'Will you tell him about our tête à tête, my dear, or shall I? He will know it all soon enough, in any case.'

Snapping free of her daze, Helen pushed past Bridgeman, the back of a shaking hand wiping the residue of his slimy kiss from her mouth. She took a few faltering steps towards Jason, gazing up appealingly into his shadowy face. He was smiling at her, she glimpsed a gleam of white teeth, but it was his lack of comfort in words or deed that turned her heart to stone. 'It's not what it might seem,' she whispered. 'I…I hope you do not believe I wanted him to kiss me.' Still he said nothing, and she knew that his silence stemmed from a suspicion that she had been enjoying Bridgeman's nauseating attention.

Anger and hurt mingled in her, churning her

thoughts to nonsense. But one vital fact surfaced to again torment her: Diana Tucker still figured in Jason's life.

So many times she had been tempted to ask Jason about her. Pride had kept the words locked in her mind, as had the memory of her naïve vow not to pry or to nag or to demand his fidelity. She had thus taken comfort from her certainty that she would *know* if he slept with another woman. Although he did not see her every night, she had convinced herself that the passion and affection they shared was special and fulfilling. When making love he was tender and patient, even when self-imposed duress corded his muscles and betrayed that he would rather plunge headlong to his own release.

Invariably their parting kiss outside Westlea House would be followed by her sound sleep, not simply got from sensual satiation, but from the tranquillity of knowing their intimacy sprang from them being friends as well as lovers. Now she knew how badly she had misjudged the reality.

She sensed that, despite Bridgeman's malice, he had not lied about Diana being still under Jason's protection. Her dream that they might build a future together had been shown as a silly fantasy, not just by knowledge of his inconstancy, but from knowing he could be so cold and aloof. Far from being her good friend, Jason might have been a callous stranger.

Now she felt a fool for having attempted to appease her faithless lover because a lecher had forced a kiss on her. She had done nothing wrong, yet Jason immediately suspected she had. She gazed defiantly into the glittering depths of his eyes.

A pitiless smile from Jason broke their combatant gazes, then he looked past Helen to where Colin stood.

'I'm not concerned with how you managed to persuade Mrs Marlowe to accompany you, Bridgeman. But I am anxious that you understand you're now *de trop*,' Jason said with eerie placidity. 'Why don't you run along…while you're still able…?'

The smirk writhing on Colin's lips began to wither. Jason Hunter was not a fellow to make idle threats of violence. He had an impressive record with both pistols and sword and was not averse to an impromptu bout of sparring. Colin clearly recalled that Peter Wenham had once riled this fellow enough, by a bit of shabby chicanery, to end sporting a shiner that took the gloss off their friendship for some while.

Bridgeman tilted his head to an arrogant angle, but was already subtly retreating. With a mocking bow for Helen, he turned and began bowling back along the path.

'Do you want me to defend your honour over it? I'll call him out if you like.'

'No…' Helen's eyes were still challengingly fixed on his rugged features etched hard and dark as granite against a backdrop of dusk.

'Did I arrive at an inopportune moment, just as you were sealing the deal with a kiss? Or perhaps you received rather than offered a seduction this time. Is that it?'

Helen flinched beneath his mordant tone, yet answered crisply, 'Yes.'

'Yes…on both accounts?'

'I don't know how you have the nerve to interrogate me over it,' Helen whispered hoarsely. 'Since we became lovers, *I* have thus far slept only with *you.*'

Jason strolled closer to her, halting beneath a little lamp that misted a pale halo above his devilishly dark features. 'I'm pleased to hear it,' he drawled. 'I would be irritated to find I'd been paying for another man's pleasure.'

Helen was stunned by his careless attitude and her glistening eyes lingered on his face.

He gave her an impenitent smile. 'My apologies for being blunt…but, as I recall, we speak plainly, don't we?' he remarked with just a hint of sneering. 'I know his terms won't be more generous than mine. So, tell me, were you preparing to end things between us to claim Westlea House as your own?'

Helen shrivelled inside beneath his ruthless gaze, but managed a controlled response. 'As you have cast me in the role of shameless hussy, I imagine you have already made a decision on it.' She lifted tear-dewed eyes to his face, then blinked furiously. 'I am not about to weep and strive to defend myself,' she whispered with shaky pride. 'I didn't want to take a walk with him. I certainly didn't want him to kiss me, but you may believe what you will about what you saw.' She pulled her shawl tighter about her shoulders and made to sweep past before the mist in her vision became water on her cheeks.

A hand shot out as she came level with him, jerking her close. 'And what I saw was you willingly taking Bridgeman's arm and disappearing with him. You might be naïve, my dear, but even you know men don't invite women to walk these dark pathways so they might talk to them.'

'Talking was exactly *my* intention,' Helen retorted in a shaky tone whilst trying to wrestle her wrist from his grip. 'And if I am naïve, then you must take some of the blame! Having kept company for some weeks with a notorious rake, I imagine that by now I ought be quite jaded!' With a final wrench she freed her wrist and made to bolt past.

'Don't run off, sweet,' Jason said with specious charm as he blocked her path. 'Bridgeman might have abandoned you, but the night's not over yet. If it's corruption you want, I'll give it to you.'

Helen shook her head at him in mute appeal as unbridled lust made dark coals of his eyes. He merely crooked his five fingers at the back of her head, bringing her close. The pretty string of pearls entwined there scattered to bounce like hailstones on parched earth. Momentarily she fought him, then his mouth took possession of hers with the sensual savagery she remembered from that first night in his coach. This time Helen intended tolerating none of it. But traitorous desire, swift and potent as liquid fire, had started to streak through her veins. She sensed the tightness in her abdomen and the drugging pliancy that stole bone from her limbs. Her body was ready to succumb to the expectation of the pleasure he gave her. Her jaw was softening, widening to receive his tongue. Familiar fingers began loosening her bodice and his hands moulded over the soft mounds of her breasts. In instinctive response her back arched in unmistakable invitation.

His palms were circling over the hard nubs of her nipples and despite her weak protestations, her breath was coming in little gasps. She pleaded for his decency with one tortured word. 'Jason…'

He laughed against her mouth. 'That's right…it's Jason,' he breathed harshly. 'Not Marlowe, not Bridgeman. At least you remembered my name.'

A taunting humour in his voice gave Helen strength to push him away. When he reached for her again with insolent confidence, a small hand traced an arc to crack hard against a lean cheek.

He certainly had not been expecting that and Helen took immediate advantage of his surprise to dart past. She flew back along the path in the direction of the sound of serenading violins.

As the dark and quiet were diluted by light and laughter she slowed her pace. Her vibrating fingers forced the buttons on her bodice back into their hooks as she continued to walk out into the milling crowd.

Of the people who had noticed Helen's disappearance, only one now saw her return.

With a twinge of sadness Emily Beaumont watched Helen emerge from the path, quite alone. Her friend's distress was not immediately obvious, but Emily sensed it nonetheless, even before she saw Helen swiftly cuff at her face, then slip into the midst of the throng to lose herself within it. With a murmured excuse for her brother, Tarquin, Emily picked a path towards her.

Emily linked arms with her friend and spontaneously angled her head comfortingly close to Helen's as her fears were confirmed. Helen's lashes were still wet with tears.

Helen gave Emily a faint smile and asked huskily, 'Have you any idea where my brother might be, Emily?'

Emily nodded. 'I have. I'll lead you to him.' She gave Helen's hand a sympathetic pat. 'And you need not fret over Bridgeman's whereabouts. I saw him leave the Gardens looking quite subdued.'

Helen shot Emily a searching look. 'Who told...how did you...?' she stiltedly began.

'Charlotte told me about...the problems,' Emily admitted quietly and gently urged Helen to keep walking. 'You must not blame your sister. She was quite distressed on seeing you go into the walkway with Bridgeman, and blurted it all out to me.' She paused. 'Charlotte was keen to get George to rescue you. She was sure Bridgeman was abducting you. I persuaded her you would be safe, for I had noticed Sir Jason had immediately set off to act knight errant.' Emily slanted a glance at Helen's averted face. 'Sir Jason *did* send Bridgeman packing, didn't he?'

Helen simply nodded and frowned into the distance.

'But...perhaps didn't act very knightly?' Emily suggested, angling her head to see Helen's expression.

'How could he think I was enjoying that horrible man's attention?' Helen bit at her trembling lower lip. 'Is Charlotte somewhere hereabouts with Philip?'

'She and Philip have taken a walk towards the grottoes.'

Helen gave an unconscious little sigh of relief.

'You may tell me to mind my own business if you want to,' Emily said gently. 'But...I know what it is to be the butt of gossip. I also know what it is to be burdened with a brother's selfishness. People might think that I happily tolerate Tarquin's faults. It's not the truth. But he is my brother and I do love him despite all the heartache he causes us.'

Helen turned to give her a wavering smile. 'Where would we be without our families?' she ruefully murmured.

'I think I would be...contentedly raising a brood of children.' Emily divulged that in an ironic tone but Helen sensed it veiled a poignant truth.

Emily answered her unspoken question with a single nod. 'Yes...I would have married a gentleman but for Tarquin spoiling things... Oh, it doesn't matter!' she said briskly. 'It was some years ago now.'

They walked in silence for a moment, then Emily nodded her blonde head. 'There is George and his devoted wife,' she commented acidly. She tugged gently on Helen's arm to slow their pace. 'Before you go, Helen—and I know you will make George take you home—I want you to understand that there is very little that you could tell me that would shock or offend me.'

Helen gave her a long and searching look before saying quietly, 'You are kind, Emily, but, if you knew more about me, I think you would be shocked.'

'And if you knew more about me, I think you would be shocked,' Emily returned. She unlinked their arms and gave Helen a smile. 'So, if you want to talk to someone about any burdensome topic such as…sisters, brothers, lovers…' She caught Helen's eyes in a meaningful gaze. 'You know who to choose.' Quickly she gave Helen's arm a squeeze. 'George has seen us and is coming over.' Helen's brother received a little wave before Emily turned and set off back the way she had come.

Chapter Sixteen

'If you're looking for Mrs Marlowe, you're wasting your time. She's gone.'

Jason pivoted about to see his brother standing behind him with his hands plunged deep into his pockets. 'What do you mean...*gone*?' he demanded in frustration. His eyes narrowed dangerously. 'Did she leave with Bridgeman?'

'Helen went with her brother,' Mark informed soothingly as he strolled closer. 'She looked a little...strained, so I assume he has taken her home.' Mark kept a tactful rein on his curiosity despite being keen to know what had caused Jason's mistress to depart so abruptly. From the dark scowl and unguarded comment thrown at him, he guessed it was due to his heartthrob brother imagining he had a rival.

Mark suppressed a wry smile twitching at his lips. The idea of Sir Jason Hunter—rich as Croesus and devilishly handsome to boot—being jealous of the likes of Colin Bridgeman, who allowedly could boast he had plenty of money if little else, was ludicrous and unprecedented. But when a man was enamoured he acted very oddly. Mark had marvelled before when strong, confident gentlemen of his acquaintance had become enfeebled wretches whilst courting the women they loved.

He had no wish to see his distinguished brother reduced to that pitiful condition, so was ready to act as arbitrator if he could. Despite their fights and arguments, Jason and he were fond of one another.

Mark had never experienced such emotional delirium over a woman, and thanked his lucky stars for it! But then he knew there wasn't a woman alive capable of bringing *him* down.

Oddly, had his attention for the best part of the evening *not* been concentrated on the infuriatingly alluring chit who happened to be Tarquin Beaumont's sister, he might have noticed his brother pursue Helen and Bridgeman into the walkway.

It was through being captivated by Emily Beaumont that he had first sensed something was amiss between his brother and Helen. He had observed Emily flit gracefully through the crowds to gain

Helen's side as she emerged, alone, from the dark pathway. Within a moment of them coming together Emily had been discreetly comforting Helen, in the unmistakably tactile way women had. Shortly afterwards Mark had his suspicions confirmed that Helen was upset when a sheepish-looking George Kingston had accompanied his widowed sister to his carriage. Mark had seen Charlotte leaving a few minutes later with Philip and Anne Goode. That party had looked to be in good spirits, indicating they had been in ignorance of Helen's distress.

Mark surfaced from his reflection and noticed Jason was still glaring at the road as though he might conjure up the carriage that had spirited Helen away.

That his brother was in love was indisputable, yet Mark sensed Jason was under the impression he was adequately concealing the strength of his feelings. Even a subtle interrogation was unlikely to extract anything from Jason whilst he was in this mood other than a few choice epithets.

'I take it you'll be leaving now.' Mark was speaking to Jason, but had difficulty removing his gaze from Emily's pensive profile. He heard a grunted affirmative, but it was a moment later that he realised his brother was already striding away towards the exit.

Mark sent a shrewd look at his old friend Tarquin.

He hadn't spoken to him yet this evening; it was high time he remedied that.

Tarquin greeted Mark with a thump on the shoulder and immediately drew him into the circle of young bucks. Some of them seemed to be attempting to impress his sister with tales of their prowess in tooling the ribbons. Despite an absent smile here and an abstracted murmur there, Emily still seemed to be locked within her own consciousness…until her brother mentioned the name Hunter.

Emily snapped from her reverie and ran her eyes coldly over the man who had joined them. Within a second her disgust was directed elsewhere, for a couple of young ladies close by had suddenly remembered to say hello to her.

Moira and Felicity Watson had virtually ignored her since they arrived despite their family group being just a few yards away. Tarquin's incarceration had rendered her *persona non grata* to hypocrites she previously had classed as friends. Now, because Mark Hunter had graced her circle with his presence, the cousins remembered the Beaumonts existed and fluttered close with breathy enquiries of how they all did.

After a terse response Emily showed them an elevated shoulder. It was a manoeuvre that brought her about to again face Mark. She tipped up her proud, heart-shaped face to challenge his stare. Her head bobbed a curt acknowledgement, but her blue eyes were icy with dislike.

Mark absorbed her antipathy and forged a stoic smile. He was sure he didn't give a damn if she liked him or not. He had come over to discover what the hell was going on between Jason and Helen. His brother had left Grosvenor Square earlier that evening in a good mood. The fact that Jason had been more than usually generous with his money and his property since he'd fallen in love was no inconsiderable incentive for Mark to try and smooth things over between the lovers. He had been about to ask to borrow Jason's racing curricle to take him swiftly to Newhaven. A boxing bout with a new French fighter had been arranged and he had promised his cronies, who had arranged to bring over the foreign pugilist on a yacht, that he would put in an appearance on the coast and run the book.

He saw Emily was about to put distance between them, so said in a solemn murmur, 'Forgive me for mentioning a rather delicate matter, but I noticed that you were talking privately to Mrs Marlowe. I have just been similarly occupied with my brother.' A meaningful throb quietened his voice to little more than a murmur. He sighed and shook his head sadly. 'It's a pity when misunderstandings lead to rifts between people who care about one another.' His frank gaze lingered on her face. He could tell she was torn between her loyalty to Helen and a desire to do what she could to restore her friend's happiness.

'Indeed, it is a shame, sir,' Emily breathed tartly. 'But not surprising that such misunderstandings originate in male egotism.'

Mark relaxed a little. If he was careful, he might yet learn what the problem was. 'My brother is proud, I'll admit; but then no man likes being taken for a fool...'

'And no woman likes being taken for a cheat, especially when she had done nothing but try to self-lessly protect a sister,' Emily hissed angrily. Suddenly aware that she had said too much she blinked rapidly at her dainty shoes. 'I beg you will please forget that I told you that. I know you are aware, from your brother, what went on. But I would hate either Helen or Charlotte to think I had betrayed them with talking loosely to—'

'To...?' Mark prompted. 'Who am I exactly, Miss Beaumont?' he asked softly. 'Lucifer? Sir Jason's brother? A scoundrel to avoid?'

Emily swallowed. 'You are the man who had my brother thrown in gaol,' she retorted. 'And I do not like you, nor ever will!'

Mark tactically shifted position so that he and

Emily were slightly cut off from the rest of the group. 'That is for another time,' he said gently. 'Helen Marlowe is your friend and Jason is my brother. We are simply trying to help reconcile two people. I guess from what you have said that Kingston is hoping to use one of his sisters to keep Bridgeman at bay. Is that it?'

Emily swiftly looked up. *'Is that it?* You did not know?' Her small mouth slackened in shock. 'Oh, you beast! You have tricked me into telling you what you did not know.' She backed away from him a pace, her features contorted in anger, her complexion white as chalk. 'I don't know why I'm surprised,' she choked in a whisper, for her brother had turned about to look at her. 'I always knew you for a blackguard. It was stupid of me to forget, even for a moment.' With that she whipped past him and began to give the nearest of Tarquin's friends her undivided attention.

It was whilst Jason was pacing to and fro on the pavement by his carriage, undecided whether to follow Helen to Westlea House and grovel an apology, or find Bridgeman and let him explain himself...before he knocked his teeth down his throat... that Diana Tucker emerged from the shadows. It was the distinctive perfume she used that first alerted him to her presence. Turning his head, he saw sinuous curls, pale as moonbeams, as she lifted the hood of her cloak.

Diana moved towards him, her hips undulating beneath the light silk of her clothing. She, more than any other, was convinced that Jason and Helen Marlowe were sleeping together. After all, it could be no coincidence that she had received a parting settlement from her wealthy lover just a few days before he was seen squiring Mrs Marlowe to the opera. The pique she had felt at being so efficiently discarded in favour of a woman older and, in her opinion, far less comely, was still uncontrollable.

But tonight she had realised, with great elation, that all was not well between the lovers. Her eyes had followed Jason most of the evening so she had seen him enter the dark walkway. Constantly watching for his return, she had thus observed Helen hasten out looking tearful. When Jason had stridden out a few minutes later, Diana had been relieved to see his face so grimly set. It had been the fateful incident she needed to approach him and renew their relationship. So, for some minutes, she had been stalking Jason here and there about the Gardens with the sole intention of getting him alone so she might seduce him into taking her back.

He had handsomely pensioned her off with a

house and a generous sum of money, but she missed the prestige, and the envy of other women, that came with being mistress to one of the *ton*'s most desirable gentlemen.

'Will you take me home, please, Jason?' Diana huskily entreated. 'I've got separated from my friends and they've left without me. You won't make me hail a hackney, will you?' She slanted up at him a coy smile. She was close to him now, her rounded hip pressing into the hard muscle of his thigh.

Jason leaned back against his carriage door. He nodded along the street to a smart coach fronted by two pairs of splendid thoroughbreds. 'Frobisher's vehicle,' he said succinctly. 'He might have found his senses and decided not to marry your friend, but I'm sure he still likes Mrs Bertram well enough to give her a ride home. If you ask nicely, I expect he'll take you, too.' Jason gave her a cynical smile. He hadn't paid much attention to Diana this evening, but he was well aware that she had arrived with Lord Frobisher's party and had her gallants with her.

Diana pouted up at him. 'I'd rather ask *you* nicely to take me home, Jason. You haven't so soon forgot how very *nice* I can be to you…have you?' She suddenly went on to tiptoe and placed a moist kiss on his lips. His lack of enthusiasm was emphasised by a curse beneath his breath. Wounded by the careless rebuff, Diana nevertheless persisted with her seduction. Her tongue tip darted to tease the lobe of an ear before he forcibly held her away.

'Good evening, *Sir Jason.*'

Jason recognised the voice that had called the sly greeting and he immediately choked a stronger oath. With a brief farewell to his former paramour, he strolled to give instructions to his driver to take him to Grosvenor Square. It was only then he turned to acknowledge Iris Kingston. She was arm in arm with a young fop who looked to be still wet behind the ears. They were given a nod and a curt, 'Good evening,' before he was swiftly in his coach and on his way home.

Iris sent Diana a scoffing smirk, then watched her flounce back towards the Pleasure Gardens. Iris guessed that the common baggage had looked indignant because she had been unsuccessful in luring Jason back to her. But the realisation that he might have spurned Diana because Helen still had her claws in him was irritating. Colin was also in Helen's thrall. In fact, both the affluent gentlemen that Iris wanted at her beck and call were infatuated with her skinny black-haired sister-in-law and it greatly irked.

Iris allowed her youthful escort to nudge her into a gap in the hedge and fumble with her clothes, but even as she murmured encouragement to him, her mind was investigating how she might bring Helen Marlowe down a peg or two.

George Kingston was slumped, semi-conscious, in an armchair, but he raised his bleary eyes as his wife came into the sitting room. A brandy glass was waved at her as he slurred, 'Ah, there you are, m'schweet. Home a' lasht. Join m'in a drink?'

Iris gave him an apathetic glance but did help herself to the decanter. Suddenly she shot a canny look at her husband. He divulged to her very little lately. But he was quite obviously drunk and might just let slip what had occurred to make Helen demand George take her immediately home.

She strolled to the fire and held out her palms to the embers dying in the grate. 'I saw Sir Jason just as we left the Gardens. He was in the Tucker woman's embrace.'

George snuffled a laugh. 'I doan' think so.'

'He was, I tell you,' Iris sweetly remonstrated and playfully tickled George's cheek with a fingertip.

Even intoxicated, George understood his wife well enough to send her a smile that was deeply cynical. He took a swig of brandy.

'I watched that harlot kissing him in the street. Bold as you please!'

George swished the amber liquid in his glass and

shook his head at it. 'Bridgeman's the problem, not her, but Jay hates me still for Beatrice…so p'raps he used Helen…'

Iris's eyes narrowed in interest as she tried to decipher her husband's drunken ramblings. 'Beatrice?' she repeated softly. 'She is Jason's sister, surely.'

George nodded, a shock of dark hair falling lankly towards his nose. 'Schweet Beatrice,' he mumbled into his drink. 'He's never ever forgiven me for that.'

'You seduced her? You seduced Beatrice Hunter?' Iris whispered in astonishment.

George looked up glassily. 'No! An' I din't abduct her either. She came willingly.' He swayed his head and nuzzled the rim of his tumbler. 'Should have let us be. Would have married her…said I would. Made us turn back. Not even half-way to Gretna… Shame…'

Iris stood for some minutes, digesting the information. When next she looked at her husband, she saw George's chin was propped on his chest. She removed the glass from his limp fingers and deposited it on a table. With a slyly satisfied smile on her lips, she took herself off to bed.

Mark Hunter found his older brother in much the same inebriated state as Iris Kingston had found her husband.

Jason, however, being renowned for the ability to imbibe an astonishing amount before keeling over, was more lucid than George had been. Mark eyed the depleted decanter, precariously perched on the edge of the desk in Jason's study. He then took another, deeply respectful, look at Jason. He had seen old Cedric fill to the top the large crystal bottle not an hour before they left the house earlier in the evening.

Jason thrust himself back in his chair and eyed his brother from beneath a lowering brow. He then propped his head against the chair back. 'What time is it?' he asked on a sigh.

'Time you went to bed,' Mark returned easily.

In response to that dictate Jason emptied what was left in the decanter into his glass. He despatched the brandy in a single swallow.

'Not tired, eh?' Mark said drolly. 'In that case… there's something about this evening's fiasco you might like to hear. It concerns that weasel Bridgeman and how he managed to get Helen to go with him.'

Jason snapped his head forward and silently studied his brother with eyes that resembled molten lead. 'I'm listening…'

Jason's deceptively gentle tone of voice sent a *frisson* through Mark's body. At that moment he almost pitied Bridgeman… George Kingston, too. For without a doubt Helen's brother was up to his neck in it all, and a day of reckoning was fast approaching.

'Mrs Kingston is here to see you, ma'am.'

Helen looked up from the journal she had been idly flicking through. Her heart sank and just for a moment she considered sending Iris away. Obviously the rumour mill had already set to grinding over her hasty departure from Vauxhall Gardens and her sister-in-law had come to pry, or gloat, depending on how much she had managed to discover about what went on.

Charlotte's thoughts of pleading a migraine, or some similar ailment, to avoid seeing Iris were obviously in tune with Helen's.

'Oh, send her away, for Heaven's sake!' Charlotte dropped to the sofa the little handkerchief she had been embroidering and wrinkled her brow at Helen. 'She is only here to quiz us over Bridgeman. Perhaps she saw you disappear with him at Vauxhall. Do you think George has told her he wants to marry me? She's probably jealous. I know she has a fancy for the wretch.'

'I'm sure George has said nothing,' Helen soothed quietly. 'He would not boast of his involvement in such sordid dealings…' In her mind she concluded…but Bridgeman might….

But it was too late for either sister to plead an indisposition, for Iris had grown impatient waiting to be admitted. She barged past Betty and sailed into the room.

Charlotte gave Iris a mumbled greeting, then fidgeted on the sofa for a moment. 'Oh…I recall I've a letter to finish. It's upstairs.' With that Charlotte sprang out of the chair and was soon making her escape.

'Fetch some tea, please, Betty,' Helen commanded from weary hospitality.

Iris stripped off her gloves and removed her stylish bonnet from her neat coiffure. 'You look washed out,' she remarked with a hint of satisfaction. 'And I'm not surprised at all!'

Helen gave her sister-in-law a penetrating look. Iris obviously was hoping a show of faux sympathy might lead to a heart to heart between them. Helen had no intention of telling her a solitary thing, but she took note of the comment on her appearance and tidied the wisps of raven hair that had escaped their pins. She knew she looked pale and tired; it was a consequence of having wept instead of slept for most of the night. 'Is George not with you?' Helen asked simply for something to say. She resumed flicking over pages in the journal.

'No, I didn't want George to come with me. In truth, I'm glad Charlotte is from the room. I wanted to speak to you alone.' Helen received a meaningful stare from blue eyes that watched her from beneath sooty lashes. 'I have something important to tell you and there is no use in being mealy mouthed. First, I shall frankly say that I'm aware you and Jason Hunter are lovers. Or perhaps I should say I'm aware you *were* lovers…' Iris cocked a knowing eyebrow at Helen.

'You said you had something *important* to say…?' Helen coolly returned, despite feeling her cheeks warming.

Iris smiled. 'It's no use coming over prim now. Everybody has guessed you have been carrying on a liaison with him.' Iris settled back into the sofa and smoothed her skirt. 'I know we have not always seen eye to eye, but I have come to do you a service.' She gazed pityingly at Helen. 'He has treated you cruelly and you ought know why. I'm sure I would not like it at all if a gentleman slept with me simply to avenge a wrong done his sister.'

With a deal of embellishment, if no actual lies, Iris recounted what George had said about his having compromised Beatrice Hunter. She added that George suspected Jason had long harboured a desire to wreak revenge for it.

Whilst that bombshell was causing a stricken look to tauten her sister-in-law's chalky complexion, Iris delivered her pièce de résistance. She solemnly recounted having quit Vauxhall yesterday evening only to see Diana Tucker brazenly kissing Sir Jason by his carriage, in full view of those passing by.

'*We* know she is not a lady…but it was hardly the behaviour expected of a gentleman, either.' Iris took advantage of Helen's silence to add, 'Why…you could not have been gone from him even an hour….'

Chapter Seventeen

'What in damnation are you doing here at this ungodly hour?'

George had his head propped in both hands, his elbows resting on the table, but he had glanced up to deliver that testy remark. He had a hangover that made it seem a blacksmith had set up business inside his skull. A regular thump was affecting his vision and the oak panelling in the dining room seemed nauseatingly atilt. Having sheltered his throbbing brow a few moments longer in his cupped palms he managed to rouse himself sufficiently to bark at his hovering butler to be gone.

'Women or money? It must be one of the two to bring you here so confoundedly early.'

'It's both,' Jason told him and, taking a chair opposite, sat down, uninvited, at the breakfast table.

George wrapped himself tighter into his dressing gown and took a nibble at dry toast. The tasteless morsel did nothing to settle his queasy stomach. His unwelcome visitor was eerily quiet and that started him fidgeting. Silverware was pushed about on mahogany. 'You've found out that I owe that bastard, Bridgeman, money and he's threatening me with the duns. What of it?'

'I found out that you're not averse to pimping to clear your debts.'

George felt fiery heat prickle beneath his silk collar. 'Bridgeman wanted to marry Charlotte,' he snapped, tossing a spoon in irritation. 'If encouraging an eligible fellow makes me a pimp, then every fond mama with a chit to offload is a procuress.'

'And Helen? Did he want to marry her, too?'

George rubbed a hand over his bristly jaw and slanted a proper look at the man opposite. Jason had a similar drink-dissipated appearance to the one he'd seen reflected in his dressing mirror not an hour since. 'You're still too far in your cups…as I am,' he mumbled. 'Best leave this till another time….'

'Did he want to marry Helen, too?' Jason roared.

George started and a hand sprang to his pounding head. 'Of course not! He's wanted her for years, but not as a wife.' George felt the burning on his neck again but managed to sneer, 'He just wanted to sleep with her…same as you….'

Jason violently gained his feet. 'Helen went with Bridgeman last night to try and persuade him to leave Charlotte alone.'

'I know…she told me when I took her home.'

'What else did she say?'

'If you think I'll repeat to you a private conversation and betray my sister's trust…' A burst of contemptuous laughter interrupted George.

'You've been betraying your sister's trust for years. Helen trusted you to do what your father asked, and care for her and Charlotte. She trusted you to let your sister marry the man she loved.'

'Just as your sister trusted you to let her marry the man she loved,' George spat and pushed himself upright. He stood unsteadily with his fists balled on the table as support. 'But you couldn't do it, could you? You had to spoil it for us.'

Jason walked towards George, his face grimly set. 'Is that what your spite and resentment is all about? You and Beatrice?' he demanded to know.

George's eyes dropped away from the steel-grey stare. In resignation he flapped a hand before showing Jason his back.

A vicious grip on George's shoulder spun him around so they were again face to face. 'My sister was sixteen when you persuaded her to run off. The consequences for her future would have been unspeakable had the scandal leaked out.'

'I would have married her,' George gritted in a voice that had lost none of its belligerent edge.

'She was too young and too innocent and you knew it. But you were always too damned selfish…just as you are now.'

'And you were always too damned horny…just as you are now. Iris told me she saw you kissing Diana last night. You went out for the evening with Helen, but soon found another woman to take her place. Yet you have the gall to come here and act noble on Helen's account!' George jeered.

'Oh, I didn't come here to act noble, George,' Jason softly enunciated. 'I came here to do this.' A single punch knocked George down into his chair. It teetered on its back legs for a moment before crashing over on to the polished parquet and sending George sprawling. 'That's long overdue and not nearly enough. But it'll do for now,' Jason said before quitting the room.

Cedric's rheumy eyes flowed over the neatly dressed young woman. She looked more modish than when last she'd arrived, alone, demanding to see the master. But her haughty look was unchanged.

'Sir Jason's not here,' he told her and started to shut the door.

Helen stepped on to the threshold to prevent him dismissing her. 'Is Sir Jason soon expected back?' she asked firmly.

'Eh?' Cedric cocked his good ear at her.

'Is your master soon expected home?' Helen asked with more volume.

'He might be…' Cedric said unhelpfully. His infirm memory suddenly pounced on something important. He recalled getting a flea in his ear for having treated this chit impolitely last time she came asking for the master. Cedric belatedly dipped his wispy head and opened the door a little wider.

'I'll wait, thank you.' Helen slipped neatly past the old retainer and into the magnificent hallway of Jason's Grosvenor Square residence.

Her heart was beating energetically, deafening her with the roar of fast-flowing blood and rendering her oblivious to Cedric's mutterings. Fearing he might again put her in the cupboard to wait, she swiftly stepped to a hallway chair and sat down. From under her bonnet brim she watched Cedric give her a stern stare, then move away on slow feet.

Helen watched his shuffling retreat, then closed her eyes as the enormity of what she'd done overwhelmed her. She had again acted with a brazen contempt for etiquette by coming here alone and uninvited. But having found the temerity to act quickly to end their affair, she did not want her courage to ebb away.

Suddenly it occurred to her that Jason might be so early abroad because he had gone to Westlea House to perform the same task as had brought her to see him.

It was finished between them, she understood that, and wanted it that way, but her pride demanded that she be the one to formally conclude their relationship.

Iris and Bridgeman were both spiteful people, but Helen instinctively knew that they had told her facts, not falsehoods. Undoubtedly some of what Iris had said had been intentionally exaggerated and hurtful, but oddly it had been enlightening, too. Pieces of a puzzle had slipped into place concerning the hatred that had sprung up between George and Jason a decade ago. George had compromised Beatrice and made Jason bitter and vengeful. As for Bridgeman exulting that Jason was not faithful to her, she had at the outset of their affair not expected he would be. Bridgeman had simply brought again into focus a wounding truth she had tried to ignore. Despite her boasts in Hyde Park, when she'd propositioned Jason, she had failed miserably to act with sophistication and accept she was to him simply a bed-partner.

Jason had been generous to her, but then he was a wealthy man who could afford to pay well for his pleasure. He had been a clever lover but, of course, he had much experience with a variety of women to draw on. He was courteous and charming, but then he was with most people—it was in his breeding. With women he desired, he was essentially the hard-hearted rake of his notoriety. And she was a perfect fool to have thought herself capable of tolerating loveless couplings with a man who simply wanted to slake his lust with a willing woman.

Most of all, she was a fool for knowing it all and still loving him.

Helen felt tears prick at the backs of her eyes and dashed them away with gloved fingers. She glanced about at her surroundings, apathetically taking in the opulence. Every surface was polished, every crystal droplet gleaming and every second silent. The last time she'd been here she'd had no opportunity to ponder on elegant furnishings and wonderful architecture. But his mansion didn't impress her. She would rather have the shabby comfort of her Westlea House than this beautiful shell that so well matched its owner.

She collected her thoughts and forced her mind

to practicalities. She ought to concentrate on securing her home and the cash she had been promised…

'Helen?'

Helen jumped to her feet at the sound of her name. So entrenched in her thoughts had she been that she had missed the noise of a key turning smoothly in the lock.

They faced each other for a moment in tense quiet, then Jason closed the door and walked towards her.

Helen desperately blinked away the mist in her eyes and moistened her lips. 'I'm sorry to have come here, but it is too late to fret over gossip, and best that things are swiftly concluded.' She tilted her chin and squarely met his eyes. Her golden glance flitted over his haggard features and crumpled clothes. He looked the worse for a night of roistering, yet was still heartbreakingly handsome. His dishevelment was out of character and made him look boyish and vulnerable. She felt tempted to touch back the knot of locks on his brow.

It suddenly occurred to her that he might not have set out early this morning, but had rather come home late. Perhaps that kiss with Mrs Tucker had led to him spending the night with her. He certainly had the look of a man spent….

Helen winced. And she had been foolish enough

to think he might have bothered going out early to see her! Fingers that moments ago had been yearning to soothe him were clenched into fists at her side. She would not be sidetracked by petty jealousy into forgetting to claim what he had agreed to give her.

'Come into the study where we can talk,' Jason urged gently. He absently swiped a hand over the dusky growth on his chin, as though regretting his unkempt appearance.

Helen gracefully glided away, evading his outstretched hand, then faced him again. The silence, the cool marble surroundings, lent her an air of composure. 'There is no need for me to tarry,' she quietly told him. 'This is private enough and what I have to say will not take more than a moment.' She noted the change in his demeanour as he felt the force of her frigidity.

'I would be grateful if you would arrange for my settlement to be dealt with as soon as possible. And I trust that what happened between us yesterday evening will in no way affect Philip's future prospects. That is all I have to say. Good day to you, sir.' Helen's husky speech had barely concluded before she was stepping past him. She was fumbling to open the huge door when Jason joined her there and smoothly performed the office.

Wordlessly he indicated she should go out. She did so, hastening down the steps. As she reached the bottom and turned towards home, a hand gripped her arm, halting her.

'Get in,' Jason ordered in an uncompromising tone whilst yanking wide his carriage door.

Helen tried to liberate her elbow but his fingers tightened.

'Get in, Helen…please,' he added hoarsely. 'Don't make me abduct you.'

With a sob of frustration Helen gave him a glare but allowed him to help her climb up. With an agile spring that belied his look of enervation, Jason was soon in and sitting opposite her. Storm-grey eyes lingered on her face before he instructed the driver to take them to Hyde Park.

'Why are we going there?' Helen demanded.

'Why not? You seduced me there, it's fitting you discard me there, too.'

His darkly ironic tone brought a tinge of pink to Helen's ivory cheeks. 'I do not find anything amusing in this. You may take me home and nowhere else.'

'Philip and Anne are visiting Charlotte. Are you sure you want to talk there?'

Helen's eyes whipped to him as he settled back into the squabs. 'You have been to Westlea House?'

'Yes.'

'Did you go there to advise me my settlement is being arranged?' Helen whispered.

'No.'

'Why, then?'

'I promised you'd be the first to know if ever I fell in love or wanted to marry.'

She had not for a moment anticipated that. A hand spontaneously sprang to her abdomen to subdue a nauseating lurch. After a long moment she managed to whisper, 'And which is it? Love or marriage?'

'Both.'

'I see. You need not feel obliged to elaborate.' Helen kept her face turned to the street scene. Children playing with a hoop seemed to her quite fascinating. She craned her neck to keep watching them, even though the happy tableau had splintered into fragments. 'I can walk from here, please put me down…'

'Don't you want to know who she is?'

Helen shook her head, fiddled with her bonnet so the brim shielded her face. 'I can guess.' A little laugh bubbled in her aching throat. 'Gossip has started, I'm afraid. This morning my sister-in-law told me she saw you kissing Diana Tucker at Vauxhall.'

'It's not her.' His voice hinted at contemptuous

disbelief. 'And I didn't kiss her. It's true she kissed me, and asked me to take her home. I refused and went off on my own.'

Helen swallowed and stole a glance at him. Just as quickly she dragged her eyes away. What did any of it matter now? Nevertheless she could not prevent an acid observation. 'You have the look of a man who has not yet this morning seen his own bed…or his razor or his valet.'

Jason smiled ruefully. 'That's all perfectly true, Helen. But I have seen your brother and Bridgeman this morning. And I have seen Charlotte.'

'You have been to see George? Why?'

'To impress on him how much he disgusts me.' Jason absently flexed the fingers on his right hand.

Helen noticed his scraped knuckles. 'You've hit George? Why? Because of the way he treated Beatrice?'

'No; because of the way he's treated you. And before you ask, yes, Bridgeman felt my displeasure, too.'

'You should not have,' Helen murmured, aghast, simultaneously becoming aware that the coach had drawn to a halt in the park. Sunbeams filtered through branches to warm her face. 'Bridgeman might be vile, but he did not force me to go with him.'

'But he forced his attentions on you.'

'You would not believe my word yesterday evening when I told you that, but you believe him!' Helen angrily blinked teary eyes. 'Is your conceit soothed from knowing I didn't willingly endure that kiss?'

'I know I've been a fool, Helen,' Jason quietly admitted. 'But I was jealous.'

'Jealous of Bridgeman?'

'No...not really.' Jason's tousled head dropped forward and a hand spanned his brow. 'It's not him.' The words emerged through muffling fingers that massaged at his face

'Who, then?' Helen demanded in shock.

'Harry Marlowe.'

Helen stared searchingly at him. When he continued to rub his weary features, she reached to pull his hand away. 'Why? Why are you jealous of Harry?' she asked as her golden eyes scanned his beautifully dissolute face.

'Because you love him, and you were his wife, and that's what I want.' Jason suddenly flung himself back against the seat. 'Don't look so petrified, Helen,' he said with quiet self-mockery. 'I know I can't make you love me, or marry me. I'll marry you on your terms, or continue to protect you. But if you want me out of your life for good, I won't bother you again.' He fell silent, staring through the carriage window. A muscle leaped by his mouth, then he turned to her. 'I'll arrange for the transfer of the deeds.' With that gruff proclamation he abruptly opened the door. 'Graves will take you home. I'll walk.'

Helen slid speedily towards him on the seat. Quickly she closed her fingers over his on the handle. Their faces were so close now she could see the glisten of moisture in his eyes. 'You went to Westlea House this morning to tell me that you love me and want to marry me?'

He said nothing, just continued to look at her. But she could read the truth in his soulful long-lashed eyes.

Helen gave him a shy smile and a hand fluttered to cup his stubbly cheek. 'I won't ever love Harry less…but I think, in time, I might love you more.'

Jason's eyes closed and his face sought the shelter of her cradling palm.

It was when the hot salt stung her skin that she launched herself at him, forcing him back onto the seat. She clung fiercely to his neck and covered his face with tiny kisses. Settling herself on his lap, she murmured, 'I love you, Jason. I love you so much. You've been so kind and generous…'

Helen felt herself unceremoniously tipped on the

seat behind him and Jason loomed over her. 'I don't want your gratitude. Just tell me again that you love me,' he demanded in a voice that was rough with need.

'I love you… I think I always have…even when I was a girl.'

His mouth plunged on to hers, hard and warm. It was a kiss like no other they had shared…not skilful or calculated. It was, Helen realised, with a sense of serenity, simply raw adoration.

Jason raised his head, his self-conscious smile betraying that he knew he'd been clumsy.

Helen wound her arms about his neck, keeping him reassuringly close.

'I'll get a special licence. Do you mind if it's a quiet affair, and soon?'

Helen shook her head. 'I've nothing planned for tomorrow,' she said teasingly.

'Tomorrow might do,' he said quite seriously. 'Do you want to go for a walk? Or to Westlea House? We must make arrangements,' he continued in a husky, urgent voice.

Helen nestled her head against his shoulder, feeling utterly content and blissful. 'I'd rather you took me to Chelsea, Jason,' she suggested softly.

Chapter Eighteen

'You're very good at this.'

'You bring out the best in me, sweetheart.'

Helen gave him a speaking look and turned her head on the pillow.

Jason supported his weight on brawny forearms, dipping his head to nudge Helen's face up to his and take her lips in a wooing kiss. His eyes, dark with desire, meshed with hers and he smiled crookedly. 'It's true…' he softly emphasised. 'You bring out the best in me…just you…no one else.' His thumb traced gently where his mouth had plundered hers and plumped the skin to dual scarlet bows. 'Do you believe me, Helen?' Jason asked gently. 'This is unique, I swear.'

She swung back her head, coating his fingers with the black silk of her hair. 'Yes, I believe you. But…'

'But…?'

'I've been jealous, too,' she quietly admitted whilst watching one of her fingers caress the lean flesh of his hand. 'It was silly of me to say that I would not care if you did not devote yourself exclusively to me.' She curled the stroking finger back into her palm. 'In fact, I have been tormented, thinking of you doing this with someone else.'

'I have not, Helen.' Jason's voice was thick with reassurance. 'I swear to you that since we first went to Hyde Park together I've not been with another woman.'

Helen swung her face back and her eyes clung to his. 'Mrs Tucker still lives in one of your houses.'

'Who told you that? Was it George making more mischief?'

'No. Bridgeman taunted me with it. He said Diana was still ensconced in one of your houses.'

'Bridgeman knows nothing,' Jason said with a scornful laugh. 'Had he bothered to check his facts, he would have found out that the property is now Diana's. I gave it to her as a parting gift.' Jason's mouth set grimly. 'I wish now I had not let Bridgeman off so lightly when I saw him earlier. Just for upsetting you over that he deserved another—'

Helen placed a finger on his lips. 'Hush, or I will think you a ruffian to get into two scraps in one day.'

She suddenly chuckled. 'But I'm glad you hit Bridgeman, he deserved it…horrible man. He would have tried to coerce Charlotte into marriage and thought nothing of it. And he tried to intentionally hoodwink George with his contract. I don't want George to go to gaol.'

'He won't. I've paid Bridgeman his money.'

Helen hugged him in gratitude then ran loving fingers over the ridges on his chest, luxuriating in the touch of silken skin sheathing rough muscle. 'So a notorious rake has been faithful to me, has he?'

'Absolutely.'

Helen undulated unconsciously beneath him in cat-like contentment. Their slick skin was bonded, their sated bodies still in congress, yet she felt the stirring inside her that told her he was ready to love her again. She felt the warm rush of excitement that made her breasts heavy and her hips instinctively tilt. 'I'm a wanton,' she sighed huskily and nipped his shoulder with teasing teeth.

'Obviously I bring out the best in you,' Jason murmured suggestively.

'You do…but Harry will always have a place in my heart. Do you mind?'

Jason shook his head. 'I'm glad you were happy with him. But I'll make you happier…'

'I wish George was happy.' Helen sighed. 'I know

he is a selfish schemer, but it is hard to hate one's own kin. And now I know what it is that has made him so sour.' She met Jason's smouldering eyes. 'I never guessed about him and Beatrice, you know. I had heard that you fell out over a woman, but that was all I knew.' She frowned. 'I imagined Beatrice stayed away from Charlotte's betrothal party because she had guessed about us and wanted to avoid me. It was George she didn't want to see, wasn't it?'

'Yes.' Jason twisted a smile. 'In fact, as soon as she heard George was in town with his wife, she found an excuse to return home.'

'Does she hate him?'

'Actually, I think she still has a scrap of tender feeling for him. Perhaps I was wrong and I should have let them be.' Jason grimaced indecision. 'At the time my mother was distraught and imagining all sorts of ruination and disaster. I couldn't be sure George would act honourably and, had the marriage not taken place, Beatrice's reputation would have been irreparably sullied. She was only sixteen.' Jason gave a sigh. 'He should not have done it...and it is pointless dredging it up—nothing can be changed. But I hope, as brothers-in-law, we might again be friends.'

'I would like that,' Helen said, a little wistfully, for something else was troubling her. 'When Iris told me of it this morning she said you were bitter over it all and that's why you took me for your mistress…as an act of revenge.'

'You don't believe that, do you?'

Jason's voice held such arrant scorn that Helen quickly shook her head.

Jason forked long fingers over Helen's sharp little chin, keeping her facing him. 'It's utter rubbish, not least because, if I'm truthful, I never held George wholly responsible for what went on.'

'Beatrice happily went with him?'

'Yes…but that is not exactly what I meant.' He slanted her a crooked smile. 'George didn't start the madness of lusting after teenage sisters, I did. I told him during a drunken spree, sometime in our misspent youths, that I found you attractive. He then declared that he felt the same way about Beatrice.' He gave Helen a wry smile. 'I wanted you, but I would never have acted on it. George took it further. He and Beatrice started meeting secretly. Then one night they eloped.' A gentle finger traced a curve on Helen's cheek. 'Had I never admitted to that secret yearning for you, perhaps George would have controlled his feelings until Beatrice was older.'

Helen gazed up at him with wide golden eyes. 'You wanted to marry me when I was fifteen?'

Jason subdued a wolfish smile. 'No…when I was

twenty-four I never thought about marriage. But I certainly thought about—'

Helen gave his arm a silencing thump to spare her further blushes. 'I had a crush on you, too. *My* intentions were honourable,' she said, mock-prim. 'I dreamed of marrying you.'

'And now you are.'

'And now I am,' Helen echoed softly, wondrously. A wounding memory haunted her mind. 'Bridgeman called me Hunter's whore and said other people were saying it, too. He never imagined you would make me your wife.'

Jason dipped his head to tenderly kiss away her sadness. 'I think I fell in love with you from the moment you opened the door to me at Westlea House. You looked like a little waif.' He threaded his bruised fingers through the silky black tresses crumpled on the white linen. 'It didn't matter that you were shabbily dressed or had your hair loose. I thought I had never seen a woman as beautiful. I delayed making you my mistress because I intended you to be my wife, Helen.' He kissed her with seductive sweetness. 'Why worry what's been said? We know you've always been Hunter's Lady….'

Epilogue

'**M**iss Beaumont.'

Emily turned her head on hearing her name. Her heart started to thud as she saw the identity of the gentleman approaching. Not that her odd excitement sprung from liking him, rather he unsettled her.

'Mr Hunter,' she greeted him and sketched a polite bob.

Mark Hunter studied the fair face turned up to his. 'I haven't seen you since the wedding. I think we ought take a little credit for bringing about that very happy occasion.'

Emily immediately smiled at the reference to Helen and Jason's nuptials, and the prior events at Vauxhall Gardens. 'The whole day was wonderful, was it not? Even the weather was glorious.'

'They deserved the best.'

Emily nodded vigorously, her blonde hair rippling prettily. 'Oh, indeed,' she agreed. A silence developed between them so she made conversation as they walked on towards the water in Hyde Park. 'I hope Charlotte's wedding next month is just so blessed with everything good.'

Mark smiled. 'They have Westlea House as a wedding gift. That's certainly good.'

'It will be quite a beautiful home when the work is finished. Charlotte and Philip are lucky indeed to have such a generous brother-in-law.'

'I think perhaps the pair owe thanks to Helen for their good fortune. I know she wanted the newly-weds to have a home of their own.'

'It must be hard to start married life with no privacy, surrounded by one's family.' Emily had said that quite pensively and her eyes instinctively slanted to her brother, who was grouped close by with his friends. She frowned and began to turn away.

Mark glanced at Tarquin, too, and understood why Emily had suddenly withdrawn from him. Tarquin Beaumont was in the company of a notorious gamester and money was clearly changing hands.

Emily was about to fly to her brother's side to attempt to keep him from more trouble. Annoyed that he was to lose her enchanting company, Mark said gruffly, 'Your brother must discipline himself and learn what company to avoid. It is not something you can do for him.'

Emily whipped her head about to give him a haughty stare. 'I quite agree he should pick his friends carefully. I recall you were the Judas who had him thrown in the Fleet.'

'If you will let me explain, there are things you don't know about that,' Mark said on a sigh.

'I know enough,' Emily countered icily. 'I certainly know I do not like you, Mr Hunter, and no sweet talk will change my mind.' Within a moment she had spun on a heel and headed off towards her brother.

Mark Hunter watched her go, an odd expression, part amusement, part exasperation, on his face. 'And I know, Miss Beaumont, that if I wanted to change your mind, it wouldn't be through conversation....

The Wanton Bride

Chapter One

'Nonsense, my dear! There is nothing sinister in it. Boys like to go off gallivanting once in a while. You're worrying unnecessarily, I tell you!' Mr Cecil Beaumont gave his beautiful blonde daughter a beaming smile. 'Don't look so glum. He'll turn up when he's good and ready.'

'Tarquin is not a boy, Papa,' Emily Beaumont pointed out quietly. 'He is a man of twenty-seven and I suspect he has got himself into one scrape too many. Perhaps he has not succeeded in stalling his creditors and is in trouble.' Her silver-blue eyes took on a faraway look as she pondered on instances when her older brother had brought himself close to ru-ination through gaming and wild ways. But he had never yet disappeared for more than a few days before turning up, like the proverbial bad penny, sober and remorseful. 'Perhaps we ought to check with the authorities in case he is again in the Fleet.'

Mr Beaumont waved a dismissive hand. 'No need…no need, my dear.' He picked up his pen, idle on a page of his ledger, and set about using it.

His daughter was not so easily put off. Emily paced to the window of her father's den, stared out sightlessly, before wandering back into the room, deep in thought. With a sigh she sank into an old armchair.

Tarquin had been due to come to their parents' home in Callison Crescent and take their brother Robert to the outfitters. But he had failed to arrive at the appointed hour five days ago and had not contacted his family to make his excuses or his apologies. Emily thought it highly irregular behaviour, even for someone as self-centred as her brother.

Mrs Beaumont's reaction on that afternoon was to mutter about *the inconsiderate knave* before she got her husband's valet to take Robert to the tailors instead. When Emily had earlier today approached her mother about Tarquin's lengthy silence, she showed herself no more concerned over her eldest son's whereabouts than did her husband.

Mr Beaumont raised an indulgent paternal eye to

his daughter. He tossed his quill on to the blotter and clucked his tongue. 'Come, my dear, no long face, I beg you. If Tarquin had been threatened with prison, he would have by now summoned my help, you may take my word on it.' Cecil gave a cynical little laugh. 'I'll not go looking for him to sort out his troubles—if troubles he has—for they always find me soon enough.' A nod concluded his philosophy and he resumed his writing. A quiet moment passed. Warily he peeked up to find his daughter still in the room and looking no less melancholy. 'Emily!' he expostulated with a hint of impatience. 'If you're unable to put your mind at ease over it, I'll call in to Westbury Avenue and see if his landlady knows where he might be.'

Emily brightened. 'You promise you will do that, Papa?' she asked.

Cecil nodded affirmation. 'I can go that way to Boodle's later.'

A smile erased the strain from Emily's lovely features. Her father bowed his head over his ledger once more, gave a couple of short coughs, firmly letting Emily know their conversation was definitely concluded.

Emily rose gracefully from his armchair and went upstairs to her bedchamber.

Feeling lighter in spirits, she gazed out on to the street scene. She watched with an amount of amused interest as their neighbour's footman strutted back and forth on the pavement, trying to catch the eye of the housemaid scrubbing the front step of the house opposite. The young woman's complexion was as fiery as her hair and she looked too hot and bothered to presently entertain any thoughts of flirtation. Emily glanced up at a clear azure sky, then at fat green buds beginning to break on the lime trees guarding the crescent of townhouses. She decided she would call on her friend Sarah Harper who lived just a few turnings away. They could go for a stroll if Sarah was amenable to the idea of whiling away the afternoon with a chat and a browse in the shops. The day was clement and after a week of unremitting rain it would be nice to get out of the house and into the fresh air.

Emily was donning her coat by the front door when her mother appeared and frowned at her. 'You must take Millie with you if you are going abroad,' she lectured. 'That crone made a point of telling me that she recently saw you out without even a maid.'

Emily signalled her insouciance with a delicately arched eyebrow. She knew exactly to whom her mother was referring, for the two women were arch-enemies of long standing. 'Well, Mama, you must tell Violet Pearson that I am a woman of four and twenty and perfectly able to take care of myself.'

'Your age is not the point, and you know it,' Mrs Beaumont began, but her intention to furnish a lesson on etiquette and how it applied to spinsters came to nought. Her daughter gave her a little wave and skipped down the front steps. For a moment longer Penelope Beaumont stared at the front door. She shrugged—she was long used to her daughter's headstrong ways. It was just a nuisance when hags, with nothing better to do than cause trouble, sought to bring it to her attention. She turned about and headed towards the parlour and a fortifying nip of sherry.

'It *is* very odd behaviour,' Sarah commented and looked thoughtful. 'Surely your brother would at least pen a note to let you know if he is out of town.'

The two young ladies linked arms and promenaded towards Regent Street. They had decided to peruse the window displays of the new French *modiste* who had recently opened for business.

Sarah's frown lifted in tentative enlightenment. 'Perhaps Tarquin has fallen in love and has been lured to the country to do his courting.'

Emily chuckled. 'I'd like to think such a noble reason exists for his absence. Unfortunately, Tarquin is besotted with Lady Luck. No real woman could compete with such a possessive mistress.' She flashed Sarah a wry smile. 'I expect Papa is right and I am worrying needlessly. My thoughtless brother is probably just gone off on a revel with one of his chums. But it is bad of him not to say so and odd that he has let Robert down. He and Robert are friends, despite the age gap between them.' She frowned. 'It was not nice to see Robert's disappointment. He has gone back to school now and missed seeing Tarquin entirely.'

Emily's arm was given a tug as Sarah drew her towards Madame Joubert's shop. Behind small mullioned panes were draped a shimmering array of silks, artfully arranged to highlight their quality.

'The sea-green colour is divine…but the gold is an unusual shade.' Emily tilted her head to peer through the door. 'They have more inside…'

Sarah interrupted Emily's appreciation of the sumptuous cloths with a hissed, 'Look who is coming!' Emily's ribs received a dig. 'You ought ask *him* if he knows of Tarquin's whereabouts. They are friends after all.'

Emily glanced along the road and her eyes fixed

immediately on the man to whom Sarah had breath-lessly referred. Indeed, it would be hard *not* to no-tice him. Mark Hunter was tall and broad with darkly attractive features that excited female atten-tion. Emily recognised the elegant lady at his side who had her hand curved possessively over his arm. It was an open secret in polite society that Barbara Emerson was Mark Hunter's mistress.

'I see Mr Hunter has his *chère amie* with him,' Sarah whispered.

'I think it is more than *that* between them,' Emily returned on a little huff of laughter. 'I've heard a ru-mour that Mark Hunter is expected to marry Mrs Emerson. I imagine she considers herself to be his unofficial betrothed.'

Sarah arched an eyebrow. 'I wonder who started that rumour?' she said drily. 'And until *he* makes it official, there is still hope for us all. Goodness, he is handsome!' she breathed. 'I think I might swoon.'

Her friend's theatrical tone made Emily cast at her a small scowl. Sarah was quite aware that Emily did not like the man. 'Handsome is as handsome does…' Emily muttered in response to Sarah's teas-ing. Her eyes returned to the object of Sarah's ad-miration and lingered. Indisputably Mark Hunter *looked* a personable gentleman, but Emily had reason to believe him mean and callous. Was he not the fellow who had in the past had Tarquin imprisoned in the Fleet because he owed him money? Yet despite that betrayal her brother still liked Mark and classed him as one of his friends. On the few occasions Emily had quizzed him over his odd attachment to a man who had betrayed him, Tarquin had simply said Mark wasn't a bad fellow.

Emily pondered on Sarah's comment that this meeting might prove useful. Perhaps Tarquin's friend might know if he had recently gone off to Brighton or to the Newmarket races or some other such place where fashionable gentlemen chose to congregate. It was an opportunity to find out and she ought take it.

Her eyes flicked up as she realised that the distinguished couple were almost upon them.

'Miss Beaumont…Miss Harper.' Mark dipped his dark head and slowed his pace, allowing the young ladies time to respond. Sarah did so immediately. A shy smile accompanied her curtsy.

Emily sketched a bob and muttered his name. He was steadily watching her and boldly she met his eyes. They were an unusual shade of blue, she realised, not unlike the lustrous peacock silk she had moments ago admired in Madame Joubert's window.

A faint smile touched Mark's lips as he acknowledged her cool response and she glimpsed humour far back in his vivid eyes. Of course, he was aware that she didn't like him given that she had once frankly told him so. She hoped he was also aware that she found his good looks and ready charm quite resistible, even if her entranced friend did not. Emily shot a stern look at Sarah.

Aware that her lover seemed more interested in gazing at Emily Beaumont than conversing with her, Mrs Emerson quickly filled the silence. 'I have not seen you in a while, Miss Harper.' She turned to Sarah. 'How is your mother? When last we spoke she was afflicted with the rheumatics.'

'She is improved, I thank you, ma'am,' Sarah replied. 'When the weather is better, her condition is too.'

Barbara Emerson murmured her pleasure at knowing it, then turned to Emily. 'And you look very well, Miss Beaumont. Are your family in good health?'

Emily gave the elegant woman an affirmative and a fleeting smile. She guessed that Barbara Emerson was probably no more than a year or two older than was she, yet Barbara had an effortless air of sophistication that made her feel girlish in comparison.

Barbara had married a wealthy man at nineteen, been widowed and left his property and fortune at twenty-one and was now the mistress and aspirant future wife of one of society's most eligible bachelors. Emily charitably allowed that Barbara had earned her quietly superior attitude.

Noting that her attempt to distract her lover's attention from Miss Beaumont had failed, Barbara subtly urged Mark to move over the shop's threshold by squeezing the muscle beneath her fingers.

Emily felt Sarah's elbow nudge her side as wordlessly her friend reminded her to speak of Tarquin before the opportunity was lost.

Mark smoothly extricated his arm from Barbara's control in a way that was uncompromising yet courteous. With a faint flush livening her olive complexion, Barbara swished about and started to peruse the silks that had drawn Emily and Sarah to a halt by the window. Sarah stepped over to her and gamely indicated the colour she preferred.

'Is your brother at home, Miss Beaumont?'

'No, he went back to school this morning,' Emily immediately answered.

A wry smile tilted Mark's mouth. 'I meant your older brother,' he gently corrected.

'Oh…I thought you were referring to Robert—I

imagined you would know Tarquin is not with us.'
Emily's small tongue stroked moisture to her dry
lips. She felt faintly embarrassed by her gaffe, but
her nervousness stemmed more from being constantly under his penetrating gaze. 'Actually, I was
about to ask if you know where Tarquin might be.'

Mark frowned—he had discerned the quiver of
anxiety in Emily's voice. 'I have not seen him since
last week at White's when we played cards. I went
this morning to his lodgings in Westbury Avenue,
but his landlady said she'd not seen him for some
days. I assumed he was staying with all of you at
Callison Crescent. I'm not pursuing him for a gambling debt, I assure you,' Mark added mildly, noticing her sharp look. 'Tarquin expressed an interest in
coming to Cambridge with me, that is all.'

Emily recalled then that Mark Hunter had a vast
country estate in Cambridgeshire. Tarquin had visited it before and returned quite in awe of its size and
splendid appointments. But now her thoughts returned to a place closer to home. She grimaced with
disappointment as she recalled her conversation earlier with her father. 'Papa said he would call in at
Westbury Avenue this afternoon. From what you
have said, he will be wasting his time.' An unconscious sigh escaped Emily. 'It is too bad of Tarquin

to go off like that without a word.' She raised anxious eyes to his face. 'Do you have any idea at all where he might be? I know he pursues unusual entertainment. Are there any boxing bouts or cockfights that might have taken him out of town?'

Mark looked down into a heart-shaped face that was tense with concern. She wanted his help and he would have loved to be able to give it. Unfortunately he had no idea where Tarquin was.

Despite knowing that Miss Emily Beaumont didn't like him, Mark had always harboured a soft spot for Tarquin's sister. It was not simply her looks that attracted him, although she was exquisitely pretty and had an alluring little figure. Presently her curves were primly hidden beneath her velvet coat, but he'd seen her dressed in less and admired the way her body tautened silk in all the right places. And on such occasions when she'd quickened his pulse, he'd brooded on trying to alter her opinion of him. Inwardly he smiled, for it would be no easy task. And therein lay another reason she held a fascination for him. Emily Beaumont had a robust character and was not too timid to challenge him or to speak her mind. A lamentable amount of young ladies tended to blush and stammer in his presence. Emily was more likely to flash him a glare from silver eyes than flirtatiously flutter those wonderfully long lashes at him.

But she was looking at him now in mute appeal and that surely indicated she was open to being persuaded he was not the heartless fellow she'd previously thought him. Mark was reasonably sure that her brother was simply lying low to avoid paying his dues. But he was willing to keep his thoughts to himself and act knightly for the beguiling chit.

'I've not heard of any such events taking place,' Mark said levelly. 'But that does not mean none exist. I can make some proper enquiries and try to find him, if you'd like me to,' he offered huskily.

Emily gave a spontaneous smile. 'Thank you, sir. I would indeed like you to do that. It would be reassuring to know that Tarquin is simply acting thoughtlessly and selfishly as usual.' She had, she realised with a pang of regret, betrayed criticism of her brother's character. Previously when with this man she had always been defensive if mention was made of Tarquin's shortcomings. But her patience was wearing thin where he was concerned. He had let them all down in the past with his antics and they had rallied to support and to protect him. But Tarquin gave little back—even in the way of thanks—and Emily was aware that her parents' lack of concern over his whereabouts sprang from a relief that their eldest son had taken himself and his problems away for a while.

Vexation caused a sigh to escape Emily. She would like to similarly forget Tarquin. Considering he had once driven away the only man she had ever loved, it seemed absurd that she could not banish the bothersome wretch from her mind.

Emily surfaced from her introspection to become conscious of a pair of deep blue eyes steadily watching her. Mark Hunter was aware of a momentary lapse in her role as loyal sibling. She guessed he was also reflecting on her reason for suddenly warming towards him.

Just minutes ago she had greeted Mark Hunter with distinct coolness. Now she felt awkward. They both knew that her abrupt change of attitude was simply due to the fact that she needed his help. That glint in his eyes was mockery, she was sure, and probably signalled that he thought her a hypocrite. And why should he not? She was on the verge of acknowledging it herself! Emily briskly dipped her head and took a step away from him.

'Were you about to go in and make some purchases?' Mark asked conversationally, seeking to delay her departure.

Emily shook her head. 'No…we were just window-shopping. If you do come across my brother, Mr Hunter, I'd be grateful if you'd remind him where the Beaumonts live. Perhaps he might think to call in and say hello. Good day, sir.'

A smile curved his lips, acknowledging her ironic tone. 'I won't forget, Miss Beaumont. I'll let you know if I discover Tarquin's likely whereabouts.'

After a murmur of gratitude Emily approached her friend and Mrs Emerson. Sarah was still persevering in trying to engage Barbara in a chat about French fashions. Barbara's responses had been limited to a variety of tight-lipped expressions.

After polite farewells Emily and Sarah walked off along Regent Street. They had distanced themselves by only a few yards when Sarah glanced back over a shoulder. 'He's still looking at you,' she hissed into Emily's small ear. 'And Mrs Emerson has an unlady-like scowl on her face.'

'He could be looking at you,' Emily immediately pointed out. 'Barbara is probably in a fit of the sulks from having delayed her shopping spree. I don't say I blame her. Those silks looked quite wonderful. It is a shame we didn't see what else was on the shelves.'

'Let's go back,' Sarah breathed. 'Why should we not? We were at Madame Joubert's first, after all.'

'Don't be silly; it would look as though we're following them.' Emily gave Sarah's arm a little tug to turn her about. 'And stop staring at them, for goodness' sake!'

Chapter Two

'Stop staring at them, for Gawd's sake!'

The young woman's booted toe made ungentle contact with her companion's shin. He yelped and swore beneath his breath at her. 'Wot you do that fer, Jenny?' he snarled.

'To stop you gawping like an idiot,' Jenny Trent hissed back. 'This ain't the time and place to be seen.' The young woman shot a look from under dropped lids and cursed quietly. 'I reckon the nob she was talking to has spotted us watching her. We don't want to be tangling with the likes of him!'

Mickey Riley affected nonchalance as he turned to look across the street. Fleetingly he met Mark Hunter's steady stare. His attention soon returned to his companion. 'Fellow's looking at you, Jenny.' He leered at the pretty woman at his side. 'I know his sort. Quality with cash and an eye for petticoat, he is.' He chewed his lips and gave Jenny a sly look. 'We could've found richer pickings than Beaumont.'

'Bit late to be thinking that now!' She pinched his arm, urging him to move on. 'You and your daft ideas!' she scoffed.

Mickey Riley eyed the distinguished gentleman propped against the doorjamb of the posh shop, whose pretty ladybird was pointing out to him something she liked in the window. The fellow didn't seem that interested; he soon glanced again across the street. 'I reckon he's taken with you, Jen. Give him something to look at,' he urged his shapely young companion.

Jenny scowled up at Mickey, but did instinctively twitch at her skirts thus revealing a pair of shapely calves and ankles. She shook back her auburn curls, setting them bouncing beneath the elaborate concoction of feathers perched on her head.

'Good girl,' Mickey praised with an appreciative grin and threaded her arm through his.

Mark Hunter watched the couple disappear into the Regent Street throng. Had Mickey Riley known his thoughts, he might have felt less cocksure. It was not Jenny who had taken Mark's interest, but Mickey himself.

Mark allowed Barbara to steer him inside the shop. He made appropriate noises as she indicated the things she liked, but his thoughts were elsewhere.

It seemed a rather odd coincidence that Emily Beaumont should mention Tarquin and cockfights to him just moments before he clapped eyes on a fellow he had last seen arguing with Tarquin at a cockfight in Spitalfields Market. It had been a heated enough exchange for Mark to enquire after the fellow's identity. Tarquin had obliged him with that information when he subsequently joined him at the ringside of a boxing bout, but had seemed reluctant to divulge more about Mickey Riley, or the subject of their disagreement.

The incident had been some weeks ago, but Mark had a good memory for faces, and Riley's appearance was quite striking. He looked to be about Mark's own age of thirty-two, yet had hair as grey as smoke and a complexion that had been ravaged by the elements to nut brown. Riley also had a misshapen nose that led one to believe he was, or had once been, a pugilist. Notwithstanding those blemishes, he was well built, and an oddly handsome man.

When Mark had witnessed the altercation between Tarquin and Mickey—who was quite obviously of a different social class—he had not been surprised or concerned. Tarquin's love of gaming brought him into contact with all sorts of people at all sorts of venues. His friend would wager on a street scrap between two bruisers or a race of thoroughbreds at Epsom. Unfortunately, wherever he went, Tarquin had an unholy knack of backing a loser.

Most gentlemen with such an appalling record of luck would find diversion of a different kind. Yet after almost a decade, and a small fortune squandered, Tarquin still followed the philosophy that the next stake would bring it all right.

Mark's thoughts returned to Mickey Riley. If Tarquin owed him money—perhaps from a bet that night in Spitalfields—Riley didn't seem the sort of fellow to take the loss lightly. Of course, Tarquin's debts were not his business…at least, not until he decided to call in the loan he had made him last year, and added to them, Mark wryly reflected.

But the sardonic tilt to his lips was soon gone. Mark's mood became sombre, for he had an uneasy feeling that Mickey and his female companion had been watching Emily. Or it could have been Sarah Harper they were interested in, but instinct persuaded him it was not.

It seemed absurd to suppose that Riley might accost Emily because her brother owed him money.

But it was certainly not unheard of for even well-connected creditors to pursue the relatives of those who tried to renege on a deal. Big and brash as Riley looked, perhaps he was too craven to approach Mr Beaumont senior with his complaints and was stalking his daughter instead.

Mark darted impatient looks about the cloyingly scented shop. Madame Joubert was rustling hither and thither, her arms full of froth, as she tempted Barbara to make her purchases. As he watched the pretty trivia pile on the counter, he wondered whether he was letting his imagination run riot. There was little substance on which to found his suspicions.

He had no proof that Riley and his female companion were doing more than enjoying a leisurely afternoon stroll. If they had been watching Emily and her friend, was it necessarily from sinister motives? Two attractive young ladies, obviously of enviable status, were bound to draw the attention of those less privileged.

It was a reasonable explanation, but ultimately did not quell Mark's suspicions. He had a sudden urgent desire to quit the *modiste*'s, immediately track down Tarquin, and demand he tell him what the hell he had lately been up to.

* * *

'Man over there give it to me. He told me to bring it to you.'

Emily looked down at the ragged child who had moments ago yanked rudely on her coat to gain her attention. The boy had then stuck out a grimy hand that clutched a note. Tentatively Emily took the paper and then peered in the direction that the wizened-faced little urchin was pointing. She couldn't see anybody at all who looked to be the likely sender. People were stepping briskly along the pavements, going about their business with no hint of any interest in her.

She looked enquiringly at the boy, who was wrinkling his freckled nose. He cuffed at his face as he looked up and down the street. 'He's gorn,' he admitted with a shrug. 'But he was over there and he give me it and then he give me this.' Dirty fingers were opened to reveal a few coppers. 'You gonna give me anythin'?' he boldly asked and peered at Emily with one eye open and one closed against the afternoon sunlight brightening his sallow complexion.

Recovering her senses and her voice, Emily murmured, 'Oh, of course.' She fished in her reticule and then tipped a few more coins to chink on those reposing on his blackened palm. His fingers trapped the pennies, then he was haring away as though he feared she might snatch them back.

Emily walked on slowly towards Callison Crescent. She had a few minutes ago left Sarah at her door and had been barely five minutes from her own home when the lad had accosted her. Curiously she inspected the note. It was sealed, but there was no name or direction on it, just the sooty marks left by the child's fingers. She made to open it, then hesitated. With a little inner smile she wondered if perhaps she had a secret admirer. If so, she ought to, at her leisure, discover his identity. She slipped the parchment into a pocket. It certainly would not have come from the gentleman who openly admired her.

Mr Stephen Bond was not prone to such romantic gestures as employing guttersnipes to deliver her a billet-doux. But he was nice enough, if rather predictable. Emily let out a sigh. Thinking of that gentleman had reminded her that Mr Bond was due to dine with them later and of course he would be exceedingly punctual.

'I expected you home before this,' was the peevish greeting that Emily received from her mother as she stepped into the hallway. 'You have not forgot that we have company?'

'No, Mama,' Emily said. 'I know Mr Bond is coming at seven.'

'Well…good…let Millie do something pretty with your hair. The curls looks limp.' Her mother circled her and picked a loose golden tress from the shoulder of her blue velvet coat. 'Stephen is to bring his grandmamma with him this evening. She is up from Bath and seems eccentric. I was introduced to her at the Revue and couldn't but invite her when Stephen mentioned he was coming. She had on the ugliest gown I ever did see. It was a shade of purple with fawn stripes. What possessed her to wear a green hat with it?'

Emily gave her mother a wicked smile. 'If she arrives here in the same ensemble, perhaps we should demand to know.'

Penelope Beaumont chuckled, but her humour soon faded and she frowned at the door. 'And your father is late home too. It's nearly a quarter to six.'

'He said he would call in at Tarquin's lodgings. That has probably delayed him.'

'A man was looking for Tarquin.' Mrs Beaumont volunteered that information with a furrow in her brow. 'Millie ran an errand for me earlier and she said the fellow stopped her in the street. He must have watched her leaving the house or how would he know of a connection between them? She said he was polite to her despite seeming a bit of a rough sort.' Mrs Beaumont peered past her daughter as her husband entered the hallway brushing water from his caped shoulders. 'It's come on to rain again,' she gleefully remarked. 'The Pearsons will have to cancel their firework display.'

'It is as well then that you were not invited, Mama.' Emily was aware that her mother and Violet Pearson were continually sniping at one another. They had been at loggerheads since Robert planted a facer on Bertie, the Pearsons' son, thereby knocking out his two front teeth. The patresfamilias had shrugged and commiserated together about the young scamps. But Penelope Beaumont and Violet Pearson seemed determined to keep the feud alive.

'No sign of Tarquin, I'm afraid.' Mr Beaumont had deposited his damp coat on a chair and was wearily approaching the ladies. His tone had changed since that morning. Now Emily detected a distinct hint of anxiety making his voice husky.

'You went to Westbury Avenue, Papa?'

'I did, and Tarquin's landlady was pleased I had stopped off, I can tell you. I had no chance to ask her if she knew where he was. She demanded *I* disclose to *her* his direction. She is under the impression he has done a flit and will not be back.' Mr Beaumont sadly shook his head. 'Most of his possessions are gone and he owes her two months' rent. She has not seen hide nor hair of him for almost two weeks.'

'What are we to do with him?' Penelope Beaumont flapped her hands in exasperation. 'When will he settle himself down and act responsibly? I knew he was running away from his debts again.'

Cecil pursed his lips. 'In my opinion, it's more than the rent he owes that's bothering him. Mrs Dale told me a fellow with a broken nose had called at Westbury Avenue looking for him. She said he looked like a cove it would be best not to cross.'

Penelope Beaumont anxiously clasped her husband's arm. 'A man with a crooked nose stopped Millie in the street. He was asking about Tarquin. Millie said he seemed quite polite...' she added desperately.

'So he will be if he is about to demand his cash,' Mr Beaumont pointed out with a cynical grunt of a laugh. 'It's when he doesn't get it that he's likely to turn rude.'

Emily bit at her lip as she swung a glance between her parents' drawn countenances. Their brief respite from Tarquin's problems was at an end. He might still be out of sight, but imagining what sort of chaos he had created was tormenting their minds.

'I can't understand why he's not been in touch,' Mr Beaumont said. 'If he needs money, I'm usually his first port of call. I wonder if he's approached one of his friends to bail him out? I warned him last time that I'd do it no more. Mayhap he took me at my word.'

'I saw Mark Hunter when out,' Emily quickly volunteered that information. 'He also had called in at Westbury Avenue to look for Tarquin.' She immediately allayed her parents' fears as to why he would be seeking their son. 'It was not for payment of a debt, Mr Hunter assured me of that. He has not seen Tarquin recently either, but he kindly said he will make enquiries and let us know if he discovers anything.'

Cecil Beaumont nodded slowly. 'Mark is a good chap; if he says he will put himself out to do that, then I expect he will.' Cecil scraped lank greying locks off his freckled forehead. 'I suppose I ought open the post in case the bad news is come in a letter from Tarquin. Usually he just turns up and I can read it in his face.'

Emily's father trudged towards his study; her mother hurried away to check on their dinner. Before Penelope disappeared towards the kitchens, she called back to her daughter, 'Oh, for goodness' sake, make yourself presentable, Emily. Look at the time! The Bonds will be with us in less than an hour.'

As the baize door closed behind her agitated mother, Emily slowly slid her hand into her pocket. She withdrew the parchment and felt a chill settle about her heart. *Secret admirer, indeed!* she mocked herself.

She suddenly had a very strong suspicion as to who had sent her letter. The manner in which it had been delivered obviously indicated that her brother did not want her parents to know of its existence, or its content. But why had he not shown himself to her? Why had he sent the boy to deliver it? If he was too wary to approach her in the street, even for a few moments, then Emily realised he must be in bad trouble indeed. The paper was dropped back into her pocket and quickly Emily headed for the stairs and the privacy of her chamber.

'You are a pretty gel, but undoubtedly past your prime.'

Emily heard that ambiguous tribute as she was sipping her wine. She swallowed quickly, for an urge to giggle had caused her to almost choke. She coughed delicately while composing herself, then smiled at Mrs Augusta Bond. She deposited her glass back on the table.

'Emily is not yet five and twenty,' Mrs Beaumont stiffly interjected. 'Hardly in her dotage, I think.'

Augusta Bond raised her lorgnette and divided her myopic gaze between mother and daughter. 'Her chances of getting a husband are not so good as the younger gels out this year. Her looks come from her father's side,' the *grande dame* opined, then affected not to see the icy stare that comment elicited from her hostess. Augusta let her glasses fall against her ample bosom and resumed attacking her beef with her knife and fork.

Emily sensed the old harridan's grandson was looking her way. She knew Stephen would want to wordlessly convey his chagrin at his grandmother's shockingly blunt manner. Emily took pity on him and gave him a subtle smile. Immediately he returned her an apologetic grimace that caused his thick brows to disappear beneath his fringe of blonde curls.

'Miss Beaumont has an exceedingly fine singing voice,' Stephen nervously told his grandmother. When that praise failed to wring a compliment from the old lady, he added, 'And I've not encountered any young lady who can play the pianoforte so well, and without a piece of music to follow.'

'That don't mean she'll make a good wife,' Mrs Bond hissed at her grandson in an audible aside.

Emily quickly snatched up her glass and downed an unladylike quantity of wine in one gulp. Oddly she felt an urge to endorse Mrs Bond's advice to her grandson. Stephen Bond was a nice gentleman but, unless there was no option but to do it, she would not marry him. He deserved to be loved, not tolerated.

Emily's silver eyes, brimful of laughter, lifted to Stephen's embarrassed countenance, then darted to her mother's face. Penelope Beaumont's expression was a study of furious indignation.

Had Emily been in lighter spirits, she would have more fully appreciated the unexpected entertainment that had arrived punctually at seven o'clock in the stout shape of Mrs Augusta Bond. She might even have entered into the spirit of the game and given the mischievous old biddy a run for her money. But her eyes were drawn to where her papa sat quietly at the head of the table. He seemed to have withdrawn to a world of his own. Even his wife's frequent glares could not budge him from it.

Emily could guess what was preoccupying her poor papa. He was trying to fathom into what sort of trouble his eldest son had now plunged. Before dinner Emily had thought she would by now have an answer to that conundrum. But the letter she had received was not after all from her brother. However, it did concern him, and Emily was still pondering on the peculiar message she had received, and why it had come to her at all.

When Tarquin's creditors gathered, if they could not find him, they usually sought to inveigle her father into paying. But this time she had received the begging letter, albeit couched in covert terms.

A person who remained anonymous had issued her an invitation to meet them tomorrow by the pawnbrokers' shop in Whiting Street in order that she might learn something important concerning her brother. It also stated that she must keep the matter to herself to avoid a scandal.

Emily had marvelled at the audacity of the fellow. She had quickly concluded that the author must be one of Tarquin's creditors who hoped to coerce her to honour her brother's debt. She had also deduced that the likely culprit was the ruffian with the broken nose, who had been loitering about, because the message was poorly written.

Emily was not so naïve to believe that her brother gambled solely in the gentlemen's clubs with his peers, but the idea that he was consorting with a man sporting a broken nose and a lack of grammar was indeed disheartening. Nevertheless, she would keep the appointment, and she would keep it to herself. She glanced again at her father as he absently pushed food about on his plate. He was approaching his sixty-fifth birthday and had for too long been encumbered with Tarquin's problems. Emily had no intention of taking on the yoke and would make that abundantly clear to Tarquin as soon as she again got within earshot of the selfish wretch.

'Have you ever received a marriage proposal, Miss Beaumont?'

Emily focussed on the present and saw that Augusta Bond had her bright beady eyes on her.

'Has any man asked you to marry him?' the old lady insisted on knowing.

Emily glanced at her mother's hideously shocked expression. Stephen had ceased chewing in alarm and had one cheek bloated with food. Emily compressed her lips to suppress the giggle throbbing in her throat. She took a deep breath before replying calmly, 'Indeed I have, Mrs Bond. I was engaged when I was twenty.'

'Cry off, did he?'

'Umm…no. I think I did, actually,' Emily said and placed her napkin down on her plate.

'Emily was betrothed to Viscount Devlin.' Mrs Beaumont issued that information in a glacial tone.

The old lady raised her lorgnette and peered at Emily with a glimmer of respect. 'Managed to hook a title, did you? No chance of getting him back now he's married to the Corbett chit. I hear she's already increasing.'

'I'll see if the next course is ready,' Penelope enunciated frigidly and surged up majestically from the table.

Emily glanced at her father to see he was now very aware of the tension in the room. He was looking in concern at her as though fearing she was upset. She reassured him with a smile before sending a challenging look at Augusta.

The old lady's eyes narrowed behind the glass, but Emily had the oddest impression that, before she let fall her lorgnette, Augusta winked at her.

Chapter Three

'That woman is the rudest person I ever did meet!'

Emily had barely managed to put a foot over the threshold of the morning room when that exclamation assaulted her ears. She had hoped that a good night's sleep might dilute her mother's ire, but it seemed as strong as ever.

When their guests had left at ten of the clock last evening, Mrs Beaumont had needed several draughts of sherry and the ministrations of both her husband and daughter to calm her enough to get her to bed.

'And her grandson is so…*pleasant,* so…*inoffensive,*' Mrs Beaumont emphasised with a quivering finger. 'Do you think it is her age? She looks to have reached her three score years and ten. Perhaps she is becoming a little confused.'

'I think she knows exactly what she is about,' Emily said with a light chuckle. 'I imagine Mrs Bond likes to be shocking.'

Penelope Beaumont clucked disgust at that. She pushed the jam pot towards her daughter as Emily sat down opposite her at the breakfast table.

Emily commenced spreading blackberries on to her toast, saying, 'Mrs Bond might be getting on in years, but she seemed to me to be in robust health and, in an odd way, I quite liked her.'

When Penelope heard that, her chin sagged towards her bosom.

'Oh, come, Mama, you must admit Augusta has a certain lively spirit, and she plays a mean hand of piquet. Papa lost a crown to her.'

Penelope snapped together her lips. 'And that compensates for her insults? How dare she speak so! You are a beauty in your prime.'

'She said nothing that was not true.' Emily took a fond glance at her mother from under long brunette lashes. Penelope had long harboured hopes that a knight in shining armour would carry her only daughter off to his Mayfair mansion and a life of untold luxury. Emily's eyes shaded wistfully. The knave had tarried too long. Her mother was on the point of urging Emily to settle for Mr

Bond and a villa in Putney. Emily pushed away her plate and wiped crumbs from her slender fingers. 'You know I'm too old to successfully compete with the débutantes for a husband. And I do actually take after Papa's side of the family. The miniature of Grandmama Beaumont could be my likeness.'

'And what about Augusta's appalling insensitive remarks about your aborted betrothal?'

'She did not know of it, Mama, I'm sure. She simply asked if I had received any marriage proposals.'

'I'll wager she *did* know of it and was out to be provocative,' Penelope snorted in muted outrage. 'Dreadful woman! You might have again burst into tears over it all.'

'I have not burst into tears over it all for a long while,' Emily said softly. 'And I promise I will never do so again. As for Augusta, I think she genuinely knew nothing about it. She lives in the country and the scandal was not so great.' She paused before reciting, 'When Tarquin Beaumont gave Viscount Devlin a beating, thereby ruining his sister's chance of happiness with the Viscount, I imagine it got scant mention in Bath drawing rooms. The gossip in London lasted barely a week, thank heavens.'

'It was only so soon forgot because that hussy

Olivia Davidson ran off with her sister's husband and set all the cats' tongues wagging.'

'And how grateful I was for poor Miss Davidson's disgrace,' Emily reminisced wryly. 'I still feel a little guilty when I see Olivia's sour face,' she added.

'It's her own fault she's ostracised by everyone, including her own kin. Silly fool should have known he'd slink home with his tail between his legs and it would all end in tears.' Penelope flapped a hand. 'Oh, enough about them! We were talking of *your* fiasco. I still say you acted too proud and too hasty, Emily. You should have married the Viscount, you know.'

'Indeed?' Emily gave a sour little laugh. 'Nicholas had made it clear by then he regretted an association with our family. I had no intention of binding him to his word and having a husband who might grow to despise me.'

Penelope waved that away, but her further arguments were immediately interrupted.

'We have been through this before and I refuse to rake it all over again. It is done with.' The grit in Emily's tone was at odds with the easy smile she gave her mother. Gracefully she rose from the dining table and went to the window. 'I am going out early today. Madame Joubert has some fine new silk…'

'I'll come too. I need some buttons—'

'No.' Emily realised she had declined the offer of her mother's company far too abruptly. Penelope looked rather taken aback, so she hastened to say, 'I was going to find something nice for your birthday. It won't be a surprise if you come too.'

Penelope flushed in pleasure and murmured, 'Oh, I see…'

Emily felt a little guilty at the excuse, though she had not told a lie. She would call in to the *modiste*'s on Regent Street and would find her mama something special for her birthday. Nevertheless, her real reason for going early abroad this morning was to keep her rendezvous on Whiting Street with the person who had sent the note. And she had certainly no intention of letting her mother in on that.

Penelope Beaumont could become disproportionately agitated over a trifling upset. If a storm was about to break over Tarquin's debts, it would be prudent to shield her from the worst of it for as long as possible.

'Mr Bond is here, ma'am.' Millie had slipped into the room to announce they had a visitor.

Penelope frowned—it was hardly yet the hour to be receiving callers. She gave her daughter a quizzical look.

'I expect he has come to apologise for his grandmother's blunt manner.' Emily gestured that she had no objection to seeing him.

'We will receive him in the parlour, Millie,' Penelope told the young maidservant.

Once in the parlour, and in the company of their diffident guest, Mrs Beaumont proceeded to pour tea while Emily and Mr Bond made polite observations on the vagaries of spring weather. Stephen was handed his cup and saucer and accepted the invitation to sit down whereupon, without preamble, he set about doing his duty.

'I must apologise for calling on you so early but I wasn't sure…that is to say…' His eyes darted between the two ladies as though searching for assistance. He cleared his throat and blurted, 'I wanted to again thank you for such fine hospitality yesterday and to make sure that you had not…been perturbed by my grandmother's blunt manner.'

Stephen glanced at Penelope Beaumont. Something in her expression caused him to quickly add, 'My grandmother does not intend to upset people, but she can be rather too outspoken.' He took a gulp from his tea, then clattered the cup down to rest.

'Does she not understand that being too outspoken is likely to upset people?' Penelope asked stiffly.

Stephen coloured and coughed. 'I don't think she does, ma'am. But if you thought any of her remarks offensive I will, of course, unreservedly apologise on her behalf.'

Emily put her tea down on a side table and kindly said, 'I thought your grandmama was quite a character. I enjoyed meeting her.' Emily's smile turned wry as Stephen looked most surprised to hear that. 'If Mrs Bond is not soon returning to Bath, you must introduce her to Mrs Pearson.' Emily sent her mother a twinkling look. 'Do you not think, Mama, that Violet Pearson might benefit from an acquaintance with Stephen's grandmother?'

Finally that morning Emily had drawn a twitch of amusement from her mother.

'Do take another cup, Mr Bond,' Penelope urged amiably and advanced with the pot.

Emily checked the wall clock and stood up. She needed to be on her way if she was to keep her appointment. 'I'm going out shopping, but do stay and finish tea,' she added as Stephen leaped to his feet.

'I'll gladly give you a ride,' Stephen volunteered eagerly, raking his fingers through his springy blond curls. 'Actually I ought to be getting along too. I have an appointment in Holborn.'

'I accept your kind offer, in that case,' Emily said.

* * *

Despite his noticeably wonky nose, it was not the fellow's looks that drew Emily's attention, but his manner. He had the demeanour of a person oblivious to the fact that he was under observation. Back and forth he strutted beneath the brass balls of the pawnbroker's shop, every so often peering at the passing carts with obvious disappointment. Then, a few yards away, a hackney cab pulled up at the kerb. That sent the fellow darting into the shop doorway, only to reappear a moment later when a stout gentleman alighted from the vehicle and purposefully bowled off up the street.

Emily guessed he had been expecting to catch sight of her before she noticed him. Doubtless he imagined she would arrive at the pawnbroker's in a vehicle rather than on foot. But Emily had not wanted to be quizzed by Stephen over why she was to be set down in an area so lacking fashionable shops. Instead, she had asked him to deliver her to a salubrious part of town that was within easy striking distance of Whiting Street. Having first declined Stephen's offer to meet her later to take her home, she had then watched his rig turn the corner before briskly walking east.

It was a fine spring morning, but chilly gusts of

wind made her keep her cloak pulled tight about her. She again sent a discreet look across Whiting Street at the fellow she was sure had sent her the note.

Although his burly figure didn't intimidate her, she did feel nervous. This was an area generally populated by gentlemen. They came to these premises to meet their men of business and pore over contracts and unintelligible papers. A lone female loitering about was likely to incite curiosity. Emily knew that her own papa often had assignments on this street with his attorney. Fervently she prayed that he had not arranged a meeting with Mr Pritchard today.

'Emily? Emily Beaumont?'

That cultured voice, once so well known to her, made Emily freeze, then pivot slowly about.

Viscount Devlin had been about to get into a crested carriage, but now he hesitated and sauntered, with much use of his ebony cane, along the pavement towards her.

Emily had wondered how she would feel if ever she and this man were to meet, alone. Of course, since the end of their betrothal many years ago, they had met socially. But that had been in polite company when they both were mindful of etiquette and speculative stares.

Notwithstanding the fact that Emily knew the love of her life was now a husband and prospective father—for she had heard that his wife was increasing before Augusta mentioned it—she wondered if the Viscount's roguish charm would still impress her. The closer he came, the more she feared the potency of his attraction. He was still youthfully good looking and could have passed for a man half a decade younger than his thirty-one years. His fair hair was artfully dishevelled and his hazel eyes warm as they settled on her face.

'Are you waiting for your father?' he asked, surprise leavening his tone, as he took a glance along the street. Emily imagined he expected to spy Mr Beaumont emerging from a nearby portal.

'No…I'm not,' Emily answered too quickly and truthfully. She sought for an excuse for her odd presence on Whiting Street. But she need not have worried over any further interrogation from the Viscount—he now seemed distracted by her small tongue as it trailed moisture over her full pink lips.

Emily felt her heart begin to race beneath his languid appraisal. The heat smouldering in his eyes brought instantly to mind images of things they had done together that she thought she had buried deep in her past. A burst of knowledge brought with it a guilty exhilaration: Viscount Devlin still desired her.

'When was it that last we met?' the Viscount asked huskily, his tawny eyes moving to her body. 'It must have been a year ago. I swear that every time I see you, Emily, you have grown more lovely.'

Emily sensed her heart increase tempo, but flashed him a cool look from silver eyes. 'And I swear, sir, that I think you must be still recovering from a night of roistering to say such a thing to me.'

'Can I not compliment you?' he asked gravely. 'Why are you so prickly, Emily? Has the hurt not yet healed?'

Emily blinked. Part of her wanted to laugh scornfully at his terribly inappropriate remarks, but there was also a shameful part of her that would rather listen to more of his flattery. Mentally she shook herself and took a step away. He might tell her she was lovely, and look at her as though he wanted to kiss her, but her memory was not so short. A few years ago, after Tarquin had thrashed him, there had been nothing but disgust and anger in his eyes when he saw any Beaumont, including her.

'What you are referring to belongs to the past, sir,' she said stiltedly, 'and there is certainly nothing more to be said about it.' She bobbed and made to whip past him, but a hand shot out, arresting her.

'Don't fly away, Emily,' he softly pleaded. 'I have long thought that there *is* more to be said. I have wanted to see you alone; have hoped we might meet by chance like this. I think of you often. I think of what might have been…'

Emily twisted her wrist from his restraint and took two crisp backward steps. She darted a look here and there to see if they were under observation and was annoyed to notice that they were. The bruiser who had summoned her to this dratted neighbourhood in the first place had now spotted her! Emily frowned and sighed softly. The situation had become farcical. She was not now likely to discover Tarquin's whereabouts.

'Do you know him?' Viscount Devlin asked.

'Who?' Emily blurted and her eyes darted quickly to the Viscount's face.

'The fellow across the road who appears to be staring at you.'

Emily spontaneously shook her head. It was not a lie; she did not yet know him, but she was certain she had been within a few minutes of remedying that when Nicholas Devlin had turned up. In a way it was fortunate that the Viscount had come along when he did. A moment or two later and doubtless he would have seen her talking to the fellow and that would certainly have given rise to awkward questions.

Emily was aware that her brother and her erstwhile betrothed still shunned one another. Whereas Nicholas might show *her* a little sympathy and kindness, Tarquin would receive no such consideration. If her brother was again in bad trouble, she was certain that Nicholas would revel in knowing it.

Viscount Devlin shot a thoughtful look at Mickey Riley, for he knew the identity of the fellow, and how he made a living. In the past he had made use of his services for he had under his wing some extraordinarily pretty young women. Nicholas also knew that where Riley went, trouble usually followed. But he didn't fear him; in fact, he knew that Riley was cunning enough to keep a respectful distance between himself and his superiors. A smile twitched Nicholas's lips as he noticed that his steady regard was making Riley nervous. A moment later the man swaggered off along the street.

Emily watched the fellow departing too, realising quite miserably that her efforts to get here on time had been squandered. Her rendezvous was to come to nothing. She also realised, with a start of alarm, that Nicholas's expression had turned shrewd. She guessed that he was about to interrogate her properly as to her reasons for being here, unaccompanied, on Whiting Street.

Quickly Emily shifted her gaze to an imposing pillared doorway some yards to her right. She could just decipher what was written on a bright brass plaque: Woodgate and Wilson, Attorneys at Law. The door was ajar and a sombre hallway could be spotted within.

'I must be going or I shall be late for my appointment.' She gave Nicholas a brief nod.

'You have a meeting to keep?'

'Yes…with Mr Woodgate. It is a private matter. Good day to you, sir.'

Emily turned and, with her skirts clutched in her quivering fists, confidently went up the steps and through the door that led, she imagined, to the offices of Mr Woodgate and Mr Wilson. What she would say to either of those gentlemen when they begged leave to know why she was trespassing, she had yet to decide. But at least she had put some distance between herself and the very disturbing presence of Viscount Devlin.

Nicholas watched Emily disappear, a smile thinning his lips. Mickey Riley had been interested in Emily Beaumont and she had been aware of him,

Nicholas was sure of it. In addition, Emily had been lying about having an appointment with Mr Woodgate. The practice dealt almost exclusively in marine law and insurance; besides, unless the lawyer had been disinterred for the occasion, she would not find Woodgate within that building. The man had been dead for some few months now. With a look of intense concentration drawing together his brows, the Viscount strolled back to his carriage and got in.

Sinking back into the hide squabs, he wondered what the devil was going on and decided his curiosity had been roused enough for him to make some investigations and try to find out.

Emily crept the musty corridor and ducked back from a doorway on glimpsing a young clerk scribbling in a ledger. His bony profile was just visible behind a pile of papers balanced on the edge of a desk. He must have caught her shadow, for he peered sideways into the corridor before resuming writing.

Emily loitered quietly in the hallway, her mind working furiously. If she were challenged, she would simply say that she had got lost and entered the wrong building. She would only need to tarry a short while for, once the Viscount had gone, she would make her escape. Inwardly she cursed. She had learned nothing today other than that the fellow with the broken nose, who had been loitering outside their house and making enquiries about Tarquin, *was* the sender of the note. He obviously had not liked being under scrutiny and had scampered off when it became clear that she and the Viscount had spotted him. Emily paced back and forth, wondering if she might manage to apprehend him and discover what on earth was going on. She silently went towards the door. If the coast were clear, she *would* try to catch up with the rogue.

'Miss Beaumont…what are you doing?'

Chapter Four

'I'm avoiding someone, sir.'

Despite the bizarre situation in which she found herself, Emily had spoken with admirably firm clarity. The only hint of her discomposure was in her unblinking, wide-eyed stare that clung to Mark Hunter's saturnine features.

He propped a negligent elbow on the wall as though prepared to wait for her to enlighten him further.

Emily slipped into a momentary daze that locked further explanation in her throat. His expression betrayed that he imagined she was stubbornly reticent, not tongue-tied. Obliquely she realised he must have emerged from one of the corridors that led off the main hallway. Mark Hunter obviously was a bona fide client of Messrs Woodgate and Wilson and had every right to be here to conduct his business.

'Avoiding someone?' Mark prompted easily, as though the incongruity of conversing with her in a musty office in the City rather than in an elegant drawing room in Mayfair had not occurred to him.

'Yes,' Emily breathed. 'The door was open and I just quickly darted in as I didn't want to speak to him any more.'

'If he's making a nuisance of himself, I'm sure I can persuade him to desist.' Mark had spoken quietly yet Emily sensed in him an alarming purposefulness. He came closer as though he would pass her and go to confront the fellow in the street.

'No! Thank you for your concern, but it is not that at all…' The thought that Viscount Devlin might be still loitering outside and faced being accused of bothering her made Emily's stomach churn queasily. As Mark drew level with her she grabbed hold of one of his arms to physically prevent him going out and causing a disturbance.

Barely had her small fingers curved over hard muscle when a *frisson* of something akin to excitement jolted through her. Suddenly she was very aware of how small and fragile she felt with Mark Hunter's tall, powerful frame looming over her. The corridor was narrow and shadowy and a musky sandalwood scent seemed to emanate from the warmth of his body.

Nicholas Devlin was a well-built man, but he had nothing like the height and breadth of Mark Hunter. Nicholas had different colouring too, being fair, not devilishly dark as was this gentleman. Emily's eyes levelled on a powerful shoulder clad in excellent grey superfine before slowly raising to a lean, angular face. Her breath caught in her throat as his gaze became sleepy and settled on her parted mouth.

Mark felt blood thicken his veins. He had an almost undeniable urge to trap her against the wall and kiss her senseless. She was the most unbelievably desirable little minx, even garbed in a voluminous cloak that disguised all her sweet curves. The distinctly wary look she was giving him did nothing to subdue the throb in his loins. Miss Emily Beaumont might not like him, but he feared he might like her… a little too much…

A dry cough shattered the tension and made Emily snatch her hand from Mark's sleeve and spring back from him like a scalded cat.

'Is everything in order, Mr Hunter?' The voice was nasal and insinuating.

Emily darted a sideways look at the gentleman

who was peering over the rim of his spectacles at them. He was of middle years and was wearing sombre clothes and a grim expression. His lids descended low over eyes brimming with disgust directed at Emily.

'I assure you this lady is not a client of mine, Mr Hunter. I'll send for a runner and have her immediately ejected if she is troubling you...'

'She is not,' Mark enunciated very coolly, very quietly. 'She is a friend and I am taking her home.'

Emily felt blood flood her face. The lawyer—for she guessed that was who he was—thought she was... Shock and outrage vied for precedence. The infernal cheek of the man! It was true she was not supposed to be here. It was also true he had come upon them when she had hold of Mark Hunter and their bodies had been pressed close together in a gloomy corridor, but... Emily's fury started to fade. The bald facts, so examined, did hint that a dalliance might have been taking place. That thought caused a fresh surge of colour to brighten her pale cheeks.

Mr Wilson now looked no less embarrassed than did Emily. He shuffled on the spot and mumbled an incoherent apology while pulling and pushing his spectacles back and forth on his hooked nose. Suddenly he slipped back out of sight through a doorway. He had made his escape at the right time; Emily's indignation had rekindled and she had been considering dodging past Mark so that she might go and remonstrate with the pious busybody.

As though sensing belligerence was keeping her small frame tight as a spring, Mark turned her firmly about and, taking her by the elbow, propelled her back out into the sunlight and down the steps. He glanced up and down the street. There was nobody loitering in the vicinity.

'Your troublesome fellow seems to have gone. Who was it?' he asked easily. 'An acquaintance…a stranger?' He raised a hand to signal and an impressively smart curricle drew to a stop at the kerb. The tiger nimbly disembarked and held the reins for his master, awaiting instruction to take his position at the rear of the vehicle.

Emily quickly took a step away from him, her mind in turmoil. She had set out this morning with just her brother creating havoc in her thoughts. Now two other gentlemen were also disturbing her peace of mind, and for the same reason: this afternoon both had wanted to kiss her, she was sure of it.

A short while ago Viscount Devlin had made no secret of the fact that he found her attractive: he had openly told her so. Nothing that could be construed as flattery had passed Mark Hunter's lips, yet she knew that just moments ago he also had looked at her with lust in his eyes. The lawyer would have been more justified in directing his scruples at his client than at her! Heavens above! She didn't even like Mark Hunter, let alone want him to kiss her… Emily frowned at her shoes; an odd fluttery feeling had revived in her as she recalled the sensation of their bodies touching in the corridor.

Mark watched flitting emotions animating Emily's sweet features. He guessed that the lawyer's assumption that she had been a soliciting harlot still disturbed her. She had every right to her indignation. The man had made a crass remark and deserved a reprimand.

'Mr Wilson is a cynic and a fool to have supposed a lady of your beauty and stature might be up to no good. All I can say in his defence is that the poor light must have prevented him getting a proper look at you.' Mark paused, aware that mentioning the incident had caused her fiery embarrassment. Gently he added, 'I will admit he is a fellow not much acquainted with charitable thoughts. But he is an excellent lawyer. Do you want me to fetch him so he might properly apologise?'

Emily looked up into eyes that were warm and rueful. 'You would do that?'

'Of course,' Mark said and stepped away from her. He came close again. 'But only if you promise to wait here until I return so I might take you home.'

The idea of again being trapped in close confinement with Mark Hunter, this time in his vehicle, made Emily blurt, 'Thank you for the kind offer, sir, but there is no need for you to trouble yourself. I can hail a cab.'

Mark casually repositioned himself and in doing so blocked Emily's retreat. She halted abruptly to avoid bumping into him.

'I hope you are not going to make of me a liar, Miss Beaumont.' Mark's tone was mock-grave. 'Mr Wilson is even now spying on us to see if we *are* friends and I *do* take you home.'

Emily glanced quickly at the building and immediately noticed a blind dropping back into place at a square-paned window. Renewed mortification sent heat fizzing beneath her cheeks. 'Insufferable man,' she muttered.

'I take it that was directed at Mr Wilson, not at me,' Mark drily remarked.

Emily looked up at him through a web of lashes and reluctantly returned him a small smile.

'Shall I reprimand him before we leave?'

Emily shook her head, setting her blonde tresses

dancing beneath her bonnet. 'No; it was not entirely his fault that he mistook the situation. What he saw must have looked…odd…' She bit her lip and frowned across the street.

Mark held out a hand to her and she permitted him to help her aboard his curricle. 'Genteel young ladies are not often seen alone in these parts. They come usually with their male relations if they have business to conduct.'

That seemed to Emily to be a purposeful observation. She guessed he might next enquire what her business had been coming here in the first place. Keen to continue an easy dialogue, she quickly said, 'I expect Mr Woodgate is nicer than Mr Wilson. It *was* Mr Wilson who appeared, was it not?'

'Indeed it was.' Mark set the beautiful greys in motion and drew smoothly into the flow of traffic in the street. 'Mr Woodgate was a very decent chap. Mr Wilson was a better fellow too before his partner died. I think he now finds it all too much to deal with alone.'

'Died?' Emily echoed, aghast.

'Mr Woodgate died suddenly of a heart attack some months ago now.'

Emily inwardly cursed that she'd made a mistake. Obviously Nicholas Devlin would have known that

Woodgate was dead. It piqued Emily that her erst-while fiancé knew she had lied about an appoint-ment simply to dodge into the building and get away from him.

'Are you not going to tell me who you were hid-ing from? Is his identity a secret?'

It seemed Mark Hunter's thoughts were in tune with hers so Emily sought a brief explanation. 'He is just an acquaintance; a gentleman I have not seen or spoken to for some while.' To prevent a further interrogation she continued, 'I have to purchase a birthday present for my mother. Would you be good enough to set me down in Regent's Street? I should like to go to Madame Joubert's.'

Mention of the *modiste* brought to mind the last time they had met. On that occasion Sarah had been with her when Mark and his mistress had chanced upon them window-shopping. Mark had volun-teered to try to discover Tarquin's whereabouts while Sarah and Barbara Emerson had looked at the silks. Quizzing Mark now over her brother might yield some information about Tarquin and have the added benefit of distracting him from questioning her further about Nicholas. Emily frowned at her hands for, in truth, she had no idea why she did not want Mark Hunter to know she had been avoiding the man who had come within a hair's breadth of being her husband.

'We have still not had word from Tarquin. Have you discovered anything that might shed light on what he is up to?' Emily's eyes shadowed as she recalled her parents' anxiety over the lengthy silence from their eldest son. 'My father is now quite concerned about him. Tarquin usually contacts him if he has problems, and we are sure he has. His landlady has not seen him for weeks and he appears to have left without paying his rent.'

Mark reined in the greys and glanced at Emily's profile. She was chewing at her soft lower lip and slender fingers were intertwining nervously in her lap. Suddenly she turned and shot up at him a look of pure entreaty.

Mark felt the tightening in his gut that was not solely a lustful reaction to her sweet appeal. Emily Beaumont was getting under his skin in a way that disturbed him. In the hallway of the lawyer's office he had been on the point of kissing her when they were interrupted. In truth, he was sorely tempted to divert to a quiet spot and do it now…but equally he wanted to find Tarquin and bawl him out for putting her through such torment. Mark's jaw tightened as a liquid silver gaze clung to him. He snapped his eyes to the road ahead.

He had an idea where Tarquin might be hiding out, and he had discovered a bit about what the miscreant had recently been up to before he dropped from sight. It was not the sort of thing that could be recounted to the man's unmarried sister.

Mark's brother had volunteered some information when asked whether he had seen Tarquin recently. Sir Jason Hunter and his wife, Helen, had been returning from a performance in Drury Lane when they had spotted Tarquin drunkenly consorting with low life in a dark alleyway. Jason had drolly recounted how a particularly comely harlot had seemed to have a tenacious grip on his affections.

A grim smile twitched Mark's lips. Perhaps Tarquin had taken seriously the sarcastic advice he had given him some months ago and was sampling a variety of vices instead of expending all his resources solely on gambling.

Emily's soulful eyes were still on him and she was waiting patiently for his answer. Carefully he told her the bare bones of what he knew. 'My brother and sister-in-law saw Tarquin about two weeks ago. I promise I will continue to investigate.'

'Where was that? Where did they see him?' Emily demanded to know. Mentally she made a note to call on Lady Hunter. Helen and she had been friends since before Helen's marriage to Sir Jason Hunter.

'They spotted him in the Covent Garden area when they were returning from the opera.'

'Was he at the theatre too?' Emily asked quickly. 'Who was he with? We might be able to extract more information from his companions,' she said excitedly.

'He wasn't in the theatre and his companions, from their description, will be hard to find. Jason only caught a glimpse of him from his carriage when journeying home. I promise I will find your brother,' Mark said huskily as he drew the curricle to a halt outside Madame Joubert's.

Emily held Mark's gaze and in her mind whirled conflicting thoughts. Part of her was tempted to divulge to Mark that she had a little information on her brother too. Should she tell him that she had received a letter summoning her to Whiting Street? Mark might recognise the description of the fellow with the broken nose and be able to shed some light on his identity, and how he might be connected to Tarquin. But Emily's natural caution with this man kept the words hovering on her tongue tip.

Mark Hunter had once had her brother sent to gaol over a paltry debt of a hundred pounds. They were friends again, but how dedicated was Mark

Hunter to helping Tarquin? Emily didn't really trust him or his loyalty to her brother.

Earlier she had reflected on the differences between Mark Hunter and Nicholas Devlin, but they had at least one thing in common: both had a keener interest in her than in her brother. And it was an interest she had no intention of encouraging. Both gentlemen were spoken for; yet today she had had first-hand knowledge of how fickle-hearted they were as husbands and lovers. With just a little encouragement—and a little privacy—she could have been kissed by either of them. The fact that they both were firmly attached elsewhere, yet would like to engage in a little dalliance with her made Emily seethe with indignation. Perhaps they imagined that, as she had reached an age when it was considered she might be left on the shelf, she would be grateful for their lecherous attention.

'I'll wait for you to make your purchases and take you home.'

Emily allowed the young tiger to help her dismount. Yes, indeed, Mark Hunter was definitely showing her a little more consideration than was due to the sister of one of his friends. He was angling, she was sure, to seduce her, and doubtless he thought his good looks and affluence would make her fall into his arms. Perhaps he imagined that she was so desperate for his help in finding Tarquin that she might act like a gullible fool. But she had acted so once before, with Nicholas, and had vowed never to do so again.

The Hunter brothers had long been known as rakish characters. Jason had reformed when he married Helen Marlowe and was now a devoted husband. Acidly Emily wondered whether Mark would similarly change when Mrs Emerson finally got him to the altar.

Subduing a sour smile, she swung about to look up at him from the pavement. He returned her gaze with a steady intensity that confirmed her suspicions. He wanted her.

'Thank you for the ride, sir,' Emily began lightly, 'and for the offer to wait, but I have other things to do besides shopping.' Before entering the *modiste*'s, she hesitated, beset by an urge to turn her head and see if he was still watching her.

Slowly she pivoted around and noticed that the curricle was quite still and so was he. Their eyes tangled for a moment, then Emily looked away. Her mind foraged for something to say to explain away her reason for stopping to stare at him. 'Of course, if you learn any more about Tarquin's dealings, then, good or bad, we would welcome news of him.' Without waiting for his reply, she quickly whisked about and entered the shop.

Chapter Five

'What did she say?'

Jenny Trent's excited query drew nothing but a dark scowl from Mickey Riley. A sulky shrug slipped her hand from his shoulder and he slumped down on to a threadbare sofa. A stove was burning in the cramped back parlour they rented, but washing draped over a chair was blocking its meagre heat. Belligerently Mickey kicked away the obstruction and it overturned scattering the clothes onto grimy floorboards.

'This place is a dump. Don't you ever clean up, woman?'

Jenny slid a wary glance at Mickey as she put the chair back on its rickety legs. She picked up her stockings and petticoats, giving them a shake, before neatly arranging them on the slats again so they might dry.

'She won't fall fer it, will she?' she said as she hung the last scrap of linen on black oak.

'Dunno yet,' Riley snapped.

Jenny eyed Mickey's surly features, then perched on a stool opposite him. 'She didn't turn up,' she muttered scornfully. 'I told you it would be a waste of time.'

Mickey Riley surged to his feet, fists balled at his side. 'I did right, I tell you,' he bawled. 'She was there, and on time, but an accursed nob went up to her. Then he saw me, and looked a bit curious, so I didn't hang around. I know him. You do too. It was Devlin and I ain't getting on his wrong side.'

'Devlin?' Jenny echoed, startled. Oh, she knew *him* and hated it when she caught his attention and he chose to spend cash on her. That fine and dandy appearance of his hid a nasty rough streak. 'Do you think Tarquin's sister told Devlin about the letter you sent?'

Mickey shook his head. 'When he clocked me I walked off, but not far. I watched them from an alley. They was only together a few minutes. Looked to me like she was keen to dodge him 'n' all. She nipped in Wilson's office and Devlin went off in his carriage.'

'Did you wait for her to come out?'

Mickey nodded and grunted a laugh. 'Waste of time it were, too. When she came out of Wilson's she was with another fellow. It were the same swell she was talking to by the posh French shop. She must've liked him good 'nuff—she went off with him in his flash rig. And that were the end of me chances.'

Jenny chewed her lower lip pensively. For a few moments the tiny room was quiet except for the sound of her tapping her small booted feet in rhythm against the dirty bare boards. 'You gonna try fer another chance to meet her?' she suddenly piped up.

Mickey's curt nod answered her.

'Won't do no good.' Her derision was emphasised by an impatient hand flick. 'We ain't never gonna find Tarquin like this. We should forget him and find another punter.'

A string of curses from Mickey met that suggestion.

Jenny more volubly repeated her idea.

'Hold your tongue, woman,' he roared. 'Can't you see I'm thinking?'

'Penny for your thoughts…'

Mark surfaced from his sightless contemplation of the ceiling as his naked mistress leaned over him and kissed him on the lips. A corner of his mouth tilted in appreciation, but his hands remained pillowing his head, his blue eyes watching the spectral shadows above him.

'What are you thinking about?' Barbara asked huskily, stretching out sinuously on the feather mattress beside him. She slid a finger softly over the muscled ridges on his torso, then let it drift lower. Her tone had hinted at pique, but she was canny enough not to vent it. For some weeks now she had sensed that her hold on this charismatic bachelor was weakening. She didn't want that; she wanted his ring on her finger and her belly swelling with his child. After many years together as friends and lovers she wanted a promotion in Mark Hunter's life.

They were of similar age and a decade ago had been planning to marry, although no formal arrangements were made. Then Mark had taken himself off on a Grand Tour despite Barbara's protestations. Barbara had been desolate to discover that he was not after all crooked as tightly about her finger as she would have liked. It was shortly after Mark sailed for France that she, while still in a temper, accepted a proposal from someone much older and far richer. She had long regretted resorting to such tactics to punish Mark for abandoning her.

On his return to England, Mark had seemed insultingly philosophical over his loss. Barbara had been wounded to the core by his attitude—simply imagining his foreign *amours* made her jealous. But they had again become lovers when her husband died.

Not so long ago she could inflame him with a touch, a kiss, into passionate hour-long lovemaking. Now she had to work at wooing him. Her fingers fanned on his firm flesh in strong, sensual massage and she leaned close, seductively swaying her breasts against his chest.

Absently Mark tasted her eager lips and a hand cupped behind her raven head. He allowed her to arouse him, quite selfishly, for some minutes while the haunting image of blonde hair and silver-blue eyes danced erotically behind his lids. With a low curse he banished the tantalising images of Miss Beaumont and, turning swiftly, paid attention to the woman he was with.

Mark Hunter was not the only gentleman behaving with a distinct lack of gallantry because Emily had captivated his mind.

Barely ten minutes after arriving in his wife's bedchamber, Viscount Devlin shrugged into his silk dressing gown and strolled out again. If he was aware of the Viscountess's glittering eyes watching him, he gave no sign that her frustration and sadness bothered him.

He had married her five months ago and got her with child almost immediately. He had also just claimed his conjugal rights but was, as usual, left unsatisfied. Instead of heading towards the four-poster in his chamber, he strolled to the large window that overlooked Cleveland Street. Nicholas gazed into the night sky and brooded on the woman he knew certainly could extinguish the fire in his loins.

It was not that he wished he had married Emily Beaumont. He had a wife who was infinitely more suited to the role. Frances was attractive, placid and amenable. Most importantly, she had brought with her an enormous dowry and impressive family connections.

Emily had none of those material advantages. But she was beautiful and, as he had discovered to his delight, passionately responsive. In Nicholas's opinion, Emily Beaumont, but for an accident of gentle birth, would have made a most exquisite courtesan. She had a natural vivacity tempered with shyness; she had the body of a sensual goddess but was engagingly innocent. When he had met her at Almack's, she had been an entrancing mix of child and woman and he had wanted her—desperately. Thus the urge to propose to her had come from his loins, not his heart, and virtually as soon as it was done he had been cursing himself for an impetuous fool.

From the start he had known that she would not allow herself to be seduced by a man who did not love her or want to marry her. So he had told her what he knew she longed to hear and mercilessly fostered her devotion to him. With her father, he had spoken of honour and security and sounded noble and sincere.

But he was cursed with the Devlin trait of profligacy, as had been his father before him. As his spending continued apace and his bank balance sank to an alarming level, he had wondered constantly how he might extricate himself to hunt a fortune without bringing opprobrium down on his head.

Fortuitously Tarquin Beaumont had saved him the bother of pondering long on devious tactics. He had not forgiven Tarquin for that beating, but their enmity had served a very useful purpose and set him free to stalk an heiress. And now, with his wife increasingly fat and boring, possessing Emily again was becoming an obsession.

When he had told Emily this afternoon that he had been thinking of her, he had spoken the truth. For months past she had constantly been in his mind. He rarely saw her, for socially they moved in different circles. The opportunity to meet her alone had seemed just yesterday a hopeless ambition. But today it had come about. She might act coolly towards him, but he could tell she was not indifferent. Emily was older, more worldly-wise and, with a little subtlety, he was confident he could seduce her again.

Now that his wife had brought him such riches, he didn't see why he should not slake his lust with a woman of refinement rather than Mickey Riley's sluts. He had the wherewithal to set up a mistress in style in a fashionable part of town. And he knew exactly whom he wanted to visit. All he had to do was get Emily to accept his proposition…

Nicholas smiled at the twinkling stars; perhaps discovering why Emily had been acting so deviously in Whiting Street, with Mickey Riley watching her, might help bring it all about.

'Emily!' Helen Hunter rose from the chair and rushed to greet her visitor. 'How good to see you. My! You're an early bird!'

Emily embraced her friend and accepted the offer to be seated in Lady Hunter's elegantly furnished rose salon. With a little grimace she said, 'I know it's quite unfashionable to be out of doors at this hour, but I have something pressing I need to ask you.'

Helen scooped up from her seat the journal she had moments before been reading and dropped it to the carpet. She sat down and gave her friend an enquiring smile. 'Well, now, I'm intrigued as well as pleased by your visit. Please ask away without delay.'

Emily bit her lip, then blurted, 'I saw your brother-in-law yesterday and I wanted to quiz you over something he said.'

Helen settled back into her armchair with a wry expression. She knew very well that Emily did not like Mark, and why that was. She also knew from her husband, Jason, that Mark's motives for having Emily's brother imprisoned had been altruistic rather than spiteful. 'Has Mark said something to upset you?' It was doubtfully suggested—Helen knew that her brother-in-law went out of his way to be pleasant with Emily. In fact, she had a strong suspicion that Mark liked Emily and was quite hurt that she felt so differently towards him.

'No, he has not upset me…not intentionally, in any case. Mark told me something about Tarquin. Well, in truth, I rather prised the information from him.'

Helen chuckled. 'Would you care to start again?'

Emily gestured apology for the garbled explanation and, with a sigh, removed her bonnet and gloves and settled back to gather her thoughts.

'Let's have some tea,' Helen suggested. 'If we are to get our teeth into something—and I rather think we are—we shall need some refreshment.'

Helen Hunter and Emily were close friends who had over the years confided secrets both good and bad. In fact, just two weeks ago, Emily had been entrusted with the wonderful news, before it was officially out, that Helen suspected she was expecting her first-born. Thus, between sips of tea, Helen had no qualms in directly answering Emily's questions about when last she had seen Tarquin. She told her friend that she had witnessed him embracing a hussy in an alley close to Covent Garden. Helen was then surprised to learn that Tarquin had, afterwards, seemed to have disappeared.

Following that first burst of vital dialogue, the two young ladies sat in pensive silence for a few minutes and finished their tea.

Emily suddenly deposited her cup, in a clatter, on a side table. 'Tell me honestly, Helen…do you think he has been set about? Are you thinking, as I am, that these…these rough people might have robbed Tarquin? Beaten him? They might not have meant to do him real harm but…do you think a terrible accident might have occurred? Oh, where *is* the wretch?'

Helen jumped to her feet and flew to Emily's

chair. 'Hush,' she soothed, crouching down to comfort her friend. 'It is surely not the case. If every gentleman who consorted with a Covent Garden nun was attacked and disappeared, Almack's would be sadly bereft of bachelors on a Wednesday evening.'

Emily managed a chuckle at that wry observation. 'Do you suppose he is simply still on a drunken revel?'

Helen elevated her dark brows. 'If he is, he *will* return with a sore head, beating or no beating.' Helen took Emily's agitated fingers into her own. 'Shall I ask Jason to try to find him?'

Emily vigorously shook her head. 'Mark has already offered to make some investigations. I would not put Sir Jason to the bother of it too.' Suddenly a look of enlightenment lifted her features. 'I wonder if that is why the ruffian with the wonky nose sent me the letter: to tell me he knows Tarquin is unwell and cannot get home. It might not be about a gambling debt at all, but I expect he will, in any case, want some money for his trouble...'

Helen's astonished laugh curtailed Emily's further ramblings. 'I think you must immediately explain some more. Letter? Ruffian with a wonky nose? What *is* going on?'

'That is what *I* should like to know,' Emily returned pithily. But she went on quickly to explain all about her fruitless trip to Whiting Street and that she had had the bad luck to meet both Viscount Devlin and Mark Hunter there.

As Emily would have rushed on, Helen put up a silencing hand. 'Wait a moment. I must know more of this. You have been talking to the man to whom you were engaged? I thought you and Viscount Devlin kept at a distance.'

'We do…or we always have. He approached me in Whiting Street and acted far too friendly for a married man.' Emily arched a dainty eyebrow. 'To escape him I dodged into a building and that's where I bumped into your brother-in-law.' The memory of being pressed against Mark in the dark corridor had spontaneously filled Emily's mind, making her feel rather hot. Briskly she forced herself to concentrate on the mystery of Tarquin's disappearance. 'Mark gave me a ride home and told me you and Jason had spotted Tarquin, but he would not elaborate.'

She understood now why Mark had seemed reticent about identifying Tarquin's companions that evening. It was certainly not considered the done thing for a gentleman to bring to a lady's attention that her brother had been cavorting with loose women, even if the lady in question had just been mistaken for a loose woman herself! She bit at her lip to prevent a wry smile as she wondered what Helen would think on learning she had been mistaken for a harlot.

'Mark must have thought it odd for you to be alone in such an area. Did you tell him you had received a note and had gone there to try to discover Tarquin's whereabouts?'

Emily shook her head. 'I wanted first to find out what the fellow was up to. It would not be the first time Tarquin has created a scandal that we must all try to keep secret.'

'Mark is a trustworthy fellow, you know,' Helen said softly.

Emily put up her chin. There was one thing on which she and Helen tended to be at odds: the worthiness of Mark Hunter. 'He has been horrid to Tarquin in the past.'

'I know you think so…but…oh, let's not debate it now,' Helen said quietly.

Emily's lips twitched in conciliation. 'I would rather you did not tell anyone what we have discussed this morning.'

Helen dipped her head. 'And I will not,' she said huskily. 'Your secrets, as ever, are safe with me. Just as I know mine are with you.'

The two young women exchanged an empathetic smile.

'Brothers!'

'Indeed,' Helen agreed ruefully, for she was no stranger to the selfish behaviour of an older brother. She lifted the teapot, then replaced it. 'I think we need something a little stronger,' she announced and went off to fetch a decanter and two crystal glasses.

Half an hour later, and fortified by a measure of sherry, Emily stepped again into the sunshine in Grosvenor Square. As she walked with the glow of the sun on her head and the sherry a warm coat on her insides, her thoughts again turned to the men troubling her peace of mind. She knew Tarquin ought to dominate her musings, but her memory kept returning to Nicholas Devlin's declaration that he missed her; strangely, she also found herself thinking of the look in Mark Hunter's eyes when they had been pressed close together in the corridor.

With an impatient sigh she increased her pace. The only person who had been likely to shed some light on Tarquin's circumstances was the fellow she'd gone to meet. And how on earth was she to find the rogue now?

She was close to home when she glanced up,

frowning, and through the shimmering atmosphere saw a man coming straight towards her. The fellow was darting furtive looks to the right and left, displaying a crooked nose in profile. Suddenly he darted into an alley between two houses and urgently beckoned to her.

Chapter Six

'**W**ot luck bumping into you, miss.' Mickey's gruff greeting was accompanied by the doffing of his hat. In fact he had been, for some while, loitering about the streets close to Emily's home in the hope of having an opportunity to waylay her.

'What do you have to tell me about my brother?' Emily had briskly recovered from her astonishment at being brought face to face with the ruffian. 'Be assured that you will not collect any winnings from me. I never settle my brother's gambling debts.' She adopted a prim look to impress on him that she was not to be fobbed off with any fantastic yarns designed to make her part with cash. She doubted she would get the whole truth, but was optimistic she might glean a few clues as to what was going on.

Mickey's blue eyes slipped a look left and right and over her shoulder as though to ensure they were private enough. He refused to be rushed into disclosing too much too soon. While he considered tactics he muttered, 'Be more private up there.' He walked away then, with a wag of his head, urging Emily to follow him.

After a moment's hesitation Emily did. It was a narrow gap between the buildings, but an area that was still visible from the main street.

'Ain't about gaming, so don't fret on that. I sent a boy to deliver you a note,' Mickey said as they came to a halt in the alley.

'Yes, I realise it came from you,' Emily retorted sharply. 'I came to Whiting Street and caught sight of you. Why did you leave so suddenly?' She studied his swarthy features. She guessed he was not much older than Tarquin, yet his hair was quite grey and his weatherbeaten skin deeply lined. At close quarters he had an oddly striking, confident appearance. She guessed many people knew him, but she had no idea who he was. 'What is your name and why have you bothered me?'

That enquiry earned her just a crafty squint.

'I put myself to some trouble to meet you in the

City,' Emily pointed out impatiently. 'I hope you are not again wasting my time.'

'I saw Devlin talking to you. I didn't fancy getting tangled with him.'

'You are acquainted with the Viscount?' Emily asked, astonished. She might have thought this fellow of some renown, but had not imagined he might boast an association with a peer of the realm.

Mickey scolded himself for having let that slip. He was canny enough to appreciate that one of his rich and influential clients would not want to acknowledge that he existed.

''Course we ain't acquainted,' Mickey scoffed. 'Just know of him, that's all. And I ain't wasting yer time. Wot I'm about is trying to do you all a favour in case things turn real bad.'

'Has my brother been hurt?' Emily demanded in a whisper. Her mind raced back some years to the time Tarquin had settled a debt at dawn on Wimbledon Common. 'He has duelled before and taken a blade in the shoulder.'

Mickey looked rather startled at knowing that. 'Didn't take him for a fighting fellow.' He shifted his weight. 'Last time I clapped eyes on him he looked right as rain,' he added.

Emily felt a release of tension at knowing it.

''Course if you don't value yer family's reputation, then it's me as is wasting time. I'll be getting off.' Mickey made no move to go and continued slyly peering at Emily from beneath wiry brows.

'Value my family's reputation?' Emily echoed. A ball of lead had settled in her stomach. She had always suspected that eventually something unpleasant would be revealed.

'If you know where Tarquin is you'd be best off telling me,' Mickey urged. 'Then I can warn him 'cos it's sure to leak out if he don't pay up.'

Emily was taken aback as much by the news as by the familiar address he used. Tarquin would surely not class this fellow a friend. 'I do not know where my brother is presently,' Emily said coolly. 'The only reason I came to meet you yesterday was to discover his whereabouts from you.' Disappointment sent a surge of water to her eyes. Angrily Emily dashed it away unwilling to let the rogue see her distress. 'What might leak out? You said this was not about money.'

'Didn't say it weren't about money…said it weren't about gaming.' Mickey Riley's expression had hardened and his voice was little more than a sibilant hiss.

His change in attitude made Emily warily put

distance between them. 'Quickly explain, for I have tarried here with you long enough.'

Mickey shifted sideways to prevent her slipping past him on the path. With a sinister calm he said, 'If you know where he is you'd best let on or I'll have to come knockin' on yer father's door. Poor lass has got nowhere to go, y'see...' Suddenly he interrupted himself with a low curse and shot a frown over Emily's shoulder. With almost comic clumsiness he backed away a yard or two in a few seconds. 'Best finish this another time,' he muttered, then set off briskly up the alley.

Emily spun about to see what had made the fellow abruptly turn tail. She immediately recognised the imposing dark-haired gentleman who was standing by a smart landau. At their ease, and seated in the landau, were her friend, Helen, and her husband, Sir Jason Hunter. The couple were carrying on a laughing conversation with Mark Hunter, who had splayed a hand idly on the glossy coachwork.

Mark was no longer chatting to his brother and sister-in-law, although his smiling expression remained unchanged, and the couple were in no way alerted to the fact that his attention was actually at a distance.

Abruptly Mark gave the landau a final tap and stepped away from it. Emily watched Helen wave at him as the vehicle moved smoothly away heading west.

She had no doubt that Mark had watched her talking to the ruffian, and seen the fellow slope away. She had no doubt too that Mark was about to approach her and ask some awkward questions. He stood sentinel at the mouth of the narrow alley for a moment, trapping her, before strolling very purposefully towards her.

'Miss Beaumont…'

'Mr Hunter…'

The hint of challenge in her tone pulled his mouth wryly aslant.

'Were you again tolerating the company of your troublesome fellow?'

Emily knew immediately to whom he referred, although, of course, Mark was still unaware that Viscount Devlin was the man who had forced her to seek sanctuary in Mr Wilson's office. 'Umm…no… it was not him I was avoiding on Whiting Street.'

'Ah,' Mark said. 'I thought perhaps it might not be him. Of the two of you Riley seemed the more eager to get away just now.'

'Riley?' Emily echoed, testing the name. 'You

know him?' She unconsciously stepped close to Mark to hurry his reply.

'I take it that he did not introduce himself. He must improve his manners.'

Emily coloured faintly at his ironic tone.

'His name is Mickey Riley and I am intrigued to know why you were talking to him.'

While awaiting her answer, and expecting it in any case to be evasive, Mark pondered on the time Mickey Riley and his lady friend had seemed to be watching Emily outside the *modiste*'s shop. He had wondered then if Riley would have the audacity to approach Emily over an unpaid debt of Tarquin's. In his wisdom, he had deduced that Tarquin owed money to Riley over that cockfight. Now his suspicions were straying elsewhere.

He had heard that Mickey Riley procured for a slightly better class of petticoat than the usual drabs who congregated about Covent Garden. Mark, having learned from his brother that Tarquin had last been spotted with a comely harlot in that area, thought it likely that Riley was chasing Tarquin's payment for another vice. In fact, Mark was fearful Mickey Riley was bothering Emily in his role as pimp, not bookie. Tarquin might be ignorant of the fact that his sister was being dragged into his sordid world, but nevertheless it seemed to be the case.

'Why were you talking to him?' Mark's voice was harsh with suppressed anger. Had Tarquin been within reach he would have throttled him. 'Was Riley asking you for money?'

Emily immediately bridled at such a curt interrogation. 'I do not see, sir, that our private conversation is any of your business.' She tipped her blonde head to a confident angle and made to pass him, but a hand shot to the redbrick wall, blocking her path.

'Tell me what he wanted.'

Emily curled five fingers over the solid arm beneath his sleeve. The muscle tightened very little in response to her fierce attempt to move him. Unwilling to participate longer in an undignified tussle, she snatched back her hand and stepped away from him. 'I repeat, sir, that my conversation with Mr Riley is none of your business. And your arrogance in demanding to know of it is breathtaking.'

'Your naïveté is breathtaking, Miss Beaumont, if you expect to deal with Riley alone. Besides, you made all of this my business when you solicited my help in finding Tarquin. A moment ago you did not even know Mickey Riley's name. I would hazard a guess you certainly know nothing about his character or what he does.'

Emily slanted him a mutinous look. Reluctantly she allowed that what he had said was correct. Mark obviously knew that a link existed between Riley and Tarquin and to deny it would be pointless. She had to admit, too, that Tarquin's lengthy absence was becoming a sinister mystery and she felt unequal to solving it alone. She had thus far been allowing her natural antipathy towards Mark to get the better of her. His arrogance needled her, and she certainly did not trust him, but he was rich and powerful and he was Tarquin's friend. She needed just such a gentleman's support for she was sure that Riley would soon return. Without money or physical strength to oil his tongue, she would get nothing from him but more riddles and garbled threats.

She could reveal all to her father, but she was quite sure now that no mild explanation was to be had for her brother's disappearance. When they had been dining with Stephen and his grandmother earlier in the week, her father's melancholy had concerned her. His strained features haunted her mind again now. He was worried for both his sons, not just his firstborn. Emily understood why her parents had encouraged Tarquin to move out of the family home and into his own apartment. They wanted to put distance between Robert and his older brother's excesses in case Robert might follow the example of the brother he idolised.

Conscious she had been some minutes lost in introspection, Emily shot a glance up at Mark. She forged a small smile; it elicited a cynical look.

Mark was not for a moment fooled by her *faux* cordiality and a grimace of impatience impressed on her that he still required an answer to his question.

In a snap she explained, 'Mr Riley sent me a message to meet him in Whiting Street. The note hinted I would get news of Tarquin.' A terse hand flick ridiculed the likelihood. 'It transpires he doesn't know where my brother is. In fact, he expects *me* to disclose to *him* Tarquin's whereabouts.' A glance from beneath her lashes revealed Mark's expression to be unyieldingly stern. 'A moment ago I told Riley I don't know where my brother is, but I'm not sure he believes me.'

'Did you not tell him all that yesterday?'

Emily shook her head. 'I didn't manage to speak to him because…' She hesitated and frowned.

'Because a troublesome fellow scared him off.'

'Yes,' Emily muttered.

'And who was that?' Mark drawled, but his easy tone held an edge of steel.

Emily turned her head, ignoring his probing. 'I have bowed to your bullying and explained about my conversation with Mickey Riley. Please do not annoy me by being too impertinent.'

Emily watched as he leisurely strolled closer. He halted inches away, so close that his broad shoulders completely blocked her view of the road. Slowly he withdrew a hand from where it was lodged in his pocket. Long lean fingers trapped her chin, turned her to look at him.

'I am trying very hard, Miss Beaumont, not to wash my hands of all of this and leave you to your own devices.'

Emily gazed up into eyes of peacock blue and felt her stomach lurch at the threat she read there. Again she bit back defiant words and impressed on herself that this man would have better luck than would she in unearthing Tarquin. His ruggedly handsome face was very close to hers; she blinked as she noticed his long lashes drooping lazily to conceal that he was watching her mouth.

'But you will not abandon me, will you, sir?' The challenge was issued in a voice of silky insolence, and immediately Emily regretted what she had done.

'Will I not?' Mark asked with specious softness. 'And what makes you so sure of that?'

Emily attempted to jerk her face free, but his grip tightened just enough to keep her still.

Very well, if he wanted to know, she would tell him that she knew no noble reason existed for his unexpected helpfulness! But several silent moments later Emily was still finding it difficult to reveal her conceit and accuse him of lusting after her. The more she tried to concentrate on whipping up righteous indignation, and the courage to slander him, the more intensely conscious she was of his touch scorching her jaw.

'Why will I not abandon you?' Mark demanded with veiled amusement. He propped an elbow on the wall and leaned closer. After a moment he felt a surge of tenderness soften his mockery, for her embarrassment was causing her complexion to glow rosily. 'Come, say it. I promise I won't object if you tell me that I'm a fool too susceptible to your beauty and too tolerant of your acid tongue. It's the truth after all.' His fingers extended, caressing a fiery cheek before he abruptly dropped the hand to his side. But he didn't move away and mere inches separated their bodies.

Emily snatched a peek at eyes blackened with desire. *Don't annoy him, you need his assistance,* was the thought racing in her mind. But despite his undeniable usefulness, what really kept her so still and quiet was a longing to again have his cool fingers curving soothingly on her hot cheek. She craved to know how it would feel to have Mark Hunter kiss her.

The yearning was undeniable and, of its own volition, her body seemed to sway forward, her face tilt to tempt a mouth that looked firm and warm...

Mark dipped his head the few inches required to skim together their lips. When she didn't immediately skitter away from that gentle salute, he took immediate advantage. His palms slid to cradle her jaw's sharp fragility and keep her close.

Emily sensed the pressure of his mouth increasing, coaxing her to part her lips while the long fingers, circling softly on her cheeks, continued to skilfully subdue any sensible thought she had of objecting to the liberties he was taking. She yielded to his wooing and her full lips parted to allow his tongue to languidly taste hers. In a daze she rested her weight against him, revelling in the icy fire that was coursing through her limbs. A slow hand travelled to her nape to smooth sensitive places and a delicious shiver passed over Emily, making her sigh against his mouth.

Mark drew her further into his embrace, greatly

aroused by her unexpectedly eager response. His mouth plundered hers sweetly, defying her to protest as his hands slipped beneath her coat to caress her body.

A shock shivered through Emily as his thumbs brushed firmly over her rib cage to stroke the two tender nubs peaking beneath her bodice. Her back was beginning to arch invitingly when suddenly she tensed and her eyes flew wide. A hawker's raucous shout reached her from the street and made her once more alert to where she was…and with whom. She jerked back.

Emily twisted her face free, horribly, shamefully aware that she was behaving like a brazen hussy with a man she knew was firmly attached elsewhere…and in broad daylight too!

She snatched herself from Mark's embrace in two shaky backward steps. Her breathing was ragged as she whispered, 'Thank you, Mr Hunter, for proving to me what I had suspected about you all along.'

Mark's eyes narrowed on her flushed face. Her frigid tone and sparking eyes indicated he was to hear nothing complimentary. 'And what do you suspect about me, my dear?' he gritted out. The first exquisite taste of her had ended too soon and he felt cheated and frustrated.

'I suspect, sir, that you will expect me to reward you for any assistance you give in finding Tarquin.'

'Do you? And what exactly am I expecting to receive?'

Emily blushed scarlet. 'You know very well. And I will not talk indelicately for your titillation.'

Mark tilted his head up and his hands gestured at the sky in exasperation. 'God's teeth! It was just a kiss…and not a very satisfying one at that.'

Emily blanched in mortification. Despite being ashamed of acting the wanton, she couldn't deny she had thought their kiss had been thrilling…but not for him, it seemed.

Mark noticed the fleeting hurt that puckered her features. 'It was nice…sweet…but unfinished,' he explained gently. When she simply tilted her chin and flounced away from him he added, 'You're not yet a woman. When you are you'll understand—'

'Oh, I understand very well,' Emily snapped. She pivoted back to face him to add coolly and quietly, 'I am twenty-four years old and you need not patronise me.'

'I'm not patronising you, I'm appreciating your innocence.'

'Please don't,' Emily countered fiercely. 'Your esteem is not appropriate.'

The silence that followed seemed to echo hollowly between the two high walls on either side of them. Emily jerkily swallowed, immediately regretting that her temper had caused her to unwisely hint at something very private. With her skirts clenched in quivering fists, she attempted to slip past him.

Mark refused to stand aside, although he kept his hands firmly in his pockets. 'My esteem is not appropriate?' he repeated softly. 'Now it has been bestowed I think you owe me an explanation for throwing it back in my face. What is incorrect about my good opinion of your innocence?'

Emily nipped her lower lip in small teeth to prevent an outburst. She had no intention of resuming their previous dialogue. In an icy tone she demanded, 'Please let me pass at once. I have been out too long and my parents will be worried for my safety.'

'I understand their fears; you might have been waylaid by a reprobate.'

'Indeed,' Emily countered with acid amusement. 'But rest assured, I will not mention meeting you.'

Mark gave her a sardonic smile. 'And Riley? Will you tell them about him?'

Emily sent him a stare that might have turned a lesser mortal to stone. Mark unflinchingly returned her regard.

'No. Will you tell them?'

'Not if you'd rather I did not.' He adopted an ironic innocence. 'I swear I require nothing for that favour other than you let me immediately escort you home.'

After a moment of inner turmoil Emily finally capitulated and said sourly, 'Why, thank you, sir, I accept your kind offer.'

Once handed into his curricle, she girded herself for a further interrogation. But he said nothing more at all; the journey passed in silence.

When he politely helped her down in Callison Crescent he said, 'I shall increase my efforts to unearth your brother, but for my benefit as much as yours. There are some pressing matters I would discuss with him.' His vivid eyes veered to her tense face. 'In short, Miss Beaumont, when I drag him back I shall require nothing for the service.'

Emily began her muted thanks, but before their conclusion he was back on the seat and setting off again at speed.

Chapter Seven

'I'll tell you what I told the rest, sir. I haven't seen Mr Beaumont for a good while now. And, if you catch up with the slippery devil, you can tell him from me that I want my rent. If I don't soon get it, I'll set the duns to find him.' With that fervent threat Mrs Dale tried to close the door in Viscount Devlin's face. The toe of one of his polished boots was swiftly wedged on the threshold and prevented her doing so.

'The rest?' Nicholas asked and gave the landlady a smile. 'Other people have been here looking for him?'

Mrs Dale allowed him to push the door a little wider open, her eyes slipping over him in sly assessment. He was Quality, no doubt about it, and might pay her for her time and trouble if she answered a few of his questions. He was probably in a similar situation to hers: owed cash by that wastrel and with no idea how to run him to ground. At the beginning she'd thought Mr Beaumont a fine fellow, with his nice clothes and posh voice, and had no hesitation in renting him rooms.

This house on Westbury Avenue was one of the sounder properties Mrs Dale owned and was in a nice part of town, too. Yet, in her bitter experience, the well-heeled taking suites in Chelsea were no better at paying their rent than were the poor souls cramped in an attic in Whitechapel.

'You said other people have been looking for Mr Beaumont,' Viscount Devlin prompted with ill-concealed irritation at her brooding silence.

The landlady crossed her arms over her shrivelled chest and leaned on the doorjamb. A grimace was aimed at the heavens. 'Mr Beaumont senior came looking for him. Oh, and before that there was a fellow looked like a street bruiser with a bent nose and hair as grey as fog. But a young feller, he seemed, for all that. Then there was a gentleman like yourself… Quality, he were, with fine clothes and a handsome face.' Mrs Dale simpered sideways at the Viscount. 'He had dark hair though, not fair like yours, and might have been taller too.'

'Thank you.' After a cursory nod Nicholas was down the steps and by his carriage.

Having taken up a comfortable position for a lengthy chat, Mrs Dale looked disappointed to see him go so soon. With a cluck of the tongue she turned to go back inside. Realising the nob had left without so much as handing over a farthing she swung back to snarl, 'Tightfist', before slamming the door.

Nicholas got into his carriage, whistling. He had got what he wanted and more besides. Mrs Dale's description of the bruiser was detailed enough for him to be sure that it was Riley who had called looking for Tarquin. He had suspected that Mickey Riley was somehow involved in Tarquin's disappearance. The fellow described as Quality was probably an acquaintance from one of the gaming clubs who was keen to call in his IOU quickly. He was not surprised to learn that Mr Beaumont senior had also been looking for his son. The family would, by now, know he'd absconded. Emily would thus be aware…and concerned…that her brother was in trouble.

She had been in Whiting Street at the same time as had Mickey Riley. Both had seemed oddly alert to the other's presence, yet keen to keep it concealed. Only one reason could account for a meeting between them: Tarquin. Emily must have been summoned by Riley to learn what her brother had been up to. And in return, of course, he would expect a payment.

Nicholas settled back into the squabs with a satisfied smile on his lips. He rapped for his driver to set the coach in motion. One of these nights he ought to make use of the services of that pretty little girl of Mickey's…Jenny, he believed was her name. And while he was there he would have a little talk with Riley and discover if there was a way that Tarquin Beaumont's latest misdemeanour—whatever it was—might benefit them both…

'If you'd rather not attend, I shall convey your regrets.'

It was the pained tone of voice rather than the words spoken that penetrated Emily's deep thoughts. A swift glance at Stephen detected that he was pink with embarrassment. She guessed that he had been talking to her and she had, unwittingly, been ignoring him. 'I'm so sorry, Stephen. What did you say?' Emily blinked beneath her mother's rebuking look.

Before Stephen could answer her Penelope did. 'Stephen was just inviting us to Lady Gerrard's soirée. Isn't that wonderful?' She shot a look at her daughter that dared her to disagree. 'The invitation was issued to Stephen's grandmother, who is her friend, but it has been extended to us too.' Their guest received a grateful smile.

Emily's small teeth sank into her lower lip as she tried to quickly summon up an acceptable excuse. In truth, she lately felt little like socialising. She had a vital and difficult task to undertake and that, together with incessant worries over Tarquin, was dampening her humour.

That morning she had received a note from Nicholas Devlin in which he stressed his pleasure at having finally had a chance to talk privately to her. The note had ended with him expressing a *great desire* that they might soon find another such opportunity. Emily had been stunned to receive it, and her first instinct had been to throw it on the fire. She might once have loved him, and been on the point of becoming his wife, but it had all turned to ashes years ago. He had married another woman and Frances was increasing with his child.

The Viscount's letter to her, like his attitude on Whiting Street, was highly irregular to say the least. Emily had a suspicion that it was not a simple friendship that Nicholas was angling for, but a more intimate relationship. But it was finished between them. She was a mature woman now, not a silly girl just out of the schoolroom. She was able to control her senses and her future, and she had no intention of allowing a married man to so much as kiss her.

If she simply ignored his letter, he might be encouraged to send another. She had to let him know immediately, and in strong terms, that pursuing her was a lost cause—he would never again seduce her into wantonness.

Hard on the heels of her virtuous resolve came a very disturbing truth: *Another gentleman had very recently and very easily made her act the wanton and the incident was impossible to put from her mind.*

Emily fidgeted on her seat as phantom pressure from warm hard lips teased her mouth. She spitefully sank her teeth into the tingling skin to stop the sensation.

Tarquin… Viscount Devlin… She could accept that those gentlemen would be bothering her peace of mind, for both had given her due cause. But the most persistent images in her head were of Mark Hunter and what had occurred between them in the alleyway. And she wanted to dismiss that as inconsequential…as he had.

It was simply pique, she told herself. No woman

would like to have a kiss—whether it had been welcome or not—dismissed by a gentleman with such a lack of gallantry. Neither could she be pleased with herself for having hinted she was unchaste. Would he have already forgotten what she said? Or was he mulling it over and deeming her quite capable of being a sullied woman?

This time it was a long and sibilant sigh from her mother that startled her to the present.

'My…you are in a daydream today, Emily.' Penelope chirped a brittle laugh. 'Perhaps another cup of tea might liven you a little and help you concentrate.'

Emily murmured an apology. Indeed, she felt guilty for having again failed to talk to Stephen. He was a fine gentleman and deserved better than being ignored while her mind was preoccupied with the less worthy. 'You must thank your grandmother, Stephen, for thinking of us and securing such an invitation—'

'Well, that's settled then,' Penelope Beaumont interjected swiftly, before Emily could conclude her declination.

'The invitation is also extended to your friend Sarah Harper.' Stephen's muted pleasure at her acceptance spoke volumes. Emily realised he was well aware that she would rather not attend. 'Grandmama mentioned to Fiona Gerrard that you might like a young lady of your own age to accompany you. Not that there won't be other young ladies present, of course. But you might not know any of them well enough to chat to...' he finished lamely.

'If you are to be there, Stephen, I shall have a friend to talk to,' Emily said and gave him a comforting smile. She could not now cry off without causing a fuss and thus graciously accepted her defeat. 'But I'm certain Sarah would be pleased to go too. I shall call on her later and find out for sure.'

When Stephen had gone Penelope surged to her feet and clapped her hands in delight. 'Only think...Fiona Gerrard's soirée! Augusta might be a rum old bird, but she has very influential friends, it seems. I expect she has secured us such a prized invitation to make up for being impolite when she came here to dine.'

'Perhaps.' Emily gave a slight smile. 'A mere few days ago you were hoping Augusta would be on her way back to Bath by now.'

'I know...and I don't mind admitting that I hoped the old harridan might make the journey in a hearse.' Penelope smiled wickedly. 'Now I'm hoping dear Augusta might stay in London all Season. Who knows how many times we might be guests of Lady Gerrard? It might be a very happy time for you.'

Emily slipped her mother a shrewd look from silver eyes. 'In what way are you hoping I might benefit, Mama?'

'I think you know quite well, young lady.' But Penelope went on to explain, 'Lady Gerrard is known to have a host of eligible bachelors in her circle. We must make sure you look your very best— you might catch the eye of one of them.'

'And what of Stephen?' Emily asked wryly. 'Is he now to be discouraged?'

'Not at all!' Penelope gasped. 'We need a nice gentleman in reserve. By Michaelmas you *must* be spoken for. You cannot sit another year on the shelf. Oh…here's your father home at last.' Penelope rushed into the hallway to recount to him her exciting news.

Having listened with furrowed brow to his wife, Mr Beaumont nodded absently and made to walk on towards his study.

Penelope looked affronted by his lack of enthusiasm. 'Well! I really think you could show a little more interest in such a promising opportunity for your only daughter. Your only daughter who, I might add, is worryingly close to her twenty-fifth birthday!'

Cecil turned about and gave an apologetic sigh. 'I'm sorry, my dear, but lately I am too concerned over Tarquin's whereabouts to take heed of much at all. I have been to several of his haunts and all the clubs in St. James's. Nobody has any news of him. It has been a confounded long while since I had word from my heir.'

Emily had ventured into the hallway and heard what her grim-faced father said about his errant son. Strain was etched deeply about his weary eyes and Emily felt herself seething with anger at Tarquin.

For a moment she was tempted to blurt out to her father that she knew more than he did. But what comfort would there be for him in knowing that the ruffian who had been loitering about was issuing threats in his quest to locate Tarquin? Neither would her parents relish knowing that the last news of their eldest son was of him cavorting with harlots in Co-vent Garden. Indeed, should she disclose what she knew, it was sure to increase her father's anxiety, and make her mother quite hysterical.

'He will turn up soon enough, Papa. I know Mark Hunter is searching for him, too.' Emily said encouragingly.

'Our son is the most selfish wretch imaginable!' Penelope suddenly burst out. 'All the while we must concentrate on him…only him! Well, I refuse to let his shenanigans spoil our outing to Lady Gerrard's.

We will go, and we will enjoy ourselves!' Penelope shot a look between her husband and her daughter. 'I forbid another mention of Tarquin until the weekend!'

The sleek carriage slowed to a stop. After waiting and watching for a few minutes Viscount Devlin spotted, at a distance, the fellow he had been hoping would appear. He alighted and pulled his many-caped coat protectively about his elegant shoulders. With sheer distaste puckering his features, he began to pick a path, with the help of his cane, over dirt and debris underfoot. As he walked the gloomy lane, shadowy female bodies brushed against him, murmuring lewdly. He ignored them and roughly pushed away one bold harlot who persisted in clinging to his arm.

Crossing the road he approached a gin house spewing a pool of lamplight on to slimy cobbles. As he came closer, its raucous sound deadened the monotonous hum of begging irritating his brain.

'Riley.'

His quarry spun about on hearing his name, and stared warily at Devlin as he stepped purposefully closer. 'Evenin' to you, sir.' His tongue snaked over his lips. 'Here for business?'

'Why else?' Nicholas sneered sarcastically and gave a speaking look at his squalid surroundings.

Mickey grimaced understanding, but his eyes were narrowed and alert. He hadn't forgotten that this man had seen him in Whiting Street when he was there to meet Beaumont's sister. And he was suspicious that the fine fellow was here for information, not pleasure.

'Got a new girl called Lucy might take yer fancy. Young and fresh she is,' Mickey said, hoping to distract any awkward questions by arousing the fellow's lust.

'I'll take Jenny.'

Mickey shot a look at him. 'She's laid up…no use tonight…'

'In that case, perhaps there's another bit of business we might do.' Two drunken navvies swayed past, arm in arm, roaring with laughter. Nicholas waited for them to weave away before gritting, 'Is there a better place we might go to discuss this?'

Mickey chewed the inside of his cheek. Any mention of business pricked up his ears, but he didn't trust this man. He didn't trust him one bit. In fact, he'd sooner deal with Old Nick himself.

Noting his hesitation, Nicholas purred coaxingly, 'There will be a tidy bit of blunt in this for you if things work out the way I like.'

It was what Mickey needed to hear. With a flick

of his beady eyes to right and to left, he cocked his head and led the Viscount through an iron gateway. The alleyway led to a small door and Mickey indicated the Viscount should enter.

Inside, revellers could be heard through the wall, showing they were immediately behind the gin shop. The room held the unmistakable reek of poverty, and a few battered pieces of furniture.

Noting the Viscount's disgust, Mickey said sardonically, 'Best I can do at short notice. So if it ain't a woman you're after tonight, what can I do fer yer?'

'You can tell me why you were on Whiting Street to meet Tarquin Beaumont's sister.'

Mickey's tongue tip hovered over his lips. 'Who?' he piped, all innocence.

Devlin smiled thinly. 'Don't act the fool and don't bother lying. I know you were on Whiting Street to meet her.'

'Told you that, did she?'

Devlin paced about the room, trying to find a spot where the atmosphere was less fetid. He came close to Mickey and looked directly into his eyes, for they were of similar height. 'I know Miss Beaumont is trying to find her brother, and I would like to assist. That would please her. She might in turn then please me.'

Mickey gave a sly smile. 'Ah…so you'd like to please Miss Beaumont…and have her please you…'

'Indeed I would,' Nicholas drawled

'And you think I might be able to help.'

'Yes.'

Mickey gave a chuckle. 'That's a thought, sir. That's certainly a thought, and it is wot I do best. But it's a bit risky with a classy lady 'cos there's her family to consider.'

Viscount Devlin reached into an inside pocket and withdrew a silk purse. It was bulging fit to burst the seams. He leisurely slackened the drawstring and drew forth a gold sovereign. The glinting disc was held between thumb and forefinger while he shook the sack until chinking could be heard. His top lip curled as he saw Mickey's eyes pounce greedily on the cash. 'There's twice that amount for you if it all goes to plan.'

Mickey shot a look at Devlin. He grinned, but his eyes were crafty slits. 'You've come to the right place, sir. I'm sure that if Miss Beaumont got news that her brother were laid up somewhere, say somewhere quiet and very private, and him right poorly, well, I reckon she'd go there straight off to see him.'

'I think so too,' Nicholas Devlin said dulcetly. 'I'm glad we understand one another.'

Mickey nodded.

'Did you tell Miss Beaumont where her brother is hiding?'

Mickey shook his head, snorting a laugh. 'I don't know where the wily cove is, but she knows well enough that I'm on his tail, for I told her so straight.'

At Viscount Devlin's enquiring look, Mickey brusquely explained, 'I got a bit of business of me own to sort out with Beaumont. Nuthin' that needs put a dampener on wot we just discussed.'

'Good,' Nicholas said. 'You understand that we have not had a conversation of any sort?'

Mickey gave a bark of surly laughter. 'Respectable gent like you...talk to the likes of me? Who'd believe that?'

Nicholas gave a nod.

'I'll see what I can do. Where can I contact you?' Mickey asked.

'You can't. And don't ever try to. I'll return in a few days or so.' Devlin turned towards the door, his nostrils flaring at the stench. 'Let me out of this fleapit.'

Mickey sprang to open the door.

'This new girl...she's young and fresh, you say?'

'She is indeed. Shall I fetch her?' Mickey started to close the door again.

'Not here, you fool,' the Viscount barked with utter contempt. 'My carriage is close by in Houndsditch. Send her there.'

Chapter Eight

Mark Hunter stepped swiftly into shadows to watch the black-cloaked figure traversing the rough cobbles. On reaching his carriage the Viscount sprang in, unaware he had been observed, and closed the door.

That Nick Devlin was sordid enough to seek pleasure in such a stew did not surprise Mark. Indeed, he had spotted him on other occasions doing business with whores in London's back streets. But an idea stirred in his mind that another reason might have brought Devlin here tonight. Had the Viscount forgone the comfort of Mayfair to come, as he had, in search of Riley and some answers?

The only connection between Tarquin and Devlin that Mark knew of was a mutual loathing. After a moment he grunted a soft, self-mocking laugh. He was being too fanciful. Why would Devlin give a damn about Tarquin's whereabouts? It was far more likely to be lust, not hatred, that had urged Nick to visit this haunt.

Pushing away from the wall, Mark was about to approach the gin shop when he heard soft footfalls and drew back against the brick once more. A young woman emerged from the murk and came towards him. Fleetingly their eyes met as she gazed, wide-eyed, up at him. But she didn't speak or accost him. She hurried on past, winding tighter about her head a shawl covering a thatch of curly fair hair.

Mark pivoted on a heel to watch her. He had been surprised by her looks. She wasn't raddled or dead-eyed as were many jades. But then the girl looked only about fifteen and had not yet lost the optimism of youth. She halted by Devlin's carriage and used her fist to bang on the door. Within a moment she had unceremoniously hiked up her skirts and disappeared inside. The vehicle remained stationary, although within seconds the carriage lamp began to swing on its hook.

Mark's mouth thinned in disgust as he realised that Devlin could not even be bothered to take her somewhere more discreet. But of course he had no idea he had been noticed by one of his peers, being serviced by a whore in Houndsditch. The locals sloping around might know the Viscount by sight, and know what he was about, but that would not worry Devlin. However, talk of his debauchery, in polite society salons, might.

Mark had never liked Nick Devlin. Even before he had married the sister of one of his friends, simply for her fortune, he had despised the man for his deviousness.

Mark was aware that Emily had been engaged to Devlin about four years ago. He and Tarquin had then been barely acquainted and he had not known Emily at all at that time. Before this precise moment Mark had never given much thought to what had broken the betrothal between Miss Beaumont and the Viscount, or what had ignited the burning enmity between Tarquin and Devlin. But now he viewed things differently. Lately Emily Beaumont had been arousing his curiosity…as well as his body. He wanted to know about her life, past and present, and why she would once have agreed to marry such a character as Nicholas Devlin.

Mickey Riley spat out an oath beneath his breath. Was he never to be left to his own devices this evening? Again he slipped a look from beneath lowered lashes while trying to guess what this individual wanted. He certainly wasn't a customer, but then there was always a first time for a bit of rough trade, even for fellows who seemed like they had never stepped foot outside Mayfair, and could afford a top-notch bit of muslin.

Mickey felt uneasy, for he twice had seen this gent talking to Miss Beaumont and it seemed an odd coincidence that he should turn up just after the Viscount had been by with a wicked suggestion concerning that very lady.

The fellow was getting closer and Mickey cursed again that he had ever got involved with Tarquin Beaumont. He was beginning to think Jenny was right: they should have forgotten all about him and moved on to someone with deeper pockets. Beaumont was of good stock and looked flush, but nevertheless Mickey was coming to fear the wastrel might not have two ha'pennies of his own to rub together.

The Viscount was a better class of nob; he'd seen the proof of his quality bulging in that silk bag. And there was a way he could get his hands on the cash. If Tarquin turned out to be a dud, he'd have to make sure that his sister made up for the loss…

But now this damnable fellow was prowling

about. Mickey felt his hackles stir and belatedly
tried to slip out of sight through the gate. If he'd discovered what the Viscount was about he'd be here
to do battle for the lady's honour.

As Mark watched the pimp scuttling away, he
felt a side of his mouth tug into a smile. So Riley
had guessed what he wanted and it didn't look as
though he was willing to provide any answers to his
questions. Mark quickened his pace, following Riley
through the gate and into the alley.

'You need us, Mickey?'

The bellowed offer of assistance came from the
street where a couple of strapping young men stood
belligerently eyeing the casual interloper.

Mickey slid a nervous glance up at his stalker. In
an odd way he found him more intimidating than
Devlin. He was taller and broader, but he sensed in
him a power that was not just about physical
strength. 'Do I need 'em? Or are you here tonight
just fer business, sir?'

'I'm here for information. I'm willing to pay for
your time.' Mark gave a slight smile. 'So…business
it is…'

Mickey's eyes narrowed in admiration. He was
a courageous nob, he'd give him that. He didn't
seem at all put out on knowing that, with a click of

his fingers, Mickey could set a couple of his hounds on him.

'I only got to shout and they'll be back.' Mickey flicked a hand, dismissing his associates. The fellow didn't look as though he'd come for a brawl. His manner was straightforward and his rig-out expensive. Besides, the promise of payment always mellowed Mickey's misgivings. He turned and opened the door, mockingly inviting his elegant visitor to enter.

As his eyes flitted over squalor, lit by a solitary oil lamp, a faint frown was all that betrayed Mark's distaste. He launched straight away into, 'I should introduce myself. I'm Mark Hunter and Tarquin Beaumont is a good friend of mine. Why have you been bothering Mr Beaumont's sister, and asking after her brother's whereabouts?'

Mickey cocked his head to an insolent angle. 'Not been bothering her, been trying to help,' he contradicted.

'In what way?'

Mickey turned a sly eye up to a hard, shadowy visage. 'Well, now…that's private and confidential…just between me and the Beaumonts.'

Mark reached into his coat and withdrew a bank note. 'They don't want to be bothered with it all.' He waved the money held in thumb and forefinger. 'I said I'd pay for your time and information.'

Mickey reflexively stuck out a hand, his eyes fixed on the plentiful cash.

Mark lazily crushed the paper in a broad palm. 'First answer me—and give me the truth, or you'll get nothing.'

'Beaumont's acted foolish, and I reckon if I can find him, and make him pay what's necessary, it'll save the family being made a laughing-stock. That's all I wanted to see Miss Beaumont about. You can ask her.'

'I don't need to. She has already told me what you spoke about. You haven't told me anything I, or any one else, doesn't already know about Tarquin Beaumont. The family's reputation will survive another tale of him losing his shirt at the tables.'

'Ain't gaming.' Mickey's voice was sulky.

'What, then?' Mark purred. 'Has he been keeping company with your whores, and not paying you fast enough for their services?'

Mickey gave a lopsided smile. 'Well, now, Mr Hunter, you're getting closer, but I can tell you, you still ain't quite right.'

'And I can tell you, I'm getting tired of playing games.' The hand holding the cash was thrust impatiently into Mark's pocket. 'Have you set your bully boys on him and he's fled?'

Mickey crossed his arms over his chest. 'Ain't done that at all,' he said airily. 'But he has taken off and all 'cos of a woman.'

'Go on.'

'Not until you pay, and I want that and another the same.' He nodded his head at the pocket hiding the banknote. Mickey's ferreting brain had realised that there was indeed a way to make money from the Beaumonts. He could recoup his losses twice over. Devlin would pay for fun with the sister, and Hunter would pay for information about the brother's folly.

Mark gave him the cash with a perilous glower that made Mickey quickly blurt out, 'Her name's Jenny and he took a real shine to her right from the start…'

Fifteen minutes later Mark was striding back along the slimy cobbles with an expression as dark and forbidding as his environment. *Tarquin, you bloody fool!* was the thought rotating in his mind as he vaulted into his carriage and gave directions for it to head home.

'You look like an angel.'

Emily gave her ardent-eyed admirer a smile and

absently smoothed her fingers over the ivory silk of her skirt. It had been her mother's idea that she wear the pale, dainty dress; Emily had favoured wearing blue satin, which she thought suited her colouring and looked less…virginal. But she had not felt inclined to argue over something trivial when so much that was serious was occupying her mind.

Despite still having had no news of Tarquin, she considered her mother to be right in one respect: they rarely were invited to be entertained at such a fine address.

Before leaving the house this evening she had dashed off a concise note to Nicholas and, when handing it to Millie to take to the post, had felt pleased that she had allowed it to take up so little of her time. Emily felt lighter in spirits than she had in a while. She looked about at her scintillating surroundings. They ought to enjoy the outing and forget their woes for a few hours.

Stephen politely held out an arm to her, then one to her friend Sarah. 'We must find some chairs in the music room before the orchestra starts. There is sure to be a crush later.'

As they walked, Sarah whispered, awestruck, 'I'm so glad you asked me to come with you. This is quite the most impressive place I have ever entered.'

Emily gave a slow nod as her eyes flitted over the opulent appointments of Lady Gerrard's drawing room. 'Indeed it is wonderful.'

'Her late husband died five years ago and left Fiona very rich indeed,' Stephen contributed to the conversation. 'But she has a host of influential friends to ease her pain at his passing.' He nodded to Sir Jason Hunter, who was just entering the room with his wife. 'Here is one of the most distinguished, just arrived.'

'Oh, Helen is here,' Emily said, with a pleased smile, on seeing her friend. 'Let's go and say hello.'

Barely a moment after they had joined Sir Jason and Lady Hunter, Emily's eyes were drawn away from the handsome couple and to the doorway. Framed in the aperture and, she had to admit, looking quite magnificent in a slate-grey tailcoat and buff trousers, was a tall dark-haired gentleman she immediately recognised. But what caused her to quickly blink and look away was not the fact that the paragon's eyes were steadily on her, but that his presence had caused her stomach to somersault.

Noting Emily's slight flush, Helen casually turned her head. 'Your brother has arrived,' she told her husband while giving Emily an astute look.

As Emily was murmuring about moving on to the music room with her friends, Mark joined their group.

'We were just off to listen to the concert,' Jason told his brother, his hand welcoming his wife's delicate fingers on his sleeve.

Sarah suddenly took Stephen's elbow and, ignoring his rather startled expression and reluctance to go, steered him to follow Sir Jason and his wife.

When the couples had moved away a few paces, Mark looked down at the top of a shiny crown of blonde hair. 'Am I forgiven yet?' he asked huskily.

'I'm afraid not, Mr Hunter,' Emily said stiffly. Her elbow-length lace gloves were smoothed over shapely arms and she made a move to follow her friends.

'Perhaps if I tell you that I have come here just to see you, and have some news of Tarquin, you might think more kindly of me.'

Emily immediately pivoted back to face him. She tilted her chin to a confident angle, but her hands were tightly clasped to still their quivering. 'Is that true, or just a ruse to make me stay a while longer with you?'

'Why are you afraid of staying a while longer with me, Emily?' Mark asked softly. 'Do you imagine I might try to kiss you in Lady Gerrard's drawing room?'

Emily blushed to the roots of her golden hair, but

managed to say, 'Not at all. I'm sure in company you adopt the manner of a perfect gentleman.' Her silver eyes flashed at him. 'Besides, why would you bother when you're sure to again be disappointed?'

Mark's soft laugh was directed over the top of Emily's head. 'Ah…so that still rankles, does it?' he murmured. 'I explained at the time why I said it, and paid you a compliment in the process. Which reminds me that you still owe me an explanation for finding fault with my praise.'

Emily felt her heart jump to her throat. She knew exactly to what he referred, and had no intention of resuming *that* conversation. She quickly changed subject. 'I had no idea you would be here tonight.' A hint of blame sharpened her tone.

'I gather you would rather I was not.'

'You overestimate the matter, sir,' Emily returned coolly. 'You may stay or go and it will make no difference whatsoever to me.'

Mark's eyes held hers until Emily flushed and looked away. 'Is that so?' he softly drawled. 'Well, as I came solely to see you, I think I shall go.' With a slight nod of his dark head he turned and was soon strolling towards the door.

In mortification Emily watched his broad back. He was actually going to leave, and she had not yet discovered what news he had of Tarquin. She bit down on her lower lip to control herself, for she was tempted to call him back. She had been so disturbed by those silly emotions that came to the fore when in close proximity to the dratted man that she had not quizzed him over her brother. And now she might have lost the chance.

She was obliquely aware that more people were moving away towards the music room. Strains of a melody reached her ears, but her eyes were focused on an athletic figure that would be soon lost from sight.

With an indrawn breath, and her pearly teeth clenched together, she went in pursuit of him, weaving nimbly through guests who were, in the main, proceeding in the opposite direction.

'Mr Hunter!' She was sure he had heard her call his name, but was ignoring her. With tears of frustration spiking her eyes, Emily yanked on one of his elbows, then quickly stumbled back a few paces as he turned about.

'I can't believe you would actually go before telling me what you have discovered about Tarquin,' she gritted out in an undertone. 'Your pride is too easily wounded, sir.'

'Is that an apology?'

She had expected Mark might look smug at having humbled her into chasing him, but his expression was remarkably grave.

'If you require I give one…yes…it is.' Emily tilted her chin and squarely met his vivid blue eyes.

A corner of Mark's mouth tilted and an idle glance swept the sparsely populated room. 'I don't require anything from you not freely given, Emily.'

Emily felt herself heating beneath his steady regard. So he couldn't resist reminding her that she had willingly participated in that kiss.

'You look a little flushed. Let me accompany you to the terrace for a breath of fresh air.' A nod of Mark's head indicated doors that were adjacent to them.

Emily looked to the right and to the left. The room was almost deserted. 'It is private enough here for you to tell me what you have discovered.'

'I think the terrace might be a better place. What I have to report is quite bad news and it is amazing how walls can sprout ears.' As though to prove him wise a young lady obligingly emerged from behind a marble pillar where she had been adjusting a bow on her bodice. She sent them a sly look before gliding away towards the music room.

'You have nothing to fear from me, Emily.' Mark's voice was husky with sincerity, although a vaguely mocking light was in his eyes. 'I shall do nothing to displease you.'

Emily snapped her eyes from his. He knew very well that another kiss from him was likely to have the reverse effect! Just as her defences were beginning to crumble she had a glimpse of someone who made her determinedly put back the barriers.

Mark's mistress was just taking a seat in the music room, near to the doors. Barbara didn't appear to have noticed that her lover was conversing privately with another woman. Or perhaps she had seen them talking together, but didn't care. The sophisticated brunette was undoubtedly confident enough of her position in Mark's life to ignore silly women like her who secretly found Mark Hunter fascinating.

If Mark had noticed his mistress he gave no sign. His attention remained steadily on Emily while he patiently awaited permission to escort her to the terrace.

Emily felt her temper rising. He had the nerve to say he had come simply to see her, when in fact he was here with his mistress! He had the gall to remind her of stolen kisses…to flirt with her and want to take her into the dark…despite being partnered this evening by the woman he loved!

Mark had sensed the atmosphere between them had been on the point of thawing. Now it seemed frostier than ever. He took a glance about to see what had changed Emily's humour and glimpsed Barbara staring at them. A footman closed the doors to the music room, cutting off her view of them, as Mark's lips formed a soundless oath. He had not imagined that his mistress would attend this soirée. Barbara and Lady Gerrard were not the best of friends, and he had felt confident that he would spend an evening free of Barbara's constant surveillance. For some months her possessiveness, and unsubtle hints about marriage, had been irritating him.

'It is probably best we do not talk now,' Emily said glacially. 'Might I suggest we meet tomorrow? I shall ensure that I am by the water in Hyde Park at about four in the afternoon. You may then tell me what you know.' Without awaiting a reply she turned to move away.

'If you're expecting me to be at your beck and call, you will be disappointed. I won't be there.'

Emily swirled about and glared at him in frustration. 'In that case, tell me quickly now about my brother.'

'Come to the terrace, and I shall.'

Emily stepped angrily towards him. 'I think you know, sir, that I ought not do that. And I am amazed that you would suggest such a thing when our friends and family are close by to witness it. You might not have a reputation to keep, but I have!' Emily felt her face becoming pink beneath his lazy low-lidded regard. In that instant she was sure they both had in mind her implication that her innocence was lost. Recklessly she added, 'And Mrs Emerson is sure to soon wonder where you are.'

'I didn't know that Mrs Emerson would be here tonight.'

A huff of contemptuous laughter made a pout of Emily's soft lips. She might have appeared insouciant, but inwardly she squirmed with embarrassment for behaving in such an unseemly manner. Young ladies did not hint they knew of a gentleman's *amours*, least of all to the gentleman himself.

'I was about to go home a moment ago. You might not consider me mannerly, Emily, but I assure you, had I escorted Mrs Emerson here, I would have been polite enough to inform her I was leaving.' With that cutting remark he executed a crisp bow and walked away. When he reached the door he hesitated, then looked back to see that Emily was standing quite still where he had left her.

As though in a trance she took a small step, then another and another, until she was walking quite quickly towards the French doors.

Chapter Nine

A scent of early blossom teased Emily's nostrils as she stepped on to the granite flags. Her eyes strained to identify shapes in shadows, for merely a sliver of silver illuminated the ebony heavens. After a moment she could see that the terrace was enclosed by stone balustrade; to one side was a little bench snugly set in an ivy-tangled trellis. A gusting breeze brought a tinkle of water to her ears, but she couldn't locate the fountain. Emily gazed up wistfully at a few winking stars. It was an undeniably romantic setting and, had the attractive gentleman escorting her been someone she liked and trusted, she might have been tempted to let him steal a kiss…or two…

Emily swiftly put such wild imaginings from her mind and paid attention to the undeniably handsome features of her companion. 'Have you discovered Tarquin's whereabouts, Mr Hunter?' she asked briskly.

'Finding him is not the problem. I could unearth him quite quickly if I wanted to.' Mark strolled to the stone rail and, bracing a hand against it, contemplated the gardens.

'Why on earth haven't you done so?' Emily demanded on a gasp.

'I haven't done so because at the moment it might be prudent to leave him out of sight. A scandal might break on his return home.'

Emily felt blood seep from her complexion to leave it tingling icily. His tone had been harsh, indicating that a very bleak announcement was yet to come. 'He is in bad trouble, isn't he?' she murmured.

'I suppose it could be worse. As far as I know, he isn't dead or injured…'

His sarcasm simply strengthened Emily's anxiety and she made a frantic guess at what ordeal they might yet face. 'Has he duelled again and killed a man this time? Are his family out for Tarquin's blood?'

'It's nothing of the sort, Emily,' Mark reassured, his stern profile softening. 'Your brother has undoubtedly been foolish, but not criminal.'

Emily nodded quickly, gratefully, indicating she was ready to hear the worst of it.

Mark stuffed his hands into his pockets and turned to face her. He cast down his eyes, his expression contemplative, as he sought an appropriate way of relating a sordid tale. A good deal of young men, while drunk, had been unruly and lived to regret it. Mark was no exception to that rule. But generally a gentleman strove to be discreet, and protect himself and his family from the consequences of his excesses. He certainly avoided binding himself to his sinful past. 'I told you that Tarquin hasn't been seen since my brother spotted him loitering in Covent Garden,' he carefully began to explain.

'Yes,' Emily breathed. 'And I know he was consorting with harlots that night.' She swallowed her embarrassment at the indelicate turn to their conversation. 'I understand why you said nothing; it is an awkward subject for a gentleman to discuss with a lady.' She delicately coughed. 'But I think we both know protocol is of scant importance at present.'

'Who told you about that?' Mark frowned, for his memory had immediately pounced on the fact that Nick Devlin had recently been in Riley's company. The Viscount was an unpleasant character and he certainly hated Tarquin. But surely even he would not be so mean as to bring to a sister's attention her brother's lechery?

'Helen told me she had seen Tarquin on that occasion in Covent Garden. We are intimate friends, and able to talk about anything at all…good or bad…' Emily said by way of explanation.

'As you know that much, you should also know that Mickey Riley is a pimp. I tracked down Riley in Houndsditch and he told me why Tarquin has gone into hiding.' Mark swiped a hand across his jaw as he looked down into a visage of pure pale beauty. Emily's luminous eyes were hungrily fixed on his face, but it was just information she wanted from him, whereas what he wanted… One of his hands started to travel towards her, but before he could sense the warm skin of her complexion beneath his fingers they were brought back to the cold stone ledge.

He felt selfish for wanting to touch. He wanted to offer comfort, but it was primarily desire that had urged him to reach for her. He took a few steps away, removing himself from temptation. 'Your brother took a shine to one of Riley's women,' Mark informed huskily. 'Her name is Jenny and Tarquin had visited her on several occasions. The last time they met he was allegedly very drunk and very amorous.'

Emily swallowed the hard lump forming in her

throat. She could tell that Mark was uneasy about giving full details of the disaster. Obviously it was of a vulgar nature. Suddenly she guessed what it might be. Once the awful thought was in her mind she had to know. 'Are you about to tell me that my brother has fathered a bastard?'

Mark frowned pensively. 'Mickey Riley didn't make mention of a child. But if there is one, now or in the future, it won't be a bastard. Your brother has married Jenny.'

'*Married?* Tarquin has married a *harlot*?' Emily's voice was little above a whisper and her eyes were enormous dark pools in a face that might have been carved in white marble. Suddenly she gasped a laugh. 'The rogue is lying! Riley probably hopes to extort money from us with a ridiculous trumped-up tale. Tarquin is a gamester, not a womaniser. I'm sure he has never given marriage, even to a respectable lady, a single thought.'

'I've no doubt Jenny was exceptionally persuasive,' Mark said in a tone of dark irony. 'And Riley isn't lying.' His expression became sober. 'I made him divulge the whereabouts of the minister alleged to have performed the ceremony. Today I visited Jeremiah Plumb. He is not a very savoury character, but he is a man of the cloth and remembers the couple. It seems the marriage is valid.'

Emily blinked to clear the mist from her eyes. Agitatedly she twisted this way and that before coming to a halt facing the darkling gardens. Her hands gripped tightly at the balustrade and her blonde head dipped in despair towards them.

Mark positioned himself just behind her slender form, resting his palms comfortingly on shoulders that were tense and shaking. When she did not immediately shrug him off, his thumbs stroked with tender sensuality against her flesh. 'I'm sorry to be the one to bring such bad tidings. But you did want to know.'

Emily nodded morosely. 'The selfish...stupid... wretch!' she suddenly spat though small pearly teeth. She spun about and gazed up at him with tear-glossed eyes. 'He has given no thought again to how this will hurt our parents. Or how it might affect Robert. Robert idolises him, yet he has shown him no proper example, as an older brother should. If Robert were to be led astray by such behaviour, it would break our parents' hearts.' Her muted outrage ended on a watery choke. The lulling sensation of Mark's fingers moving on her skin calmed her, and she stayed within his casual embrace, her mind furiously working. 'Now I understand what Riley is about. He is urgently seeking Tarquin so he can blackmail him. He wants money for his silence. But even if we pay what he asks, what good will it do? Sooner or later it will all come out.' Her voice trembled into depressive quiet.

Mark slowly slid a hand to her nape, soothing softly beneath silky blonde curls. His dark head bent close to her, his lips discreetly skimming a crown of scented hair. 'Hush… Riley can be dealt with quite easily. And a divorce can be arranged. It will be possible to contain the worst of the scandal, I'm sure.'

'Do you truly think so?' Emily clung to his sleeves, shook them a little to drag from him more reassurance.

'I do,' Mark stressed gently and urged her closer to him. He lowered his head and touched his lips lightly to hers. It was a mild salute, almost passionless.

The anguish churning Emily's stomach was slowly transforming into an infinitely nicer sensation. Warmth was stealing through her cool limbs, bringing a welcome relaxation to her tight muscles. What she had just learned had obliterated all memory of Mark's mistress, of her vow to shun his advances, from her mind. She simply yearned for more sweet relief from fretting on an impending calamity. She closed her eyes in wordless agreement.

Mark was swift to oblige. His mouth slid against hers with more pressure this time, tenderly persuading her soft lips to part, allowing him to taste the warm silk within.

Emily pressed closer, needing his strength and protection. When his firm hands started to trace her silhouette, she clung to him, responding to his artful caresses with sighing pleasure. A sudden noise shattered the spell.

Mark cursed beneath his breath as he noticed that the terrace doors were being brushed back and forth by a low branch of a tree. 'There's nobody there; it's just the wind strengthening,' he murmured as Emily would have pulled away.

She relaxed again, accepting the comfort of the strong arms that bound her to him. Quite naturally her face found a nook beneath his shoulder in which to nestle. But even as she craved again to feel his mouth on hers, her mind was clogged with questions. 'But…what if…what if there *is* a child?' she insisted with a hint of hysteria. 'What on earth is to be done then?'

With a quivering hand silencing her gasp of dismay, Barbara Emerson retreated from where she had been eavesdropping by the French doors. From the moment she had seen Mark talking to Emily Beaumont in the drawing room, her instinct had been to find out what was going on. Since the afternoon when they had all met by chance outside the *modiste*'s, she had been alert to Mark's attraction to Emily.

After her husband had died Barbara had taken great pains to lure Mark back to her. She had been sure that she could kindle his continuing desire for her into love. Then she would get him to marry her once a decent period of mourning was done.

But years had passed since then and, although Barbara was sure she was the most important woman in Mark's life, she had accepted she would never again be the only one. She knew of his brief liaisons with a society beauty here or a little actress there. A few months ago an Italian soprano had taken his fancy. Barbara had never let it show that any of them bothered her, but she had been relieved when the pretty songstress had flown away home. Lovely Signora Carlotti had been a worthy rival.

Now lesser mortals were aspiring to fill the soprano's place. Lady Goodrich had been risibly unsubtle in her pursuit at Vauxhall and Verity Marchant was constantly bumping her buxom hips against him.

In retaliation Barbara had taken a particular fancy to a few handsome gallants who danced attendance upon her. She had conducted discreet affairs—she knew Mark would not tolerate being the object of ridicule. But, if he had been jealous of those young gentlemen, he had admirably concealed it.

Nevertheless Barbara had always been sure that she held the key to Mark's heart, no matter their trifling peccadilloes. He might dally elsewhere, but she was the constant in his life and she had been confident that he would eventually make her his wife. Now she was frightened that her dearest ambition had been snatched from her grasp.

She flattened her back against the wall, her face a mask of shock and fury. She had not witnessed all that had gone on between Mark and Emily Beaumont on the terrace, but she had seen and heard enough to understand that she was losing him. She had glimpsed with her own eyes the kisses, the tenderness bestowed by her lover on another woman. And then the little trollop had mentioned a child! Emily Beaumont must believe herself to be increasing with Mark's bastard! And, from Mark's loving attitude towards the scheming hussy, Barbara guessed he might ask Miss Beaumont to marry him!

Barbara felt her back teeth grind in rage and frustration. She had hoped that *she* might conceive. She knew Mark well enough to realise that he would cherish and protect his firstborn, and the child's mother. But he had always been careful to let the sheets, or her belly, catch his seed, thus far denying her the right to his family and his name. Now that sly minx would usurp her place as his wife. Barbara dashed away the wrathful tears stinging her eyes and stiffened her spine. She was not about to put paid to years of devotion to Mark Hunter. He was hers and she would keep him!

Barbara glanced swiftly about the deserted room and noticed that a young fellow was wandering about, peering here and there, as though searching for someone. She thought she recognised him and, as he turned her way, a smile tilted her lips. It was Miss Beaumont's loyal puppy. He had been escorting Emily earlier and giving her moon-eyed looks. No doubt he was in pursuit of her just as she was in pursuit of Mark. In a flash of inspiration she recollected his name was Stephen Bond and his grandmother was Augusta, a friend of their hostess.

Barbara stepped over to Stephen and gave him a bright smile. Her fan was theatrically employed to cool her flushed face. 'It is so hot, is it not? I expect you slipped away from the concert to get some air. I did too.'

A neutral smile and a polite nod were his response. Stephen made to move on to look elsewhere for Emily.

'Might I ask you to accompany me to the terrace, Mr Bond?' Without awaiting a reply, Barbara attached her hand to the crook of his arm. 'I expect we will both benefit from a little night air.'

Stephen grimaced in barely concealed annoyance—it was the second time that evening that a woman, not of his choosing, had urged him to act as her escort. But he was too much of a gentleman to refuse. His frustration was limited to a terse, muttered agreement. An angry blush stained his fair cheeks as he allowed Barbara to steer him towards the terrace. As they approached the doors his misgivings increased. He looked askance at her. Without apparent cause she had suddenly burst into shrill laughter.

Barbara had a very good reason for creating a din. It was her intention to alert her faithless lover to her presence. She didn't want anyone else to witness that he was paying ardent attention to another woman. Especially not this fellow! Were Stephen Bond of a jealous, fiery nature—Barbara took a glance at him and curled a smile at the improbability—a rumpus might ensue and then her humiliation would become common knowledge.

Her loud giggling had the desired effect. With a groaned oath Mark gently put Emily from him and, threading her arm formally through his, began to lead her back towards the drawing-room doors. They were a few paces away from the light when Stephen and Barbara appeared on the terrace.

'Emily! There you are. Are you not well?' Stephen asked in concern, immediately quitting Barbara's side.

'I...just felt a little hot,' Emily explained with a strained smile. 'I'm better now.'

'That is good,' Barbara said sweetly. 'I have some salts you may borrow if you think it might help.'

Emily gave a quick shake of her head and murmured thanks.

'If you are a little feverish, you ought to hurry inside, Miss Beaumont, in case you take a chill.' Barbara gravely advised. 'Besides, I expect your mother has missed you too. She will have been imagining all sorts of odd things to be responsible for your absence.'

Emily avoided Mark's eyes as she joined Stephen. She had gone with Mark to the terrace determined that she would not again succumb to his skilful flirtation. Yet he had easily brushed aside her principles and her inhibitions and started to seduce her.

Just a short while ago she had criticised Tarquin for jeopardising her family's reputation. Yet had she not acted with equal disregard for decency? She had known very well that Mark was spoken for. She had also known that his mistress was close by, yet still she had let him kiss and caress her.

And how very firmly attached he was too! Emily had obliquely observed Barbara glide to Mark's side, then curl white fingers possessively over an elegant dark arm.

'Thank you, Mr Hunter, for your kind escort,' Emily said with stiff formality, and guilt writhing in the pit of her stomach.

'You're very welcome to it, Miss Beaumont,' Mark returned easily. His eyes rested for a long moment on Stephen, making the young man shift rather uncomfortably.

When Emily pulled gently on Stephen's arm to indicate it was time to go inside, her escort's relief was obvious enough to tug a side of Mark's mouth into a smile.

'Where have you been hiding this evening, Miss Beaumont?' Augusta Bond raised her lorgnette and peered shrewdly at Emily. 'You missed some good music, you know.'

'Emily was taking the air on the terrace, with Mr Hunter, Grandmama.' Stephen had answered after a short pause, for Emily seemed to be in a daze that had deepened a dent between her delicate brows.

'Ah…' Augusta said, and gave a significant nod. Her gimlet eyes shifted behind the glass to the people just entering the room. Barbara Emerson had a fierce determined smile on her face as she looked at her lover. Augusta was not fooled. It was not simply that the gentleman looked detached, and had his eyes on Emily. Augusta could easily tell when a woman was worried that she was about to be pensioned off. She had been cast aside herself by gentlemen friends before Mr Bond had swept her up the aisle.

'I'm sorry, Mrs Bond…did you say the concert was enjoyable?' Emily babbled, for she had sensed Mark's presence in the room, and his eyes on her.

'I did. And I'll also say that I had a notion you might do better for yourself than Nicholas Devlin.' The old lady had lowered her voice to add that. She gave Emily a subtle smile. 'I should like a glass of champagne. I think you deserve some, too, miss.' Augusta turned to her grandson. 'Miss Beaumont and I are off to have a chat to Fiona before the orchestra starts up again. Fiona knows all the latest gossip and I must have something to tell them back in Bath.'

'Are you soon going home, ma'am?' Emily

asked, desperately polite, as she tried to concentrate on anything at all other than what had occurred on the terrace with the imposing gentleman they were about to pass.

'I'm not sure when to leave,' Augusta replied. 'But before I go, I'd like to see Stephen happy.'

'Yes, of course...' Emily frowned and stole a glance at Augusta's profile. 'You think he is unhappy, ma'am?'

'Indeed, I do. And he always will be while he hankers after you,' Augusta said bluntly. 'You're a nice gel, Miss Beaumont, but you're not right for my grandson.'

'What a fine evening it was to be sure. Even the presence of that vinegar-faced Violet Pearson could not ruin my enjoyment.' Penelope slipped off her shawl and did a little twirl on the rug. 'Our hostess spent far more time talking to us than the Pearsons.' A wicked smile animated Penelope's face. 'We have Augusta to thank for being so favoured, and for making Violet so obviously *furious*.'

Emily gave her mother a smile and sat down in a chair in the parlour. They had not long ago arrived home. All Emily desired now was to sleep. Her head ached from her efforts to either make sense of the troubles that rotated dizzily in her mind, or banish them completely. Her eyes felt hot and weary. But her mother was eager to talk, for she had very much enjoyed their outing, and it would be churlish to deny her a brief résumé of gowns, gossip and guests.

'Well, I do think you could show a little more enthusiasm, Emily.' Penelope had guessed that her daughter was keen to retire. 'Lady Gerrard seemed to like you very much. And so did her nephew. I saw Stephen give him a scowl when he twice asked you to dance.' Penelope chuckled. 'It will not hurt Stephen to know he has a rival. Although I'm not sure the Brettles have as much money as one would expect for people related to the Gerrard clan.'

'It was all very pleasant indeed,' Emily said with a fleeting smile. 'I'm quite tired, Mama. I think I'll go up, for I can hardly keep my eyes open.'

Penelope shrugged and pouted in disappointment. 'Oh, by the by, where did you get to during the concert?'

'I was on the terrace…getting some air…I told you,' Emily said quietly.

'Ah, so you did. You were with Tarquin's friend, Mr Hunter.' Penelope gave a sigh. 'I expect you were trying to find out what he has discovered about the rogue. Must you tell me anything?' she asked in a martyred tone. 'I know your papa has no news of him at all.'

Emily felt her heart slow to a painful thud. She had hoped to avoid any mention of Tarquin, for she didn't want to lie. Stubbornly she clung to a forlorn hope that a mistake might have been made. Perhaps things were not as bad as they seemed, and she would do anything rather than unnecessarily upset her parents with a false alarm. 'Mr Hunter has not finished his investigations, Mama. We will know more soon, I'm sure.' With a murmured 'good night', Emily quickly slipped from the room.

Chapter Ten

'I think you owe me profuse thanks…but I will settle for a full account of what went on.'

Sarah had teasingly uttered that as soon as Mrs Beaumont closed the parlour door behind her. Moments before they had all enjoyed tea and ginger cake, whilst savouring every aspect of Lady Gerrard's magnificent party. But Penelope had now quit the room so the young ladies might enjoy a private cose.

Emily sent her friend a repressive look as she laid aside her napkin.

Undeterred, Sarah continued to grin mischievously at her whilst collecting spicy crumbs from her plate. 'I've been dying to know…did he kiss you?' She popped a sticky finger in her mouth.

Emily's cheeks grew rosy but she managed an insouciant little chuckle. 'I take it you are referring to my walk on the terrace with Mr Hunter last night.'

'Of course! It was good of me to divert Stephen, was it not?' Sarah arched an eyebrow. 'You did not seem put out to be left alone with Mark. I don't think you take against him as much as you would have me believe,' she slyly added.

Emily had mixed feelings about that! But it was true that she owed Sarah her thanks for having commandeered Stephen. Hot on the heels of that thought came another that made her ruefully acknowledge she was a coward. She would rather still be in blissful ignorance of her brother's calamitous *mésalliance*, and her own shameful behaviour.

'What happened?' Sarah insisted on knowing. 'That's the second time I've noticed Mark Hunter pay you particular attention. And he gives you the most smouldering looks. I wish a rich, handsome bachelor would stare at me like that.'

'You would not if you knew his reasons,' Emily returned pithily and then regretted having further whetted her friend's curiosity.

'Did he take shocking liberties with you in the dark? I've heard he's a rakish character.' Sarah settled comfortably into the sofa, eyes round as saucers. She shivered, massaged at gooseflesh on her arms.

'What did he do…say?' Sarah persisted with her inquisition. 'Is he angling to pay court, do you think?'

'Don't be a henwit! You know very well that Mr Hunter is already spoken for.' Emily scolded lightly. 'He spent more time at his mistress's side than he did at mine.'

'Perhaps he did. But his eyes were on you most of the while. And I'm sure she knew it,' Sarah said with a gleeful chuckle. 'I doubt you'll be receiving an invitation to Mrs Emerson's soirées!'

'Well, that's a relief!' Emily muttered seriously. The thought of attending a salon hosted by Mark's mistress made her feel quite ill.

'We are friends! You must have something a bit outrageous to tell me.'

'If I did, it would concern Tarquin.' Emily gave her friend a rueful look. 'There is only one reason Mr Hunter and I need to converse in private, to discuss my troublesome brother! They are friends, and Mark has been good enough to try to find out what the miscreant is now up to.'

Sarah looked genuinely disappointed at that explanation. 'You don't think he might be more interested in you than your brother?'

Emily flapped a hand, outwardly dismissing the notion as absurd. But she averted her face to shield her expression. Although Mark had declared he wanted nothing from her for his services as detective, it seemed that he always did get a sensual reward…and with very little coaxing…

Sarah sank back into the cushions, contemplating her clasped hands, her mood now oddly subdued.

Emily took the opportunity to steer the conversation to another gentleman. 'Thank you for keeping Stephen company yesterday.'

'Oh, I didn't mind at all,' Sarah glanced up. 'In fact…' A grimace turned up her snub nose and she simply shrugged.

'Go on,' Emily gently prompted. It had never before occurred to her that Sarah might hold a torch for Stephen.

'It doesn't matter,' Sarah muttered.

'I think it does,' Emily countered softly.

'I just think Stephen is very nice,' Sarah self-consciously admitted whilst twirling a chestnut curl about a finger. 'And if I thought he might stop vainly pining for you…for I know you will never want him…I might tell him so and see what happens.' She clucked her tongue. 'How daft I must sound! You are blonde and beautiful and I am dark and plain.'

'You are *not* plain, you are pretty!' Emily stressed. 'You are younger than me by three years, and have a fine complexion. You never blush an ugly red as I do. Brunettes are the rage this season, too,' she added with an emphatic nod.

Sarah seemed deaf to her friend's compliments. 'Besides, if Stephen gave up the chase so easily, when he is obviously in love with you, he wouldn't be nice at all, would he?' she reasoned.

'Yes, he would!' Emily forcefully begged to differ. 'He would be a fickle character and not to be trusted.'

'I don't think Stephen loves me. It is an infatuation. And we all are entitled to be in thrall to that, at least once.' Emily gave her friend a twinkling smile.

'Are you hinting that I have an infatuation for Stephen?' Sarah asked, rather sharply.

'No! I am saying that I understand how easily one might confuse the two emotions, for I believe I did. For a long time I thought I truly loved Viscount Devlin. Now I am not sure whether it was love or infatuation. I know I found the idea of being in love very appealing, perhaps very deluding too…'

'You don't know how it feels to be in love?'

About to answer in the negative, Emily hesitated—her mind had veered to the memory of being enclosed in Mark's protective embrace. That recollection led to another: the sensation of a sultry warm mouth moving on hers and firm, confident fingers arousing her body. 'I'm not sure,' Emily blurted, her cheeks pink.

It seemed too absurd that she had immediately associated a gentleman she didn't know very well, or like very much, with love. But perhaps she *was* coming to know Mark, an inner voice whispered, and perhaps because of that she *didn't* dislike him as much as once she had. Heaven only knew he had been of immense help so far in piecing together the puzzle surrounding Tarquin's disappearance. It would be an ingrate indeed who would still disapprove of a gentleman who had gone to so much trouble for her family.

'Perhaps Stephen is not wasting his time waiting for you, then,' Sarah said stiffly, having stabbed a guess at the identity of the fellow occupying her friend's thoughts. 'Please forget I told you I liked him, which I do, of course, but not in *that* way. I would not want you to think you have a rival, or that I was presumptuous.'

'I was not thinking of Stephen just now. He is not the one…that is… Oh! Don't be like that, Sarah,' Emily pleaded as her friend got quickly to her feet.

'I must be going,' Sarah said tightly. 'I told Mama

I would accompany her to Baldwin's for some velvet.' With no more ado she stepped briskly to the parlour door and quit the room.

Emily felt quite melancholy as she walked with her friend to the vestibule. A tension now existed between her and Sarah and yet there had been no real disagreement between them, just talk of gentlemen. As Emily watched her friend descend the steps and turn towards home, without a backward glance, she sighed and wondered if finding a husband was really as beneficial as their mothers would have them believe.

Sarah Harper was not the only young woman who was, that morning, despondent in the knowledge that a gentleman did not reciprocate her feelings.

Barbara Emerson had just received a message from her maid that Mr Hunter had called and was waiting below. Mark never waited below. He had for many years visited her at this house and, whatever the hour, had felt comfortable coming to her boudoir. Whether he arrived to talk or to make love, he never before had stood on ceremony. Now he did, and she feared she knew why.

She had been aware for a while that his ardour was cooling. When he had brought her home last night, despite her best efforts to lure him indoors, he had gone off without even giving her a proper kiss.

Before Claudine's gaze darted away, Barbara had seen the mingling of pity and embarrassment in the girl's eyes. Even her French maid knew Barbara was about to be cast off. She trusted Claudine to be loyal and discreet, but soon it would be all over town that she was no longer Mark's mistress, or his future wife. Speculation would start as to who had usurped her, but they would not guess. Only she knew the identity of the brazen hussy who had stolen Mark away.

Barbara paced to and fro, her face set in rigid lines, her lacy negligee sailing out from her voluptuous body with the vigour of her movement. She could plead an indisposition. Of course he would not believe her, for not once had she refused him an audience. Either he would leave or he would relent and come up to find her. And then she might be able to use her wiles to stop the awful words in his throat, before he could utter them.

'*Madame* is indisposed, sir.' The petite maid peeped at a hard, dark face, then quickly her eyes sought the floor.

'In that case, convey my commiserations to *ma-*

dame,' Mark said quietly. 'And tell her I will return tomorrow.'

If Mark was aware that he was being observed from between the curtains in the window above, he gave no sign. Springing aboard his curricle, he set the fine animals to a trot. His flinty demeanour was not caused by the woman he anticipated might not gracefully accept he no longer wanted her, but by the friend who was creating havoc in the lives of so many people.

With an effort he banished Tarquin, and his exquisite…captivating…sister from his mind and forced himself to concentrate on what was to be done to make the break with Barbara as painless as possible. If she continued to try to delay the inevitable by refusing to see him, then he would send her a note. But that seemed the coward's way and he would sooner act honourably. He didn't want to hurt her, but neither could he continue to condone her fantasy that they had a future together.

After Barbara's husband had died, and they had resumed their affair, he had bluntly told her that he could not again promise her his fidelity or his love. There had been a tacit understanding between them that he would want his liberty, and from time to time, other women. He had appreciated that Barbara was too proud to nag him over those liaisons. For his part, he had never mentioned those *special* gallants who escorted her home, then discreetly slipped out in the small hours.

Despite their passing fancies, they had continued to share mutual pleasure, and Mark had not previously wanted to put an end to something that suited them both. But lately her hints that they should marry were becoming less subtle and were apt to grate on his nerves. She had become disturbingly possessive, and kept him under surveillance when they were out. He knew it was not a coincidence that she had come on to the terrace at Lady Gerrard's. She had probably been stalking him for a while before she showed herself. His tolerance of it all was spent, and he realised that his desire for her was too.

To safeguard fond memories, and Barbara's dignity, he had hoped to end it without rancour. Mark sent a rueful look skyward. Worthy sentiment…but would he be as determined to act with such ruthless efficiency if it wasn't for the matter of Miss Emily Beaumont?

Emily knew of his long-standing relationship with Barbara, and he imagined she deemed him a faithless rogue. But she still responded to him sweetly, despite her misgivings, and he was encouraged to believe she might yet grow fond of him.

Stolen kisses were one thing, but she would shun his formal courtship unless he honestly declared Barbara was out of his life. His smile turned wry as he realised he was gratified to know Emily considered Barbara her rival. And she did; he had noticed a decidedly antagonistic glint in her silver eyes as Barbara had made her appearance on the terrace with Stephen Bond. That conceit caused Mark to choke a laugh. Of course it was possible the cause of her pique was seeing her beau escorting another woman.

Musing darkly on that particular admirer—a fellow who had done nothing to merit uncharitable thoughts—made Mark grudgingly acknowledge he was jealous. Stephen Bond had a *tendresse* for Emily. Tarquin had told him so some months previously. His friend had also helpfully imparted the news that Emily liked the fellow, but was not expected to accept his proposal even if, at some time, Mr Bond found the temerity to issue it. Stephen was beneath his grandmother's thumb. The woman held the purse strings, and her grandson's inheritance, in her grasp.

With that thought encouraging him, Mark flicked the reins over the greys' backs, urging them to a faster pace. His concentration returned to Emily's brother. It was high time he had a few strong words with Tarquin, and he had a good idea where he might find him.

Emily restlessly paced the floor of her chamber. She had been feeling odd since Sarah had left. Although she could settle on nothing specific that she had said or done wrong to cause a rift with Sarah, none the less a pang of guilt would not be banished. With a final tug of the brush through her thick hair she tossed it, in a glint of silver, on to the bed. Aimlessly she went to the dressing chest and peered in the glass at her reflection.

Large silver eyes darted from pert nose to wide mouth to sharp little chin. She frowned as though she might find the answers she sought in her features. Was she being cruel to Stephen? She certainly liked him…but as a friend. Would she ever accept being a true wife to him? Bearing his children? Perhaps if he knew how she felt he might declare her a fraud, and their friendship a sham.

Augusta Bond knew the truth. Since the woman had first met her she had been adamant that she was not right for her grandson. Did Augusta consider her a heartless tease? She didn't want to hurt Stephen any more than she had wanted to upset her friend Sarah.

With a sigh Emily tipped the glass away from her and went to the door. She *had* been selfish in keeping Stephen dangling on a string...*in reserve*, her mother would put it, in case no better bachelor could be found to take her from the shelf. It was time to set him free to make an attachment with someone else...someone like Sarah.

'I was hoping to bump into you again, miss.'

Emily spun about at that sibilant hiss to see Mickey Riley peering in her direction from a nearby shop doorway. Once certain that she had noticed him, and in a scene that Emily felt she had played out before, he sloped nonchalantly along the pavement a yard or two, then darted into an alley.

After a moment Emily followed him, her expression grim.

Although she had hoped to quickly deliver the letter in her pocket to Stephen, it was opportune that Riley had accosted her. She would dearly love to give him a piece of her mind! She suspected that Tarquin's marriage had not been an unlucky aberration, but had been plotted in advance. It might not have come about but for this avaricious fellow.

'We ought to stop meeting like this, Mr Riley,' Emily said with harsh sarcasm.

Riley's lips pulled into a sideways grin. 'I'm flattered yer took the trouble to find out me name.'

'Please don't be. It was no trouble at all,' Emily returned icily. 'I do know who you are and much more about you besides.'

Riley cocked an insolent eyebrow at her, daring her to voice what she knew.

'You go first, and make it quick.' Emily crossed her arms over her waist in a display of impatience. 'I have no intention of spending more than a minute or two with you.'

'Well, that's a fine way to greet a feller who's been stood around hoping to give yer some news about yer brother.'

'I already have some news about my brother, Mr Riley,' Emily snapped in an underbreath. 'Believe me, I would rather not know it. So, if you are about to tell me that he has been coerced to wed one of your…' Emily swallowed the vulgarity. 'One of your female associates,' she resumed stiltedly, 'you may save your breath.'

'So you found out about Jenny, did yer?' Riley cupped his stubbly jaw in a hand and glanced at her from beneath lowered lids. His devious mind turned over recent events. He came to the swift conclusion that Mark Hunter had relayed to Miss Beaumont the unsavoury news. In which case that gentleman and this lady were *very* close. It was hardly a topic of light conversation. Riley had thought that if Mark Hunter were to babble to anyone about it he would have chosen old man Beaumont. Mickey gave his chin a final tickle. He'd need to tread carefully if he was to successfully play all sides against the middle or he'd risk losing a tidy profit.

With a careless gesture he said, 'Now yer know why I was keen to find Tarquin. Don't fret now. There's a way to square it afore all hell breaks loose.' He gave her a sympathetic smile. ''Course yer won't want to worry yer ma and pa with it all. But keeping it quiet and putting it right'll cost.' Riley snaked his tongue over his lips.

'And how exactly are you going to put it right?'

'Well, now—that's for me to know, and for you to pay to find out, ain't it?'

Emily gave a little scornful laugh. 'You fool! Are you about to ask for payment for a silly scheme to pretend the marriage didn't take place? Jeremiah Plumb performed the service and is a bona fide clergyman, so I understand. What will you do? Bribe him to delete the records and in doing so embroil my brother in yet more trouble?'

Mickey gave her a startled glare.

'It *was* your intention to do that, wasn't it?' Emily said with quiet incredulity.

'You think you're pretty clever, don't yer, miss?' Riley hissed. 'But that ain't what I wanted to speak to you about, although it do concern your brother.' Mickey felt cheated. He had thought his plot quite ingenious, yet it had taken her no more than a few minutes to unravel it.

When he had set out today he had been unsure whether to go ahead with the Viscount's wicked plan to entrap this lovely young lady for his own base needs. Now he thought it might serve her right. She could do with taking down a peg or two.

'Tell me quickly what it is, then,' Emily demanded. 'I have an important letter to deliver.'

'I've got a message for you from your brother.' Mickey jutted his chin. He'd got her attention now! An immediate gleam of concern had widened her eyes. He held out a hand. 'Crown'll do it.' Mickey felt a sense of triumph that the little madam was paying him for her ruination. His fingers sprang like a trap over the coin that Emily had furiously slapped there. 'Yer brother sent Jenny a note and off we went to see where he's holed up. He's got no money, so it were pointless looking to *him* to square Plumb and give me a little consideration for me efforts.' A sneer curled Mickey's top lip. It was the truth. He had certainly wasted his time with the loser. 'He's been drinking too much and sleeping rough since he bolted. Now he's taken a chill and it's turned nasty.' Mickey slipped a look at Emily to see her reaction to the tale so far. He could tell she was anxious to hear more. 'Jenny reckons all he needs is a dose of summat, and a hot meal inside of him, and he'll be good as new.' Mickey shook his head in a show of exasperation. 'Yer brother's fretting he might turn up his toes, and wants to see you. But he don't want to see yer pa just yet 'cos he's ashamed…naturally.'

'Why did *Jenny* not come to see me sooner?' Emily wailed in a stifled tone.

'*I* take care of things where Jenny's concerned,' Riley stated threateningly. 'Anyhow, it were only a day or two ago we got wind of it all.' He gave her a fierce look. 'Yer brother made it clear he only wants to see you. If you turn up with anyone else, he won't show his face.'

Emily's complexion was now quite ashen with strain. 'Are you lying? Is this a ruse to extort more money from me?'

'I could've arst fer more just now, miss,' Riley

pointed out, adopting a pious look. 'And I don't want to see him push up the daisies any more'n you do.'

'He'd be no use then, would he?' Emily breathed furiously. Riley might have scoffed at Tarquin's impecunious state, but Emily was sure the villain had not yet given up hope of finding a profit in her brother's calamitous marriage. 'Tell me at once where he is.'

'I've got a rig. A jarvey won't be keen to go that far. Be quicker 'n' cheaper if I take you. Won't arouse suspicion with yer parents if you're there 'n' back double quick.'

Emily cast a look at her feet; her head was feeling dizzy with milling anxieties. Riley was right on one score. Hiring a vehicle and driver would be costly, and take time. If he was telling the truth, and Tarquin was ill, she needed to see him immediately, and try to talk some sense into the dolt. It was inevitable that he must return home and face the music, ashamed or not, if he was to get better. Slowly she nodded, whilst prevaricating, 'I can't go right now. I need to get something from the apothecary for Tarquin. There is a potion that calms fever. I will meet you later this afternoon.'

Emily did not for a moment trust Riley, and was nervous about going anywhere alone with him. She urgently needed assistance, and there was only one person to turn to…Mark Hunter…

Chapter Eleven

'Mr Hunter is out, Miss Beaumont.' Such was the butler's polite response when Emily gave her name and requested an immediate audience with his master.

Geoffrey Lomax cast a dubious eye over the lovely young woman. It was obvious that she was a lady of good class, and that made her behaviour the more bizarre. It was not at all proper for an unaccompanied spinster to pay an impromptu call on a bachelor. His stern look softened a mite as he noticed her downcast expression. He deduced it was a matter of vital importance that had made her act bold and look glum. 'If you would like to leave a message for Mr Hunter, I will make sure he has it directly he returns,' he promised.

Chaotic thoughts cluttered her brain, keeping Emily wide-eyed and mute before the manservant. What was she to do? In a short while she was to meet Riley, and he had made it clear he would not wait if she were late for their rendezvous. But she desperately wanted Mark apprised of this latest development. Trusting Riley to his word carried a grave risk to her personal safety. The matter was too confidential to leave a verbal message with the butler, but a communication of some sort must be made. 'Might I beg leave to have a pen and paper in order to write your master a note?'

A nod and a smile from Lomax invited her in to Mark's mansion on Belgrave Crescent.

Emily stepped over the threshold and into a vast hallway. Absently her mind registered its opulence; smooth flags on the floor were of the same pristine marble as the graceful pillars that soared out of sight. Whilst the butler disappeared to fetch writing implements for her, she noted the stark elegance of Mark Hunter's home. She paced nervously, oblivious to being surreptitiously observed from outside.

When Barbara's equipage had drawn up at the kerb a few minutes ago, she had been immensely frustrated to see Emily hurrying up the wide stone steps. She had been on the point of using them herself!

She had swallowed her pride, and her fears that she might be hastening her own demise, to come to see Mark. Her hope had been to find him in a mellow mood and thus receptive to sharing sweet reminiscences of their youth. Barbara's scowl deepened. The sight of the Beaumont girl had shaken her optimism, seeded doubts that Mark might be swayed by appeals to his memory...or his virility.

The footman closed the huge doors, cutting off Barbara's view of Emily, thereby prompting a few unladylike expletives to roll off her tongue. She slammed her back against the squabs. It seemed that Miss Beaumont was soliciting Mark's attention without so much as a maid in tow as token chaperon. But there was little satisfaction in knowing that her rival was a brazen baggage.

A furrow marred her brow as she sought for a reason why Emily might act with such audacity. Barbara was still ruminating on that conundrum when she heard the door again being opened. Quickly she shifted forward on the seat and twitched aside the blind. She watched as Emily descended the steps and headed off at a fast pace.

A smile curled Barbara's tinted lips for Emily's countenance had been puckered with strain. Perhaps Mark had been disgusted by her shocking intrusion and had sent her off with a flea in her ear. She had not been inside the house above ten minutes.

Assisted by a footman, Barbara was soon out of her carriage and mounting the steps.

'Mr Hunter is not at home, Mrs Emerson.' Mr Lomax coupled the information with a dour expression. He had never warmed to this woman despite knowing she had, for many years, retained her position as the master's favourite lady friend. His lids descended over eyes studying Barbara's lush figure swathed in muslin and a flimsy silk cape. Obviously the woman had attractions…if no sense on how to keep warm on a chilly day. And Mr Hunter was certainly a red-blooded gentleman.

Barbara sailed past Lomax and into the house with all the pomp of a woman who believed it her right to do so. She twirled about and gave the butler a perfunctory smile. 'How disagreeable to have missed him. But he was not expecting me, so I cannot scold him.' Her features were a study of insouciance as she glanced about. Her dark eyes darted back to a piece of parchment resting on an ebony surface. Idly Barbara moved in that direction to check her appearance in a gilt-framed mirror positioned over the console table. Her bonnet ribbons were loosened, then made more secure, but all the while covert glances were scanning what she now recognised to be a letter. On it she could decipher Mark's name, and it had undoubtedly been written in a female hand. Barbara's heart jumped a beat, for she had noticed something that indicated it could be from only one woman: the ink was still moist! Swiftly she turned her back on her reflection and re-garded Lomax, but her hands were gripping the edge of the table behind her.

Her mind was suddenly overwhelmed by the whispered words she had overheard on Lady Ger-rard's terrace. *But what if there is a child...what are we to do then?* Did Emily Beaumont now know for certain she was increasing with Mark's child? Such staggering news would certainly prompt her to dis-regard etiquette and urgently seek him. And she *had* looked violently troubled when she left this house a short while ago.

Barbara's fingers tightened on ebony as she strove to contain her tormented imaginings. 'I shall not leave a message and you need not tell Mr Hunter that I called.'

Mr Lomax elevated a quizzical eyebrow. 'As you wish, ma'am.'

Barbara's exploring fingers located paper and snatched. Suddenly she surged towards the door, rapidly covering marble in small steps. 'I think that is all,' she said as she swept past Mr Lomax. A regal nod at the footman bid he attend the door.

'Does your wife know what you get up to?'

The drawled irony made Tarquin shoot up out of the armchair. The young woman who had been balancing astride his lap tumbled awkwardly sideways. She quickly scrambled to her feet whilst smoothing down her skirts and giving Tarquin's arm an admonishing thump for such rough treatment.

'What in damnation…?' Tarquin's unshaven jaw dropped to his chest. Agitatedly he scraped his fingers through his lank, flaxen hair, all the while gawping at Mark. 'You just gave me the fright of my life, Hunter. What in damnation are *you* doing here?' he snarled, fumbling at his breeches, his face ruddy with embarrassment.

'What am *I* doing here?' Mark echoed in a tone replete with sarcasm. He looked about the comfortable, if spartanly furnished, room. 'Last time I saw the deeds I owned this lodge. I thus feel quite entitled to use it. More to the point, Beaumont, is what the hell you are doing here. Besides worrying the life out of your family, of course. But then I suppose you've not given much thought to any of that, have you?'

'I hope you're not going to preach,' Tarquin muttered. 'You're no saint by any means.'

'True; nevertheless you need a lesson over this.' Mark moved purposefully closer, but halted when Tarquin's companion skipped to shield him with her dishevelled figure. She continued to button her bodice, but up went her chin, and she challengingly met Mark's eyes.

A contemptuous look was directed over her head at Tarquin before Mark strolled away to examine what was on the small dining table. He picked up a fork and turned over the remnants of a half-eaten meal of cheese and venison. A bottle of claret had a small amount left in it. Mark recognised the wine as from his cellar—a particularly good vintage—and it prompted him to wryly smile and wonder what provisions, if any, were left in the store. Mark poured what remained of the claret into a tumbler and tossed it back in a gulp. As he replaced his glass he remarked drily, 'I see you've not gone without…' A significant glance lingered on the woman. 'Does your wife care that you've abandoned her? Or perhaps the honeymoon is already over.'

'This *is* my wife,' Tarquin admitted petulantly, and flung himself down into the chair he'd recently vacated.

'Ah…I take it the honeymoon is progressing well, then.' Mark took a more interested look at the pretty young woman and realised he vaguely recognised her. If his memory served him correctly, he had spotted Riley and her loitering in the vicinity of the *modiste*'s shop on Regent Street. On that occasion she had been wearing a flamboyant hat that had shielded her features. 'Your manners are sadly lacking, Tarquin. Aren't you going to properly introduce us?'

Tarquin did so, tersely. He gained his feet with a sigh and ambled to stand by his wife's side in a show of grudging loyalty. Jenny slipped her hand through his arm and rewarded his gallantry with a little peck on the cheek. Mark received from her a glower that dared him to comment.

'I suppose my marriage is common knowledge if you've come here looking for me. No doubt my father is beside himself and Mother is prostrate on a sofa with her salts—'

'They don't know,' Mark cut sharply over Tarquin's self-pitying whine. 'And you had best give some serious thought to what you intend to do about the mess you're in.'

'He'll cut me off without a penny.'

'Can you blame him? You must have understood the risk you were taking.'

'I hardly understood a blasted thing! I was so far in my cups, I was barely conscious throughout the service.'

Irritably Tarquin shrugged off Jenny's possessive grip and stomped to a window of the hunting lodge. He gazed out through brown bars of bark to greensward in the distance. Finally he sighed and said, 'It's a God-awful mess. I don't know what to do.'

'You've got about half an hour to decide; then, ready or not, you're coming back with me.' Mark said in a voice that brooked no refusal. He glanced about. 'I'm afraid your sojourn enjoying all the comforts of home, at my expense, has just ended. And to make sure you fully understand that...I'll take back my spare keys.'

Tarquin turned his back on the pastoral view of Enfield Chase. Reluctantly he fished in a pocket, then lobbed metal on to the table. His mumbled gratitude for enjoying free hospitality was soon followed by, 'So if it is *not* common knowledge about my marriage, how did *you* find out?'

'Riley told me. He's been trying to use your *mésalliance* to extort money from Emily. I've no doubt he would have blackmailed you instead had he discovered where you were hiding.' Mark glanced at

Jenny. 'I take it your wife has *your* best interests at heart, not Riley's?'

Tarquin looked affronted at that but, nevertheless, shot a dubious look Jenny's way.

She had the grace to immediately blush. 'I tried to put him off going after your sister,' she insisted. 'I told him to forget all about the Beaumonts and find another punter who'd cough up easy. But he's a stubborn blighter. He wouldn't let it rest.' She raised doe-eyes to her husband. 'I could've let on to Mickey where you was hiding, but I never did… honest…'

'Emily's embroiled in this?' Tarquin had suddenly recaptured control of his shocked senses. His hoarse demand cut across his wife's reassurances. Her little nod sent both his hands to cup his face, and he shook his head in a show of remorse.

Jenny snuggled against him, said softly, 'I come here today to tell you about Riley and what he's up to now, 'cos it ain't right, and I want no part of it. I would've said sooner about your sister, but…' the pink in her cheeks deepened to crimson. '…you distracted me and it slipped me mind.'

Tarquin fidgeted on the spot. He couldn't deny he had given Jenny very little opportunity to strike up a conversation since she arrived about twenty minutes ago. He cleared his throat, asked stiffly, 'What have you to tell me about Emily?'

Jenny seemed suddenly tongue-tied. It was not the frowning look from her husband unsettling her, but the callous stare from his friend. Suddenly the fellow made a violently impatient gesture, making her jump and slip behind Tarquin.

'If you know that Riley is planning more mischief in order to extort money from Miss Beaumont…' Mark began.

'It isn't that,' she blurted. 'Mickey's getting paid all right, but not from her.' She looked at Tarquin apologetically. 'He's made a bargain with a fellow who's got a fancy for your sister, and wants a chance to be private with her. Mickey, the vile devil, is getting paid to set up a meeting between them.' Jenny quickly glanced away from the terrifying glint in Mark Hunter's eyes.

'What nonsense!' Tarquin snorted. 'I know Stephen Bond fancies Emily, but he's a decent fellow. He hasn't got it in him to plot a seduction, I'm sure of it.' He shot a look at Mark and paled, for his friend's features might have been hewn from stone.

'What arrangements has Riley made? How is he to lure her there? Is it to soon take place?' Mark fired the questions at Jenny.

Jenny blinked rapidly and moistened her lips. 'It's soon,' she admitted. 'I know Mickey wants to get his hands on the cash quick as can be. But that's all he's let on to me. By my reckoning he'll use Tarquin as the bait.'

'And who asked Mickey to set it up?' Mark demanded with icy quiet. 'And don't lie to me.'

Jenny simply gazed forlornly at Tarquin for support. But he seemed to have retreated into a daze. His thumbnail was being whittled away by worrying teeth.

'Tell me the name of the devil or by Heaven I'll throttle it out of you!' Mark gritted at Jenny through unmoving lips.

'Steady on, Hunter…' Tarquin snapped to attention to remonstrate on his wife's behalf.

'It's Devlin!' Jenny suddenly shouted with tears of fright sparking in her eyes. She knew that she had just burned her bridges by betraying Mickey. If he ever found out his money-spinner had turned sour due to her, he would not hesitate to seek revenge. She took a deep breath and repeated shakily, 'It's Devlin…that's who it is…the brute…'

Emily looked up at the façade of the house and frowned. Moments ago she had disembarked from

Riley's gig and now stood with him on gravel that formed a circular drive to an elegant double-fronted residence. She took a look about. The property was definitely isolated from its neighbours, but was of grand proportions, and that put it beyond Tarquin's pocket even had he been flush.

On the journey to the edge of town she had pondered on the hardship Tarquin might be enduring. Images of rural cottages with draughts whistling through windows and doors had beset her mind. She had feared she might find him a shivering wreck wrapped in rags with no fire in the grate. On looking skyward she could see curls of smoke drifting lazily upwards from twin chimneys.

Riley had told her that Tarquin was ill from sleeping rough. If he were within these doors, it would be more likely he was in fine fettle, and had been reposing on a feather bed at night.

She turned to Riley with a dubious frown and an unpleasant sensation gnawing at the pit of her stomach. 'Tarquin would never have the means to rent such a house. As far as I am aware he has no friends hereabouts who might let him use their property. Are you sure this is the right place?'

'It's the right place right enough,' Mickey returned on a bark of a laugh, but he avoided her eyes.

Suddenly he stooped and grabbed the little bag of provisions and potions she had brought with her. 'Come along, miss, won't do to dawdle or we'll never get back to town afore it gets dark.' As though to emphasise that threat he glanced up deliberately at the lowering clouds in the west.

Emily skipped after his striding figure despite the host of niggling suspicions in her mind. Before she could voice even one anxiety, the door was suddenly opened by a manservant. Emily hesitated, the hairs on the back of her neck stirring as she noted the fellow's neat uniform. It was an unusual livery of brown and gold that she recalled seeing before…quite recently. An instinct made Emily stop and take a pace back.

Riley had noticed her hesitation and, firmly clasping one of her elbows, propelled her up the steps and into the hallway. The manservant immediately closed the door and silently withdrew.

Emily spun about to gaze at Riley. But his attention was elsewhere.

'There…all ready and waiting,' he said, with a leer, but it was not her he was addressing in such a lewd tone of voice.

Slowly she became aware of approaching footfalls and twisted about. Her soft mouth slackened in amazement and her delicate brows pulled together. 'Nicholas?' She tested the name even though she could see quite clearly that it was indeed her former fiancé. She gave a little hysterical laugh. 'Oh, never say that *you* have given my brother shelter. I thought the two of you were still at odds. Do you know all about Tarquin's disappearance?'

'I'm afraid I don't, my dear, nor do I want to,' Devlin said bluntly. 'But over dinner you can tell me all about it, if you like. I'm prepared to indulge you, despite I couldn't give a tinker's cuss how he does. It's *you* who arouses my interest,' he concluded throatily.

Emily's soft lips slackened, her eyes grew round. An absurd notion that the two men might have been in cahoots to dupe her entered her mind and refused to budge.

'I take it this is mine?' Riley said and snatched up something from the hall table.

Emily whisked about to look at him, but was uncertain to what he referred. Then she heard the unmistakable chink of coins as they were dropped into his pocket.

Mickey Riley had been paid by Viscount Devlin to bring her here! Swiftly she strode to Nicholas and glared up into his tawny eyes. 'Have you plotted with this…this cur to trick me? Have you brought me here for no good reason?'

Nicholas put out a hand to touch her face soothingly. 'You're here for a very good reason, my love. I know you remember another such time when we were alone…and both so very pleased to be so. Soon you'll be glad I acted the despot.'

Emily savagely slapped away the fingers that stroked her cheek. 'You despicable beast!' She would have returned her fist to her side, but it spontaneously raised and made vicious contact with his jaw. Obliquely she heard Riley give a hoot of laughter.

Nicholas pressed a few fingers to the livid stain her assault had put on his skin.

'If it's taming you want tonight, I'll give it to you,' he said hoarsely, his eyes darkening with a mix of anger and excitement.

Emily felt fear painfully knotting her insides, but steeled her courage, determined not to panic. 'Was it not enough that you seduced me once before?' she whispered in a tone of sheer loathing.

'Of course not, or why would I go to such trouble and expense to do it again?' Nicholas tore his eyes from Emily's lovely features to give Riley a speaking look.

A ribald chuckle from Riley was the extent of

him taking his leave. The sound seemed to echo about the hallway, petrifying Emily for a moment. Quickly gathering her senses, she flew towards the open door to escape from the house but, from the shadows, the manservant appeared. The fellow turned the key in the lock and removed it. As Emily watched her gaoler disappear she remembered where she had before seen that distinctive earth-brown livery: it had been in Whiting Street. Devlin's coachman had been caped in brown and gold.

Her heart was thudding painfully slowly as she turned back to Devlin. She felt barely able to breathe let alone speak. Finally her arid, trembling lips formed brave words. 'You are a devil and I am utterly ashamed that I once knew so little about your character that I wanted to marry you.'

'Hush…' Devlin purred as he pursued her retreating figure until she was cornered. 'You have nothing to fear from me, Emily. I understand that you are angry at my scheming with that ghastly ruffian. But what could I do?' He shrugged elegant shoulders. 'You refused to meet me…sent me cruel letters spurning my love. Why? I want nothing from you that you have not before freely given.'

Chapter Twelve

'I'll swing for Devlin! I should have finished him off last time!' The dangerous sentiment exploded from Tarquin as Mark's curricle ground to a halt outside the Beaumont residence in Callison Crescent.

As they had sped through the northern suburbs of town Mark had been similarly plagued by murderous thoughts. But he had kept tightly leashed his emotions and his threats. For now, saving Emily was his only concern. Once that was achieved he would be ready to turn his mind to retribution...

'Devlin will pay.' It was a vow as cold and hard as a knife thrust. 'You may stake your life on it. But for now we must ensure Emily is warned of the dangers.'

Tarquin sprang to the ground, his features contorted with anguish and remorse. Mark knew his friend was concerned not only for the safety of his sister but for his wife too.

About half an hour ago Jenny had been set down. Shortly before she had disembarked, she had voiced her fear that Mickey would exact revenge if he discovered she had ruined his deal with Devlin. But she had bravely reassured Tarquin that she would lie low with an aunt who lived in Hackney until things could be sorted out. And there, in Brewer Street, they had left her.

'Your wife is right in one respect,' Mark said. 'Riley doesn't yet know you have returned to your family. If he tries to use your absence to lure Emily away, the trick is exposed for what it is.'

The grooves about Tarquin's mouth deepened as he manfully strove to conceal his distress. He had set in motion a disastrous sequence of events and the consequences were coming home to roost. Mark saw Tarquin's lips tighten, but felt not a twinge of pity for him. Emily was his only concern; once he knew for certain she was safe, Tarquin would be the second target for his wrath.

'It might be wise to keep the worst of it all from your parents,' Mark suggested tightly. 'Their natural outrage might create a hue and cry and give the miscreants time to skedaddle or concoct a defence.'

'There's nowhere that cur can hide that I won't find him.'

'I'll deal with the Viscount.'

Tarquin cuffed his dewy nose, then paced restlessly back and forth on the pavement. 'You may go and batter the fiend if you like, but it won't stop me killing him afterwards! I had him for a callous libertine, but not so low that he would scheme to ruin a gentlewoman he once purported to adore!' Abruptly he stalked off towards the house, but Mark called him back.

'What caused you to fight him all those years ago? Did your hatred spring from the broken engagement between Emily and Devlin?'

Tarquin shook his head and gazed fiercely into the dusk. 'The engagement was broken *after* I gave him a beating, not before.' He paused, shifted his weight from foot to foot. 'I've never told Emily this—or my parents for that matter. Emily, especially, would be mortified to know what sort of vile character she'd once loved. She was upset for months after their betrothal ended.' He gave Mark a piercing look. 'If my father had found out he would have called for pistols. But I trust you to keep this to yourself.' His unshaven chin was cradled in fidgeting fingers. 'In my opinion the Viscount was relieved the betrothal came to nought. He was a fortune hunter, and Emily's dowry was never going to be enough to satisfy his greed, or his debts.' Tarquin's expression turned sheepish. 'You probably think I've got a devil of a nerve to talk so about a fellow's gambling debts, but I would never sell my soul, or betray a woman's love, for cash.' He plunged his hands into his pockets. 'Anyhow, on one long night in White's, when we both had been several hours at the faro table, I took a short break. He didn't know I'd returned and was close behind him. I overheard him boasting about Emily to one of his cronies…lewd disrespectful talk…about how fortunate he was that his betrothed was a hot wanton, as though already he had bedded her.' Tarquin drew in a sharp breath. 'He was drunk, it's true, but there was no excuse for such despicable slander. Devlin's a weasel. I should have finished him off then, when I had the chance.'

Mark felt a tightening in his gut and his back teeth clenched together, making his jaw ache. 'I'm glad you told me,' he said with steely quiet. 'Now go…do what you must to make your apologies to your family.' Without another word he set the curricle in motion. As he pelted through the streets towards Belgrave Crescent, one thought tormented his mind. Was it slander, or had the Viscount and Emily been lovers when they were engaged?

A bittersweet memory niggled at Mark's consciousness, made him fear the truth was the answer he didn't want. Emily had ended their first kiss too soon and, in frustration, he had made a crass remark. His attempt at conciliation had been rebuffed and she had refused to elaborate on her reasons for rejecting a compliment on her innocence. Now, with wounding insight, Mark suspected he knew what she meant by it. Once she had been Devlin's mistress as well as his betrothed. Perhaps the Viscount thought he was entitled to that intimacy again… whether she was willing or not.

'Arrange for fresh horses to be brought round. At once!'

Geoffrey Lomax gazed at his master's broad back as he strode the hallway, then took the stairs two at a time. Snapping from his daze at being on the receiving end of such uncharacteristic churlishness from Mr Hunter, the butler sprang to do his bidding.

Within minutes Mark was again in the lobby, the weight of razor-edged steel in one pocket of his greatcoat balanced by a duck's foot pistol in the other. He was not a violent man, and hoped the weapons would remain unused, but he accepted he must be prepared for any eventuality.

If Devlin were not at home this evening, Riley's slum would be his next port of call. Mark suspected that a fight would erupt if Riley's two henchmen were about. A brawl, even with odds stacked against him, would not usually bother him. Without vanity he accepted his notoriety as one of Gentleman Jackson's finest. But he did not want his mettle tested. He wanted to be fit and able to protect Emily if the need arose.

Aware that his grim-faced master was on his way out without another word passing between them, Lomax hopped to intercept him. 'Umm… there was a caller in your absence, sir. I promised to give you the lady's note as soon as you returned.'

Mark halted at once and frowned fiercely at Lomax. 'A woman came here to see me?'

'Miss Beaumont was her name, and she seemed upset to have missed you. She left a note,' Lomax concisely informed his master.

'Give it to me at once,' Mark demanded hoarsely, a hand already outstretched to receive it.

Lomax hurried to the console table and gazed in vain. He crouched on spindly legs to see if the note had dropped to the floor. He scanned an arc of marble in case it had gone further adrift.

Mark walked towards him, his expression thunderous.

'I cannot understand it, sir. I put it here. I know I did.'

'Has another servant moved it?'

'They wouldn't dare…nobody has been near nor by except…'

'Except?' Mark prompted with dangerous impatience.

A grimace of disbelief distorted the butler's features, for what he suspected, yet hesitated to mention, was outlandish…perhaps calumnious. 'Mrs Emerson called, a few minutes after Miss Beaumont left. Mrs Emerson did study her reflection in this mirror, but she said not to mention her visit, so of course I would not have done so…'

Before the servant had concluded his explanation Mark loosed a terse dismissal and strode to the door, his lips a thin white line on clenched teeth.

The note reposed on polished mahogany amid crystal perfume bottles and chased silver boxes. Barbara was seated on her little velvet boudoir chair, her dark eyes resting on the tantalising white rectangle.

Abruptly she picked it up. Her pale fingers slipped
to the sealing wax, then withdrew. Irritably she
tapped the paper against a thumbnail as she strove
for the courage to open it. If Mark ever discovered
what she had done there would be no adequate explanation for such outrageous impertinence. But
now that she had stolen the note, it seemed silly to
simply imagine what it might contain. Holding it to
the window, or to candlelight, had elicited not a hint
of what message was concealed within. With a
gulped breath, and a burst of activity, Barbara tore
at the wax, quickly unfolded the parchment and
scanned the single paragraph.

*Riley has discovered Tarquin's whereabouts, and
that he is ill, and wants to see me. Riley will not disclose the exact location other than to say it is on the
outskirts of town. It cannot be too distant as he promises we will return before dusk. I do not completely
trust him, yet don't know what he might gain from
such a lie. So I shall go with him, and do my best to
persuade Tarquin that he must return to face the
music. I trust we will return safely together and that
you might continue to give your support and counsel to Tarquin. I wish I had found you at home to tell
you all this...*

Barbara frowned and read it again, then, with a

little oath, tossed it aside. It had not been worth the effort at all! She had hoped—or rather dreaded—that she had intercepted a love letter, or one that informed Mark that he'd impregnated the little trollop. But what had she got? Just drivel concerning Emily's gadabout brother and a fellow called Riley who knew where the wastrel was to be found. What cared she for any of that?

Perhaps she had been too hasty in thinking Mark and Emily were in love. Barbara picked over the words more carefully, looking for hidden meaning. Emily might have written of her regrets at not finding Mark at home, but there was no hint of passion in her prose.

A sound of pattering feet made Barbara swivel on her chair. Her maid appeared in the doorway, her small chest heaving as though she had sprinted up the stairs. 'The *monsieur* is here, *madame*, but I said he must wait below, for he looks so very angry…' The French girl shivered into silence as she sensed Mark's presence behind her.

'You may leave us, Claudine,' Barbara said, but her voice sounded shrill, and her unsteady fingers swiftly slid back and forth behind her to try to conceal the parchment with boxes and bottles.

Her fluttering fingers and flustered demeanour made a purely cynical smile touch Mark's mouth.

Barbara gained her feet in a sinuous movement and swayed towards him, arresting his progress towards the dressing table. 'This is a most pleasant surprise,' she murmured huskily and went on tiptoe with her face tilted as though to kiss him.

Mark caught the twin white limbs that would have snaked about his neck. Keeping a firm grip on her wrists, he pulled her with him towards the dressing table. A perfume pot crashed to its side, filling the air with musky scent, as he carelessly cleared the note of obstacles. But for a tic close to his mouth, Mark's face remained impassive as he read Emily's cry for help.

'I…I came to see you earlier,' Barbara started in a rush, disturbed by his peculiar stillness. 'You were out. When I said I might soon chance upon you in Hyde Park, Lomax gave me the letter to take to you…' Her words faded away to awkward silence, but it was not her fluent lie unsettling her as much as the vivid blue eyes boring coldly into her.

'Is that so?' Mark asked in a voice of silky steel. 'For the moment we will ignore the poor likelihood of any such meeting. What excuse have you for opening a letter addressed to me?'

Barbara's cheeks bloomed beneath his contempt. 'It might have been a pressing matter,' she breathed, in a burst of inspiration. 'Indeed, I deemed it to be of a vital nature, for your butler to want it so quickly delivered,' she smoothly reasoned with a winning smile. 'When I could not see you in the Park I thought I ought to open it and find out if that were so, in case I should search for you elsewhere.'

Mark grunted a mirthless laugh and extricated his hand from fingers that had crept to erotically fondle his palm. 'You're a mischief-maker, Barbara, amongst other things.' He strode away from her and was again at the door when he added, 'It's a pity it has come to this between us. I've no time now to say more, but I think you already suspect how I feel. In any case, know this: I despise liars and thieves.'

As Mark leaped from his curricle outside the Beaumonts' home, Tarquin hurtled down the steps as though he had been waiting for his friend to hove into view.

'Thank God you're back! Emily is not at home and hasn't been seen since early this afternoon,' Tarquin gabbled, his brows drawn tight together in consternation.

Mark felt a stab of anguish. It was the news he had expected, yet dreaded to hear, from one of the Beaumonts.

'My parents are not yet too concerned—they think she is probably gone off with her friend Sarah Harper. They often spend many hours together. Let's see if she is at Sarah's. It's not far…'

'She isn't there,' Mark bleakly dashed Tarquin's hopes whilst raking fingers through his dark hair. Abruptly he pulled from a pocket Emily's note and thrust it at Tarquin.

Tarquin moved to stand beneath the pale light of a gas lamp to scan it. 'Damnation! Jenny was right! He's used the very trick she mentioned. We're too late. Devlin's got her.' This last was uttered in a voice that vibrated with horrified disbelief.

'But where? Where has he got her?' Mark clipped out in a tone that hinted at desperation. He strove to stay calm. The boundary of his control was crumbling. But to succumb to rage would defeat reason. And then he would never help Emily. Her note was a tangible proof of her trust in him. In the lines of her composition he had sensed her heartfelt plea that he must come to her rescue if it transpired that Riley was up to no good. Mark tipped back his head and aimed a string of foul curses at the emerging stars. If only he had been at home when she called. But he had been in Enfield, evicting her brother from the hunting lodge. He squeezed shut his eyes, but the hideous images of Emily's torment would not quit his mind.

'Riley will have gone to ground,' he reasoned hoarsely. 'He will have suspected that Emily would not go with him without leaving a message of sorts with someone she trusted. He is wily enough to know that person would come looking for him when Emily did not return.' Mark paced to and fro, his hands plunged deep into his pockets, his face a study of savage concentration. 'Devlin will have arranged that Emily be taken to an isolated spot. Without Riley leading us there, it will be impossible to find it.'

'Jenny will have a few ideas where Riley hides out.' Tarquin's face grew animated. 'We can go and beat out of him where he has taken Emily.' Tarquin's bright expression crumpled and he aimed a grimace at the Beaumont residence. 'I've deflected my parents' questions so far with lame excuses. My father is too disgusted with me to stay in my company for long.' He paused. 'But Mother is a constant shadow. I had a devil of a job escaping just now. She attempted to drag me back by my coat-tails when I said I was off out with you.' He shook his head in despair as he dwelled on their likely reaction to knowing of their daughter's jeopardy. 'We must bring Emily back, whatever that bastard has done to her. If she is sullied, we must make sure that we are the only ones who know of it.'

'It won't come to that!' Mark gritted out and turned on Tarquin eyes that resembled ebony slits. 'We must make sure it doesn't come to that.'

Tarquin quickly nodded, keen to pacify his friend. He had known for a while that Mark was soft on Emily. His friend was sensibly attempting to direct his energy into solving the riddle of Emily's whereabouts. But until they had an inkling of where that might be they were powerless to save her, and Mark's simmering frustration was close to erupting in violence.

'If we manage to snatch Emily from his clutches, Devlin might threaten to spread gossip from spite,' Mark said. 'He knows it is Emily who will suffer most from a scandal.'

'I'll cut out his tongue if he does that!' Tarquin said. 'After that, I'll take his black heart.'

'You need to keep a cool head until Emily is safe.' Within a moment he had added on an insightful sigh, 'We both do…'

As though fearing Mark might refuse his company, Tarquin sprang aboard the curricle and settled firmly into the seat. 'There's no time to lose. Let's go and find Jenny. I'll wager she's privy to Riley's hidey-holes.' He cast a worried look homeward and noticed his mother peering at him between the curtains. 'My father will kill me if Emily is harmed!' he groaned.

'He won't. I will,' Mark vowed with perilous quiet before he joined Tarquin on the seat.

Chapter Thirteen

'You have planned this quite meticulously.' Emily raised her goblet and let ruby wine just moisten her lips. She had no intention of allowing Nicholas to get her tipsy. But there might be an advantage in fostering his mellow humour and letting him think she was tolerant of his company and his hospitality. The less he thought she was inclined to escape the more likely she was to successfully do so.

The initial shock of having been kidnapped had lessened and Emily had come to the conclusion that expending energy on angry complaints would be foolish. Better, surely, to employ the same craftiness that had been used against her.

She guessed she had now been in captivity for some hours although she had no idea of the exact time. It seemed the only people at the house were the manservant who had opened the door, and a young maid who had shown her to a chamber to make ready to dine.

Despite her fright and simmering anger, Emily had been grateful for the sanctuary it provided. She had been tired and dusty after her headlong trip with Riley and felt unprepared to pit her wits immediately against her captor.

The chamber had been warm and steaming scented washing water had helped to soothe her fraught senses. Emily had dismissed the maid despite the girl's insistence that she must press her crumpled dress and style her hair. Emily had had no intention of allowing herself to be primped for the benefit of the scheming lecher waiting for her below. She had also wanted the maid gone from the room in order to investigate possible escape routes. But a swift inspection had revealed that every window was sealed and the door had been locked from outside. That discovery had set Emily's pulse racing alarmingly. In a moment desolation had overwhelmed her and brought scalding tears to sting her weary eyes.

From the moment Riley had departed, leaving her alone with the Viscount and his minions, she had not given up hope that she might soon manage to flee. But it seemed that Nicholas had schooled his servants well. Both his butler and his maidservant had cooperated in her incarceration.

By the time the maid had returned Emily had curbed the craven instinct to wail and plead for liberation and was more composed. With the girl's encouragement she had freshened herself with the lavender-water and untangled the knots from her blonde tresses well enough to tease them into a plain chignon. Her pride in her appearance had been solely for her own benefit. She had resolved not to appear before Nicholas looking a wreck lest he believed he had managed to cow her. She would not snivel, nor would she outwardly quake even if her insides felt like jelly. She would certainly never willingly do his bidding. Once she had believed he cherished her, and had proved she trusted him by gifting him her body. Now she would fight him with her last breath rather than tolerate even a kiss from him.

As she had followed the girl down the wide carpeted stairway, Emily had been oblivious to her plush surroundings. Her thoughts had been with her parents. She had drawn comfort from the recollection that they had an invitation for this evening. If they returned late from the opera they might retire without ever knowing their daughter's bed was empty. There was yet time to avert their heartache…and a scandal. But she must get home, and to do that she must pray that Mark came to her rescue in time.

She would remain optimistic, she vowed beneath her breath, her fingers stressfully tightening in her lap. By now Mark would have her note and be immediately suspicious as to Riley's motives for taking her out of town. He would go to Callison Crescent and, without alerting her parents to her jeopardy, discover she had not returned home. Then he would search for Riley and interrogate the duplicitous pimp until he admitted he had tricked her into going with him, and revealed her whereabouts.

Having thus boosted her morale, she resented the small inner voice that would rob her of such sweet confidence. *But what if Mark cannot find Riley?* it whispered. Perhaps he might be injured in the pursuit of the villain. And plainly there was a chance he might not yet have returned home to take delivery of her note. He was a leading light of polite society with family, friends and a mistress to occupy his time. He might not return to his own home or bed at all tonight…

Emily forgot her rule to be abstemious. She took

a spontaneous gulp from her wine to steady her pounding heart. If only Mark had been at home when she called! Abruptly she deposited the glass on the table, fearing it might shatter in her bone-white clutch. She fought down the panic tightening her chest and gulped in a steadying breath.

A calculating look flew from under her lashes at the man seated opposite her. To keep at bay his advances, she must engage him in conversation. Eventually she might prick his conscience, and persuade him to go home to his wife.

'You have been deep in thought, my love. Have you concocted a plot to escape?' Nicholas's torrid gaze swept over her, lingering where the rapidity of her breathing was straining the buttons on her bodice.

Emily felt her cheeks tingle; he was close to reading her mind. 'Escape?' She gurgled a laugh and made a dismissive gesture. 'Do you expect I might resort to running around aimlessly in the cold and dark?' Her tone was scornful, yet in truth she would most definitely choose the night, and the unknown countryside, over him.

'Is this house yours or have you acquired it simply as a theatre for seduction?' She inwardly praised herself for sounding so calm when it was hard to keep her teeth from chattering. Her sleek fair head turned this way and that as she studied the stylish furnishings bathed in an ambience from logs burning in the grate. 'It is a fine stage. Should I be flattered that I merit such lavish treatment?'

Devlin gave a throaty chuckle. 'I am pleased to know that you are still my proud, intrepid Emily. No tears…no tantrums…you know deep in your heart, my love, that we are destined to be together, do you not?'

'You have not answered my question, Nicholas,' Emily scolded breathily.

'The property was one of many that came to me on marriage as part of my wife's dowry. But what matter its origins? I'm glad you like it—we shall make regular use of it. It shall be our special place to meet. Perhaps—if you greatly please me—I might eventually make it yours.'

'How kind… But I'm not sure that I like it that much,' Emily returned acidly. 'And I doubt your wife would appreciate the use to which you put her property.'

'It is no longer her property and we will not speak of her again.'

'Why ever not?' Emily demanded pithily. The longer they conversed about his duty to his family, the more confident Emily became that he might relent. 'Would you deny your wife's existence? Or that of your unborn child?'

Nicholas forcefully thrust away his plate, making Emily start and drop her fork. It seemed she had softened him not one jot.

'I suspect you are about to moralise and we both know you are hardly a lady fit to do so.'

'And you are hardly a gentleman to have reminded me,' Emily returned. She had expected a reference would be made to their one night of passion and had steeled herself to parry it. Yet she could feel tingling in her face and queasiness in her belly from the shame of it. Her brazen riposte remained blocked in her dry throat.

'I am not complaining about your passionate nature, my dear, as I'm sure you know.' Nicholas gave a lascivious chuckle as he noticed the roses in her cheeks spread to her throat.

'I thought I loved you, Nicholas, and it ill behoves you to mock my sincere emotion. Had I not been so young, and so very naïve, I would have understood that, for you, I was just sport. When I lay with you, I truly believed we soon would be man and wife.'

'And I truly regret it could not be,' Nicholas drawled. 'Alas, you tempted me with your body, my dear, but had no such desirable dowry.' He smiled wryly. 'I must say that, for just a few thousand more, I might have forgone an heiress…'

'I doubt it,' Emily snapped. His flippancy had fired her anger to such a degree her trepidation was evaporating.

'I do too,' he conceded with an impenitent smile. 'A woman with thirty thousand, and a property portfolio of the same value, has undeniable allure for a man with pockets to let.'

'You tricked me with lies and promises. You had no intention of marrying me, did you?' Emily accused.

Nicholas shrugged and spread his hands in a show of insolent apology.

'Our betrothal was a sham. You proposed simply so you might seduce me.'

Nicholas sighed in irritation and shoved himself back in his chair. 'Do not make me out the heartless villain.' He eyed her through lowered lashes. 'You were ripe for love, innocent yet wanton, and took little persuading that night.'

Emily's soft lips parted in shock and indignation at such brutal honesty. But then she ought to know by now that Nicholas was careless of wounding her ego. A small corner of her mind acknowledged too that, young or not when engaged, she had been a credulous fool to be so totally blind to his true character. The only consolation was in knowing that she had not been the only one taken in by his lies. He had duped her parents too with his smooth talk of love and honour.

'You will find I am very different now, Nicholas,' Emily said coldly. 'I have no liking for you, let alone any stronger feelings…'

'Enough!' Nicholas snapped before Emily could amplify her disgust. 'I would far sooner treat you gently, Emily… share the pleasure with you.'

'You are a fool if you think you can get away with this,' Emily pointed out quite levelly although her moist palms were quivering in her lap. 'How do you intend to explain away having kidnapped and forced your attentions on a gentlewoman? By now my parents will be worried for my safety. The authorities will have been notified. You will be arrested once the truth is out.'

Nicholas snorted an unconcerned laugh. 'And who will tell the truth? You? Your parents? The last thing any of you want is for our affair—now or in the past—to be common knowledge. Your reputation would be irrevocably lost and your family would share in your shame.' The wine goblet performed a balletic twirl between his fingers. 'You were willing once; who would not believe you were willing again?' He smiled, almost sympathetically. 'You would not lie under oath, Emily, and deny we were lovers. You must accept that it is meant to be. Fate and your brother's folly have happily reunited us.'

'Which house?' Mark's voice was eerily soft as he addressed Jenny, but his eyes glittered hard and bright as ebony stars. A scouting look assessed the vicinity. In the meagre light he could just see that Jenny had directed him to the heart of a London slum. Stumpy terraces wobbled like rows of rotten teeth on lanes that yawned in four directions.

Jenny was wedged between the two men in the curricle. She nodded at a property that looked slightly less dilapidated than its neighbours. A weak lamp was burning in the ground-floor window. 'I reckon he might be in there gaming. When he's flush he likes to play dice for big stakes. I came here once before with him.' She swallowed and her wide dark eyes swung between the two men. 'You both best be careful. There are coves who hang around with him who'd crack your skulls open soon as look at you.'

'Can't Riley fight his own battles?' Tarquin scoffed, seemingly unperturbed by the idea of a brawl.

Jenny's top lip curled. 'He's a coward who saves his beatings for the girls who work for him. He got that broken nose off his pa for backchat when he was a youngster.'

Tarquin's lips twitched at the anecdote then, disengaging his elbow from Jenny's fearful grip, and with a fierce instruction to her to sit tight till he returned, he followed Mark towards the building.

'If I jump, you're in big trouble.'

'So are you,' Mark returned without bothering to take a look at the man trussed beside him.

Riley wriggled in his bonds and flung himself back against the squabs. 'Anything happens to me, you'll never find her.'

'And if I don't find her…a great many things *will* happen to you. That's a promise,' Mark said with tranquil menace. His cool demeanour admirably concealed that his anguish was mounting by the minute.

He had long known Devlin for a debauchee, but never before had he believed him capable of such dastardly behaviour. In abducting Emily he had proved himself to be a ruthless criminal too. But how far would he go to assuage his lust? Would he resort to physical violence if Emily resisted his attempt to charm her into bed? Would he ply her with drink and rape her helpless, comatose body? Emily was Devlin's captive, at his mercy for him to do with her what he would! Mark felt the agony writhe again deep in his gut as vile images of Emily's torment rotated in his brain.

He loved Emily Beaumont and had wanted to ask her to marry him. Had she been his betrothed she would have been protected by his name. Devlin would not have dared corner her to demand a kiss, let alone more. How would he ever forgive himself if she were harmed? A groaning oath tore from between his lips and he urged the horses to a faster pace. He must find her and there was only one man who could lead him to her. He'd use verbal persuasion to start, but if that didn't work he'd do whatever was necessary. God only knew the villain beside him deserved a beating for what he'd done to Jenny, let alone his part in this evil plan.

Abruptly he turned his head and a gaze so replete with loathing was levelled at his reluctant passenger that Riley shrank back into the corner of the vehicle. 'You're in deep trouble,' he gritted through his teeth. 'The sensible course of action would be for you to assist in righting the wrong you've done to Miss Beaumont. In a judge's eyes, it might redeem you slightly and lessen the severity of his sentence.'

'I'll swing anyhow if Jenny croaks.'

Mark's face tautened into bleak lines at the reminder of the disturbance he'd left behind in town.

Jenny had not taken Tarquin's advice and stayed in the curricle. Instead she had slipped inside—probably to assist and keep Tarquin from harm—when a fight erupted. Riley had had his henchmen with him and, whilst Mark and Tarquin were battling with them, Mickey Riley had noticed his nemesis hovering in the corridor. Realising that Jenny had betrayed him, the ruffian had battered her savagely to the ground. Jenny was rendered unconscious before Tarquin or Mark realised she was in the house.

Within minutes Mark had left Tarquin tending to his limp, bleeding wife and set off towards the Surrey border with Riley cursing and squirming beside him. Now that his bruisers were unable to save him Riley had quietened, but Mark knew that his foxy brain was constantly calculating methods of escape.

'If you want to jump, go ahead,' Mark snarled. 'There's a good chance it won't kill you…not straight away, anyhow. The sight of your broken limbs won't bother me. As long as you're able to talk, that's good enough.'

Riley kicked out in frustration at the side of the vehicle, then slouched into the seat with a sullen scowl on his face.

Mark reined back as they approached a cross-roads. 'Which way?'

Riley remained uncommunicative. When Mark slid along the seat towards him and repeated his question in a voice of silky steel, the villain jerked his head to the right.

Immediately Mark snatched up the reins, whipped leather over the backs of the horses, and they sped off again into the night.

The meal was coming to an end and with it Emily's capacity for conversation. She felt exhausted and fearful. Nicholas would feel entitled to strike now he had acted the gallant and wined and dined her. She slipped her unsteady fingers to the dinner knife she had secreted in the folds of her skirts. She hoped she would not need to utilise it, but she had no intention of quietly going upstairs with him!

Oh, where was Mark? Why had he not come to her rescue? Once she had shunned his touch; what would she not give now to rest within his powerful embrace?

Emily dropped the spoon with which she had idly been stirring her syllabub and jumped to her feet. While she had been deep in wistful reverie Nicholas had made his move. He had gained half the length of the table, and his expression was unmistakably predatory. Before she could properly extricate herself from her chair to flee, he was trapping her against it.

With a low chuckle he twisted the dinner knife from her fist, for he had anticipated her defensive tactics. Mockingly he clucked disapproval as he dropped the silver on to mahogany. His hard fingers were tight as manacles on her wrists as he brought his face closer to hers.

Emily's back bowed as she tried to avoid his lips travelling on her throat. His murmured endearments steamed on her skin and then his mouth pounced, forcing apart her lips, so his tongue could thrust within.

Emily twisted in his grasp, but his unpleasant laugh met her futile attempts to free herself. He was enjoying curbing her struggles, she realised, and she would not knowingly give him pleasure. Abruptly she became still, allowed him to nuzzle at her neck whilst her averted eyes darted to what lay on the table that might serve as a weapon. Her flitting glance returned to the grand silver candelabra. It was quite close and its weight would do far more damage than the dainty porcelain crockery within easy reach. The knife he'd taken from her had skidded some distance on the polished surface, but a fork was tantalisingly near to the fingers she had splayed on the table edge for support.

Swallowing her revulsion at the Viscount's fingers exploring her bodice fastenings, she forced herself to relax and tolerate a kiss. Coquettishly she twisted her head away. 'Do you really regret not marrying me, Nicholas?' she gulped whilst slyly edging sideways. 'I should like to think that at least is the truth.'

'Of course it's the truth,' he growled on an impatient pant and planted his hot mouth against the rapid pulse at the base of her throat.

Emily squirmed in his grasp, loosening his hold enough to allow her to sidle a step closer to the fork, barely an inch from her outstretched fingers. 'You're not just saying it to seduce me more easily?' she wheedled.

Nicholas raised his head, gazed at her with hot amber eyes. 'I said I'd rather share the pleasure with you, Emily,' he answered huskily. 'I'm not a violent man…but I can be when I'm desperate.' He cupped her chin in a hard hand. 'I want you…I'm desperate to have you. Why are you being cruel?'

He made the complaint with such genuine perplexity in his voice that Emily could barely repress a snort of derisive amazement.

'Be kind to me, my love!' Nicholas demanded hoarsely. 'Then I shall be kind to you.' He tried to prove his point by biting against Emily's throat with less brutality.

'I'm afraid I can't, for you disgust me,' Emily gasped and, snatching up the fork from the table, used all her might to stab him in the thigh.

Nicholas yelped and tottered back, a hand massaging furiously at the wound she'd delivered.

Emily raced to grab the silver candlestick and brandished it with both hands. 'Stay away, you vile swine, or I swear I'll use this on you!' she cried.

Nicholas gave a final rub to the puncture in his flesh. 'You little bitch,' he enunciated slowly. 'You will certainly pay for that.' He twisted his mouth into a sneer. 'And if you think a candlestick will save you, you are a silly little fool.' He paced purposefully closer, making Emily retreat in time with his advance. 'You are exceeding all my expectations, my dear. Fight me if you will. I'll enjoy taming you. I should have told you that it's the chase… the victory…that I need above all else.'

Just as Emily was rallying strength to launch her missile at him, a noise made her hesitate and whip her head around. But what she saw made her realise that the interruption was a reprieve, not deliver-

ance. The manservant was hovering on the threshold
of the dining room. A neutral expression was shaping his brawny features as though it was not uncom-
mon for him to witness a young lady about to fend
off his master's advances with a flaming candelabra.

Nicholas's face was a mask of fury and a few
crude curses were spat out as he strode towards the
fellow.

The servant hastened to meet him, now with an
intensely apologetic look on his face. Quickly he
whispered a message and, in return, received a curt
nod, and a muttered instruction from his master.

'It seems that Mr Riley has returned for some
reason best known to himself.' Nicholas's tone was
rough with irritation. 'Please excuse me just for a
moment, my dear, while I impress on the dolt that
he is *de trop* and very much unwelcome.' He gave
her a subtle smile. 'I will not abandon you for long,
I promise, but be seated again.' His former suave
composure seemed to be restored. A theatrical hand
flicked specks from an immaculate sleeve. 'There is
no escape; my servants are utterly loyal to me. So…
why not relax and finish your syllabub whilst you
wait for my return?'

Nicholas had instructed his manservant to stop
the pimp setting foot inside the house. He therefore

strode out directly on to the canopied porch with a snapped, 'I hope you have an excellent reason for this impertinence, Riley…'

'He has,' Mark drawled as he emerged from the shadows cast by the eaves. 'He doesn't want a bullet lodged in his black heart.' The duck's foot pistol was held in a steady hand against Mickey Riley's chest. Abruptly Mark realigned the weapon so both men were in its range. 'As for you, Devlin, a bullet strategically placed elsewhere might suit.' Mark indicated with a wave of the weapon that they should go inside the house.

'Do you mind telling me what the hell this is all about?' Devlin blustered, affecting outrage. He sent Riley a purely poisonous look.

'I think you know exactly what this is about, Devlin,' Mark responded with icy calm. 'Where is Miss Beaumont?'

Devlin licked his lips. He had not for a moment anticipated that a knight in shining armour might turn up and scotch his plans to force Emily to become his mistress.

'I shall quite happily persuade you to answer,' Mark said. 'I have enough ammunition to make life very uncomfortable for you both.'

'Miss Beaumont is presently eating her dinner,

Hunter,' the Viscount uttered quickly. His mind ferreted for explanations as to what prompted this man's interference. He knew that Tarquin Beaumont and Mark Hunter were friends, but he sensed that Hunter's involvement might be due to a more personal interest in Emily. Nicholas had been aware that soppy Stephen Bond was sniffing about her, but not that a fellow of Hunter's stature was in the running for Emily's affections. It was time to mark his territory, even if in doing so he sullied Emily's reputation.

He gave Mark a conspiratorial smile. 'I think you must recall, Hunter, that the lady and I once were betrothed. Alas, it came to nought but we still are *passionately* fond of each other.' He spread his hands appealingly. 'There, I have said it. You are privy now to our secret. It is a delicate situation, but we are both men of the world. I know you would not intentionally ruin a spinster's future marriage prospects by breathing a word of this to anyone.'

'No…but you would, and give little thought to the consequences for her and her family,' Emily uttered in a gruff little voice. She had immediately followed Nicholas from the dining room. So confident was he of his servant's loyalty and vigilance that he had not bothered to lock her in. Now she moved forward, slowly at first, but her relief at seeing Mark prompted her to skip swiftly to his side.

A strong arm immediately secured her there, heavy and possessive about her quivering shoulders. The hand holding the pistol did not waver from its target.

Devlin's eyes narrowed on the couple. Emily had quite naturally curved into Mark Hunter's embrace as though she had done so before. He smiled grimly. 'Perhaps the two of you have been keeping secrets of your own—' he began, but his insinuation was immediately curtailed by Mark's voice.

'I know you won't object if we are immediately on our way.' Mark swung a look between the two men and his lip curled slightly. 'I imagine the two of you have scores to settle.' Keeping the gun steady on them, he led Emily towards the door.

'You must think you're pretty clever, to get the better of me,' Devlin gritted in furious frustration as he watched Emily slipping from his grasp.

'No…not really,' Mark answered. 'What I do think is that you're pretty stupid to think you'd get away with such an outrage.' Mark suddenly raised the pistol and fired a shot at the brightly flickering chandelier. The chain was severed and crystal and brass crashed to the floor, plunging the hallway into blackness. Swiftly Mark turned and, with Emily fast in his embrace, urged her out into the night.

Chapter Fourteen

'I knew you'd come to rescue me.'

'And are you glad I did?'

Emily sent her saviour a somewhat startled look. She had intended her vibrant declaration to convey her praise and gratitude, yet Mark's response had sounded cynical. 'Could you not tell how pleased... how relieved I was to see you?' she demanded, rather piqued.

'Given the circumstances it would have been ill advised to look disappointed. You might once have been betrothed to your kidnapper, nevertheless you have your reputation to consider.'

'What do you mean by that?' Emily breathed fiercely. She had been feeling quite enervated by the day's chaotic events, but now her temper was stirring, sparking vitality into her. 'Do you think I was pleased to find the Viscount had plotted to abduct me?'

'I believe that once you would have been pleased to be the Viscount's wife.'

Emily felt the full force of his trenchant blue gaze. Her chin went up, but her heart plummeted. Whilst she had been in captivity, Mark had soared so high in her estimation that she feared she might be coming to like him very much indeed. He had been her hero, the man on whom she had pinned all her hopes. She'd trusted he would bring everything right and, up until a few moments ago, he'd lived up to every expectation. In fact, so beguiled by him had she become, she had acknowledged that he stirred her heart…and body…in a way that no man had, even Nicholas…

Now he had ruined it all. He had just forced her to recall that recently she had been sure she didn't like him. Suddenly she felt quite depressed…quite sad.

'It's true Nicholas and I were betrothed many years ago,' Emily eventually said. 'He now has a wife. I hope you are not hinting I might welcome the attentions of a married man.'

'And if he were not married?'

'It would make no difference,' Emily returned immediately.

'Devlin mentioned you were still *passionately* fond of one another.'

'Well, he had no right to say any such thing! It is a lie!' Emily choked. 'I loathe him, and I don't believe he likes me much either. If he had any kind of regard for me, he would not have wanted to treat me so abominably. Not that any of it is your business.' Emily paused after that outburst, fiddled with her cuffs. 'I have satisfied your inquisitiveness simply because you have gone out of your way to assist me today.' Her voice was husky with emotion and spontaneous tears shone in her eyes. A hand sprang to her face to irritably dash the wet away.

As they had thundered towards London Mark had enquired if she were warm enough, if she wanted to make an early stop. Beneath his courteous consideration for her comfort Emily had sensed that he was in a brooding mood. She had anticipated an early interrogation, even a scolding for having put herself in jeopardy by going off alone with Riley. What she had not expected was this odd atmosphere that had erected a barrier between them. On the journey, when her attempts at conversation received a monosyllable in reply, she'd lapsed into quiet. She had at first imagined Mark was preoccupied with putting distance between the curricle and possible pursuers.

Emily now suspected the space he'd wanted to maintain was between them.

Since they had joined forces to solve the mystery of Tarquin's disappearance, she had grown accustomed to those blue eyes smouldering at her in humour or desire. Now he was different; his attitude was unerringly polite but aloof. And she didn't like it. She wanted soothing words and strong arms comforting her. She wanted his approval and his affection…

'I'm sorry, Emily, I didn't mean to upset you.' Mark pinched at strain between his brows, feeling churlish in the extreme at having let suspicion conquer courtesy. Since he had discovered Emily had been tricked into going with Riley, and for what vile purpose, he had been frantic with worry for her safety. Now, instead of cherishing the gift of her presence, and her safe deliverance, he was acting like a jealous buffoon.

Emily had endured more than enough already today, yet he had just added to her troubles. His hand slid to enclose quivering white fingers. 'I had no right to say any of that, or pry into your past. Forgive me…?'

When Emily remained silent, Mark sat back in his chair with a heavy sigh. 'For hours I've been dreading what your captor might do to you, Emily.' His admission was quiet, almost diffident. 'Devlin tried to make light of it all. He hinted you were a willing participant and had a secret life as his mistress…it maddened me.' He passed a hand roughly over his face. 'I'm a fool, I know, to suspect one word that bastard uttered might be the truth.'

Feeling reassured by the explanation for his bad mood, Emily twisted her wrist beneath his to clasp his palm. 'I was so very glad you came for me, Mark,' Emily stressed softly. 'It was only the thought that soon you would burst in to rescue me that kept my spirits up.' Her small fingers tightened reflexively about his as a wave of relief shuddered through her. 'I prayed you would get my note in time and find clues to where Riley had taken me. Had I lost hope and trust in you, I doubt I would have found the strength to resist.' Her voice trembled into silence and she stifled a sob with her knuckles. 'I stabbed Nicholas in the leg with a fork to get free and was about to throw a candelabra at him when you turned up.'

Mark chuckled softly, raised her fingers to his lips and tenderly saluted them. 'Devlin was never a match for you.'

The inflection in Mark's voice made Emily sure he was not simply referring to her plucky attack on Devlin.

Gently, reluctantly, Mark disengaged his hand from fingers that felt temptingly sensual. He used it to grab his glass and take a swallow of brandy. 'Drink your wine before it cools. It will revive you. We still have many miles to travel.' He pushed her hot toddy closer to her on the table.

Emily rewarded him with a smile and gratefully toasted her cool palms on the steaming cup. Quickly she took a glance about at her cosy surroundings.

It had been impossible to safely travel on without allowing the horses to be rested and watered. They had broken their journey at this wayside inn on the Guildford Road. The saloon bar of the Rose and Crown had been crowded with boisterous locals so Mark had taken a private room for them. The landlord—a jovial fellow with a patch over one eye that lent him an incongruously piratical air so far inland—had shown them to the back parlour of the establishment. Whilst leading the way through the narrow corridors, he had apologised profusely that they could not have the best parlour, but that, he explained, had been taken earlier by a family on their way to Guildford. The other he had available was very nice, he'd assured them, and so it proved to be. It was small, but quite clean and tidy and adequately furnished. Once ensconced in wing chairs positioned on either side of the glowing grate, Mark had assured her they would be back on the road within an hour and in Mayfair before midnight.

In truth, Emily had been grateful for the stop. Since they'd set out back to London at breakneck speed there had been no proper opportunity for much conversation to pass between them. After their recent fraught exchange, Emily wasn't sure whether she would rather maintain this amicable quiet than have the answers to the pressing questions rotating in her mind. It seemed talking invariably led to bickering. But she knew they must talk, and at great length, for there was so much she needed to know.

What news was there of Tarquin? What would happen to Riley, and to Viscount Devlin? Mark had said Nicholas would pay and so he should. Such despicable behaviour deserved punishment. But a scandal? Please, no! Her parents did not deserve to be embarrassed by their foolish daughter as well as their wayward son.

Mark watched flitting emotions etch strain on Emily's heart-shaped countenance. Wisps of fair hair had escaped from the knot at the back of her head to embellish skin made luminous by misty night air. Her eyes were languid with sleepiness, the lids low.

Mark needed answers to those questions that still pitilessly tortured him. The Viscount had schemed to trap Emily today, and she was genuinely angry over it. But had she once willingly been Devlin's mistress? If so, would he have eventually again coaxed her into consenting to sleep with him?

Mark took a swig from his brandy, aware that he felt ashamed of the quickening in his loins. She looked desirable despite her ordeal, too beautifully vulnerable to be alone with a man who wanted her as much as he did. Despite their differences, he knew she trusted him, felt safe with him, yet he could not banish the lustful thoughts pricking his mind.

He suspected she was not as innocent as a genteel spinster ought to be. But how experienced was she? Had Devlin taken her maidenhead, or had his devilish plot been devised so he might finish what he'd started years ago?

Mark rose abruptly and strolled to the window. He struck a broad hand on the frame and looked into the blackness, his thoughts as hot as his loins. If he were to kiss her…and she were to melt against him as she had done before…what harm in that? They were miles from home and prying eyes, and if she were knowing and compliant…there were rooms upstairs…

'Are you hungry? Would you like something to eat?' Mark asked abruptly. He shoved back from the window and paced to and fro to ease his rigid muscles.

'I'm not hungry at all. I ate dinner with Nicholas…' Emily glimpsed an immediate fierce light in Mark's eyes at another mention of the Viscount. Quickly she added, 'At first I thought it best to humour him as much as possible and accept his hospitality, while I waited for you.' Inclining her blonde head, she brought her cup close to her lips and took a sip from it. She was obliquely aware of Mark's jerky movement as he snatched up the decanter and refilled his glass.

'Very wise…' he eventually said with barely a hint of irony. His empty glass was replaced abruptly on the table.

'Are you still angry with me?' Emily asked quietly. She gave him a sweet, tentative smile. 'I know I have put you to a lot of trouble. I know it was rash to go with Riley. Actually, it was a stupid risk; I know it now I have had time to think sensibly on it. But I honestly thought Tarquin might be in peril.' She traced the rim of her cup with a slender finger, watching the movement as she said, 'I was terrified my brother might die all alone…cold and hungry.'

Her soft lower lip was nipped between worrying teeth. 'I didn't know what to do; that was why I came to try to find you at your home.' She sighed and shook her head. 'I hoped so much that you would be there to counsel me.' She finished what was left of her mulled wine, then made a rueful admission. 'That's not quite true. I didn't want your advice; I wanted you to take away the burden of it all and deal with it for me.'

'And I would have done that, I swear, Emily,' Mark vowed huskily. 'I'm not angry with you. But I am angry with Devlin and Riley, and with your dolt of a brother who brought about this fiasco. I'm angry with myself too.'

Emily would have interrupted at that point, but Mark gestured for her silence. 'Let's not speak of any of it again tonight.' A long finger moved on her cheek, teasing back a stray curl that spiralled close to her mouth. 'You're safe and that's the most important thing.' He tilted up her face so she must look at him. 'You're tired and overwrought, as is natural considering what you have been through. And if that were not enough to get you immediately back to Callison Crescent, there is your family to think about. We must get you home, and hope you have not been missed.' A frown corrugated his brow beneath a fall of dark hair. 'Heaven only knows what excuse will satisfy your parents if they have noticed your absence.' Mark gently urged Emily to her feet and, fetching her cloak, courteously placed it about her shoulders. 'If you are ready, it's high time we set again on the road.'

'Mr Hunter?'

Mark halted immediately on hearing his name barked in a cultured female voice. He turned his head. What he saw caused him enough dismay to make him swear beneath his breath, although his expression altered not one iota.

Emily was positioned slightly in front of Mark, and her slender frame had tensed statue-still for she, too, had recognized those haughty tones. Even before Mark's low curse reached her ears she knew she was once more that day in awful trouble. Her stomach lurched, and she pressed a hand against the wall to help support her on legs that felt boneless.

'I thought I recognised you, sir.' Mrs Violet Pearson emerged fully from the doorway of the Rose and Crown's best parlour. She pulled her shawl tight about her scrawny arms to ward off the chill. But her inquisitiveness had been roused far too much for her to yet go back inside and seek the warmth of the blazing logs.

When her son, Bertie, had gone upstairs to bed in a sulk, he had not properly closed the door behind him. Violet had cast a purposeful look at Mr Pearson, but he had contrived to nod off in the chair at that precise moment. Violet had thus stomped to perform the office herself rather than tolerate the draught. Just for the once she was glad that her husband and son could be lazy and inconsiderate for, as she put a hand to wood to push the door shut, she had spied something very interesting indeed in the corridor.

A lady and gentleman, glimpsed through the aperture, had seemed familiar to her. For the fleeting moment she had them in her sights Violet had been instantly put in mind of another kind of familiarity: the kind shared by people in love. Not that Violet had experience of such sweet intimacy with Mr Pearson, but she conversely relished the bitterness the lack provoked.

Violet was sure she could scent a rat…or rather a scandal, for although she had not got a good view of the young woman with Mr. Hunter, she had got a peep at golden hair curling beneath a bonnet. She also recalled seeing a classic profile and an enviably curvaceous figure. Few women could boast such remarkable attractions, and grace of movement. Naturally, she would never let on to the chit, or her mother, that she thought her pretty. So *could* it be Miss Emily Beaumont?

Violet knew that Mark Hunter and Tarquin Beaumont were chums, so there was a connection of sorts between Emily and Mark. But it seemed remarkably odd that the two of them might be at an inn, halfway to Guildford, at ten of the clock at night. Perhaps Miss Beaumont was with a relation who was elsewhere in the building…or perhaps she was not…

Violet's riotous imaginings turned her mind feverish and her face florid. Suddenly she jerked to her senses as she became aware that Mark Hunter was almost at the door, and on the point of exiting the building now he had returned her a nod and a muttered greeting.

Violet sought swiftly to detain him. 'Fancy bumping into you here, sir,' she called shrilly, speeding in his wake. 'Are you going, as we are, to the Festival in Guildford? Last year it was a delight; the orchestra and the singing divine…'

'No, ma'am,' Mark replied with a hint of irritation clipping his tone. 'I'm travelling in the opposite direction towards London.'

Violet Pearson was not so easily put off by a dark look and a curt response. She sidled the corridor wall, her head leading the way as she tried to get a better look at the dainty female partially obliterated by Mark's large frame. Violet's tongue flicked excitedly to her lips; she was very aware that the fellow was deliberately trying to shield his companion from view. A glitter brightened her eyes. Would she be returning to town with a juicy tale to relate concerning the family of her arch-enemy? She advanced determinedly on the couple, already savouring the piquancy of a rousing victory over Mrs Penelope Beaumont.

Mark propelled Emily forward. She understood perfectly the instruction in his firm guidance and did her part by quickening her pace and keeping her bonnet brim low to shield her features.

Violet put on a spurt, and the exertion served her well. Suddenly she got a proper look past those powerful shoulders that, preposterously, were almost as wide as the corridor. 'Why…Miss Beaumont, is it not?' she purred. 'How are you, my dear? And how is your mama? Is she here with you?'

Emily stood rigid and tongue-tied for a moment. Obliquely a corner of her mind registered that she was hopelessly, irrevocably compromised. But she turned slowly to receive Mrs. Pearson's horribly gloating look. 'No, she is not,' Emily said in a lightly quavering tone.

'Oh…I see,' Violet said, immeasurable insinuation conveyed by those few words. Barely containing her glee, she added sweetly, 'I expect you heard me say to Mr Hunter that we are off to the Festival in Guildford. Are you going there? Or are you also travelling back to London?'

Emily moistened her lips, about to speak, but Violet piped up again. 'If your parents are not here, I expect your brother is escorting you. No doubt Tarquin is somewhere about the place.' She gave an exaggerated peer about as though she might spot the fellow lurking in a corner. 'Of course, I know you would not be here alone with Mr. Hunter…would you?'

'Miss Beaumont is travelling with me,' Mark interjected coolly. He gave the woman a purely cynical stare. 'Enjoy the Festival, won't you…'

'Indeed I shall,' Violet said. She twitched a smile, and her skirts, in a travesty of respect. Even a blast of cold air as the couple went out into the night could not shift her. She stood for some minutes shivering in the draught, a wondrously smug smile on her thin countenance.

'She is a malicious witch and will delight in making trouble for our family.' Emily's face fell forward into her cupped palms. 'Oh, why did I ever set out today on such a stupid mission? Everything is now so much worse!' she wailed.

The curricle sped on through the night, but one of Mark's hands relinquished the reins to slide about Emily's shoulders and draw her close against his side. A thumb smoothed against a wind-chilled cheek, back and forth in soothing rhythm until she succumbed to his comfort. A small hand snaked about his waist and she clung uninhibitedly to him, her eyes screwed tight against the breeze and burning tears.

'Hush…' Mark said softly. 'You did what you thought best, and your brother is fortunate to have a sister as loyal and caring as you.' The equipage raced smoothly on as he encouraged her head against his shoulder.

Emily snuggled readily into the lee of his powerful body, a watery snuffle muffled against his coat. 'My intention was to shield my parents from further distress! Now look what I have done! I have increased their troubles tenfold!' She miserably shook her head back and forth. 'A wayward son is one thing. Society will tolerate a young man sowing wild oats, but not the shameless behaviour of his unmarried sister.'

'Hush, Emily.' Mark dropped his face to hers,

nudging up her chin so he might touch together their lips. She tasted salty-sweet and he relinquished her mouth reluctantly to concentrate on the dark road. 'It is not insurmountable. There are ways and means of putting this right…'

'There's only one way and you know it.' Emily choked on a hysterical giggle. 'We must announce we are to be married. And I think you know far too much about me now to ever want to do that!'

Chapter Fifteen

'You are a selfish wretch!'

'I know…I'm sorry,' Tarquin mumbled whilst shamefacedly contemplating his bitten nails. He suddenly leaned across the breakfast table, snatching at his sister's hands to impress on her his apology.

Emily shrank back, firmly crossing her arms over her waist as though to prevent him again touching her. 'Do you comprehend the extent of the chaos you caused?' A whirling hand illustrated the magnitude of it all. Emily tipped back her head in despair.

Of course she already knew the answer to that! Her brother was ignorant of a great deal of the damage that had resulted from his foolishness. The worst of which was her horribly inopportune meeting with Violet Pearson, and the ruinous effect it might have on their whole family. There was much she must tell Tarquin, and ask him, but she could barely contain her temper well enough to talk to him at all. With a depressive sigh Emily turned her attention on the coffee pot. She poured a cup and immediately gulped a mouthful of the strong, bitter brew.

'Have you yet told our parents of your real reason for running away? Sooner or later it is bound to come out. You cannot keep your wife hidden for ever.' Emily had breathed the final sentence in an undertone whilst darting a wary look at the door. She hoped they had not been overheard.

Her mother was no doubt still abed; it was not yet her usual time for rising. She was confident her father would already be out on matters of business, for he was an early bird however late he retired. But servants had a knack of gleaning titbits to chew over below stairs.

Emily again thanked her lucky stars that she had got home yesterday just minutes before her parents returned from their evening's entertainment. She had been halfway up the stairs when she heard a key in the lock, followed by their jolly conversation in the hallway. Despite her weariness Emily had instinctively sprinted up the remaining treads and out of sight. Concealing herself behind the banisters on the landing, she had called her goodnights in a sleepy voice as though she had kept awake especially to do so. Trudging off to bed, she had felt quite guilty at her spontaneous subterfuge, and then quite silly too. Forlornly she had recalled that, if Violet Pearson were bent on making mischief, her hellish jaunt with Riley would eventually be uncovered no matter how good had been her play-acting.

Emily's attention returned to Tarquin. She was still waiting to learn from him whether their parents were cognizant of the fact of their son's scandalous marriage.

'Jenny is dead,' Tarquin blurted out. His eyes glittered as he added sombrely, 'And she was not really my wife at all.'

Emily clattered her cup and saucer together and her lips parted in astonishment. 'Jenny is *dead*?' she echoed in a husky whisper. 'And you say you did *not* marry her?' She clamped a hand to her brow and thumb and forefinger pressed indentations into pearly skin. 'Was it all for nothing? Did you suspect all along the marriage was some sort of hoax?'

'No! I believed we were legally leg-shackled, I swear.' Tarquin concealed his trembling lips with a fist planted hard against them, only removing it to briefly enlighten Emily to the circumstances of poor

Jenny's demise at the hands of the fiendish Riley. He cleared his throat to gruffly continue, 'Jeremiah Plumb is a clergyman, if a shifty character. It all seemed correct. The marriage was certainly consummated…' Tarquin blinked nervously and blushed on recalling to whom he was expressing his thoughts.

'Go on,' Emily prompted, dismissing his tacit apology as unnecessary.

'Jenny regained consciousness for a short while after Mark set out to rescue you. She told me before she expired that I was not her only husband. It was Riley's idea, of course, to make of her a bigamist. At one time I think she was quite infatuated with him. But she came to know him for a selfish, avaricious swine.' Tarquin flung his spine against the chair back. 'Riley had successfully extorted money from other fellows who had been tricked into taking vows when stewed. Once sober, they readily parted with cash to seal Riley's lips.'

'He thought you would too. But you had none to give.'

Tarquin nodded slowly. 'So he had the confounded cheek to accost you instead for payment.' His mouth thinned to a white line. 'I would gladly murder the brute for that alone, never mind what he did to Jenny!'

'And in doing so most definitely embroil us all in a terrible brouhaha.' Emily pointed out angrily. 'We are not yet over one calamity before you are talking of creating another.'

Tarquin hung his head. 'I shall arrange for a decent burial for Jenny in any case,' he murmured on a suspiciously watery gurgle. 'She wasn't wholly a bad girl.'

Angry as Emily was with Tarquin, he deserved her sympathy for his bereavement. Kneeling close to his chair, she looked up into his mournful damp countenance. 'I'm so very sorry to hear about Jenny's fate. Had I known earlier, I would not have scolded you so.' Her pale fingers covered his, squeezed in comfort. 'It's a mess and no doubt about it. But I'm glad to know you cared for one another. Jenny could have gone to her grave saying nothing about the bigamy, but she chose instead to put your mind at rest over it all. She loved you back, Tarquin,' she stressed softly.

Tarquin nodded and made a snuffling noise before cuffing at his nose.

Emily let him be and sank back on her heels. Her brother was deeply upset by the death of his illicit wife. Tarquin had fallen for a harlot, a woman who had conspired to trick him, but had ultimately risked and sacrificed her own life to help him. Emily felt no disgust on knowing on whom her brother had chosen to bestow his love. In fact, she rather admired him for having the pluck to buck convention in choosing his mate. She now suspected that, at the altar, her brother had been more in possession of his faculties than he cared to admit. Oddly that gave Emily a sense of serenity.

Gracefully she gained her feet and paced to the window. She stared out into a beautiful spring morning. The sun was shining and her countenance tilted up to be warmed by its golden glow. The lime trees were more leaf than wood, for the buds were now almost fully unfurled. With a sigh Emily turned her back on the pleasant scene. 'Will you tell our parents about the real reason for your disappearance?'

Tarquin shook his head. 'I am a widower—legal or not—and it is pointless now worrying them with news of a dead daughter-in-law.'

'Indeed,' Emily quietly concurred. She paced restlessly, then shot her brother a helpless look. 'I'm afraid to say there might soon be something even worse to disturb them.' For the first time that morning she allowed herself to ponder on her own distressing predicament. How long a reprieve might she have before Violet Pearson returned to town to ruin her future?

Just a day ago—it seemed so much longer than that!—she had written a letter to Stephen Bond in which she had kindly let him know she would only ever consider him a good friend. She had acted from altruism; now she felt mean for being relieved the note remained undelivered and in her cloak pocket.

But what would she do? Would she find the gall to encourage Stephen to propose simply to protect her reputation? That would certainly prove Sarah's hints on her woeful character correct: she *was* selfish and inconsiderate.

If her betrothal were official before Mrs Pearson returned to town, would the woman admit defeat and say nothing? More importantly, if whispers *did* start to circulate about her being spotted in scandalous circumstances with a bachelor, would Stephen renege on the contract? He would have every right to do so!

'I can't guess at it. You must explain what you mean,' Tarquin prompted.

With a sigh Emily proceeded to do so.

'Violet Pearson! Of all people!' Tarquin snorted in disgust. 'I don't socialise much with you ladies, but even I know that the old hag will go out of her way to stir the cauldron where our family is concerned.' The palms of his hands made forceful contact with his thighs. 'What the deuce was Hunter thinking of, taking you, unchaperoned, to an inn where you might be spotted together? I'll have something to say to him when I see him, I can tell you.'

A gasp of astonished laughter was Emily's first response to that. '*You* will have something to say to *him*?' she echoed incredulously. 'It might have slipped your mind that in fact Mark was doing you and me a very great favour by getting involved in any of this. If you think sensibly on it, you will understand that pulling in to the Rose and Crown was a necessity, not an indulgence. Mark had risked the health of his animals by travelling many miles at full pelt. The poor things were on their last legs and, had we continued, I might never have been safely returned home at all.'

'Calm down!' Tarquin muttered. He knew he had deserved her tirade. 'I'd not see you overturned in a ditch rather than compromised.' Suddenly he gave a knowing chuckle. 'For a lady who, as I recall, didn't have a good word to say about a certain gentleman, you jumped to his defence pretty quickly *and* fiercely.'

Emily felt blood sting in her cheeks at that shrewd observation. 'And I have good reason to do so, as do you. Had Mark not turned up when he did, I might still be at Devlin's mercy, and it would be your fault!'

'Nothing for it, then,' Tarquin suddenly proclaimed in ringing tones. 'Hunter must marry you.'

Emily's gasp of bitter laughter was drowned by the sound of the door opening. Millie was hovering on the threshold of the morning room.

'A visitor for you, Miss Emily,' the maid advised, her tone displaying her surprise that a caller had arrived at such an unfashionably early hour. 'Mr Hunter is in the hall.'

After a moment of breathless indecision Emily shot a fleeting glance at Tarquin. Her brother had a smug grin on his face. 'Show him in please, Millie,' she said faintly.

On learning the identity of her visitor Emily had sensed her heart cease to beat. Now it began to throb alarmingly. Of course, she had expected he would come today to speak to her about what had happened at the inn, but she had not expected him yet and was certainly not ready to receive him.

She crossly reminded herself that, had she not made that stupid remark last night, when tired and hysterical, she might not be so flustered by his arrival.

Mark had received her impulsive jest with unsmiling gravity. His taciturn visage had remained unflinchingly facing the road ahead as he urged the horses to increase pace. The final leg of the journey home to Mayfair had passed in virtual silence.

Surely he had not thought she seriously expected him to propose marriage? As though she would! She knew he was in love and spoken for. The attention he had paid to her was simply opportunistic flirting…she knew that too…

What had alarmed him, and turned her weak joke sour, was that they both had known she had voiced what others would think. If a genteel spinster were to be unfortunately compromised by a gentleman, polite society would deem it his duty to protect her reputation with an offer of marriage. But of course it was different with them. The gentleman had already guessed that the spinster was not as virtuous as polite society assumed her to be, and was loath to make the sacrifice.

'He's here to rescue your reputation, I'm sure.'

Tarquin's hissed encouragement caused Emily to cast on him a frown. Far from being here to ask her to be his wife, Emily guessed Mark Hunter's early arrival was due to his keenness to impress on her he knew the phrase about closing the stable door after the horse had bolted. And how could she blame him for that? For his pains, he risked being vilified as her heartless seducer rather than her saviour.

Looking quite heartbreakingly handsome, and the epitome of composure too, Mark strolled in to the room. He was so elegantly groomed—charcoal tailcoat, snow-white cravat and top boots gleaming like glass—that it was obvious he deemed this visit a matter of grave importance. His immaculate appearance reminded Emily that she had been too agitated by recent events to take much time with her toilette that morning. Tendrils of blonde hair were quickly smoothed back from her pearly brow and her pink dimity skirts were given an unobtrusive shake to neaten them.

Mark looked straight at her and she gave him a small smile, hoping to reassure him that he would not suffer on her account. He was a kind and decent man, she knew that now, and she would set him free to marry the woman he loved.

Emily's smile faded away for, far from being well received, her wordless welcome had caused his expression to become faintly ironic.

Tarquin immediately strode towards his friend and stuck out a hand. 'Good to see you, Mark.' The greeting was stressed in throbbing tones that conveyed a multitude of gratitude.

After a momentary hesitation Mark met the proffered hand. 'You'll forgive me if I don't return the compliment.' He managed to extricate his hand from being vigorously pumped. 'In fact, it would not bother me if I never set eyes on you again, Beaumont.'

Tarquin had the grace to turn florid. 'Caused a bit of trouble, I know…' he mumbled and hung his head.

'You have a nice way with understatement.' Mark's response was silky with sarcasm. 'Jenny?' It was a blunt question.

Tarquin's chin dropped further towards his chest. He shook his head.

'I'm very sorry,' Mark said quietly. Within a moment he followed that with, 'I would like to speak privately to your sister.'

Tarquin's lowered eyes batted between the couple and he cleared his throat. 'Yes…of course… understand…' he mumbled, backing towards the door. Emily received a sly wink from her brother before he slunk into the corridor.

'Ah…I see he does understand,' Mark commented drily as soon as the door had closed.

Emily nodded jerkily, inwardly cursing her brother for having made it seem that there was a conspiracy between them. 'I've just told him about the unfortunate meeting with Mrs Pearson…' Her voice faded into awkward silence.

'My apologies for calling at such an ungodly hour,' Mark said. 'I hoped to catch your father at home. I know he rises early.'

'He rises very early,' Emily echoed faintly.

Mark walked closer and Emily felt her stomach somersault, for his presence held undeniable allure. She had grown used to being welcomed into his arms, kissed and caressed until her worries evaporated and he was the mainstay of her existence. She clasped her hands tight behind her back, though she ached to rush to him, have him again make everything right. She backed away a step on realising with anguished sorrow that there was actually nothing she would like better than to become Mark Hunter's wife.

'You know why I am here, Emily,' Mark began levelly.

'Yes…' Emily began. 'And before you say more, there is something you ought to know…'

'Indeed there is,' he confirmed quietly. 'A couple of my questions remain unanswered. I have managed to work out the answer to one of those myself. When you first arranged to meet Riley on Whiting Street you were loitering in the lawyer's office to avoid Devlin, were you not?'

Emily merely gave a little nod. 'And the other?' she asked quickly, keen to get to the crux of the matter and set him free.

'I asked you once why you rebuffed my compliment on your innocence. I'm still waiting for your explanation.'

She had not at all anticipated that abrupt demand. The words that had been ready to release him blocked her throat. Her small tongue tip darted to moisten lips that felt arid. 'I think you know why I said it,' Emily blurted. Silver eyes that had been shielded by twin fans of dusky lashes suddenly sparked at him, proud and challenging.

'I imagine it is to do with the *passionate fondness* that Devlin says you shared.'

Emily tilted her chin a little higher. 'You are very astute, sir.'

'How passionately fond of him were you?'

'As passionately fond as it is possible to be,' Emily answered in a hoarse little voice. 'And we need not speak in riddles. You will not offend my delicate sensibilities by speaking of carnal love.' She suddenly unclasped her hands and brought them in front of her, flexing fingers that felt stiff with cramp. 'I think you have guessed that I lay with Nicholas when we were engaged. I am not a virgin,' she quickly continued in a whisper, 'And I do not want you to feel obliged to protect me with an offer of marriage…if indeed that was your intention.' She slid him a fleeting look and noted his expression was unreadable. His stillness, his silent unflinching regard, made her desperately seek something else to say.

'It is as well you have not found my father at home, if indeed your intention was to discuss a marriage contract. But you have not wasted your time in coming here,' she intrepidly continued, despite his refusal to participate in the conversation. 'You no doubt feel an unwelcome duty has been thrust upon you. Rest assured it has not, and speaking to my father is quite unnecessary.' Emily walked to the breakfast table and began to stack the used crockery. A fork escaped her nervous clutch and clattered on to mahogany. She gave up the task and gripped the table edge instead. 'It was most unfortunate that our brief rest at the inn was witnessed, and by such a spiteful person. But there is no need for you to feel you must act to protect my good reputation.' Emily closed her eyes, willing him to speak. Any reaction…even a scornful observation that she had no good reputation to lose…would be better than his wordless audience. 'I have a gentleman friend,' she battled on. 'And he reciprocates my fond feelings.

It is now the right time for things between us to be made official.' Her silver-blue eyes were slowly raised to Mark's face.

'And you think that Stephen Bond would take to wife a wanton?'

Emily felt her complexion heating beneath his potent blue gaze. 'I do not think that our being spotted together will merit such harsh gossip being bandied about.'

'I think you know I didn't mean that.'

Emily's pink cheeks darkened to scarlet. 'Stephen will never know about that…unless you or Nicholas tell him.'

'Of course he will,' Mark jeered softly. 'He'll know the first time he lays with you…' He suddenly shot her a fierce look. 'Or perhaps he already has,' he murmured. 'Do you have a similar *passionate fondness* for Mr Bond? Or was it simply the thought of being a Viscountess that excited you?'

Chapter Sixteen

'How dare you!'

Emily felt her stomach writhe with humiliation, but stalked away from the table to face him indignantly. 'I was very young when I first fell in love and allowed Nicholas to seduce me.' She gulped in a steadying breath. 'I bitterly regret being duped by his lies, but I am no longer that silly, naïve child.' Her blonde head was flung back and she levelled on him quite a haughty look. 'You are hardly a model of virtue, and have a devil of a nerve to moralise! I wonder if Mrs Emerson realises how fickle you are.'

'Whether she does or not is of no consequence,' he coolly replied.

'And that validates my opinion of your character,'

Emily breathed. 'That you would show so little respect for the feelings of the woman you love is disgraceful.'

Mark laughed, a guttural sound of raw sarcasm that sent a shiver through Emily.

'You have no idea what you are talking about, Miss Beaumont, and I suggest you leave alone the matter of my love affairs.'

'Gladly!' Emily snapped, but still smarting from his rebuke. 'If you will do the same for me.'

Their combative gazes locked for an infinite moment. Emily looked away first when he made no move to take his leave.

'There is no need for you to stay longer,' she said stiffly. 'If a shred of conscience over my future is delaying you, let me put your mind completely at ease. I think you know I have little liking for you. I would not marry you if the only alternative was earning my keep on the streets.'

'I'm sure Devlin would be your keenest customer. He knows you suit the work,' Mark drawled, a twitch of a smile his only reaction to her gasp of outrage. But beneath his blasé exterior bubbled uncontrollable jealousy. His fears had been realised: the woman with whom he'd fallen in love had slept with a man he detested. But even if mild-mannered Stephen Bond had taken her virginity, he would have liked it no better. A primeval need to have been the first to possess her would not be denied, and was making him callous. 'You might not like me, sweetheart,' he said, 'but what does that matter? We both know we can forgo fondness and concentrate on passion.'

Emily felt her skin heating and she swung away from him, desperate to formulate a rebuttal. What he'd intimated about their compatibility was cruel, but none the less true. Even before she knew her feelings towards him were changing, she had sensed the potent allure of his virility. His mocking eyes were scorching her profile, his scathing words were echoing in her ears, yet still she craved the relief of the bittersweet sensuality he could arouse in her.

She was the one who hadn't been entirely honest. At one time she might have persuaded herself she did not like Mark Hunter; but she could not do it any more. Despite his insults, she knew she most certainly did like him. In fact, she feared she had fallen in love with him. But she'd never accept being Mark's despised wife any more than she had once wanted to endure the humiliation of Nicholas marrying her under duress. Before Mrs Pearson returned from the music festival, another solution must be found.

'Would you like me to prove to you how good

we'd be together, Emily? It'll be my pleasure to drive any thoughts of Devlin from you…'

Emily felt a *frisson* pass through her; the imagery he'd purposely put in her mind had sent iced fire streaking through her veins. Slow footfalls approached, then firm fingers were skimming the silken skin of her arms. Warm, intoxicating lips stroked her nape, slid to the sensitive hollow behind an ear. Her head angled to accommodate him, and she luxuriated in the fever he'd so easily raised in her blood. But she steeled herself against succumbing to his practised seduction. He wanted her, but deemed her of easy virtue, and was unabashed to tell her so. Desire could be enchanting, but without love and respect it was worthless to her. She had learned that bitter lesson with Nicholas.

Anticipating her imminent rejection, Mark released her, denying her even that small proud triumph. He moved away to brace a foot against the fender, a hand against the stone chimneypiece. With thoughtful nonchalance he steadily regarded her. 'Once your parents discover from Violet Pearson what has gone on, they'll be desperate to get you settled with the first man who'll have you.' He stooped, scooped up a log and lobbed it on to the embers in the grate. 'Trust me, Stephen Bond won't be applying to be your husband. He might be smitten, he might even consider a less binding arrangement with you, but he'll not risk losing his grandmother's inheritance by taking a discredited woman to wife. Once Violet spreads her poison he'll be a laughing-stock, and Augusta won't allow shame to taint their family's name.'

Emily flinched from the unpalatable truth. Augusta had openly told her she didn't think her right for her grandson; and this had been whilst the woman believed her reputation to be intact! Mrs Bond would never sanction her grandson's marriage to Miss Beaumont after she heard the scandalous rumours. Dejectedly Emily had to agree with Mark's interpretation of Stephen's character: he would not buck convention, or his inheritance, for her sake.

Having rekindled the fire Mark strolled to the door, rested back against it with his arms crossed over his chest. For a long, almost unbearable moment he subjected her to his sleepy scrutiny. 'I'll consider marrying you, sweetheart,' he said eventually. 'Not because I feel obliged to do so, but because I suspect there are sweet advantages to taking a wanton bride.'

'Was that Mark Hunter I glimpsed in the vestibule a moment ago? My, he's quick off the mark this morning! But then I fear he must have pressing matters on his mind concerning the conduct of that scapegrace son of mine.'

Penelope Beaumont sailed into the parlour, her pastel morning dress wafting about her trim ankles. 'Where *is* Tarquin, by the by? Is he in hiding from his friend's scolding?'

Emily's silence prompted Penelope to take a proper look at her daughter. Noticing the strain etched into her white features, she hurried immediately to her side. 'Whatever is the matter, Emily? You look dreadful.' Penelope gasped and put a hand to her throat. 'Never say that Mr Hunter has upset *you*? It's Tarquin who deserves his complaints!'

Penelope suddenly looked askance at her daughter. Over the years she had cringed on more than one occasion when Emily had been snappish with Mark Hunter. Previously she had marvelled at the way the fellow tolerated it with equanimity. If Emily had caught the sharp side of his tongue at last, perhaps it was no more than she deserved. 'Were you rude to him, Emily?'

Emily was about to deny any such thing, but instead forced a fist against her mouth as she was racked with hysterical giggles.

'For goodness' sake, Emily!' Mrs Beaumont

chided. 'Is it not enough that we have a son who makes a habit of acting foolishly?' In exasperation her shawl was yanked this way and that about her shoulders. 'And Mr Hunter is such an influential gentleman, too. I was hoping that you might persuade him to continue to be Tarquin's good friend. Mark always seemed to have a soft spot for you despite your petulance.' Penelope stamped to the door, then whisked about on the threshold to deliver a parting shot. 'I'm off to do some shopping and I'd sooner go alone.'

Immediately after her mother went out Emily sought the sanctuary of her chamber. But even the comfort of a little nap was to be snatched away. Her brother had soon stationed himself outside the door and begun cajoling to be allowed in to talk to her. Her refusal had prompted him to direct hissed questions through the keyhole. Was he to have Hunter as a brother-in-law? he'd repeatedly demanded to know. Or was a scandal going to break next week when the Pearson woman came back to town?

Emily had lain on her bed with her hands covering her face. She'd felt too enervated and emotional to again wrangle with any one else that morning, so she simply ignored Tarquin. Eventually he had mumbled about funeral arrangements for Jenny and gone away. From her window Emily had just watched her brother striding off purposefully up the street. About to try and again seek sweet oblivion in a catnap, she instead decided she too would go out. Perhaps the air might revive her numb mind and bring fresh ideas to lighten her depression.

She had not seen Sarah for some days and craved to have an uncomplicated chat to a friend. And why should she not try and enjoy the little interlude left to her? In a short while, when Mrs Pearson returned from Guildford, all would be deadly serious. Momentarily Emily hesitated by the front door and smoothed her gloves with agitated fingers. If she visited Sarah, Stephen Bond was sure to be a topic of conversation between them. Emily was unsure what to say about him any more. With a sigh she lightly descended the steps and headed off in the direction of Sarah's house. She would negotiate a path across rickety bridges when she encountered them! Drawing in an invigorating gulp of crisp air, she quickened her pace.

'It's good to see you, Emily.' Sarah rose from where she had been working on her embroidery and rushed to meet her friend. She took both Emily's hands in her own.

Emily returned her friend's enthusiastic welcome

by squeezing her fingers. She was glad that there was no hint of the awkwardness that had been present when last they had parted company.

'Come…sit down. I'll arrange for tea,' Sarah said, already halfway to the bell pull. 'Papa said that he'd heard your brother is back in town,' she said conversationally. 'That must be a relief for you all.' She sat close to Emily and bestowed a sympathetic look. 'Is it a relief, or has he simply brought his woes back with him?'

About to prevaricate on that tricky subject, Emily was saved the need to do so. Mrs Harper was framed in the parlour doorway.

'Oh, hello, Emily, my dear. How nice to see you. I didn't realise you had a visitor, Sarah. Are you going to accompany me? Or would you now rather not as Emily is arrived? I have not said definitely that you *will* attend…'

'Definitely, I will not, thank you all the same, Mama,' Sarah returned with a little conspiratorial smile for Emily.

'Oh…please…do not let me stop you going out,' Emily said at once. 'I can call another day.' She began to rise.

'No! I insist you stay!' Sarah cried and clutched at Emily's arm to make her again sit down.

Mrs Harper gave the young ladies a blithe smile and, with a little wave, withdrew.

Sarah turned to Emily, a hand dramatically placed upon her breast. 'Don't abandon me, please! I was ready to summon up a migraine to avoid the ordeal of weak tea and stale Madeira cake. Of course, that sour-faced old biddy makes me feel quite bilious too.'

Emily stripped off her gloves and settled back into the cushions of the sofa. For the first time in many hours she felt good humour ease the painful constriction in her chest. 'And which poor hostess, pray, has earned your wicked description?' Emily feigned thoughtfulness. 'I can think of many who the cap might fit, but you must enlighten me, lest I insult one of your mother's best friends.'

Sarah wove her needle into cloth to secure it then pushed away the tambour. She made herself comfortable, crossing her arms, before beginning, 'Violet Pearson has forgone her trip to Guildford and returned to town. No sooner is she back than she has arranged to have everyone to tea.' Sarah gave a chuckle, oblivious to her friend's stricken expression on hearing her yarn. 'Mama said the Pearsons are famous misers and there will be only one reason Violet has squandered the cost of the journey *and* paid out to entertain the moment she is home: the woman has discovered something riveting and is determined to be first with a juicy bit of gossip!'

For the second time in a week Geoffrey Lomax gawped at his master's broad back and wondered what had put the fellow again in such a foul temper. Moments before Mark had entered the house and proceeded past him towards his study with just a terse greeting emerging from between his teeth.

The butler watched him and shrugged in despair. He had been about to announce to Mr Hunter that he had a visitor, but possessed neither nimble legs to run to catch up with him, nor the vulgarity to shout the information in his wake. Let him discover for himself that his brother was in the house waiting to see him.

Mark came upon Sir Jason warming himself, inside and out, with his cognac and his fire.

'You look comfortable,' Mark drawled sardonically.

Jason glanced up from his hearthside chair and stretched his long legs out in front of him. 'Do you begrudge me my contentment?' he asked bluntly.

Mark gave his brother a quirk of a smile. Did he resent Jason's contentment? No…but most certainly he coveted it. Just a short while ago he would have pitied his brother the loss of his bachelorhood. But that was before Emily Beaumont had gazed at him with those captivating silver eyes and asked for his help in finding her brother. Now he was enslaved, heart and soul, and he wished he were not. Mark abruptly clashed together the decanter and a glass. Remembering his manners, he held out the bottle.

Jason declined another drink. He watched as his brother dropped into the chair opposite, and proceeded to sink the cognac in a single gulp.

Mark had been acting oddly for some time, and Jason had come here to discover if his wife's suspicions were correct. Lady Hunter had ordered her husband to bring Mark back to dine with them that evening, but first Jason deemed a little private chat might benefit.

Helen was sure Mark and Emily Beaumont were, despite evidence to the contrary, falling in love. Jason knew better than to gainsay his wife on such matters of excellent female intuition. But, on the occasions they had all been in company together, Jason had noticed Emily had seemed cool with Mark rather than enthralled. At Fiona Gerrard's recent soirée, the couple had spent time alone, but Jason had put that down to a necessarily discreet conversation concerning that numbskull brother of hers.

Mark was staring unblinking into the fire, and

Jason gave his moody countenance a more penetrating appraisal. He knew from personal experience that the road to love and happiness could be strewn with pitfalls, and his brother certainly appeared to be licking his wounds.

'Helen has sent me to fetch you back for dinner. And she won't take no for an answer,' Jason added when he noticed Mark considering his response. An excuse was imminent.

'Who else?'

Jason grinned—he knew exactly why his brother was suspicious. In the past Helen had been known to seat her eligible brother-in-law close to nubile young ladies of her acquaintance. 'No matchmaking, I swear,' Jason promised. 'It's just the three of us. Helen is concerned that we have seen little of you lately. What have you been up to?'

Mark watched his empty glass as it oscillated between thumb and forefinger. Abruptly he rose and refilled it. 'I've been courting.' The announcement was followed by a grunt of mirthless laughter. Mark thumped his glass down on the desk. 'That's what I've been doing. And I really don't think that tonight I feel sociable.'

'Damned tricky business,' Jason commiserated, settling a booted foot on a knee. 'Wouldn't want to do it again myself.' He gave Mark a rueful look. He knew his brother recalled the obstacles that had complicated his relentless pursuit of Helen Marlowe. 'Do you want to tell me about it?'

'No.' Mark strolled about his desk and picked up a few papers to idly scan them.

'I take it the lady has declined your kind offer, in which case it isn't Barbara you've settled on. She'd meet you at the church tomorrow.'

'You're being damned inquisitive,' Mark snarled. 'Thank Helen very much for her invitation, but—'

'I'm being your brother,' Jason interjected quietly. 'I know something is not right and I don't like to see you unhappy, but if you don't want to talk about it…' He shrugged. 'It's your business.' Jason gained his feet and looked squarely into Mark's eyes. 'I've done my best; the least you can do is return the compliment. If I turn up without you, it's likely I'll have to endure some nagging, and a very lonely night.'

'The joys of married life?' Mark suggested drily.

'Indeed,' Jason replied. 'But it won't put you off any more than it did me. If you love her, you'll take that and more…'

'I really think I ought to be going.' Emily had sat chatting with Sarah for forty endless minutes before she felt able to issue that statement. Since she had learned of Violet Pearson's aborted trip to Guildford she had subdued her agitation and attempted to maintain a façade of cheeriness. But for her good manners preventing it, she would have quit Sarah's company five minutes after having been invited to sit down and take tea.

She had instinctively decided not to confide in her friend her grave suspicions over what had brought Violet haring back to town. When Mrs Harper returned from taking afternoon tea, Sarah would know it all, and so would many others in polite society. This evening, salons and drawing rooms throughout London would be abuzz with gossip… concerning her!

Sarah gave her friend a searching look. She was aware that Emily's mood had changed after her tale about the Pearson woman. 'Have I said something to upset you? I wouldn't have spoken unkindly about Violet if I thought you liked her…'

Emily forced a gasp of laughter. 'Heavens above, I do not! You *know* I do not.'

Sarah frowned in puzzlement, but leaned forward to pick up the teapot. 'Have some more tea,' she cajoled.

Emily deposited on the table her cup and saucer

with a hand that shook and made the china rattle. 'I will not, thank you.'

Noticing that Sarah looked rather hurt, she added quickly. 'It is nothing you have said or done, Sarah, I swear. I…it is just…you are right…' she breathed with some relief as she recalled something her friend had mentioned earlier '…the return of the prodigal has not been without its worries. Tarquin would not be Tarquin if he turned up completely free of woes.'

Sarah took Emily's hands in her own and lightly pecked her cheek. 'I understand, but come again soon.'

Emily walked swiftly in the direction of home, but, at the corner of Callison Crescent, and with her door in sight, she stopped. What was she going to do? Would she go to her chamber and hide her head under the covers until tomorrow her name…her family's name…was dragged through the mud? She had thought Tarquin an unfit sibling to their young brother, Robert. How she was humbled for having deemed herself superior!

She had rashly assumed she had time to decide on a course of action. That buffer had now been whipped away and she was teetering on the brink of disaster. With a sob welling in her throat, she leaned back against a brick wall for support. She ignored curious looks from people busily traversing back and forth on the pavement and forced her mind to reflect on the only man who might be her saviour.

She had received a marriage proposal of sorts from Mark Hunter and simple pride had stopped her grabbing the opportunity. The half-hearted offer had been prompted by duty, and from his desire to make love to her. But how could she bear that? As his wife she would be safe from scourging tongues, but she could never bear the hurt of knowing her absent husband had spent the night with his mistress. She might have his name, but Barbara Emerson would have his love.

Emily smeared the wet from her eyes and blinked into the breeze. There was only one person she could talk to when she was so low.

Helen would not judge her. They were similar souls. Before she had married Sir Jason, the young widow, Helen Marlowe, had been forced to put at jeopardy her good name. Helen was no stranger to the risk of being ostracised.

Plunging her cold hands into her pockets, Emily turned and walked back the way she had come, heading towards Grosvenor Square.

Chapter Seventeen

'I'm very well, thank you, Cedric,' Emily glibly lied.

Old Cedric cocked his good ear at the visitor to discover how she fared. He had no need to ask her business, or her name. He knew very well that Miss Beaumont had come for a chat with her good friend Lady Hunter. He ushered her into the vast marble hallway of Sir Jason's magnificent townhouse.

'And how are you?' Emily asked the old retainer.

The butler wagged his head up and down. 'Mustn't grumble…mustn't grumble.' Suddenly a look of enlightenment lifted his aged features. 'I've just remembered that Lady Hunter's maid went up to dress her hair. Dinner is quite soon.'

'Oh…I will not stop, then. I had not realised it was so late.' Emily sent a glance to a stately grandfather clock set against the wall and saw it was indeed almost a quarter to seven. She had lost all track of time since she'd left the house at late afternoon. It was well past the hour to pay an impromptu social call, even on a close friend. With an apologetic little smile for Cedric she turned to the door.

'Emily!'

A great deal of warmth and welcome was in that single word. Lady Hunter was gliding down a curving staircase, looking a vision of elegance in lemon silk with her ebony ringlets swept to one side of her lovely face.

Once on the marble tiles Helen hurried towards Emily and linked arms with her, drawing her further into the house.

'I will not stop, Helen. I had not realised quite how late it is, and you are dressed to dine.'

A hand flick dismissed that as of no importance. 'Of course you must stay! Jason is not even yet home.' Helen raised her eyes heavenward. 'He is probably taking a tipple with his brother. I know he was going to see Mark.' Helen watched carefully for a reaction to that idle information. With an amount of satisfaction she noted that a reference to Mark Hunter had indeed made Emily start. Helen also noticed that Emily's heart-shaped countenance was unusually wan, and shadows bruised the delicate skin beneath her eyes.

'Come along to the blue salon. It is just finished and you must tell me if you like the furnishings I have chosen.'

Emily looked about, praised her friend's excellent taste, then the ladies took seats close together on a sofa covered in fabric of blue and white stripes. Settled barely a moment, Helen made to spring up to ring for some refreshment.

'No, I will not, thank you, Helen.' Emily managed a small smile, and to restrain Helen from rushing to the bell. 'I am awash with tea. I have just been to see Sarah Harper,' she obliquely explained. The tenuous hold she had on her composure evaporated. A hand flew to her face to shield the gleam of tears.

'What is it?' Helen asked immediately, drawing her friend into a solicitous embrace. 'Surely Sarah has not upset you? I could tell straight away that all was not well.'

'It is not Sarah…leastways, nothing she has intentionally done. But she told me Mrs Pearson is already back in town and I can't bear it.'

Helen patted at her friend's quivering shoulders. 'I know she is a witch, but we can hide her broomstick.' Helen's gentle levity could not disguise that she had been made anxious by Emily's distress. Emily was an intrepid character and not prone to waterworks.

A gurgling laugh burst from Emily, but she remained quite still and uncommunicative, rallying the courage to relate her tale.

'Has Tarquin given the tabbies something new to relish?' Helen probed. 'I had heard he is back in town too.'

'A scandal *is* about to break. But it concerns me and I don't know what to do! My parents will be heartbroken.' Emily pressed a scrap of lace to her damp eyes.

'Hush…' Helen soothed. 'It cannot be so bad. Is my brother-in-law aware of it?' After a pause, Helen rephrased her question. 'Is Mark involved in any way?'

Emily gave an almost imperceptible nod.

'Start at the very beginning,' Helen urged softly.

Disengaging herself from Helen's arms, Emily sat straight and drew a gulp of a breath to begin her woeful account. She was interrupted before she had uttered one word.

'Just the three of us to dine this evening, I see…'

The sardonic male voice made both Emily and Helen turn simultaneously towards the door.

On the threshold stood two tall, immaculately attired gentlemen. One of them seemed as though he might pivot on his heel and leave rather than enter the room.

Mark Hunter was directing a look of extreme irony at his brother, Jason. His eyes then moved to Emily and lingered.

In response to his brother's tacit accusation, Jason gave a shrug, gesturing his bewilderment. But his eyes, when they shot to his wife, were brimming with quizzical amusement, and not a little admiration.

Helen sent her husband a welcoming smile, but it faded as she realised that Emily had jumped to her feet.

'I must go, Helen. I'm sorry to have troubled you,' Emily breathed, her face flaming. She had heard, and comprehended, the irony in Mark's tone. He imagined that Helen and she had plotted this meeting, and he had been lured back by his brother to be a target for their matchmaking. He suspected she had changed her mind, and was now so desperate to get him to issue a proper proposal that she had humbled herself to trap him.

She had been on the point of asking Helen's advice, but had already guessed what it would be. There was only one sensible course of action if she was to protect her family from shame: marry Mark Hunter if he would have her.

But all that was rational had been set to flight by his scorn and arrogance. Her spirits had rallied and she was sorely tempted to loose at him an immediate defence. Angry words teetered on her tongue tip. For two pins she would have told him that, had she known *he* was in the vicinity, she would have given Grosvenor Square a very wide berth indeed. But she would not demean herself with any such petty barbs. With her head high, she steadily paced towards the door.

'Do not disturb your plans for this evening, sir. I am leaving,' Emily said with cool politeness as she came nearer to him.

'Don't go on my account, Miss Beaumont.' Mark started into the room on a direct path to meet her.

Emily's pace slowed; they were on a collision course, but she would not give him the satisfaction of stepping aside. With barely a yard separating them she came to an abrupt halt.

Mark took another step until he was within arm's length of her bristling little figure.

Emily's chin was jerkily elevated, setting her blonde curls dancing. She gazed up into a face of raw-boned masculinity. Why did he always look so devastatingly attractive? She inwardly railed as she felt her body swaying towards him. Even now, with tension crackling between them, she yearned for his strength and comfort. Hastily she put all such thoughts from her mind. In a business-like fashion she started to pull on her gloves, wordlessly impressing on him he was delaying her. A soft noise prompted her to tilt her head to one side to see past him. The door had clicked shut on the discreet departure of Jason and Helen.

'Let me pass, please,' she demanded. 'I have to go. It is dinner time.'

'Which is surely why you're here.'

Rather miffed, Emily pointed out the glaring error in his assumption. 'I'm hardly dressed for the occasion,' she said stiffly, deliberately glancing down at her plain, serviceable ensemble.

Mark gave her attire a leisurely scrutiny. 'You look fine to me.' It was husky, complimentary.

'That remark shows how little you understand women,' Emily snapped with heightened pique.

'Amen to that,' he said on a dry laugh.

Emily moistened her lips, aware of peacock-blue eyes searing her face. Feeling overwhelmed by his closeness, she took a pace away. 'I know you believe this is no chance meeting,' she blurted. 'It is. I came here uninvited, and your brother and sister-in-law have done nothing underhand. They are not accomplices in some scheme to hook you, or in any way responsible for your embarrassment.'

'I'm not embarrassed. I am, however, intrigued as to why you pay your visits so late.'

Emily flicked up at him a bold stare. 'A pressing matter brought me here.'

'A pressing matter that concerns me?'

Emily felt blood flood beneath her cheeks. 'It's none of your business.'

'I think you know that's not true, Emily,' he lightly corrected. 'And what was Lady Hunter's advice? Should you grasp the nettle and marry me?'

'I might ask you the same question, sir,' Emily returned immediately. 'What was your brother's advice?'

'Jason doesn't know I asked you to be my wife.'

'Asked me to be your wife?' Emily echoed with husky scorn. 'Is that what you said to me?' Silver eyes flared at him. 'It sounded very much as though you were suggesting I be your…' She pressed together her lips, regretting having made herself sound vulgar. Quickly she made to dodge past him.

He moved to block her path. 'And you made it sound as though marriage to me would be a fate worse than death.'

Emily became still as a surge of remorse washed

over her. He had sounded hurt as well as angry. Her eyes fluttered shut as thoughts jumbled in her mind. Had she been so concerned with protecting her own pride that she had ignored the damage done to his? Mark always seemed so effortlessly self-contained, so invincible. She had rebuffed him brusquely, she knew, but had believed he must eventually welcome his release from an onerous duty to save her reputation. Suddenly she felt the tension seeping from her body.

'We should stop acting like petulant children,' she said quietly, barely flinching from the quizzical look that remark provoked. But she could tell that he, too, would welcome a truce.

They seemed on firmer ground, and Emily intended to tread carefully so they might equably debate the matters perturbing her. 'I know you would make Nicholas pay for what he has done, but I beg you will not worsen the situation by fighting him.'

Mark's lips twitched in a rueful smile. 'I won't say it wasn't my intention, but Riley got to him first. The fiasco ended in a scrap between them. Devlin is back home, and looking very much the worse for wear. The official report is that the Viscount was attacked by felons on the road.'

Emily's little gasp earned her a frown.

'Are you worried about him?'

Emily quickly shook her head. 'No! I hope his bruises are sore for weeks!' she announced pithily. 'But I fear his battered appearance might lead to inquisitiveness, and that might, in turn, lead to awkward questions.'

'He is lying low, and packing up his household to leave town. Ostensibly, his move to the country is due to his husbandly concern for the delicate condition of his wife.'

'It is no constitutional, I'm sure.' She gave Mark a tentative smile. 'You have made him go, have you not?' Quickly she added, 'I don't want to know how you brought it about.'

Mark's lids descended over his eyes. 'I simply suggested it might be wise. Devlin is not so stupid as to fail to understand that his behaviour could have grave repercussions. He knows Riley hates him, and would betray him for a pittance. Abduction and attempted rape carry heavy penalties, even for peers of the realm.'

Emily nodded slowly. 'And Riley?'

'I imagine he will make himself scarce rather than be dealt with by his cronies. They were not happy that Jenny was mortally injured. Her death will warrant an investigation and bring the authorities down on all their heads.' Mark looked at Emily and said softly, 'I am very sorry about what happened to her.'

'Tarquin is too,' Emily replied. 'I think he truly loved her at first and still does, despite knowing she was a bigamist...'

'A bigamist?' Mark echoed incredulously. 'They were not really wed at all?' Harshness was again present in his face and tone.

'He did not know until the end.' Emily quickly leaped to her brother's defence. 'Riley made Jenny wed those men so he might blackmail them. She told Tarquin all before she died. He is very upset to have lost her and you must not be angry with him over it or I will...' Her threats faded into silence.

'Or you will what?' Mark taunted softly. 'What will you do, Emily? Tackle his problems alone next time?'

Emily winced beneath his mockery. He had every right to go this minute and harangue her brother till kingdom come. 'He is different now,' she said quietly. 'I have never known my brother show such remorse. Usually he is too eager to find a gaming table to tarry long enough to say sorry.' She gazed up into Mark's eyes. 'I truly believe this awful episode has made him mend his ways.'

'I hope you're right,' Mark replied. 'It won't be before time.'

Emily drew in a quivering breath as the silence between them lengthened. For some minutes they had been concentrating on any issue but the one that truly mattered. Now it would no longer be denied. Emily knew it was time to surrender to her fate. To grasp the nettle, as he had said…

'Our squabbles are hindering us finding a solution to our own troubles.'

'There is only one solution, Emily, and you know what it is.' Impatiently he raked five fingers through his dark hair, ruining its neat appearance. 'A notice ought to be immediately gazetted. Time is running out…'

'It has run out,' Emily whispered. She raised her eyes to meet his, for they had immediately whipped to her face. 'Violet Pearson did not go to Guildford. She has returned instead to town, and I think I need not tell you why.'

Mark twisted a smile. 'So you have been denied even a few days' respite.'

'As have you.' Her gaze clung to his face as she said, 'I'm so sorry.' She moved a little closer, wistfulness puckering her perfect features. 'Had I not asked you to help me find Tarquin…had I not been foolish enough to go off alone with Riley…you would not now find yourself in such a terrible situation.'

Mark raised a hand, touched a single finger softly to her lips to silence her. Emily's lids drooped and for just a moment she revelled in the feel of his skin on hers. She took a deep breath and turned her face away. 'No…let me finish. There is much I must say. I have not thanked you for your help and, Heaven knows, you deserve my gratitude.'

'I don't want your gratitude, Emily,' Mark said hoarsely.

'I know you do not. Despite your angry words, I know you have given your aid freely, and would do so again.' She paused, thinking back over those years she had known Mark Hunter. For most of their acquaintance she had treated him coldly because of the incident surrounding her brother's imprisonment. In her heart she had known that her loyalty to Tarquin was extreme and unappreciated. Tarquin had been wild and out of control, and Mark had been right to rein him in. Difficult as it was to now eat humble pie, she must do it for her conscience's sake.

'I don't simply owe you my gratitude; I owe you an apology too.' She sensed smouldering eyes warming her. 'I know that when you had Tarquin sent to the Fleet you were being cruel to be kind. His incarceration stopped him gambling, and losing what little assets he had left. I was wrong to put the blame for it on you. I was wrong to be insolent to you.' Emily slanted a nervous peek at him through a web of long, inky lashes. 'Tarquin is lucky indeed you are still his friend, and that you have done so much recently to help him.'

'I didn't do it for him.'

Emily took a step closer to gauge his expression.

'I did it for you; surely you realised that?' he said gruffly.

Emily searched blue eyes that were devoid of irony, that seemed soulful, and intent on analysing her reaction to his words.

'Because you want to sleep with me?' Emily whispered.

'Because I love you, Emily Beaumont.' In a low, velvety voice he added, 'And, naturally, I want to prove that to you in bed.' He came purposefully closer. 'Actually, I'd like to prove it to you now.'

Hands that were lightly vibrating were raised to tenderly cup her bashful face and turn it up to his.

'You love me, even though you know that I lay willingly with Nicholas?' Emily asked in a small voice.

'I can't pretend I like knowing it,' Mark admitted with raw tenderness. 'I admit too that, since you told me, I've acted like a sulky youth over it.' His manner was endearingly self-conscious. 'I've always abhorred hypocrites, yet now I've acted as one.' His thumbs swept soft arcs on the satin skin of her jaw. 'I owe you an apology. It's not your fault that you were seduced by Devlin's lies and promises. You were young and sincere and understandably vulnerable to a master of deceit.' Mark paused. 'I don't like knowing that you gave him a precious part of yourself, or that you wanted to marry him. But perhaps you don't like knowing that, in my youth, I loved Barbara Emerson, and wanted her for my wife.'

Emily gazed at him with eyes that had spontaneously filled with prickling tears. 'I don't like knowing it at all. I don't like the rumours that you will wed. I don't like it that she is still your mistress.' She ended her admission on a shrill note of indignation that made Mark wryly smile.

'She isn't…not any more…' he soothed. 'I have seen Barbara today and told her that it is finished between us.' Mark was prevented from adding that he'd had no intention of asking Barbara to marry him since he turned twenty-one.

Emily suddenly flung her arms about his neck, hugging him chokingly tight. 'I thought you still loved her. I thought you hoped to marry her, and would hate me for depriving you of the woman you truly wanted as your wife.'

'You're the woman I truly want as my wife, Emily,' Mark told her gravely. His lips skimmed the silky blonde hair at her brow. 'We both have loved and wanted to marry people who we now know would have ultimately made us unhappy. We must be thankful that those affairs are behind us and we are free to concentrate on our future together.' He tilted up her chin with a single digit. 'Do you agree?'

Chapter Eighteen

'I do agree.'

'And Stephen Bond?'

'Stephen is a nice man, but I do not love him. In fact, I had a letter telling him so to post, but was distracted when Riley abducted me.' Emily gave him an adoring smile. 'I love you, Mark…so very much, and would be greatly honoured to be your wife.' She paused, raised a hand to tenderly cup his angular chin. 'I love you so much more than ever I loved Nicholas…'

'Prove it,' Mark demanded, his voice gruff with need.

Emily immediately complied. She went on tiptoe to press her soft warm lips against his. But he wanted more wooing than a coy salute. Gamely she teased him with little nipping kisses until, satisfied, he allowed her tongue to slip into his mouth to tangle with his.

With a guttural sound rasping in his throat, Mark lifted her up so their faces were level and he could fully enjoy her sweet seduction. From instinct, her legs immediately separated, wound about his thighs to clasp him possessively to her. Mark forgot about flirtatious games; he wanted her... His mouth stroked back and forth on soft, willing lips, plundered with savage sensuality until the kiss was so deep their faces were still.

Easily carrying his sensual prize, he strode swiftly to the nearest wall.

With blue watered silk at her back and Mark's hard powerful body keeping her effortlessly in place, Emily loosened her cloak. With her face still upturned to his and her mouth greedily taking the onslaught of his lips, she felt for her buttons. Unsteady fingers slowly loosened her bodice by touch alone. Mark raised his head, his eyes glowing with desire as he watched her small moving fingers. Deliberately Emily opened her chemise until the sides flapped away from her alabaster skin like small lapels. With her feverish gaze still meshed with his, she pulled down the soft cotton until it framed and supported her naked breasts, raising them close to his mouth.

Mark's eyes swooped to adore the lush, milky flesh offered up to him. His mouth slowly descended to take her invitingly slack lips in a slow, rewarding kiss that made her squirm delightedly.

Emily arched her back, rotated her hips faster against the rigid heat at his pelvis, wordlessly begging for him to soothe the aching need building within her feminine core.

With his body supporting hers, he used both hands to take his gift. Long, avaricious fingers began to reverentially stroke, pamper, shape the quivering flesh he was preparing to feast on. First one, then the other, blood-red nub thickened, stiffened beneath his skilful tongue as it leisurely trailed torment. When her aching flesh was almost unbearably hot and swollen Emily fought to contain the sob of pleasure tightening her throat. In delirium her head was thrown back, twisted from side to side in wordless denial, but the groan burst from her.

Mark covered her panting mouth with his to stop the feral sound from increasing in volume.

'Hush…' he whispered against her bruised lips, his tone throaty and amused. 'That was loud enough to bring old Cedric running, and he's deaf as a post.'

Emily tensed, then, in chagrin, her eyes screwed tight shut. The haze of sensuality drugging her was ebbing away and fiery embarrassment taking its place. She was a guest in an aristocrat's mansion, yet was acting like a dockside harlot. With a subdued shriek of shame she struggled to find her feet and her dignity. She pushed at Mark's shoulders, wriggled this way and that to try to make him set her down.

Emily's writhing now drew a guttural noise from Mark. Her attempt to recover her modesty was having the reverse effect to the one intended. His arms tightened about her, subduing her protests whilst his mouth relentlessly pursued hers.

'Oh…let me go, Mark,' Emily pleaded in anguish as his lips cornered hers. 'Do you suppose they heard? What must your brother think of me? Do you think they understood what we…that is…do you think they *know* what we're doing?' She turned to him, grasped his lean, angular jaw, then rushed her soft palms up and down on abrasive skin to hurry his reassurance.

Mark tore his eyes from the delectable sight of her nude bosom heaving just inches from his hungry mouth.

'What do *you* think of me?' Emily wailed softly. His desire had harshly tautened his features and she craved some tender affection from him. Did Mark think she had just proved herself a hussy rather than a fitting wife?

He looked deep into her stormy eyes; touched his lips to hers in a lightly teasing kiss. 'I'll show you what I think of you.' But instead of a renewed seduction, he gently lowered her to the ground. His hands drew together her chemise, her gaping bodice, and painstakingly refastened them. He then slipped a hand to his pocket and withdrew a jeweller's box. Carefully he prised open the lid and turned towards her his gift. A huge rose-cut diamond caught candle flame and sparked fire. 'I brought this with me this morning. I didn't have a chance to give it to you.'

Emily's sharply indrawn breath caught in her throat. For a moment she was so mesmerised by the magnificent betrothal ring that she forgot to be concerned about his expertise in deftly fastening a lady's undergarments.

Whilst Emily gazed upon her beautiful gift, Mark gazed upon his. Her dress was crumpled, her blonde locks were tousled and her mouth was beestung from their loving. Humbly he gave thanks for his good fortune that this woman was his.

'It's wonderful,' Emily at last managed to gasp.

'I wasn't sure whether you would prefer a different stone. I wasn't sure what Devlin got you.'

Emily looked into his eyes. 'A sapphire, and I gave it back without regret,' she said huskily. 'This is the most splendid gem I have ever seen.' She gazed up into his eyes. 'You'll never get it back.'

Mark drew forth the platinum shank from its satin nest and slid it on to her betrothal finger. 'I'd best marry you then…it cost a small fortune.' He placed a light reverential kiss on her scarlet lips. 'If you are still unsure what I think of you, Emily Beaumont, let me tell you in words,' he said huskily. 'I love and respect you utterly. I want us to be married by special licence tomorrow.' He smiled ruefully, 'And I would have told you that even had I not yet sampled what sweet advantages are to be had from taking a wanton bride…'

REGENCY
Collection

*Let these sparklingly seductive delights whirl
you away to the ballrooms—and
bedrooms—of Polite Society!*

Volume 7 – 5th August 2011
Regency Mistresses by Mary Brendan

Volume 8 – 2nd September 2011
Regency Rebels by Deb Marlowe

Volume 9 – 7th October 2011
Regency Scandals by Sophia James

Volume 10 – 4th November 2011
Regency Marriages by Elizabeth Rolls

Volume 11 – 2nd December 2011
Regency Innocents by Annie Burrows

Volume 12 – 6th January 2012
Regency Sins by Bronwyn Scott

12 volumes in all to collect!

www.millsandboon.co.uk